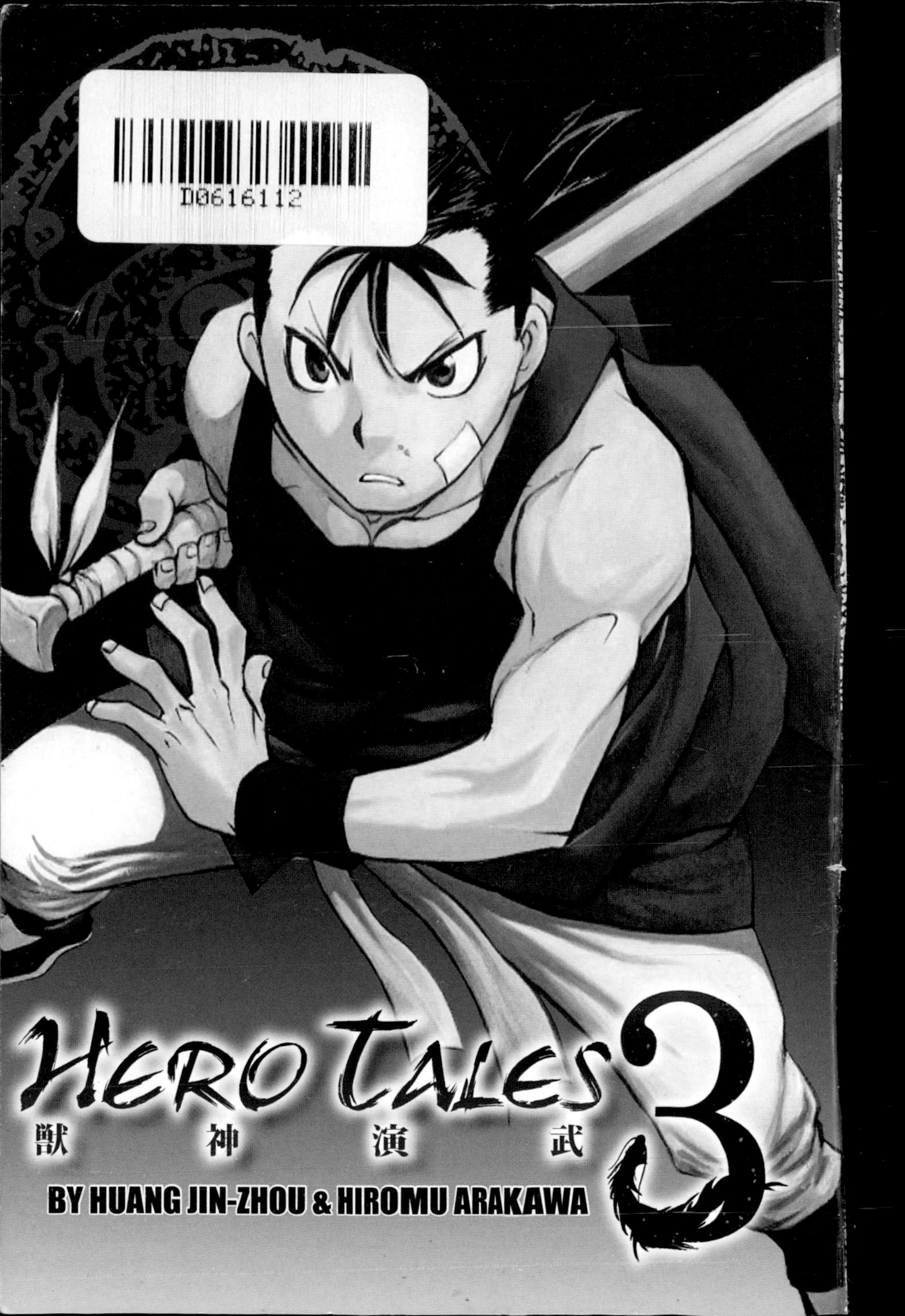
D0616112
HERO TALES
獣神演武
3
BY HUANG JIN-ZHOU & HIROMU ARAKAWA

HERO TALES

獣神演武

# 3

## The Chronicle of the Big Dipper

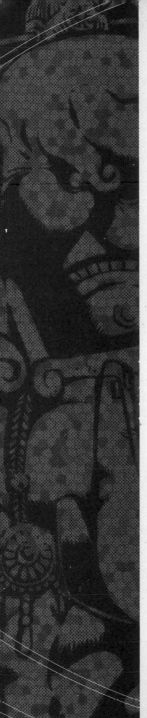

There are seven unique
stars in the heavens.
They are the seven stars
of the Big Dipper.
Seven stars, each one
assigned to a Hokushin-
Tenkun—a HERO destined
to wield the power of
his ruling star...

When the world becomes
corrupt, these avatars of the
stars will appear and restore
peace to the world of men.

But...

Like heaven and earth,
yin and yang,
there are two opposing stars
in the Big Dipper—
TONROU and HAGUN.

These two stars reign supreme
over all the Earth.

Should fate bring these
two together, these sinful
stars of disaster will throw
the world into chaos in their
battle for supremacy...

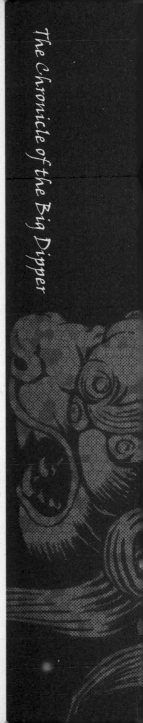

At the conclusion of his coming-of-age ceremony, Taitou is presented with the Kenkaranbu, the Champion's Sword that can only be drawn by a true hero and that represents imperial power. When the sword is snatched by the mysterious Shimei, Taitou pursues the thief to the capital city. Along the way, he meets Kouei, a wise woman and Housei's master, who warns him that the power of Taitou's star, Hagun, will only bring misfortune to those around him. The journey also affords an opportunity to see the destruction caused by the Genrou-Tou, the regiment of soldiers led by General Keirou, who possesses Taitou's opposing star, Tonrou. Infuriated by the ruin and despair of his countrymen, Taitou resolves to confront the emperor himself and demand a solution. Getting into the Imperial Palace was easy. Getting out is the tricky part . . .

**TAITOU**
★HAGUN★

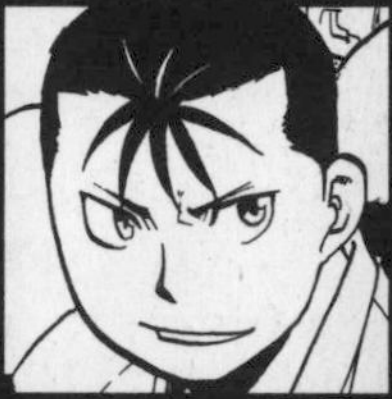

A proud and defiant warrior struggling to master his newfound power

**RYUUKOU**
★BUKYOKU★

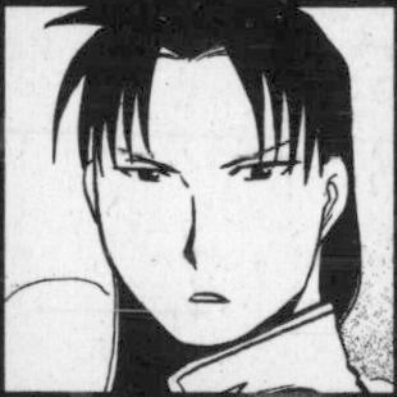

RENJOU

A Rikka priest and Taitou's guide

**LAILA**

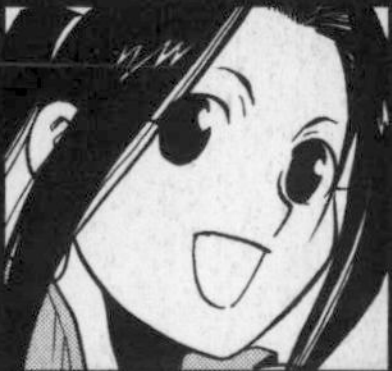

Taitou's sister

**KOYOU**

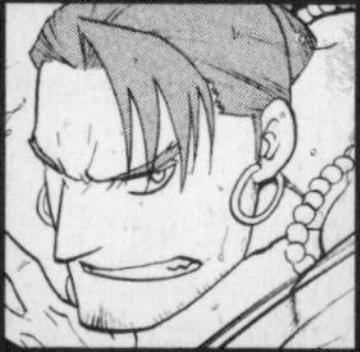

Captain of the ship *Touga*

**SOUEI**

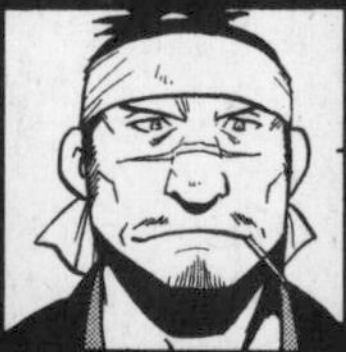

Taitou and Laila's father

**SONNEI**

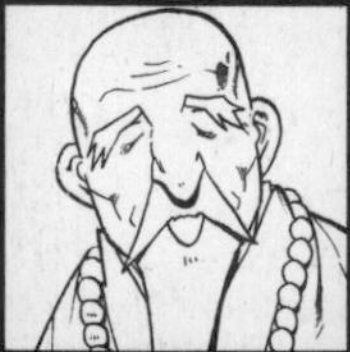

Priest of Rentsu Temple in Taizan

**RYUUSHOU**

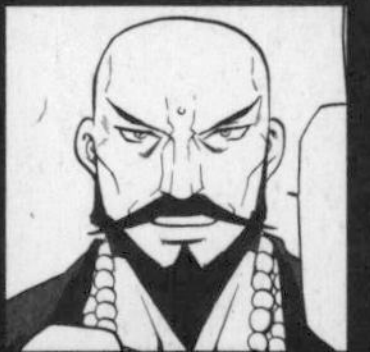

Priest of Touyuu Temple in Rakushou

**RINMEI**
★KOMON★

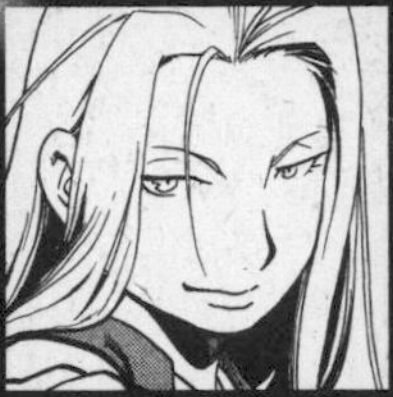

A no-nonsense aide at Touyuu Temple

**HOUSEI**
★ROKUSON★

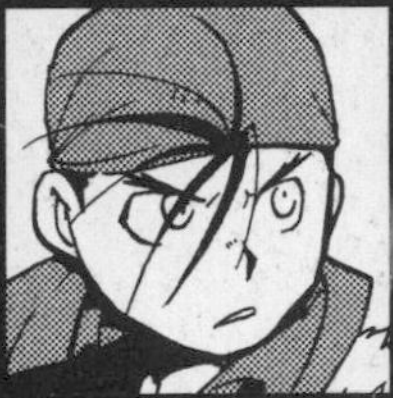

A skilled archer and traveling companion

**KEIROU**
★TONROU★

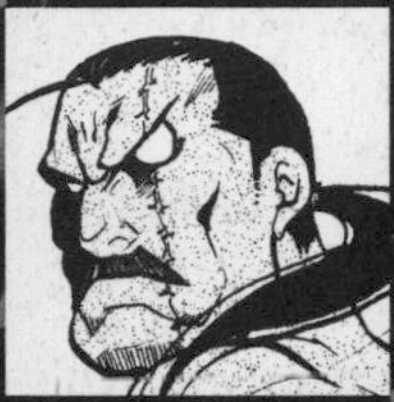

Leader of the Genrou-Tou

**SHIMEI**

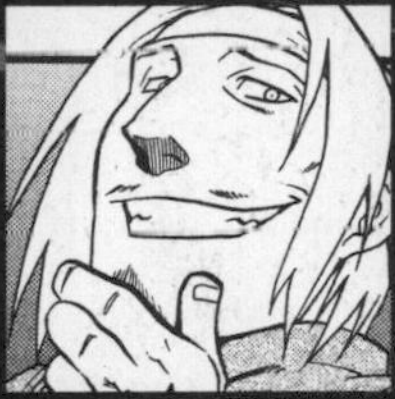

Keirou's ally, a man with mysterious powers

MONKOKU

**TAIGATEI**

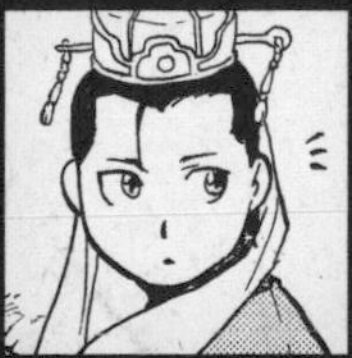

Emperor of the Ken Empire

**SHOUKAKU**

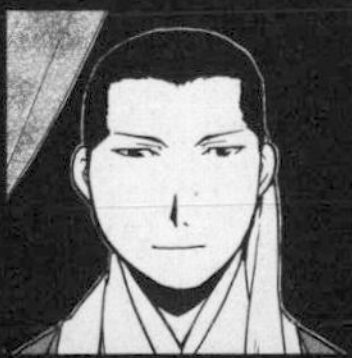

Taigatei's tutor and mentor

**CHOUKA**

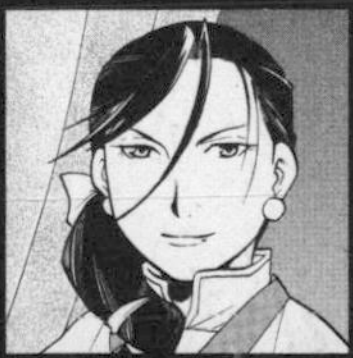

Passionate supporter of Keirou

**KOUCHOU**

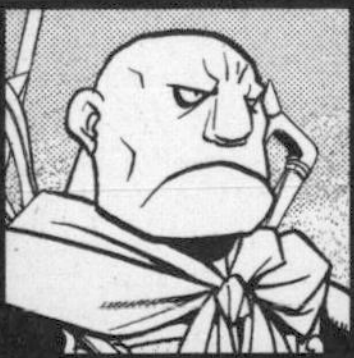

Keirou's right-hand man in battle

HERO TALES

獣　神　演　武

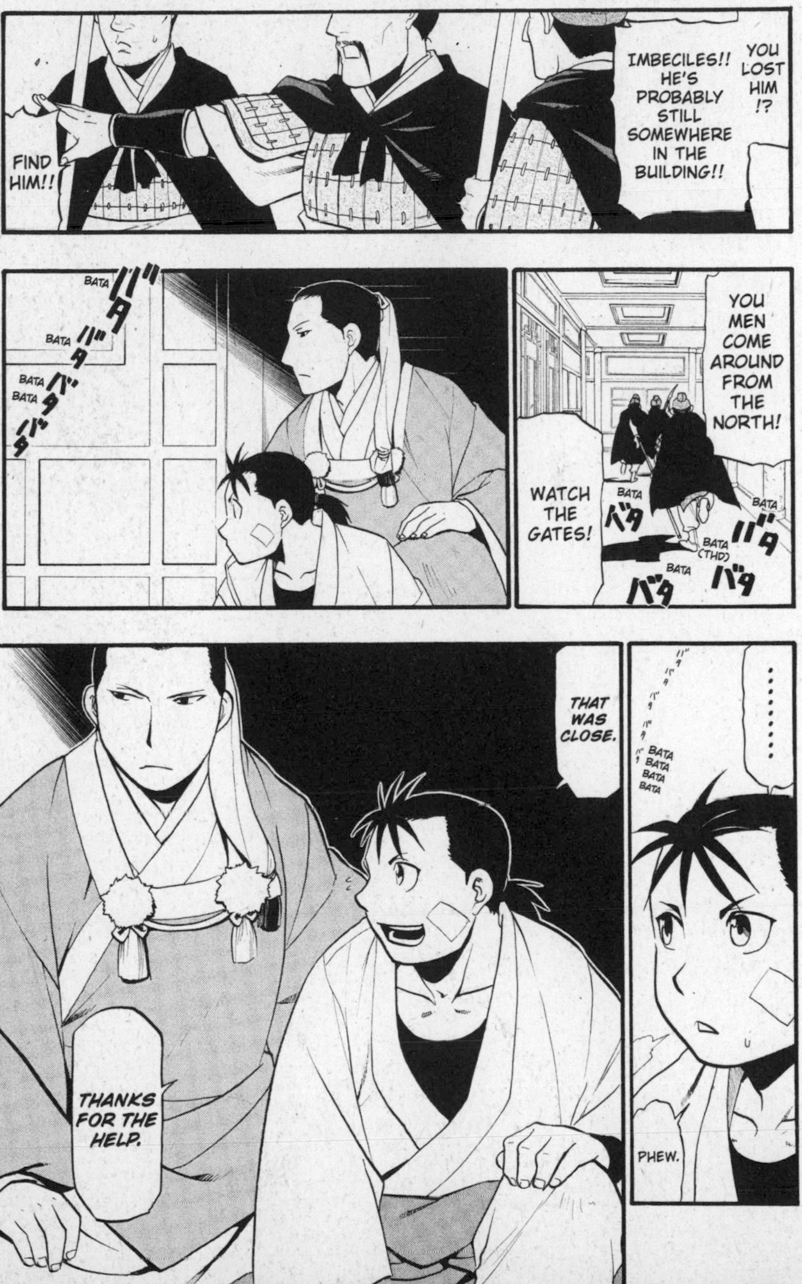
YOU LOST HIM !?
IMBECILES!! HE'S PROBABLY STILL SOMEWHERE IN THE BUILDING!!
FIND HIM!!
YOU MEN COME AROUND FROM THE NORTH!
WATCH THE GATES!
BATA
BATA
BATA (THD)
BATA
BATA
BATA
BATA
BATA
........
BATA BATA BATA BATA
PHEW.
THAT WAS CLOSE.
THANKS FOR THE HELP.

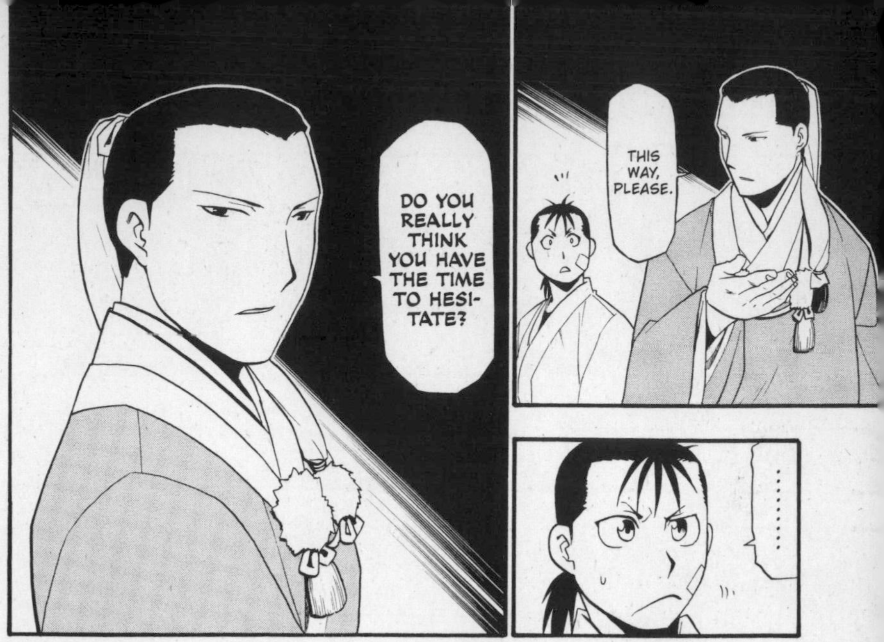
THIS WAY, PLEASE.
......
DO YOU REALLY THINK YOU HAVE THE TIME TO HESITATE?

# Chapter 8
# The Jaws of the Werewolf

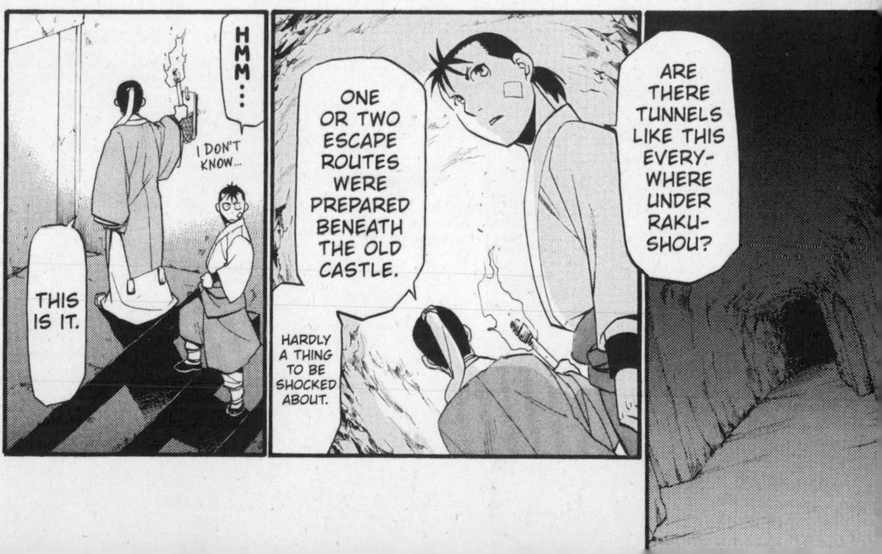
ARE THERE TUNNELS LIKE THIS EVERYWHERE UNDER RAKUSHOU?
ONE OR TWO ESCAPE ROUTES WERE PREPARED BENEATH THE OLD CASTLE.
HARDLY A THING TO BE SHOCKED ABOUT.
HMM...
I DON'T KNOW...
THIS IS IT.

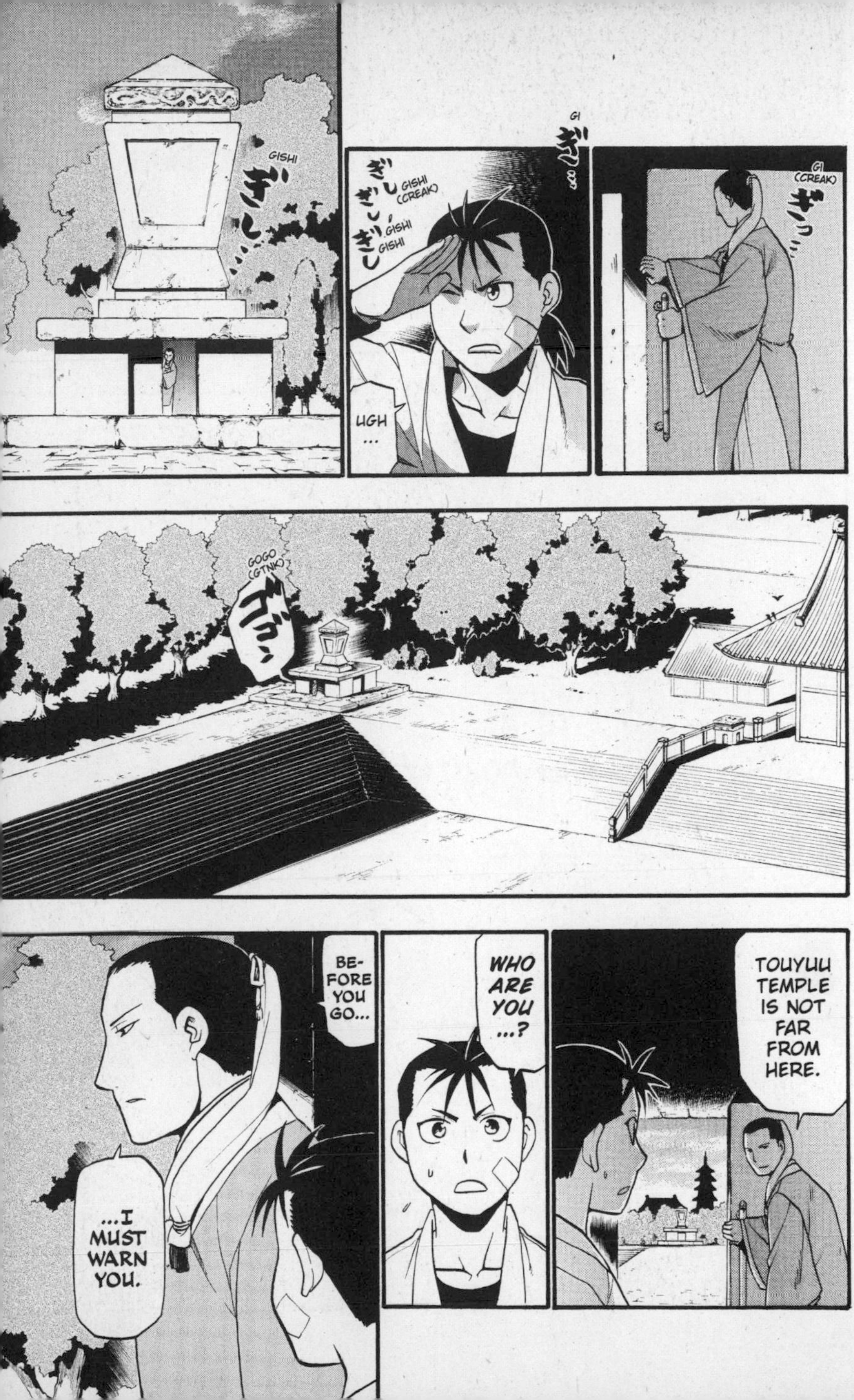
GI (CREAK)
ぎっ...
GI
ぎ...
GISHI (CREAK)
ぎし ぎし ぎし
GISHI
GISHI
UGH...
GISHI
ぎし...
GOGO (GTNK)
ゴゴ
TOUYUU TEMPLE IS NOT FAR FROM HERE.
WHO ARE YOU...?
BE-FORE YOU GO...
...I MUST WARN YOU.

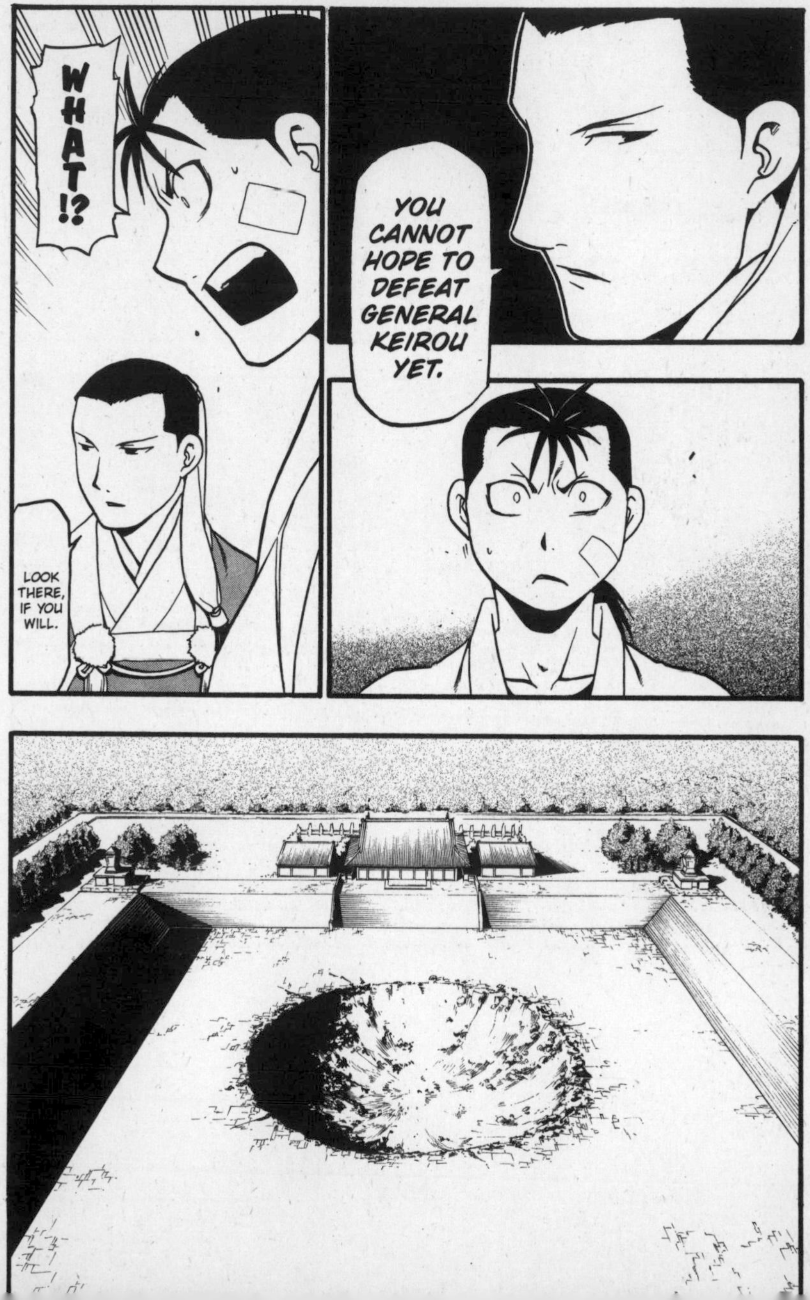
YOU CANNOT HOPE TO DEFEAT GENERAL KEIROU YET.
WHAT!?
LOOK THERE, IF YOU WILL.

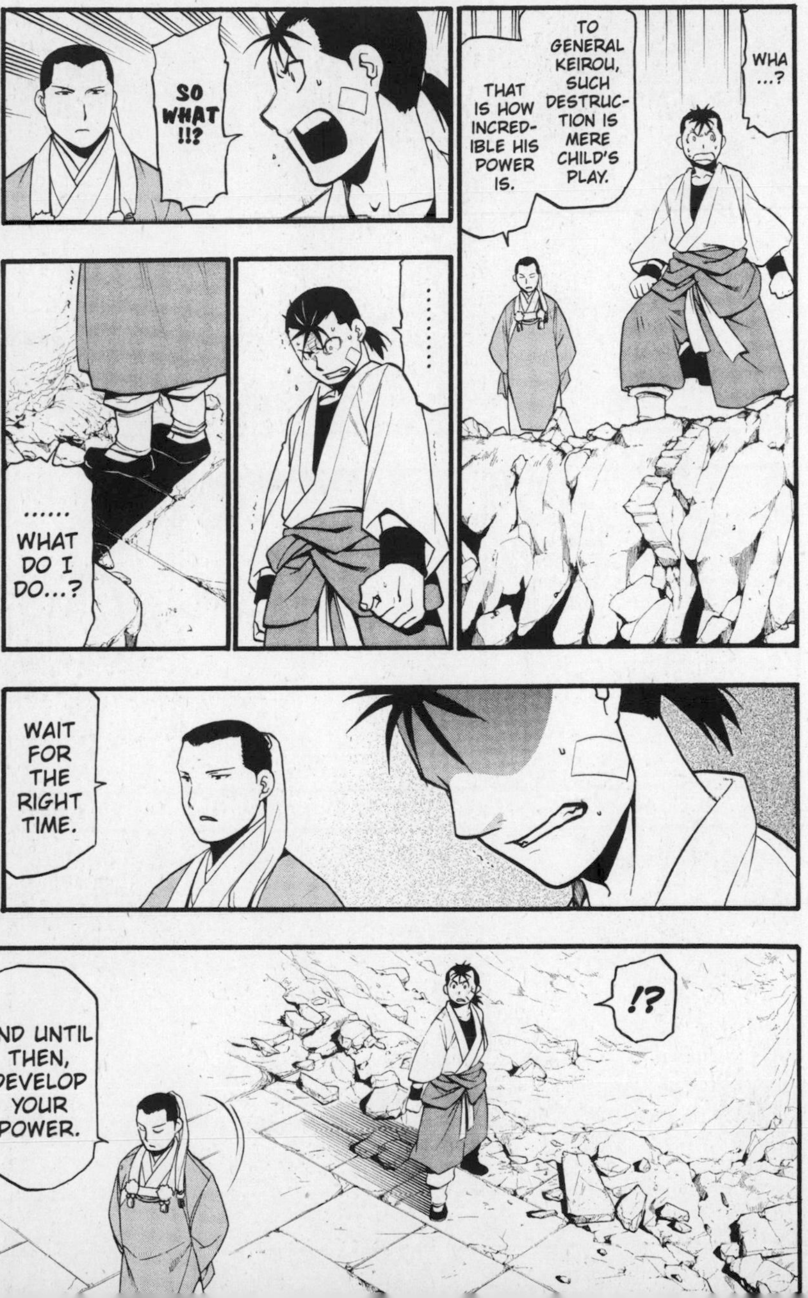
WHA ...?
TO GENERAL KEIROU, SUCH DESTRUCTION IS MERE CHILD'S PLAY.
THAT IS HOW INCREDIBLE HIS POWER IS.
SO WHAT !!?
......
...... WHAT DO I DO...?
WAIT FOR THE RIGHT TIME.
!?
AND UNTIL THEN, DEVELOP YOUR POWER.

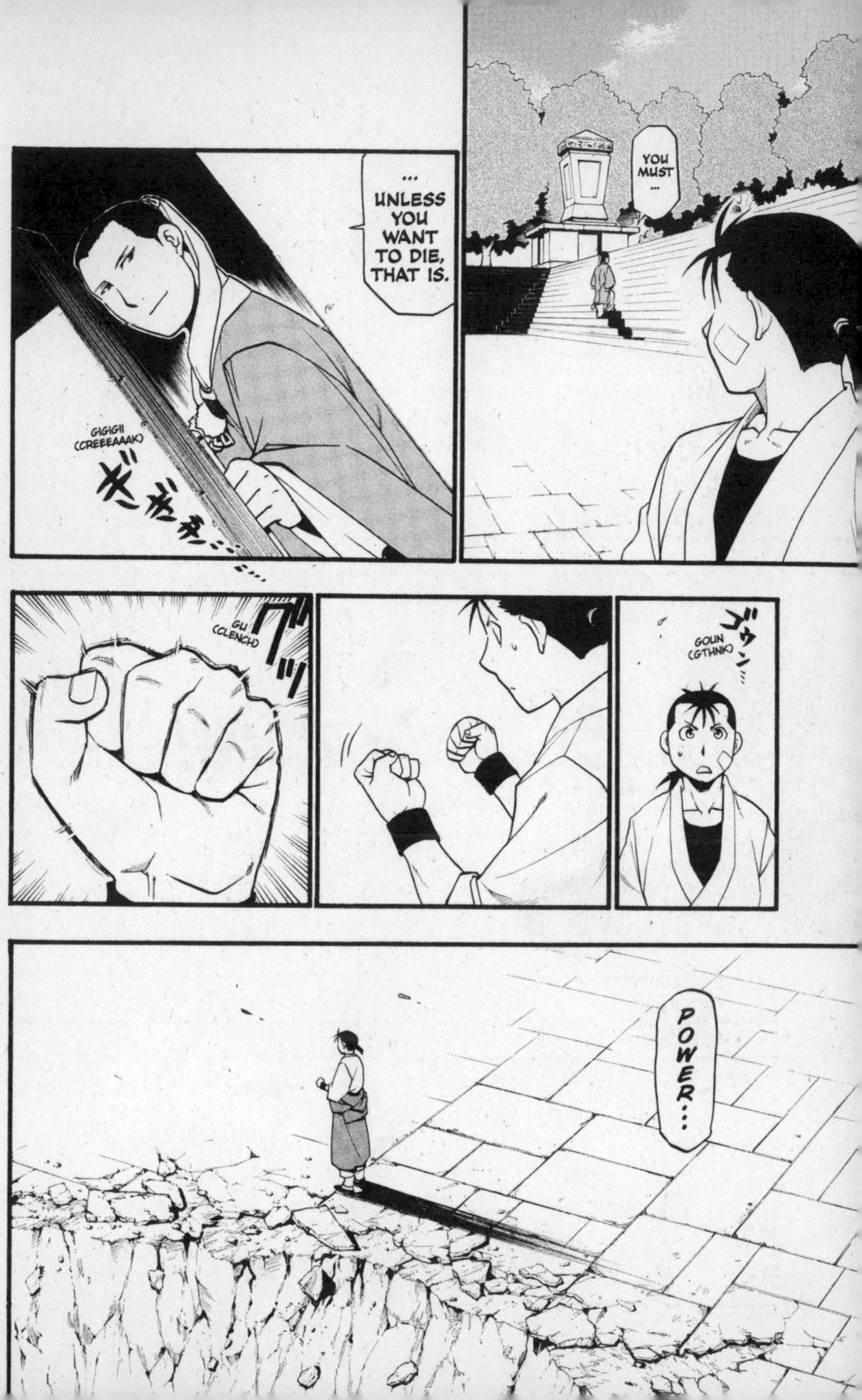
YOU MUST ...
... UNLESS YOU WANT TO DIE, THAT IS.
GIGIGII (CREEEAAAK)
GOUN (GTHNK)
GU (CLENCH)
POWER...

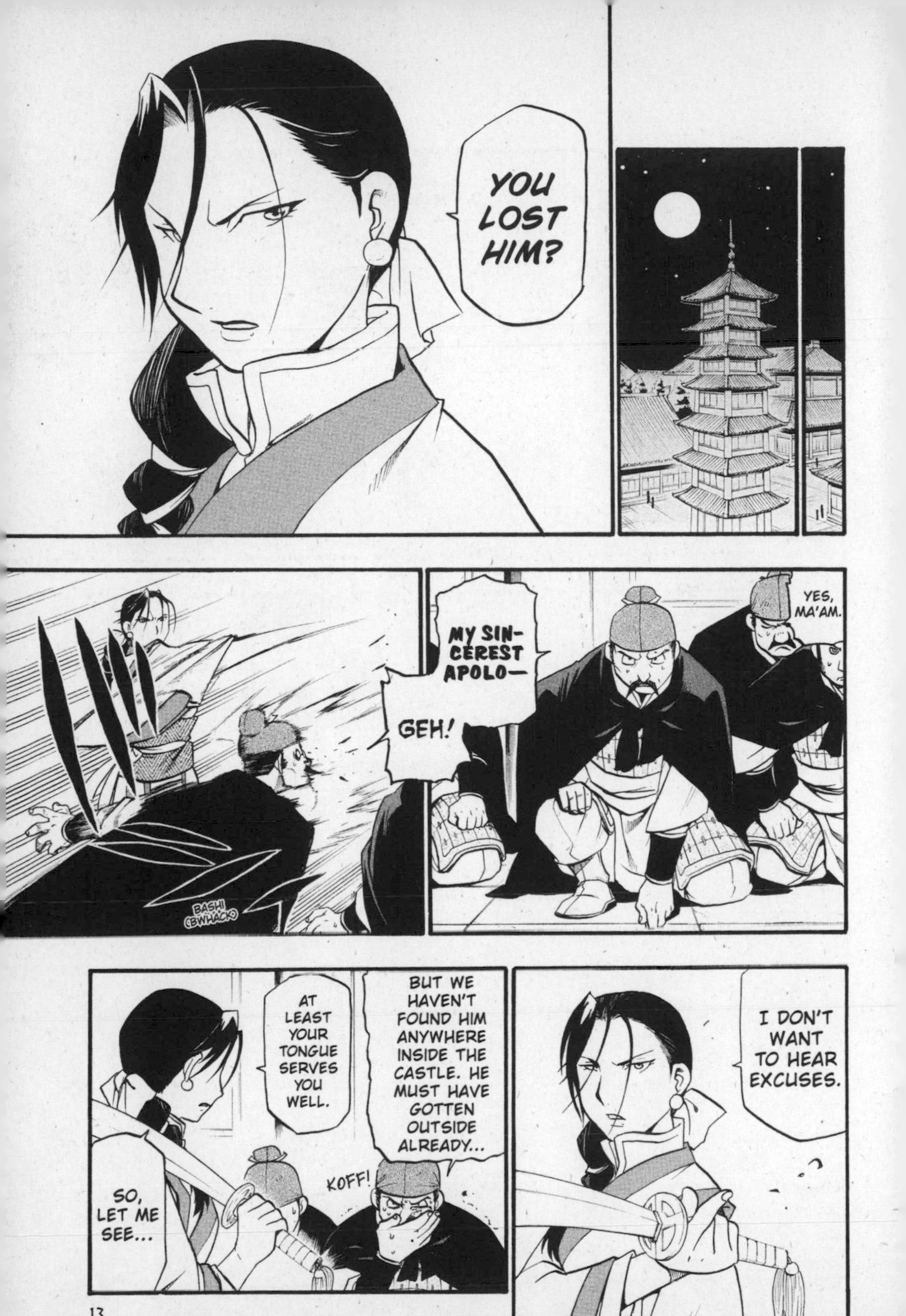
YOU LOST HIM?
YES, MA'AM.
MY SIN-CEREST APOLO—
GEH!
BASHI (BWHACK)
I DON'T WANT TO HEAR EXCUSES.
BUT WE HAVEN'T FOUND HIM ANYWHERE INSIDE THE CASTLE. HE MUST HAVE GOTTEN OUTSIDE ALREADY...
AT LEAST YOUR TONGUE SERVES YOU WELL.
KOFF!
SO, LET ME SEE...

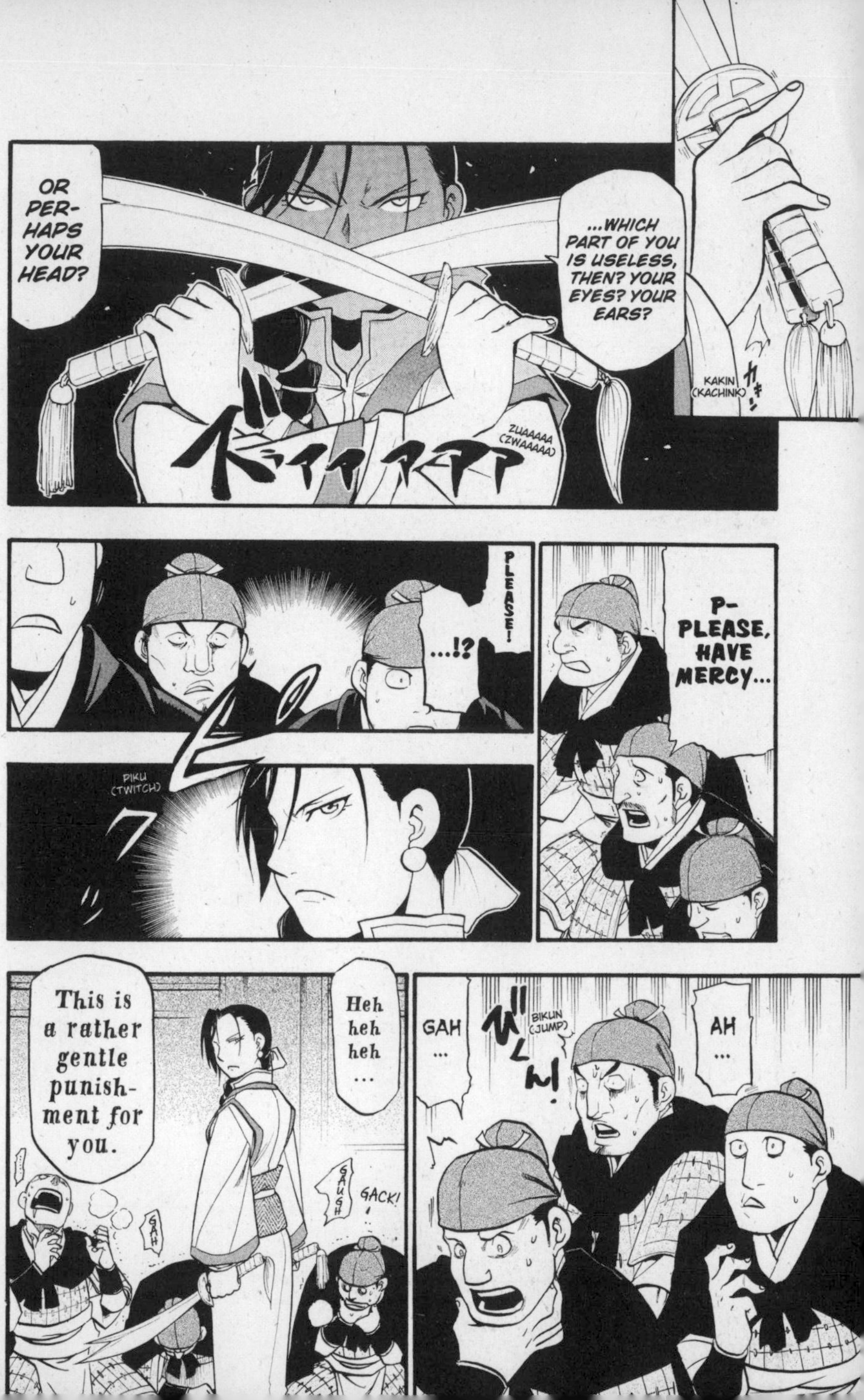
KAKIN (KACHINK)
...WHICH PART OF YOU IS USELESS, THEN? YOUR EYES? YOUR EARS?
OR PER-HAPS YOUR HEAD?
ZWAAAAA (ZWAAAAA)
P-PLEASE, HAVE MERCY...
PLEASE!
...!?
PIKU (TWITCH)
AH ...
BIKUN (JUMP)
GAH ...
Heh heh heh ...
This is a rather gentle punish-ment for you.
GACK!
GAUGH
GAH
...

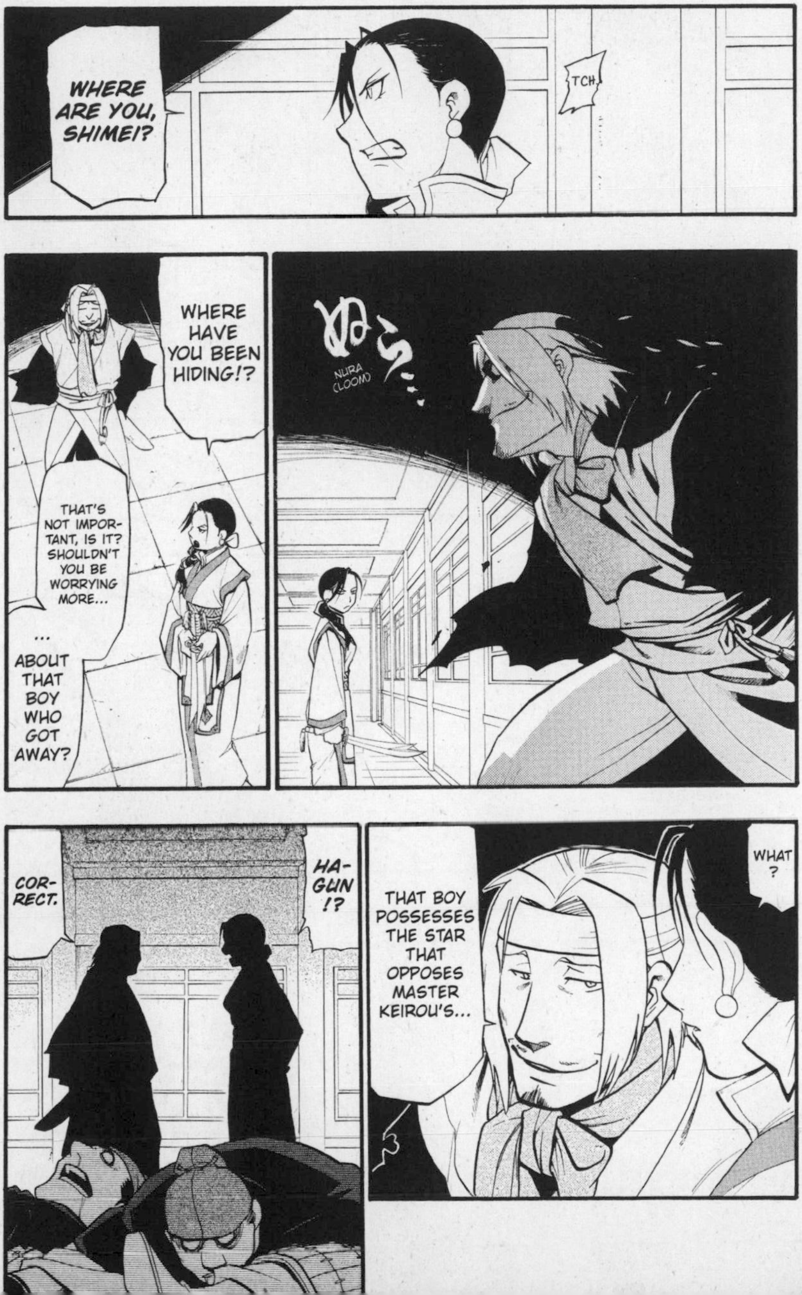
TCH.
WHERE ARE YOU, SHIMEI?
ぬら
NURA (LOOM)
WHERE HAVE YOU BEEN HIDING!?
THAT'S NOT IMPORTANT, IS IT? SHOULDN'T YOU BE WORRYING MORE...
... ABOUT THAT BOY WHO GOT AWAY?
WHAT?
THAT BOY POSSESSES THE STAR THAT OPPOSES MASTER KEIROU'S...
HA-GUN!?
COR-RECT.

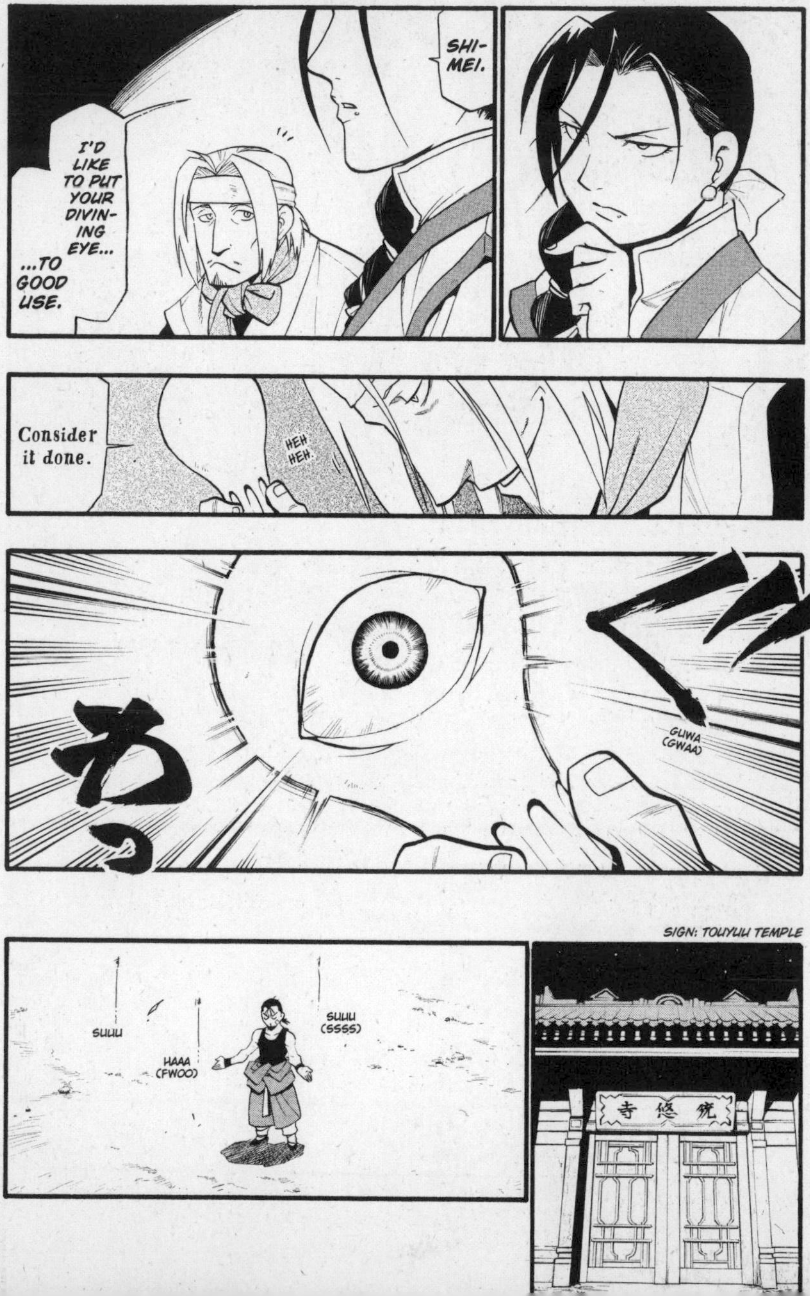
SHI-MEI.
I'D LIKE TO PUT YOUR DIVINING-EYE...
...TO GOOD USE.
HEH HEH.
Consider it done.
GUWA (GWAA)
わっ
SIGN: TOUYUU TEMPLE
SUUU (SSSS)
HAAA (FWOO)
SUUU

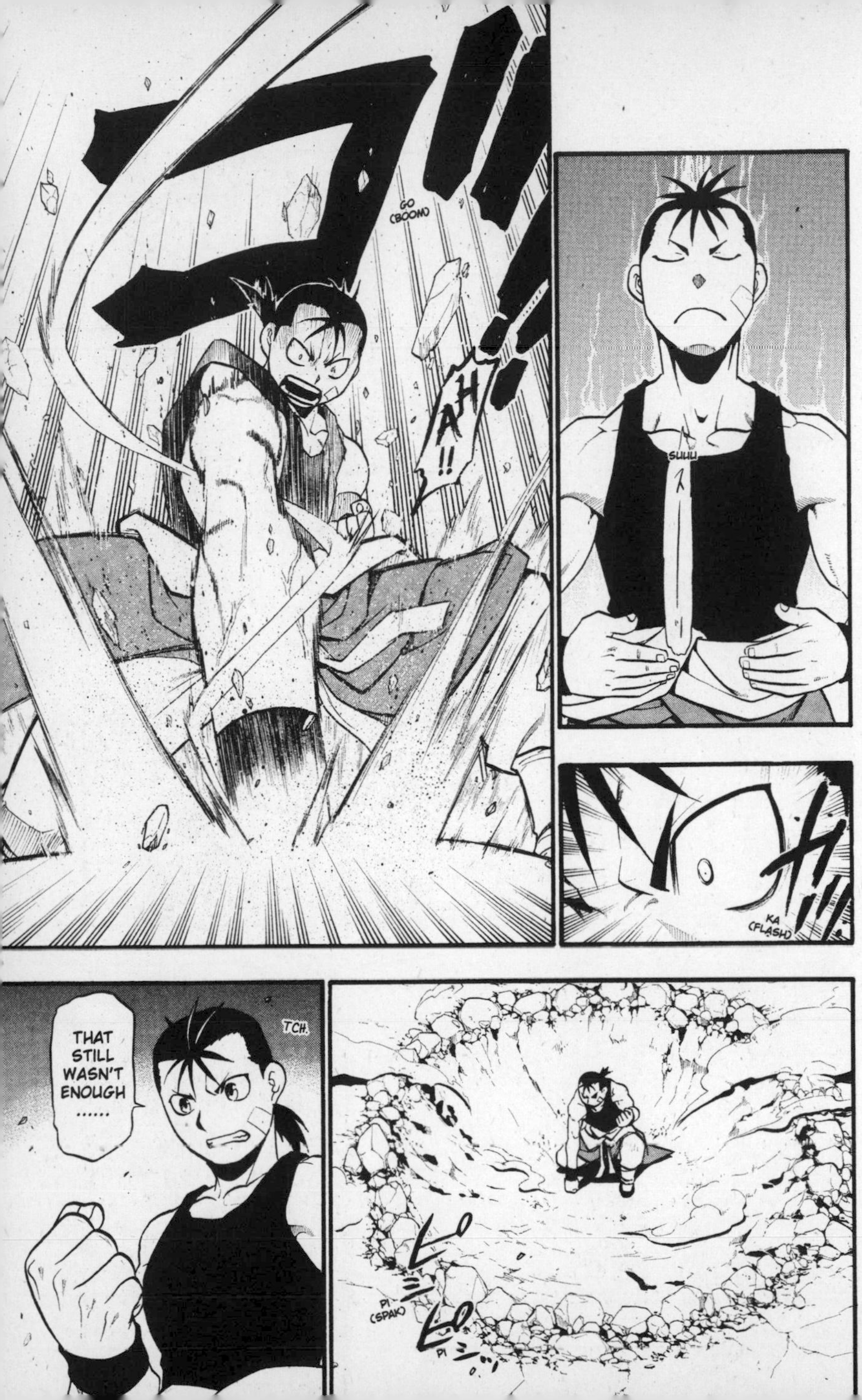
SUUU
KA (FLASH)
GO (BOOM)
HA!!
PI (SPAK)
PI
TCH.
THAT STILL WASN'T ENOUGH .......

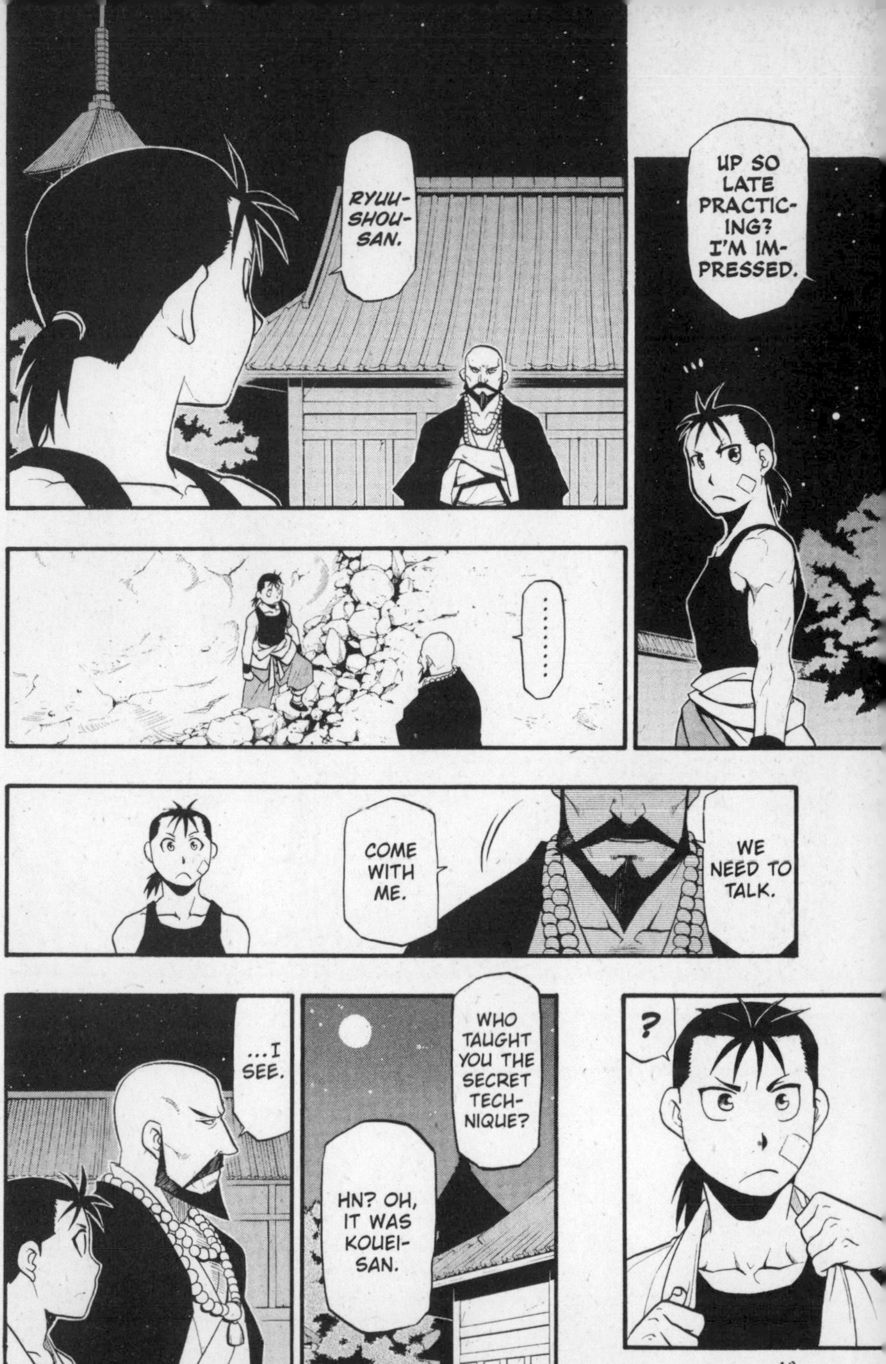

UP SO LATE PRACTIC-ING? I'M IM-PRESSED.
RYUU-SHOU-SAN.
..........
WE NEED TO TALK.
COME WITH ME.
?
WHO TAUGHT YOU THE SECRET TECH-NIQUE?
HN? OH, IT WAS KOUEI-SAN.
...I SEE.

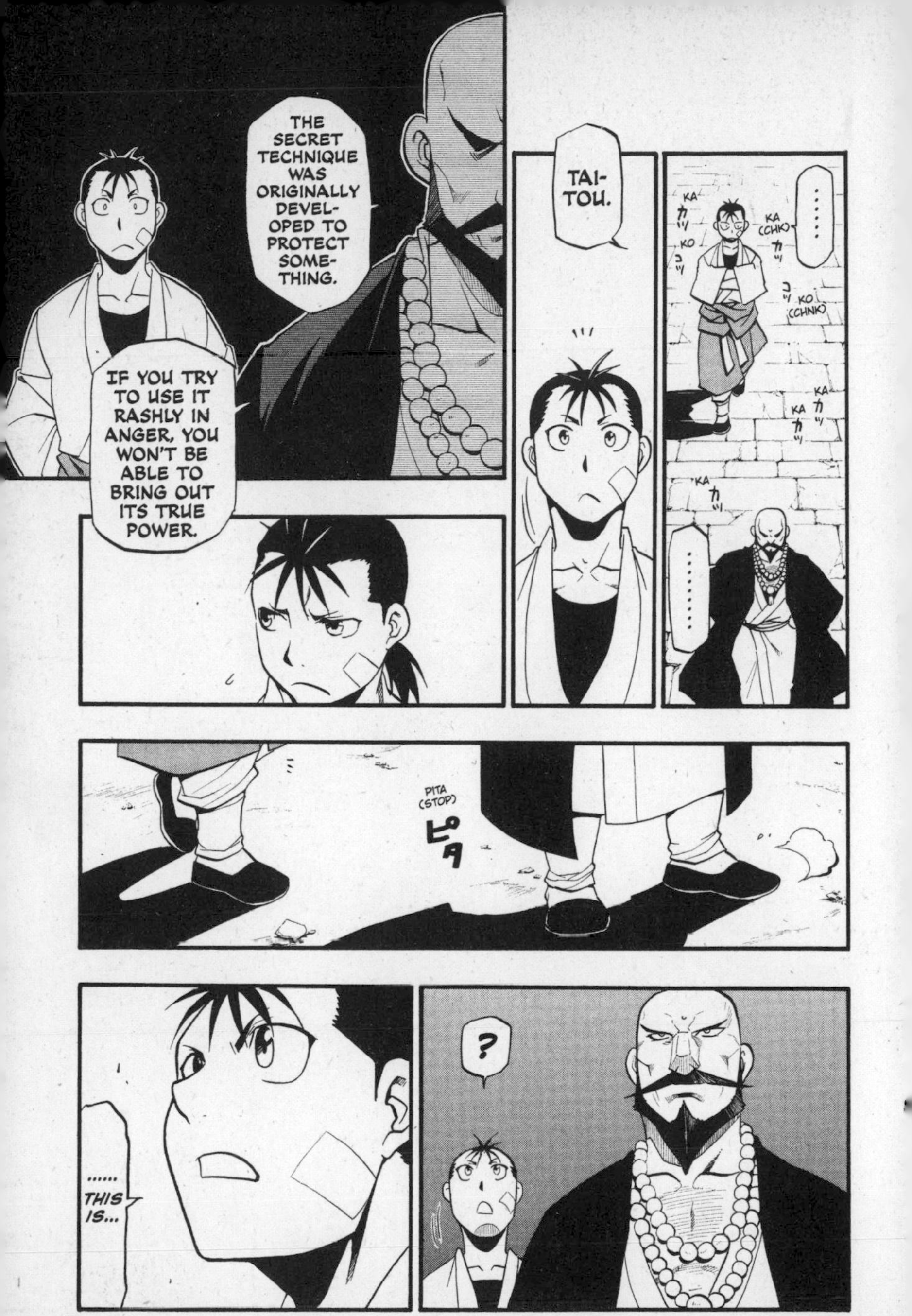
......
KA カッ
KA (CHK) カッ
KO コッ
KO (CHNK) コッ
KA カッ
KA カッ
KA カッ
......
TAI-TOU.
THE SECRET TECHNIQUE WAS ORIGINALLY DEVEL-OPED TO PROTECT SOME-THING.
IF YOU TRY TO USE IT RASHLY IN ANGER, YOU WON'T BE ABLE TO BRING OUT ITS TRUE POWER.
PITA (STOP) ピタ
?
......THIS IS...

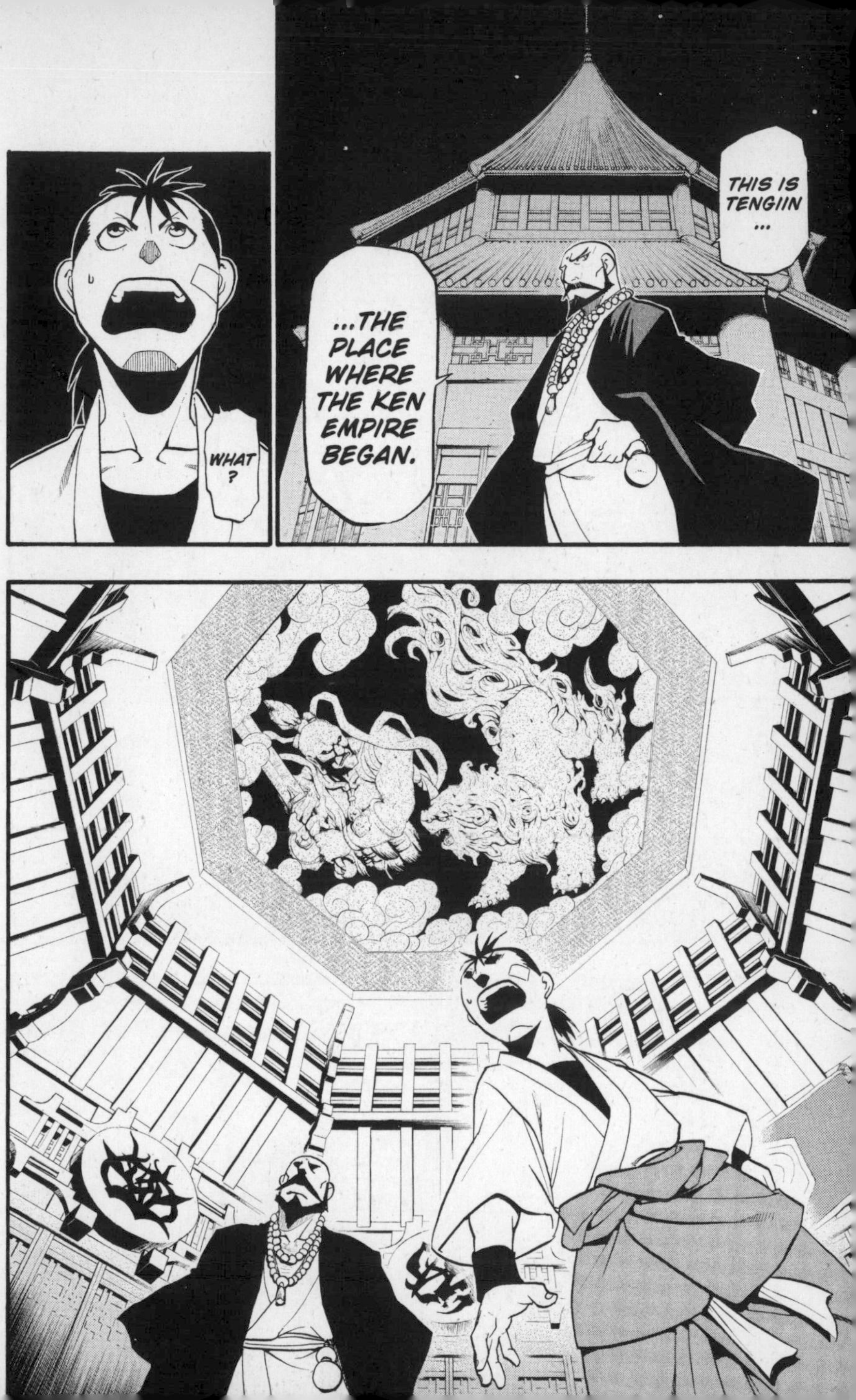
THIS IS TENGIIN ...
...THE PLACE WHERE THE KEN EMPIRE BEGAN.
WHAT ?

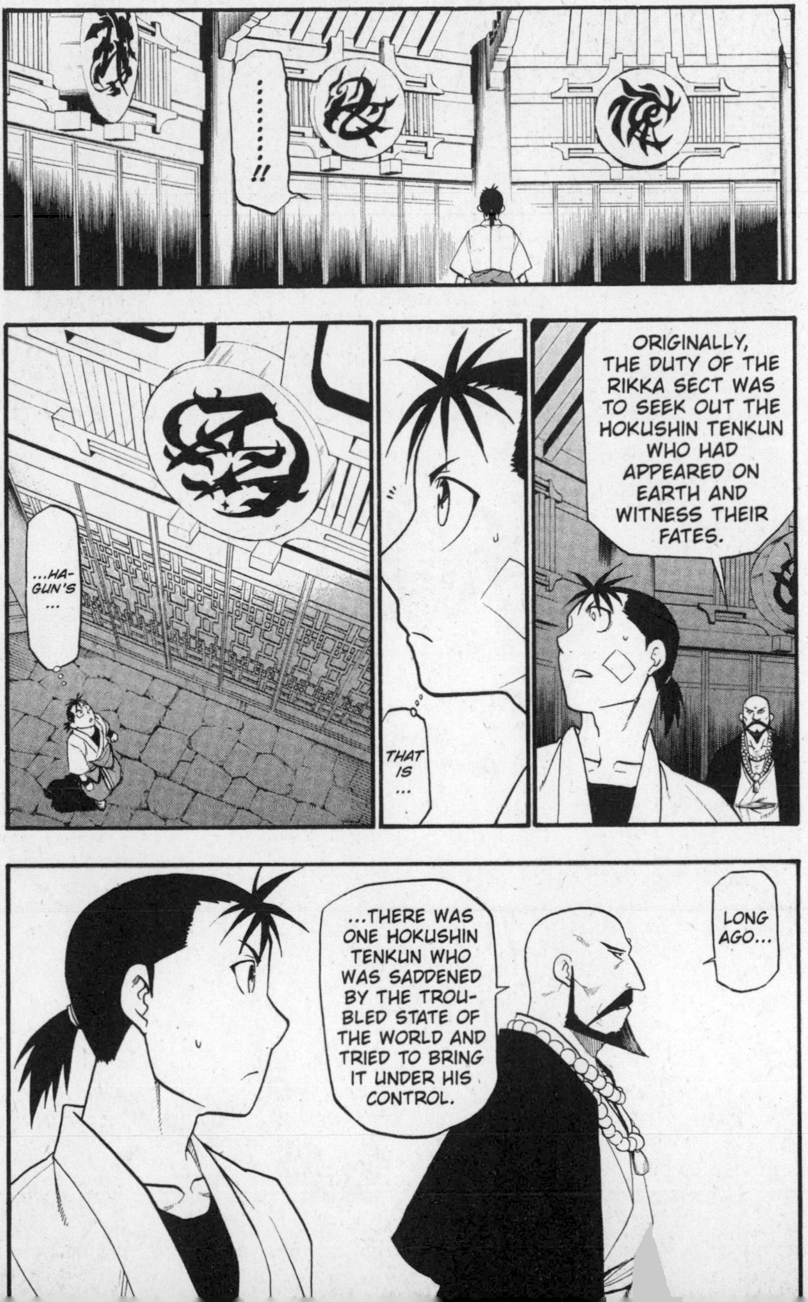
........!!
ORIGINALLY, THE DUTY OF THE RIKKA SECT WAS TO SEEK OUT THE HOKUSHIN TENKUN WHO HAD APPEARED ON EARTH AND WITNESS THEIR FATES.
THAT IS ...
...HA-GUN'S ...
LONG AGO...
...THERE WAS ONE HOKUSHIN TENKUN WHO WAS SADDENED BY THE TROU-BLED STATE OF THE WORLD AND TRIED TO BRING IT UNDER HIS CONTROL.

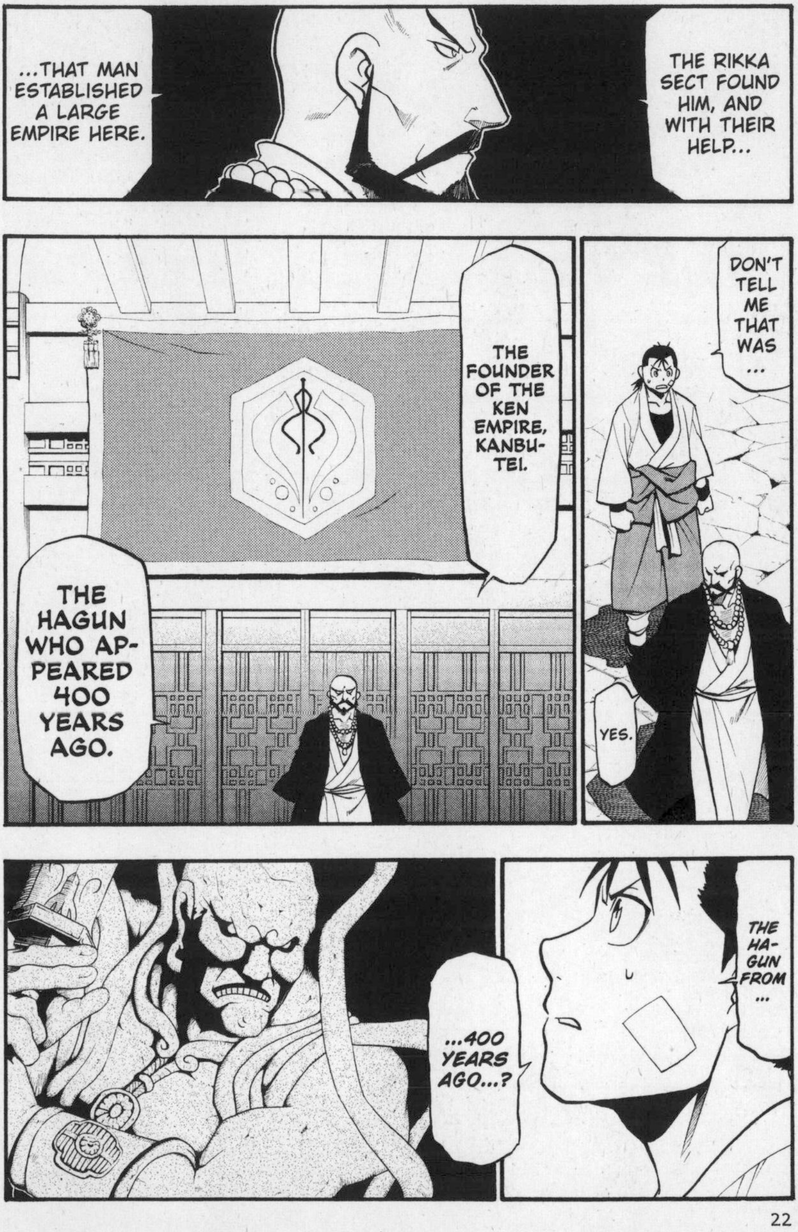
THE RIKKA SECT FOUND HIM, AND WITH THEIR HELP...
...THAT MAN ESTABLISHED A LARGE EMPIRE HERE.
DON'T TELL ME THAT WAS ...
YES.
THE FOUNDER OF THE KEN EMPIRE, KANBU-TEI.
THE HAGUN WHO AP-PEARED 400 YEARS AGO.
THE HA-GUN FROM ...
...400 YEARS AGO...?

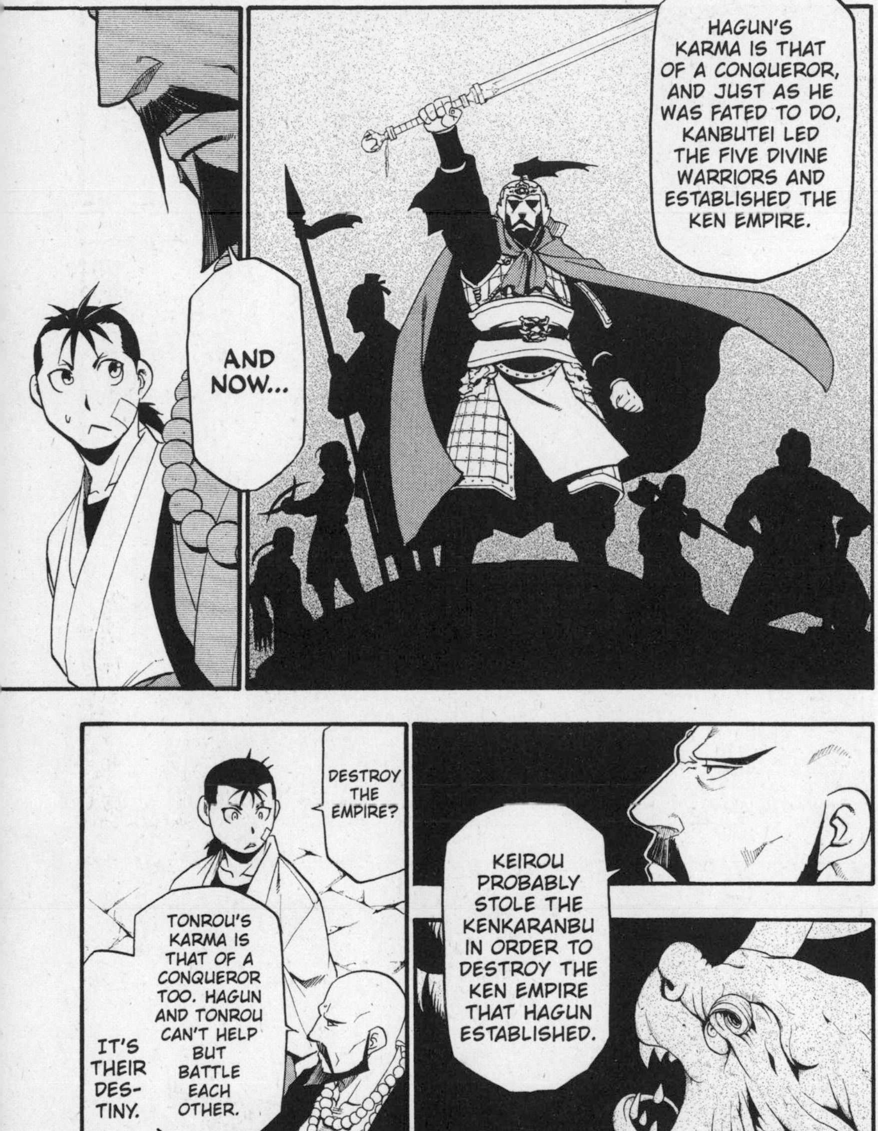

HAGUN'S KARMA IS THAT OF A CONQUEROR, AND JUST AS HE WAS FATED TO DO, KANBUTEI LED THE FIVE DIVINE WARRIORS AND ESTABLISHED THE KEN EMPIRE.
AND NOW...
KEIROU PROBABLY STOLE THE KENKARANBU IN ORDER TO DESTROY THE KEN EMPIRE THAT HAGUN ESTABLISHED.
DESTROY THE EMPIRE?
TONROU'S KARMA IS THAT OF A CONQUEROR TOO. HAGUN AND TONROU CAN'T HELP BUT BATTLE EACH OTHER.
IT'S THEIR DES-TINY.

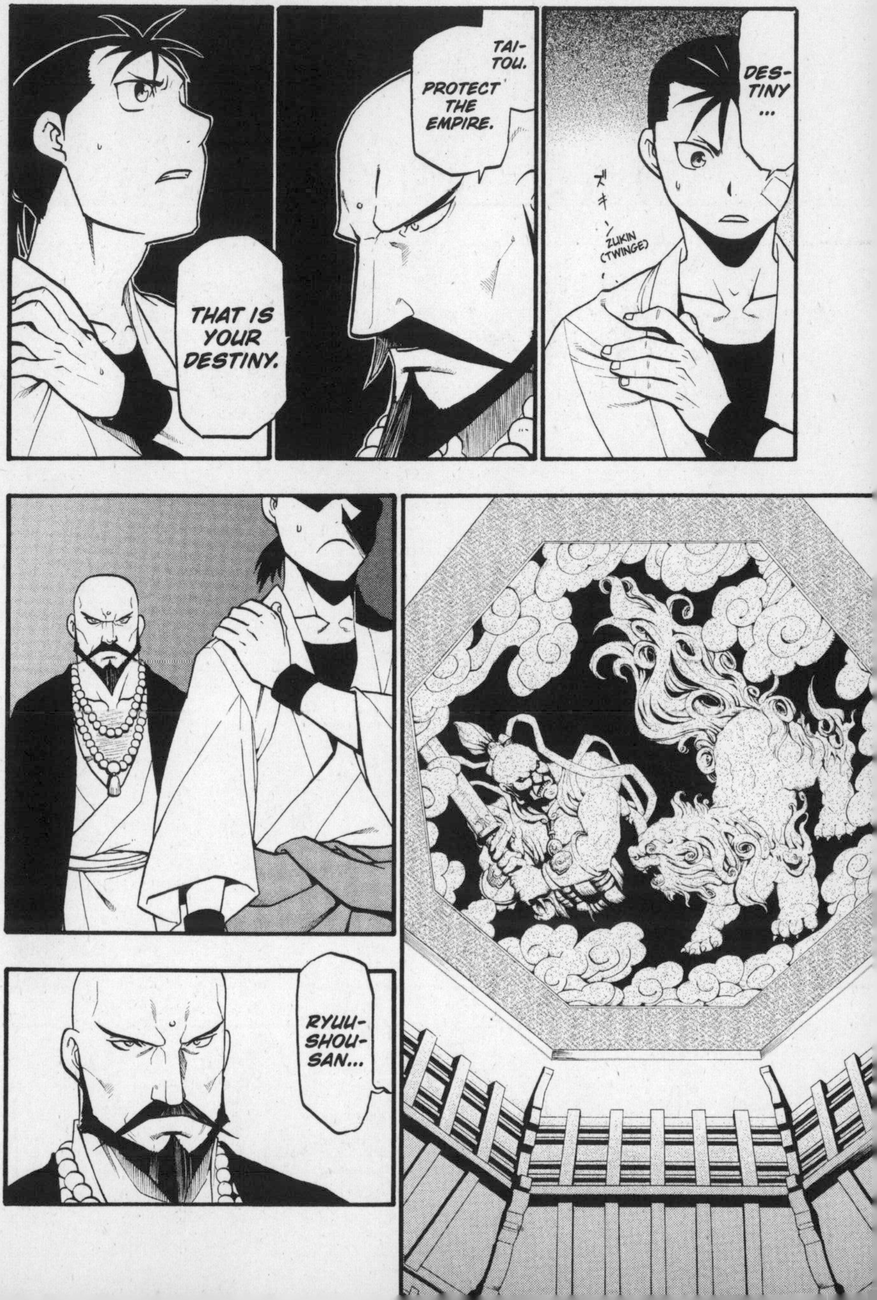
DES-TINY...
ズキン
ZUKIN (TWINGE)
TAI-TOU.
PROTECT THE EMPIRE.
THAT IS YOUR DESTINY.
RYUU-SHOU-SAN...

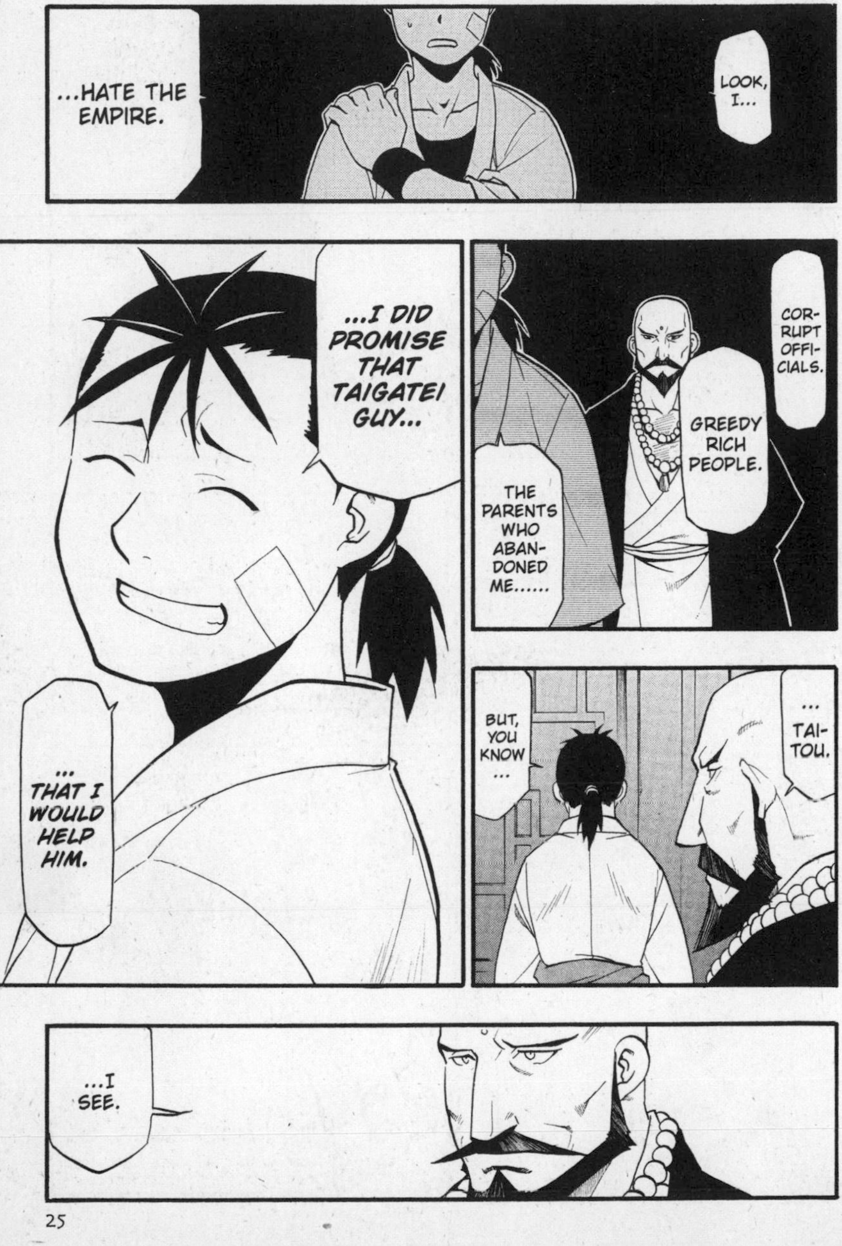
LOOK, I...
...HATE THE EMPIRE.
CORRUPT OFFICIALS.
GREEDY RICH PEOPLE.
THE PARENTS WHO ABANDONED ME......
...TAITOU.
BUT, YOU KNOW ...
...I DID PROMISE THAT TAIGATEI GUY...
...THAT I WOULD HELP HIM.
...I SEE.

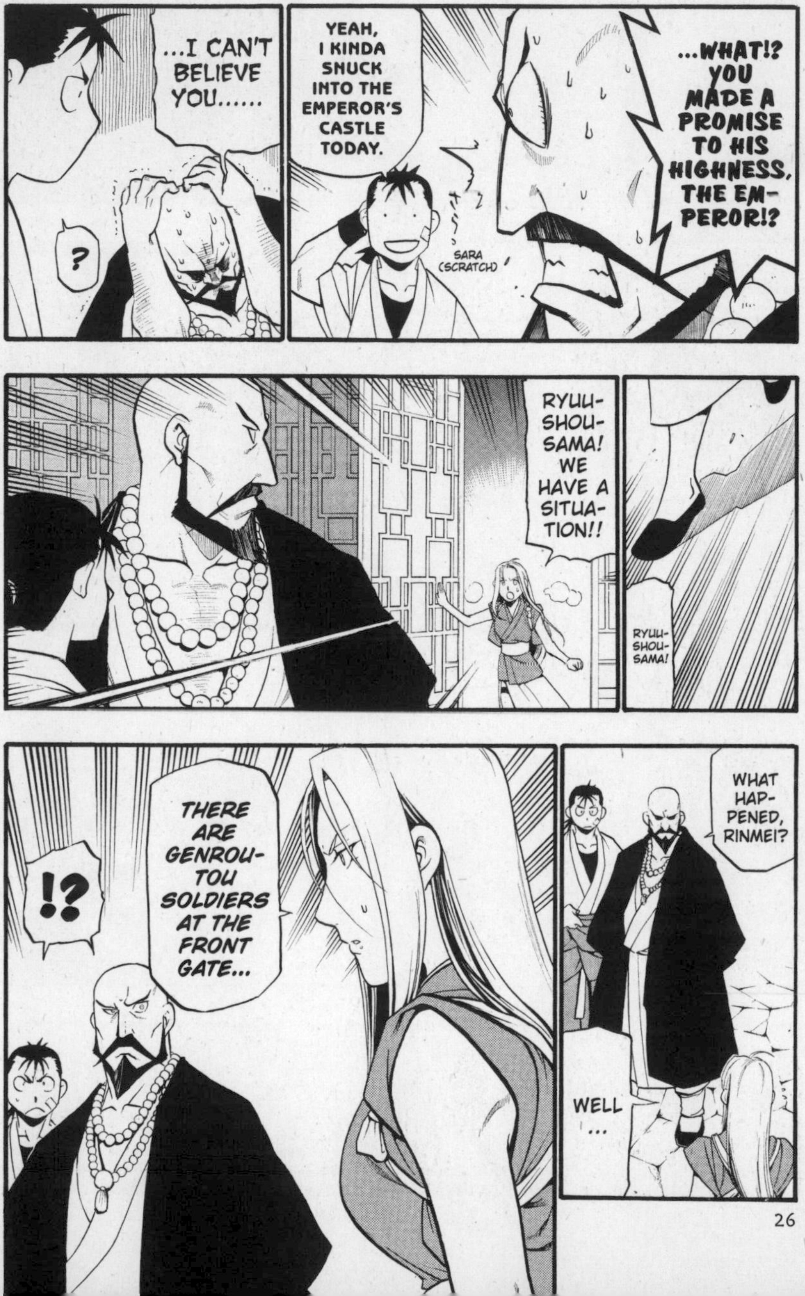
...WHAT!? YOU MADE A PROMISE TO HIS HIGHNESS, THE EMPEROR!?
YEAH, I KINDA SNUCK INTO THE EMPEROR'S CASTLE TODAY.
SARA (SCRATCH)
...I CAN'T BELIEVE YOU......
?
RYUU-SHOU-SAMA!
RYUU-SHOU-SAMA! WE HAVE A SITUATION!!
WHAT HAPPENED, RINMEI?
WELL...
THERE ARE GENROU-TOU SOLDIERS AT THE FRONT GATE...
!?

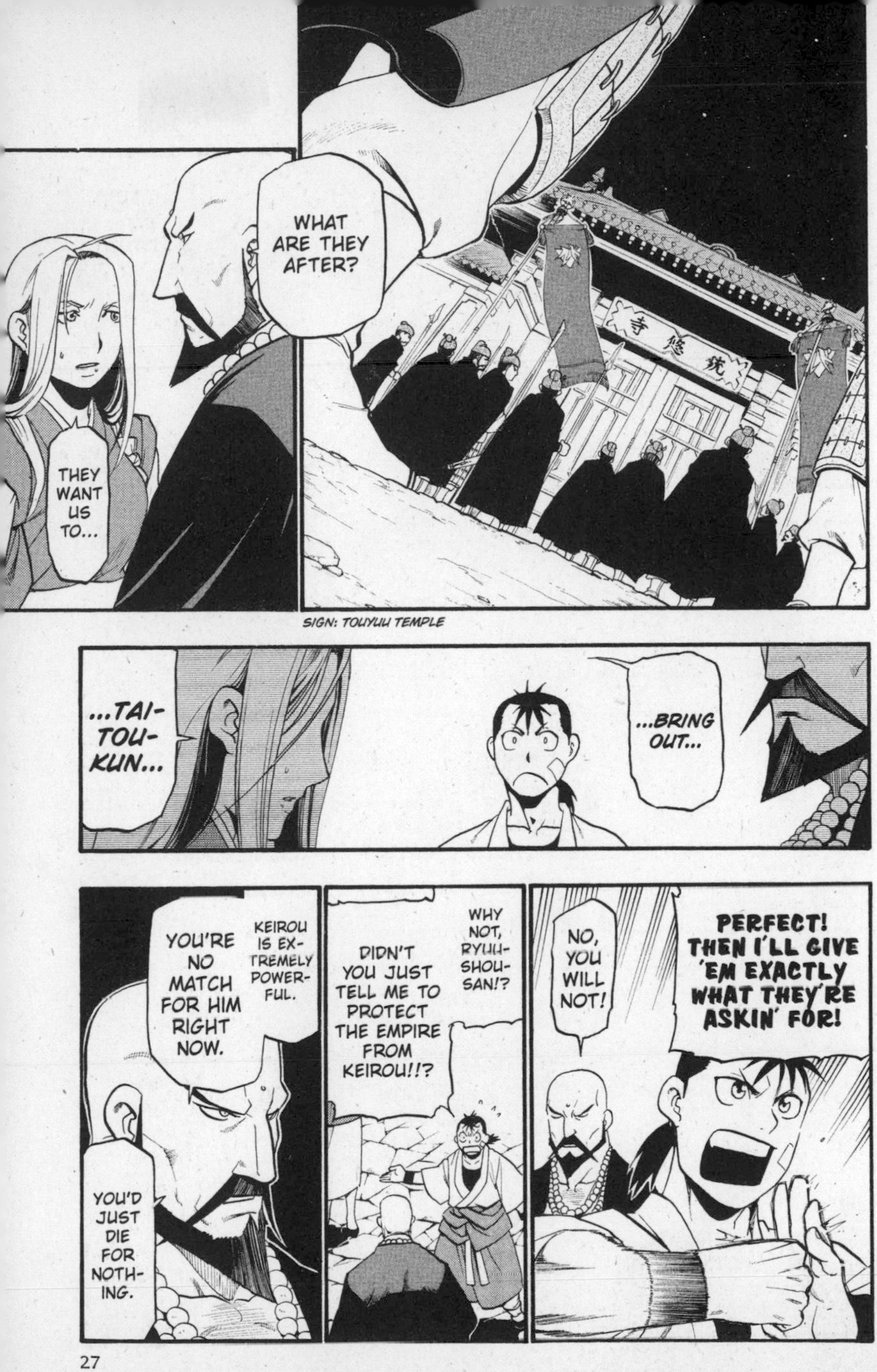
WHAT ARE THEY AFTER?
THEY WANT US TO...
SIGN: TOUYUU TEMPLE
...BRING OUT...
...TAI-TOUKUN...
PERFECT! THEN I'LL GIVE 'EM EXACTLY WHAT THEY'RE ASKIN' FOR!
NO, YOU WILL NOT!
WHY NOT, RYUU-SHOUSAN!?
DIDN'T YOU JUST TELL ME TO PROTECT THE EMPIRE FROM KEIROU!!?
KEIROU IS EXTREMELY POWERFUL.
YOU'RE NO MATCH FOR HIM RIGHT NOW.
YOU'D JUST DIE FOR NOTHING.

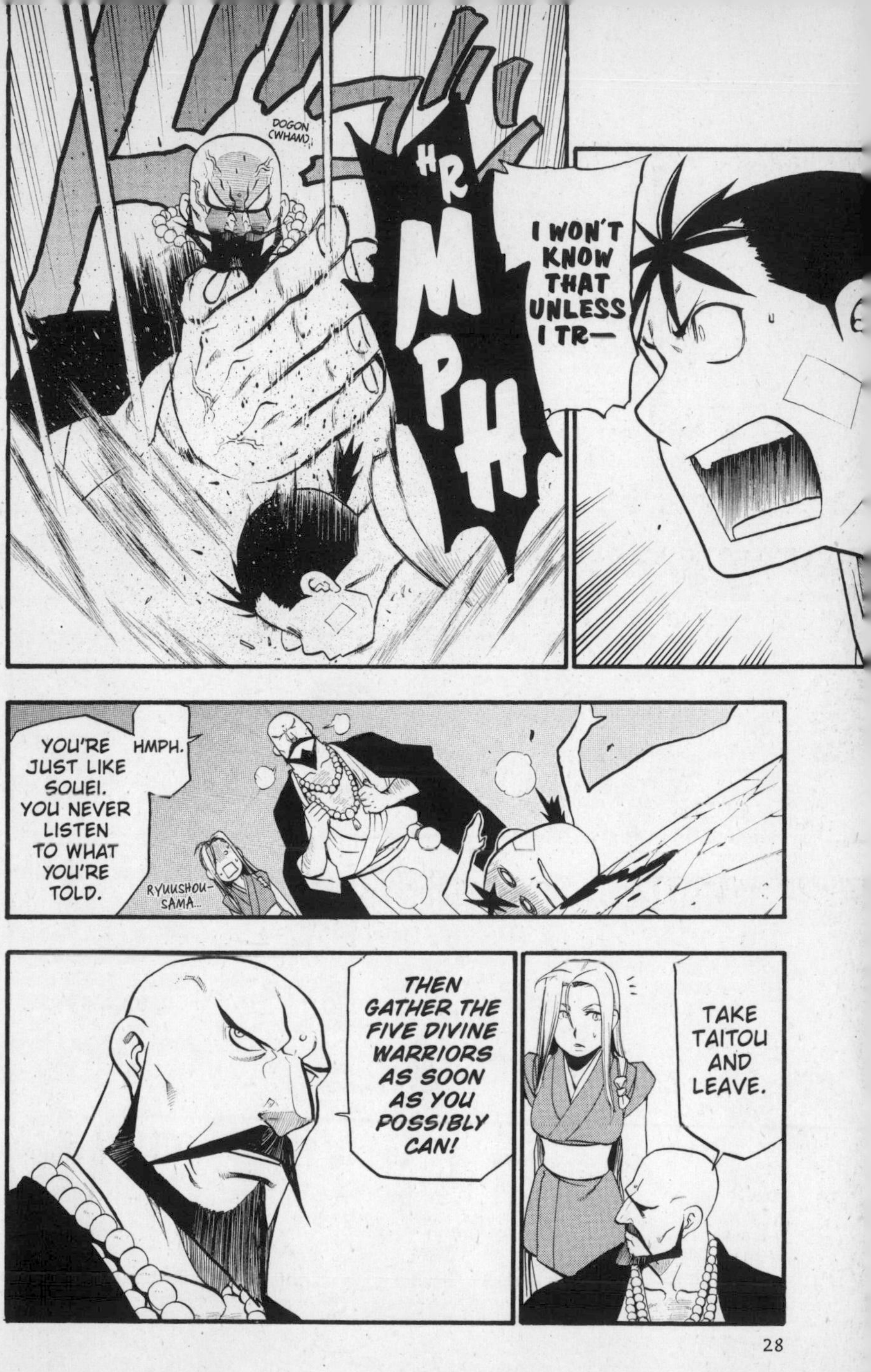
I WON'T KNOW THAT UNLESS I TR—
HRMPH
DOGON (WHAM)
HMPH.
YOU'RE JUST LIKE SOUEI. YOU NEVER LISTEN TO WHAT YOU'RE TOLD.
RYUUSHOU-SAMA...
TAKE TAITOU AND LEAVE.
THEN GATHER THE FIVE DIVINE WARRIORS AS SOON AS YOU POSSIBLY CAN!

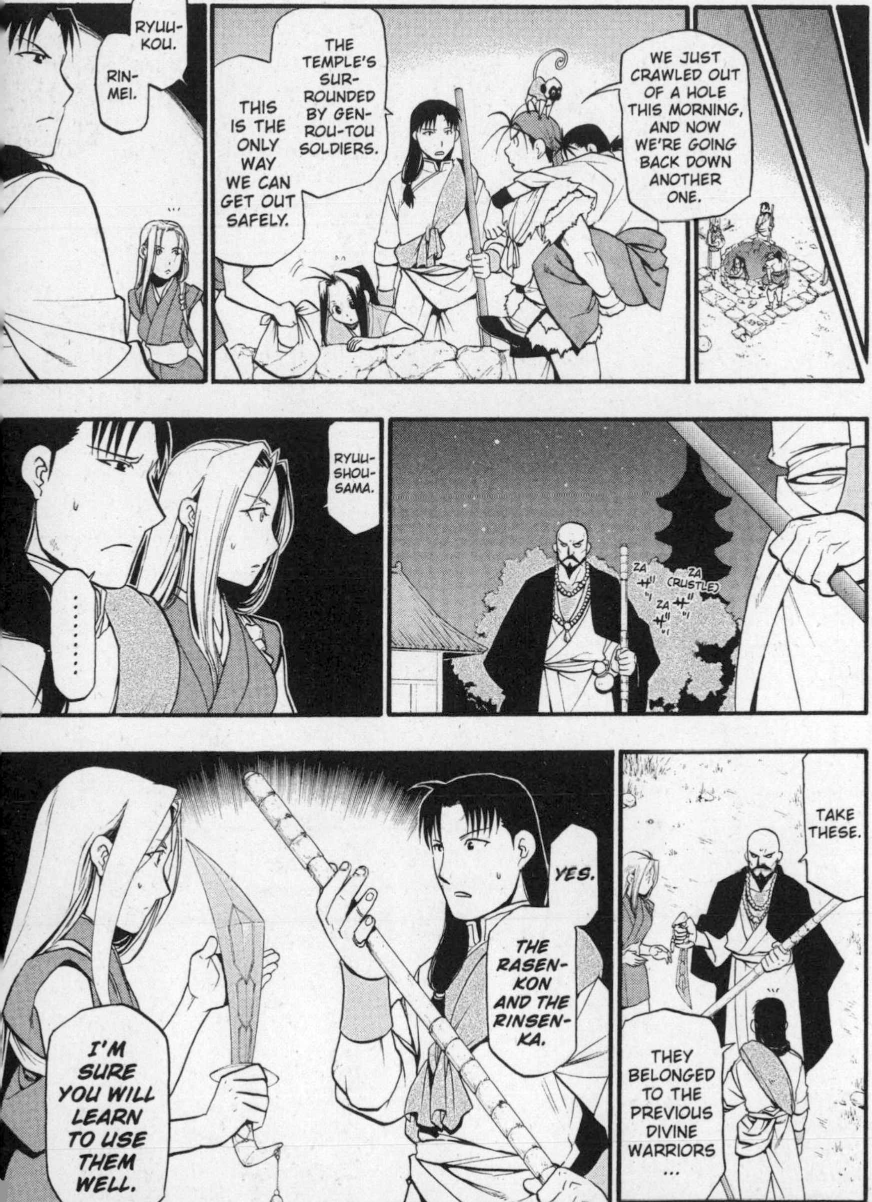
WE JUST CRAWLED OUT OF A HOLE THIS MORNING, AND NOW WE'RE GOING BACK DOWN ANOTHER ONE.
THE TEMPLE'S SURROUNDED BY GENROU-TOU SOLDIERS.
THIS IS THE ONLY WAY WE CAN GET OUT SAFELY.
RYUU-KOU.
RIN-MEI.
ZA ZA (RUSTLE) ZA
RYUU-SHOU-SAMA.
......
TAKE THESE.
THEY BELONGED TO THE PREVIOUS DIVINE WARRIORS...
YES.
THE RASEN-KON AND THE RINSEN-KA.
I'M SURE YOU WILL LEARN TO USE THEM WELL.

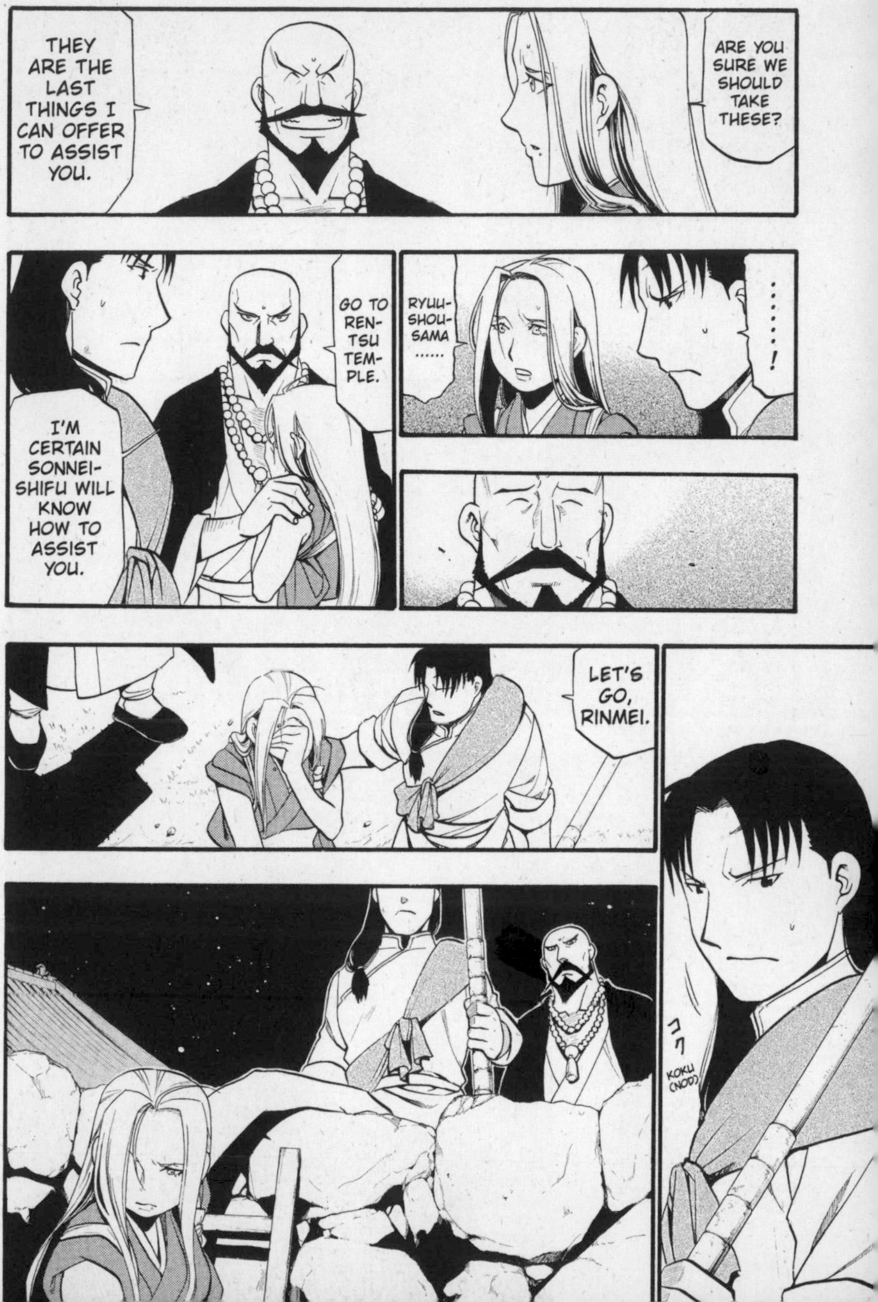
ARE YOU SURE WE SHOULD TAKE THESE?
THEY ARE THE LAST THINGS I CAN OFFER TO ASSIST YOU.
......!
RYUU-SHOU-SAMA ......
GO TO REN-TSU TEM-PLE.
I'M CERTAIN SONNEI-SHIFU WILL KNOW HOW TO ASSIST YOU.
コク
KOKU (NOD)
LET'S GO, RINMEI.

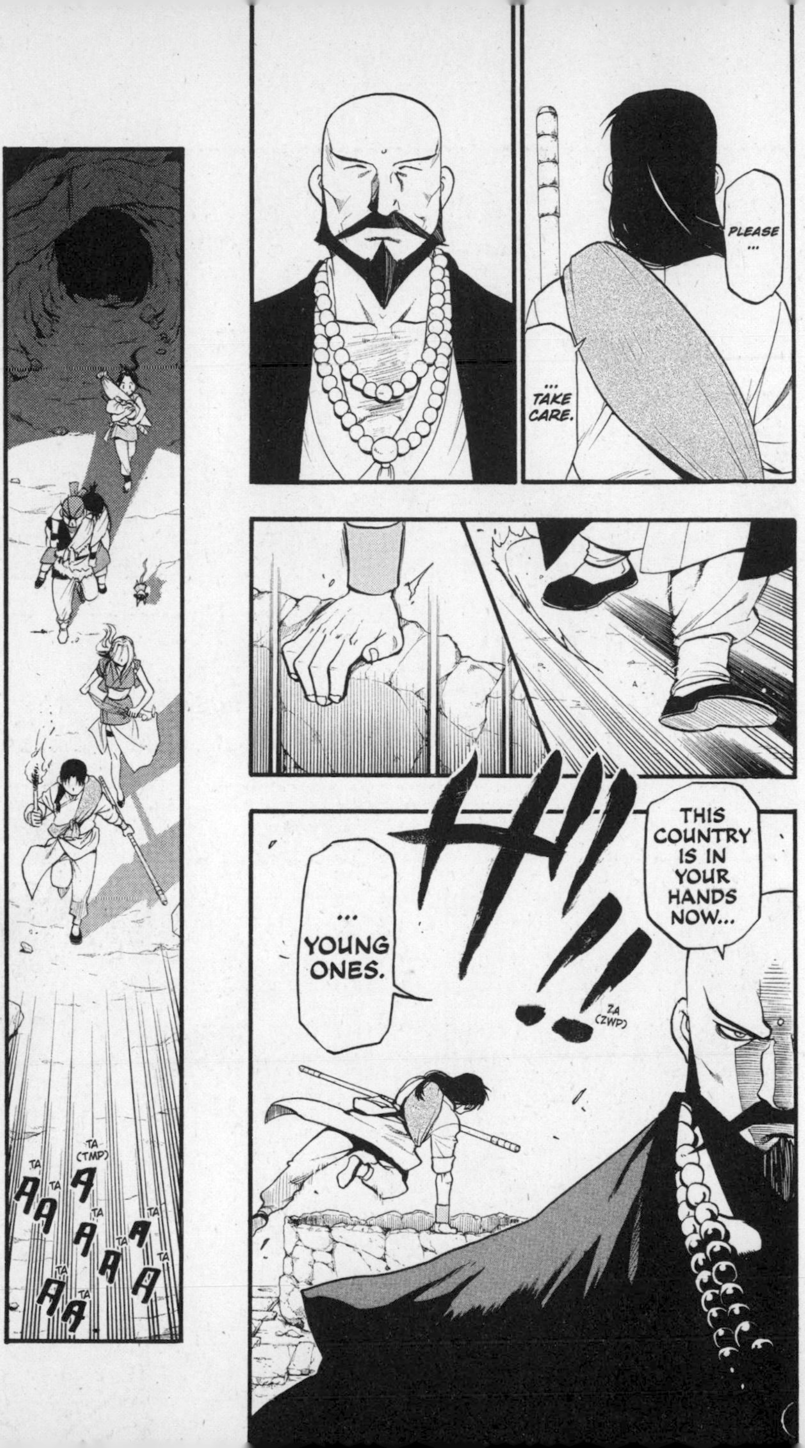
PLEASE ...
... TAKE CARE.
THIS COUNTRY IS IN YOUR HANDS NOW...
... YOUNG ONES.
ZA (ZWP)
TA (TMP)
TA TA TA TA TA TA TA TA TA

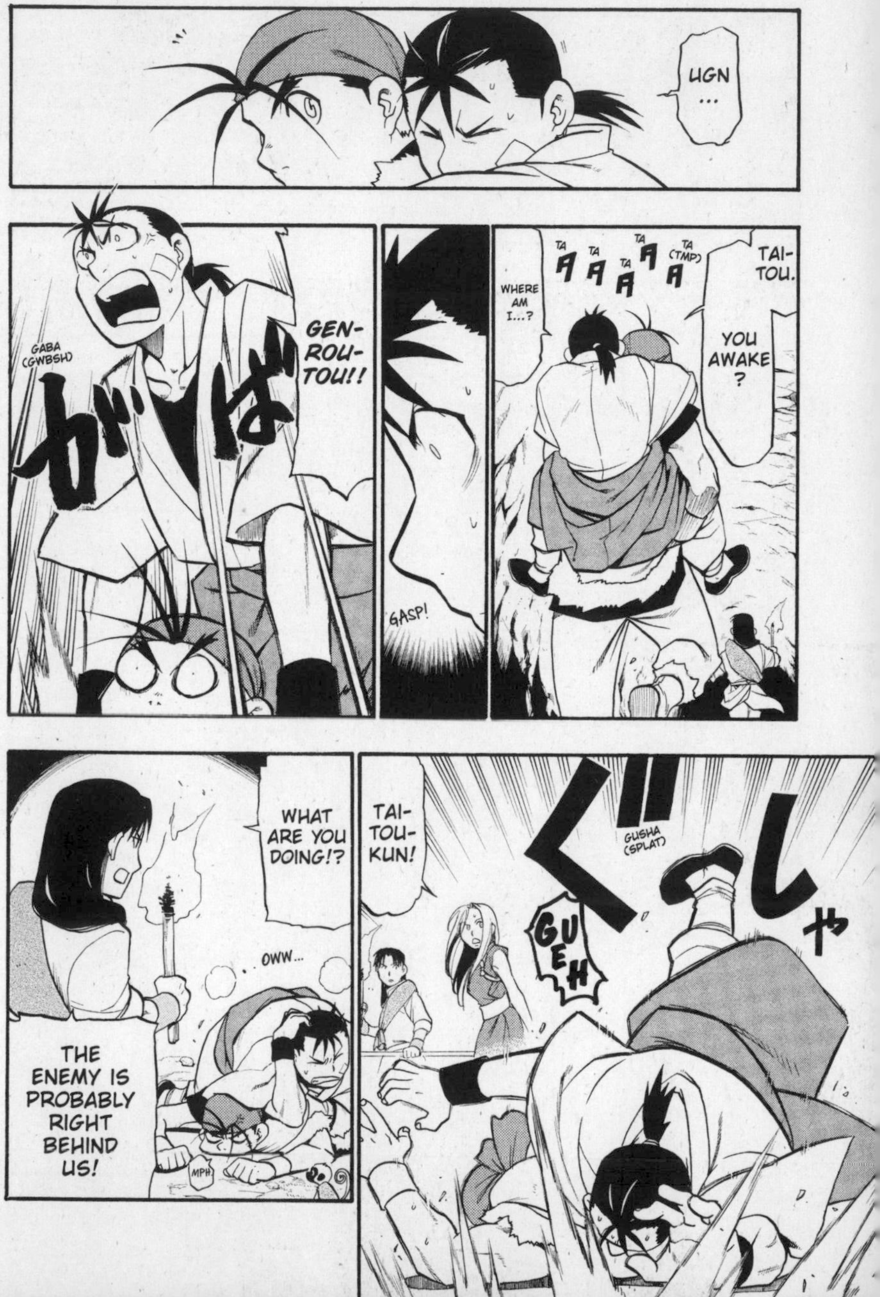
UGN ...
TAI-TOU.
YOU AWAKE?
TA TA TA TA TA (TMP)
WHERE AM I...?
GASP!
GEN-ROU-TOU!!
GABA (GWBSH)
GUSHA (SPLAT)
GUEH
TAI-TOU-KUN!
WHAT ARE YOU DOING!?
...OWW...
THE ENEMY IS PROBABLY RIGHT BEHIND US!
MPH

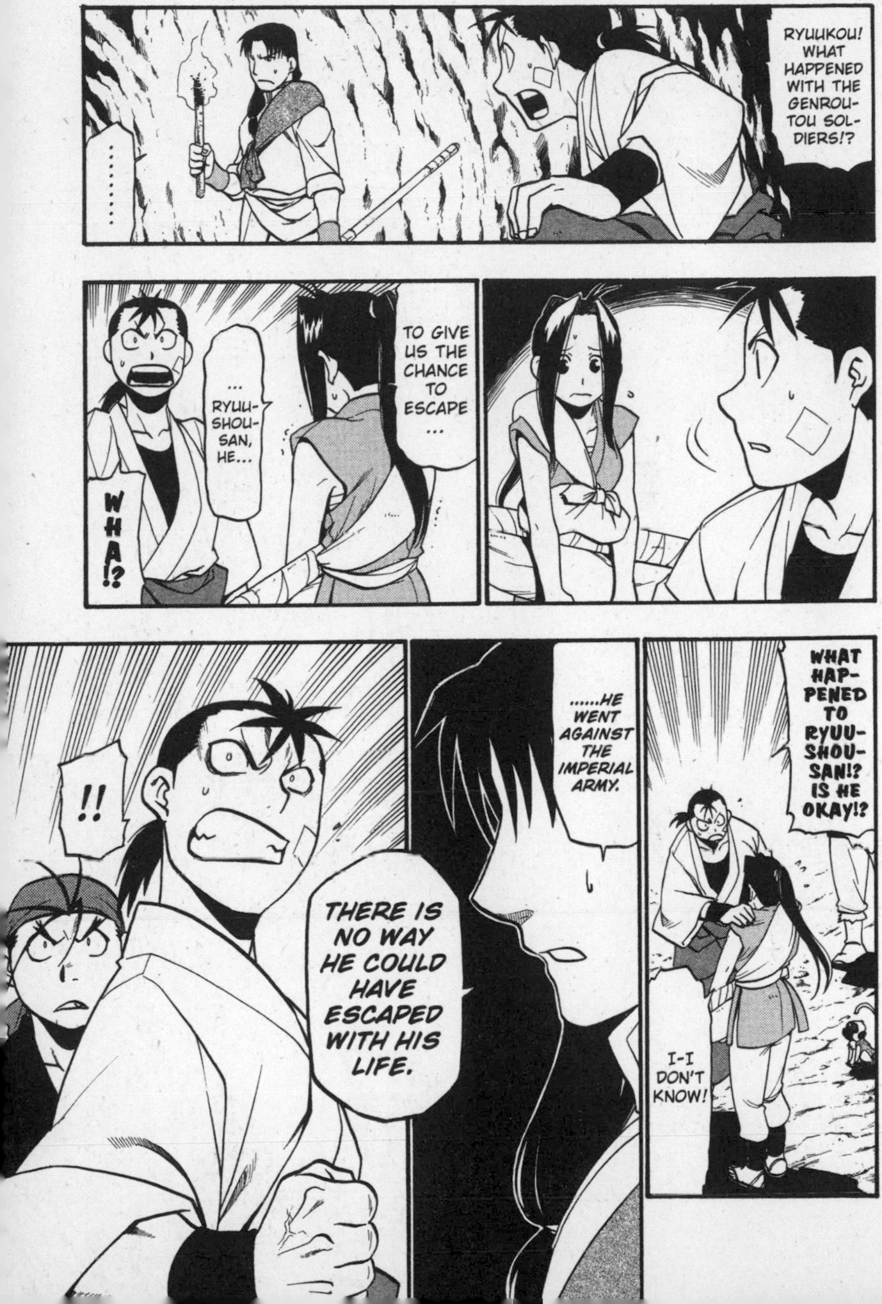
RYUUKOU! WHAT HAPPENED WITH THE GENROU-TOU SOL-DIERS!?
......
TO GIVE US THE CHANCE TO ESCAPE ...
... RYUU-SHOU-SAN, HE...
WHA!?
WHAT HAP-PENED TO RYUU-SHOU-SAN!? IS HE OKAY!?
I-I DON'T KNOW!
......HE WENT AGAINST THE IMPERIAL ARMY.
!!
THERE IS NO WAY HE COULD HAVE ESCAPED WITH HIS LIFE.

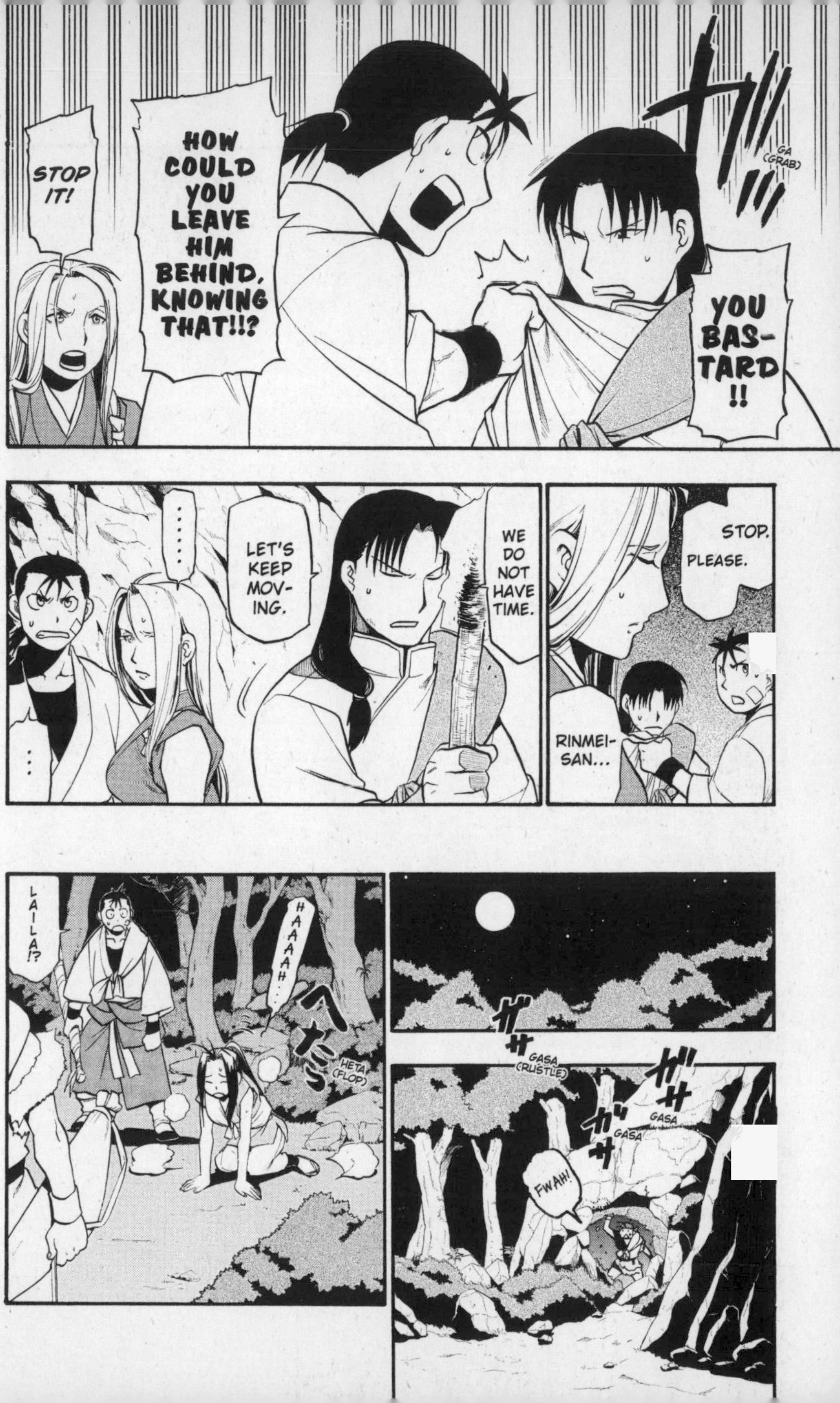
GA (GRAB)
YOU BAS-TARD!!
HOW COULD YOU LEAVE HIM BEHIND, KNOWING THAT!!?
STOP IT!
STOP.
PLEASE.
RINMEI-SAN...
WE DO NOT HAVE TIME.
LET'S KEEP MOVING.
......
...
GASA (RUSTLE)
GASA
GASA
FWAH!
HAAAAAH...
HETA (FLOP)
LAILA!?

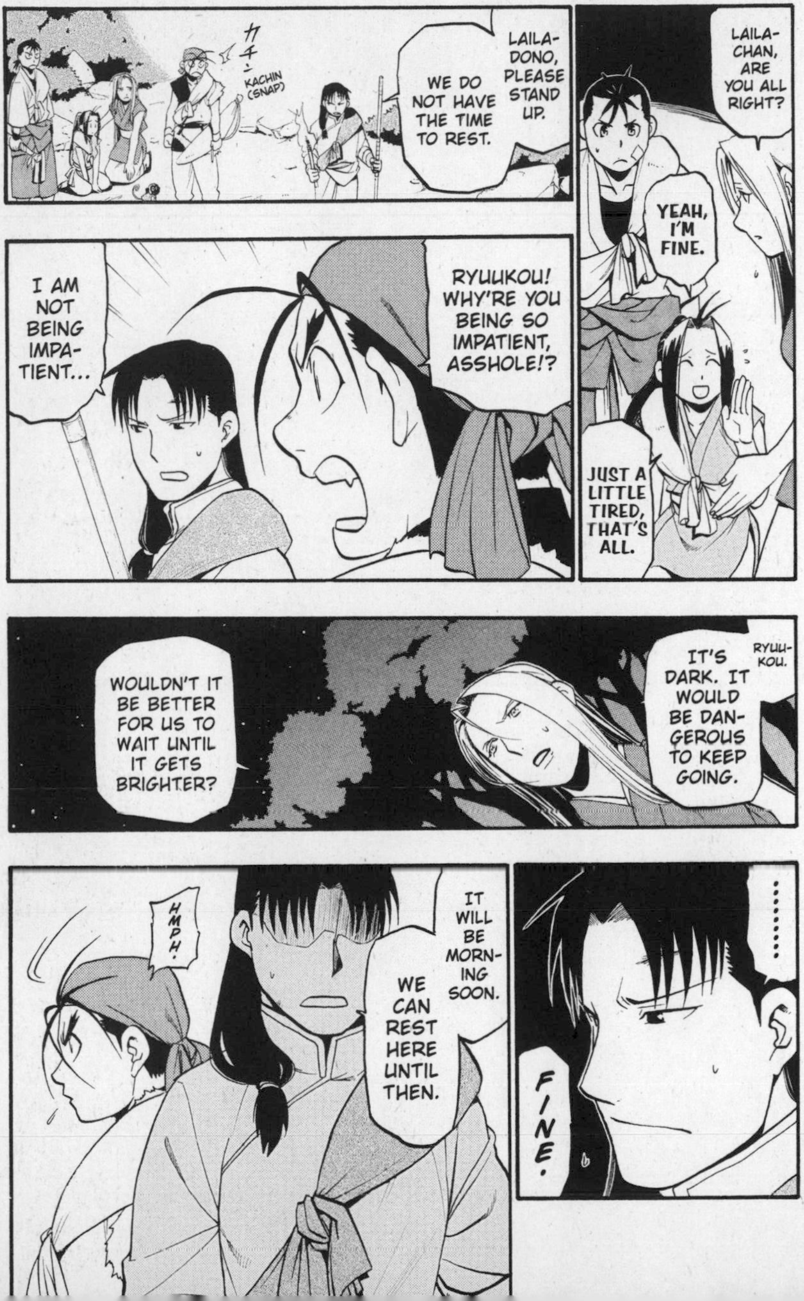
LAILA-CHAN, ARE YOU ALL RIGHT?
YEAH, I'M FINE.
JUST A LITTLE TIRED, THAT'S ALL.
LAILA-DONO, PLEASE STAND UP.
WE DO NOT HAVE THE TIME TO REST.
カチン
KACHIN (SNAP)
RYUUKOU! WHY'RE YOU BEING SO IMPATIENT, ASSHOLE!?
I AM NOT BEING IMPATIENT...
RYUUKOU.
IT'S DARK. IT WOULD BE DANGEROUS TO KEEP GOING.
WOULDN'T IT BE BETTER FOR US TO WAIT UNTIL IT GETS BRIGHTER?
.........
FINE.
IT WILL BE MORNING SOON.
WE CAN REST HERE UNTIL THEN.
HMPH.

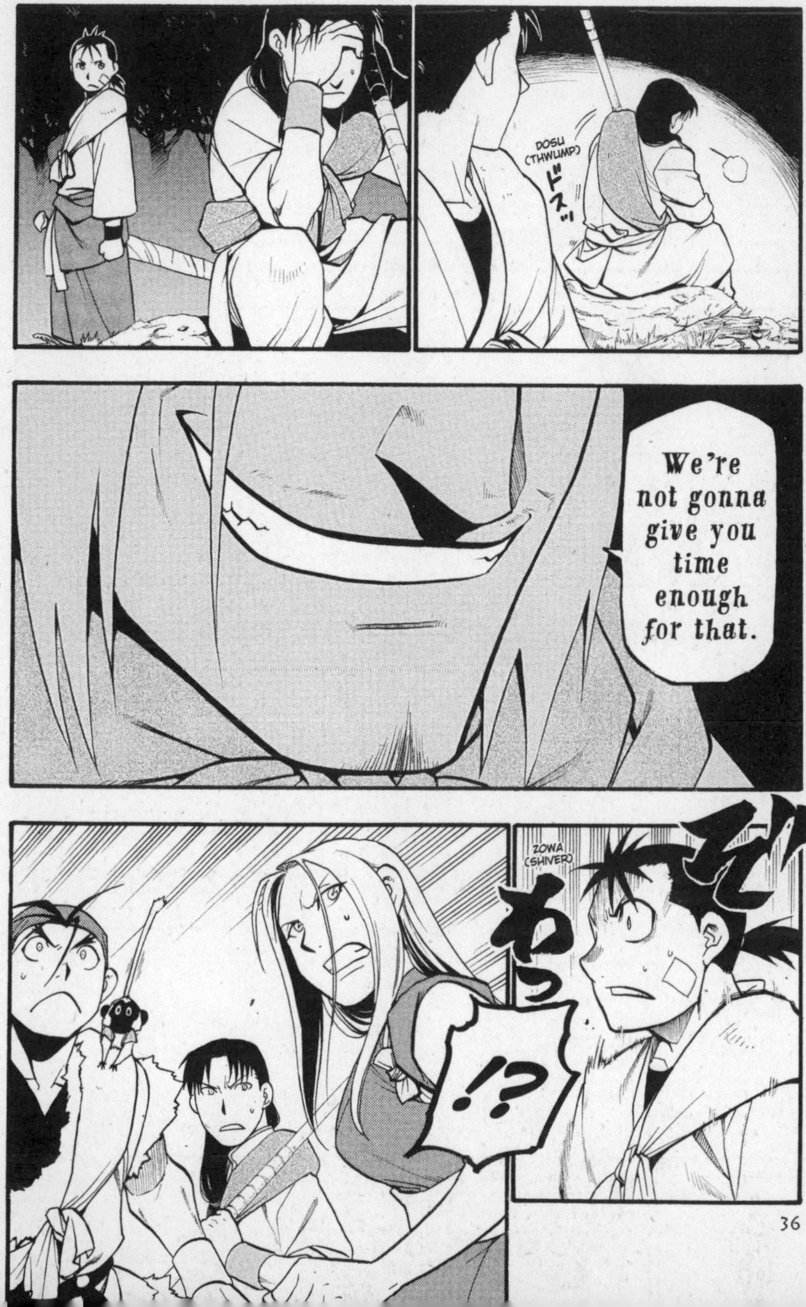
DOSU (THWUMP)
ドスッ
We're not gonna give you time enough for that.
ZOWA (SHIVER)
ぞわっ
!?

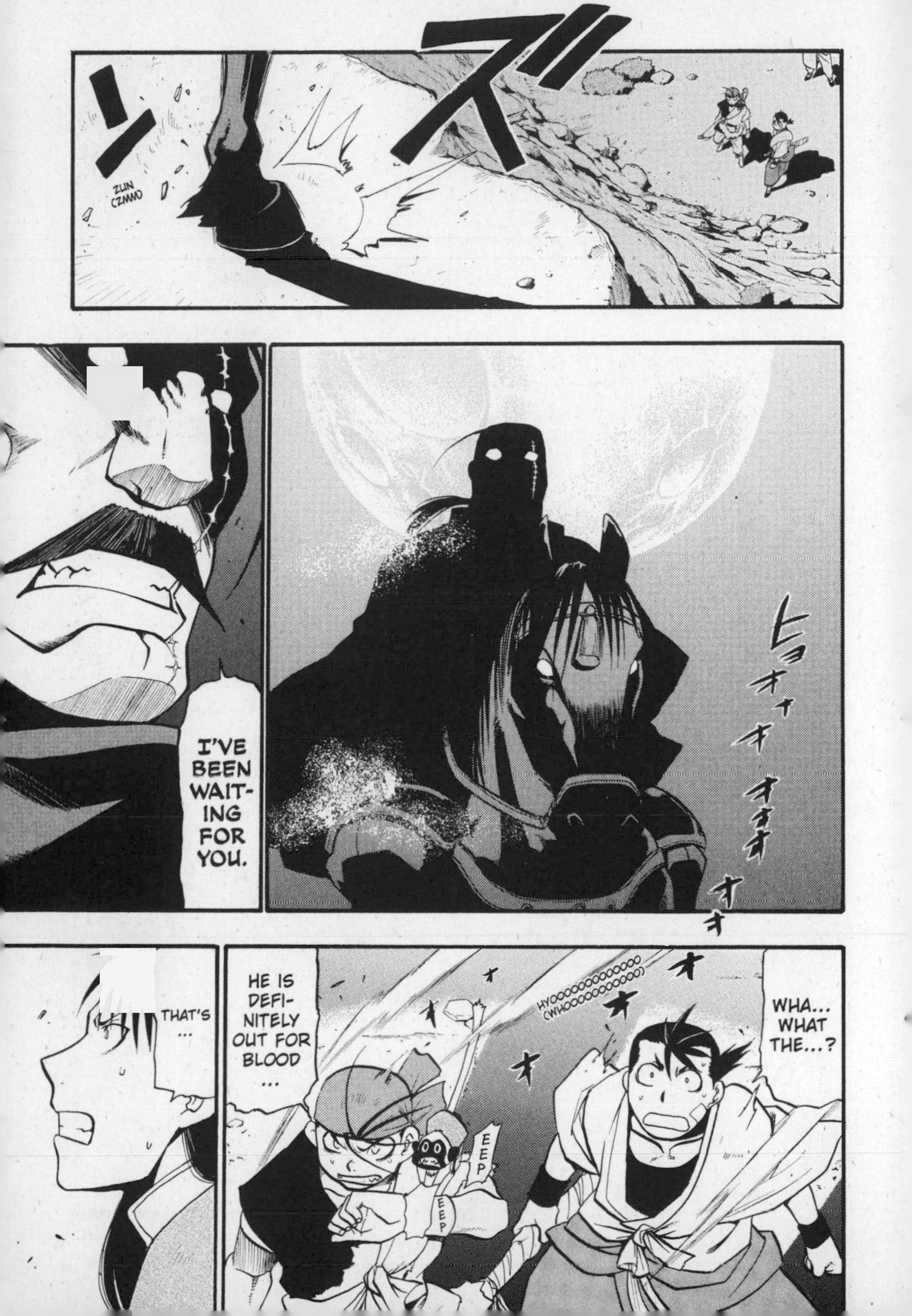
ズン
ZUN (ZMMM)
ヒョオォォォォォォォ
I'VE BEEN WAIT-ING FOR YOU.
WHA... WHAT THE...?
HYOOOOOOOOOOOOO (WHOOOOOOOOOOOOO)
HE IS DEFI-NITELY OUT FOR BLOOD...
EEP
EEP
THAT'S...

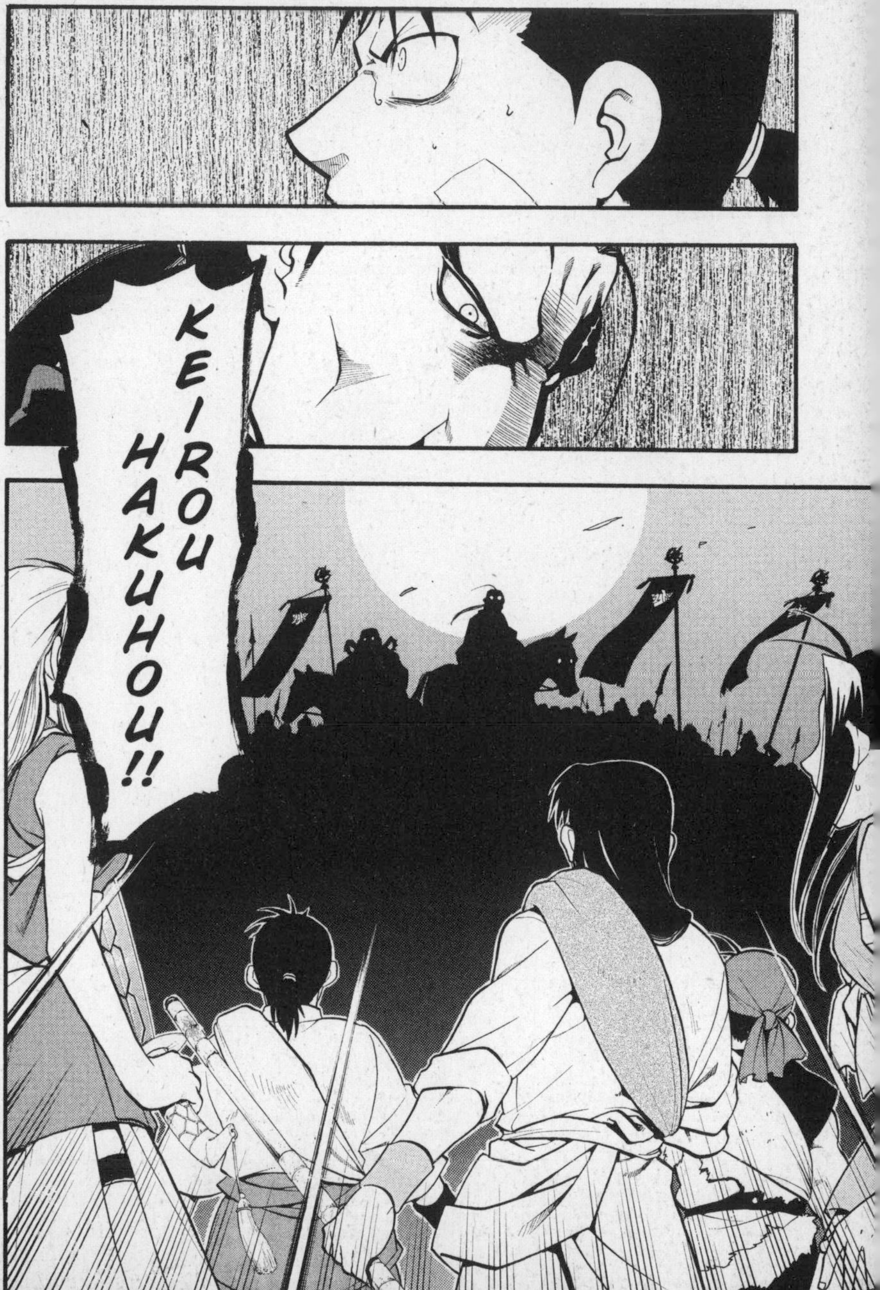
KEIROU HAKUHOU!!

# HERO TALES

獣　神　演　武

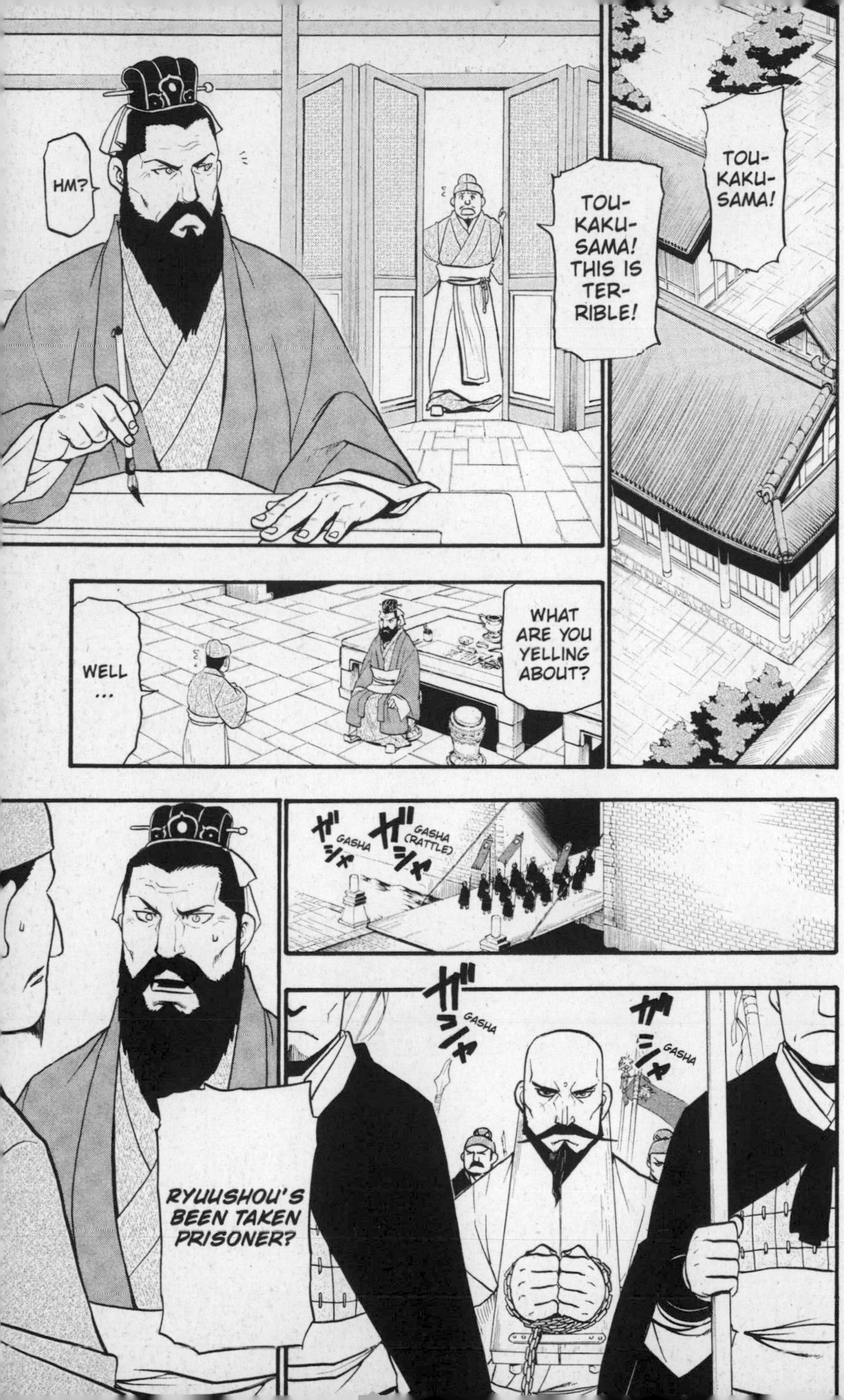
TOU-KAKU-SAMA!
TOU-KAKU-SAMA! THIS IS TER-RIBLE!
HM?
WHAT ARE YOU YELLING ABOUT?
WELL ...
ガシャ GASHA (RATTLE)
ガシャ GASHA
ガシャ GASHA
ガシャ GASHA
RYUUSHOU'S BEEN TAKEN PRISONER?

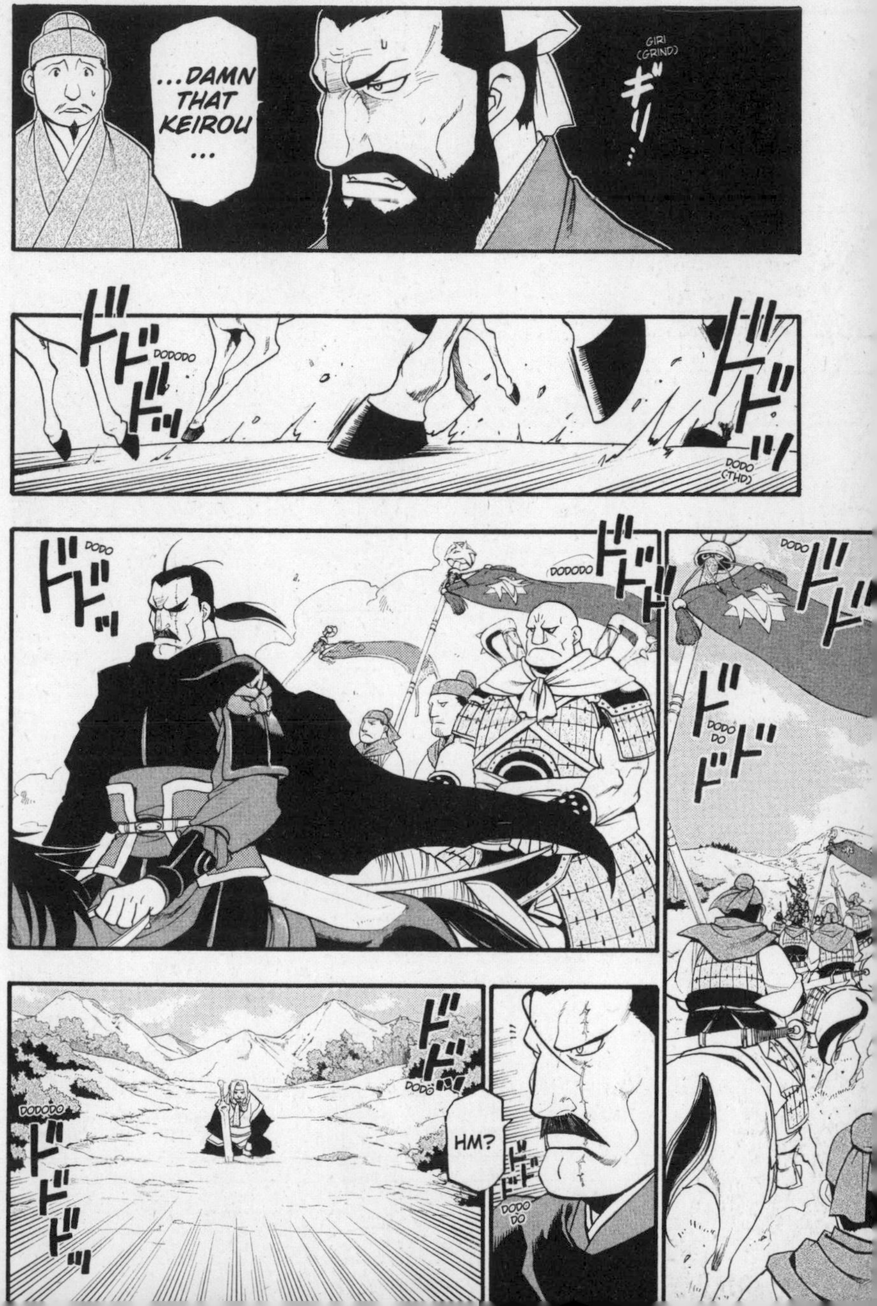
GIRI (GRIND)
...DAMN THAT KEIROU ...
DODO (THD)
DODODO
DODO
DODO DO
DODODO
DODO
!!
HM?
DODO DO
DODO
DODODO

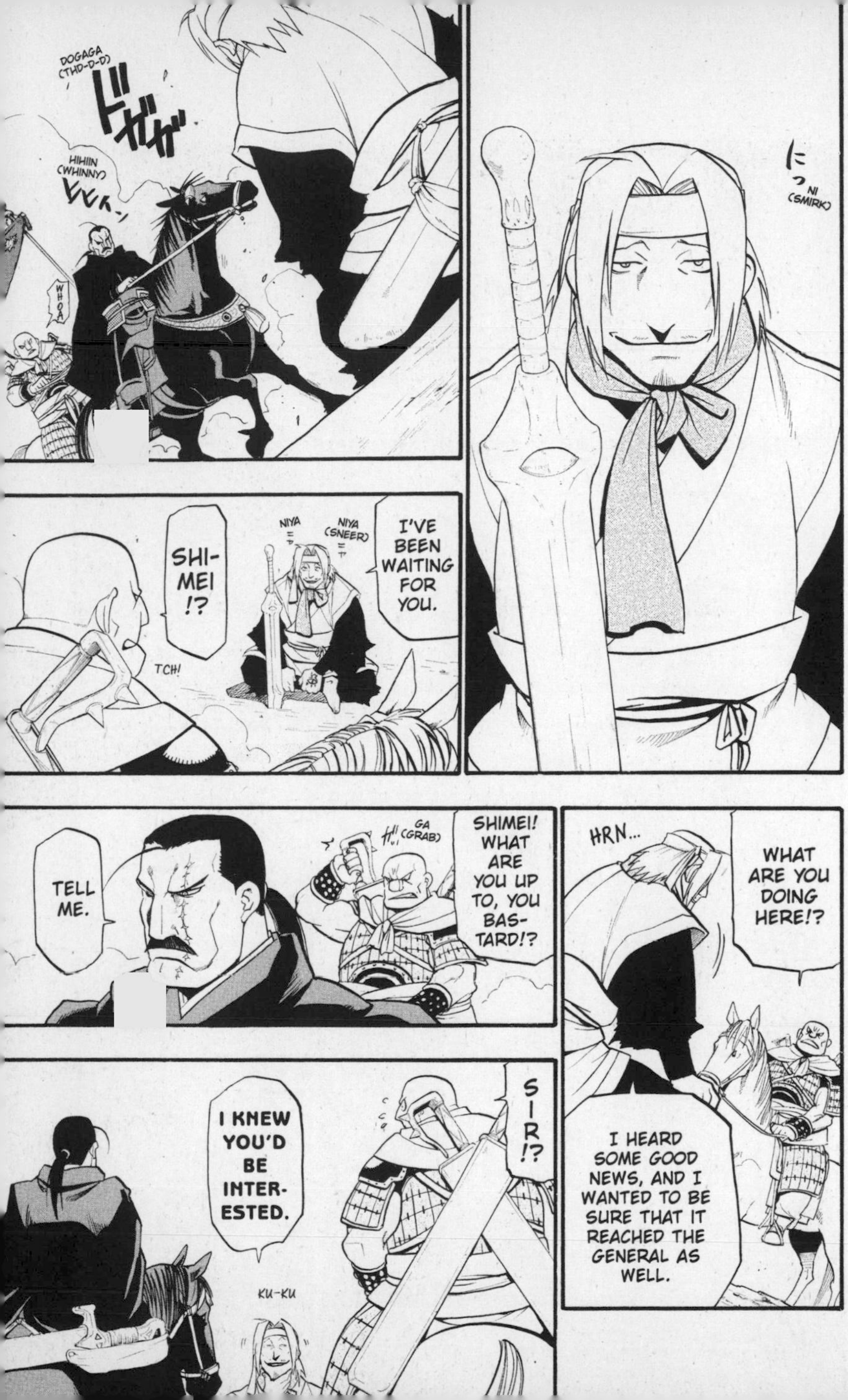
にっ
NI (SMIRK)
DOGAGA (THD-D-D)
ドガガ
HIHIIN (WHINNY)
WHOA
I'VE BEEN WAITING FOR YOU.
NIYA NIYA (SNEER)
SHI-MEI!?
TCH!
WHAT ARE YOU DOING HERE!?
HRN...
I HEARD SOME GOOD NEWS, AND I WANTED TO BE SURE THAT IT REACHED THE GENERAL AS WELL.
SHIMEI! WHAT ARE YOU UP TO, YOU BAS-TARD!?
GA (GRAB)
TELL ME.
SIR!?
I KNEW YOU'D BE INTER-ESTED.
KU-KU

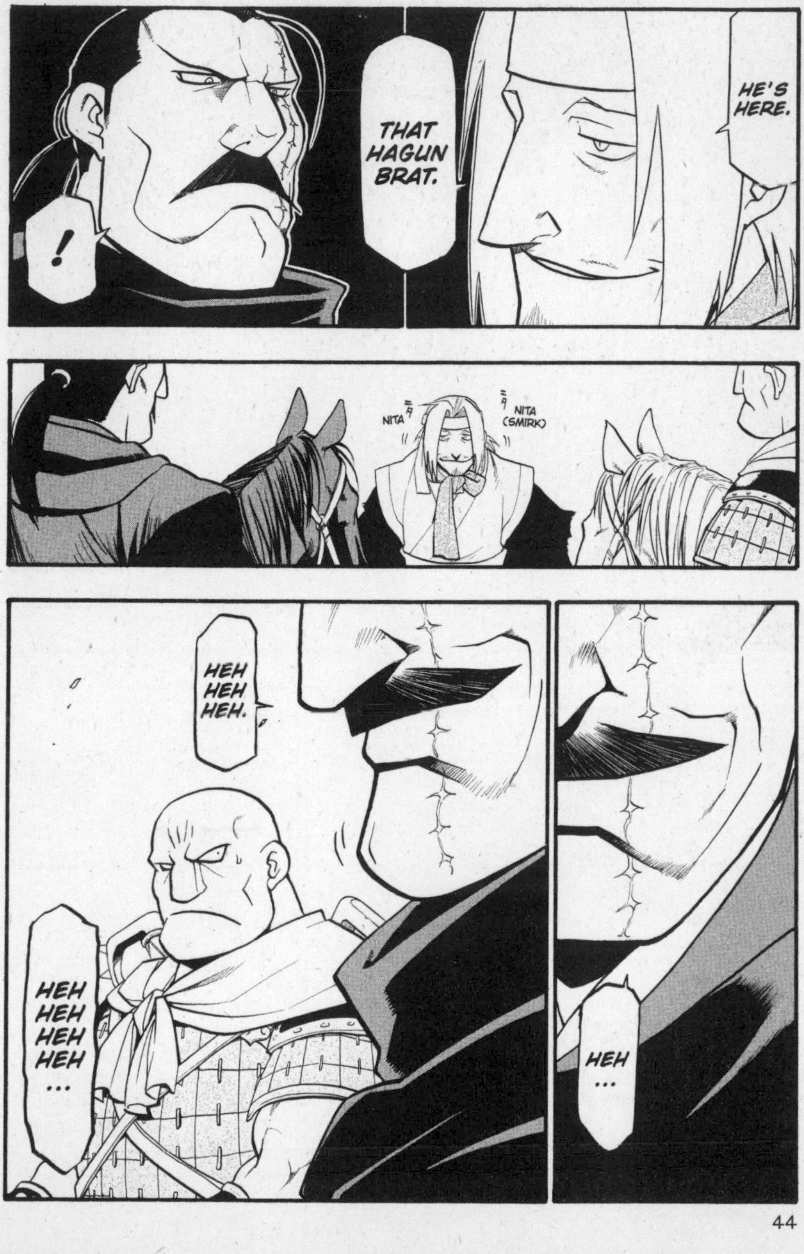
HE'S HERE.
THAT HAGUN BRAT.
!
NITA (SMIRK)
NITA
HEH ...
HEH HEH HEH.
HEH HEH HEH HEH ...

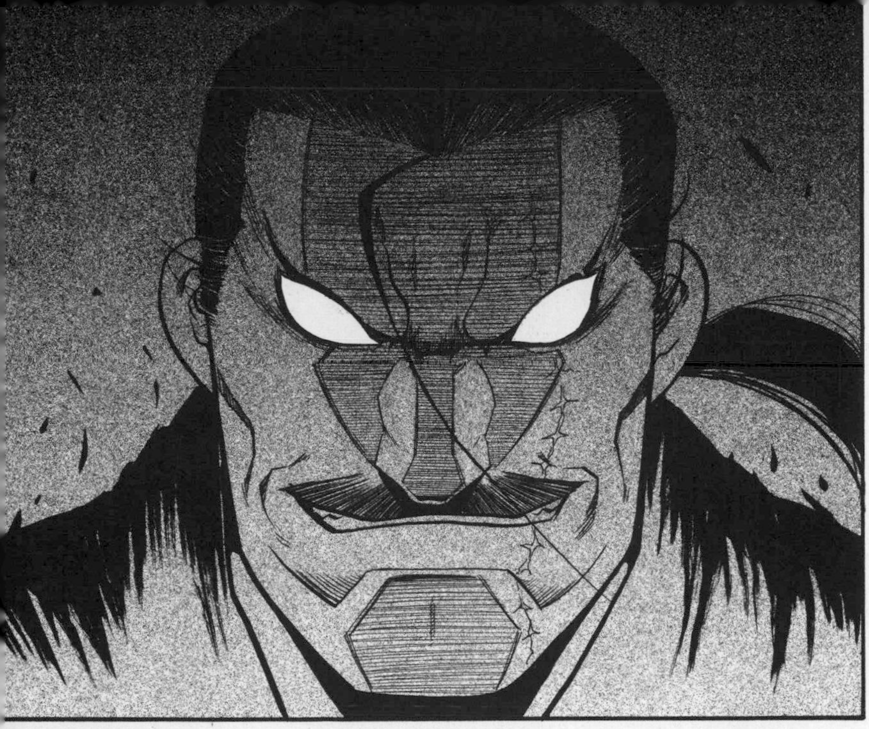

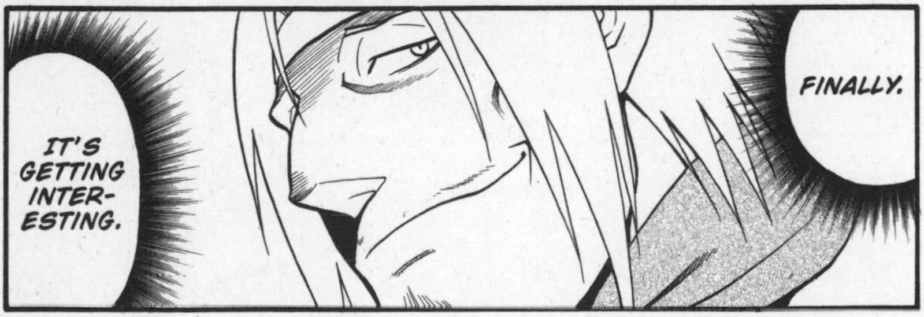
FINALLY.
IT'S GETTING INTER-ESTING.

# Chapter 9
# Night of the Sacrifice

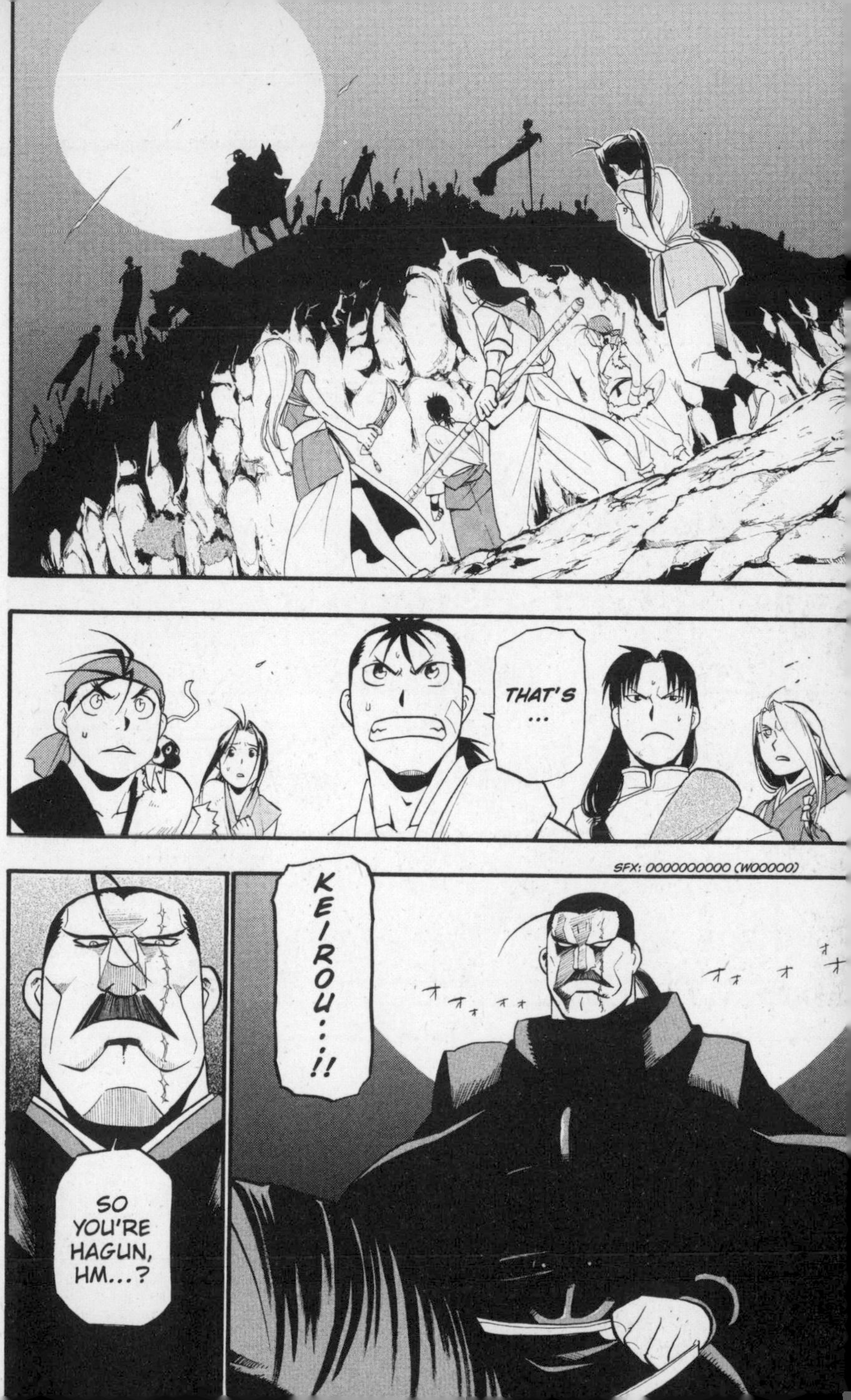
THAT'S ...
SFX: OOOOOOOOOO (WOOOOO)
KEIROU...!!
SO YOU'RE HAGUN, HM...?

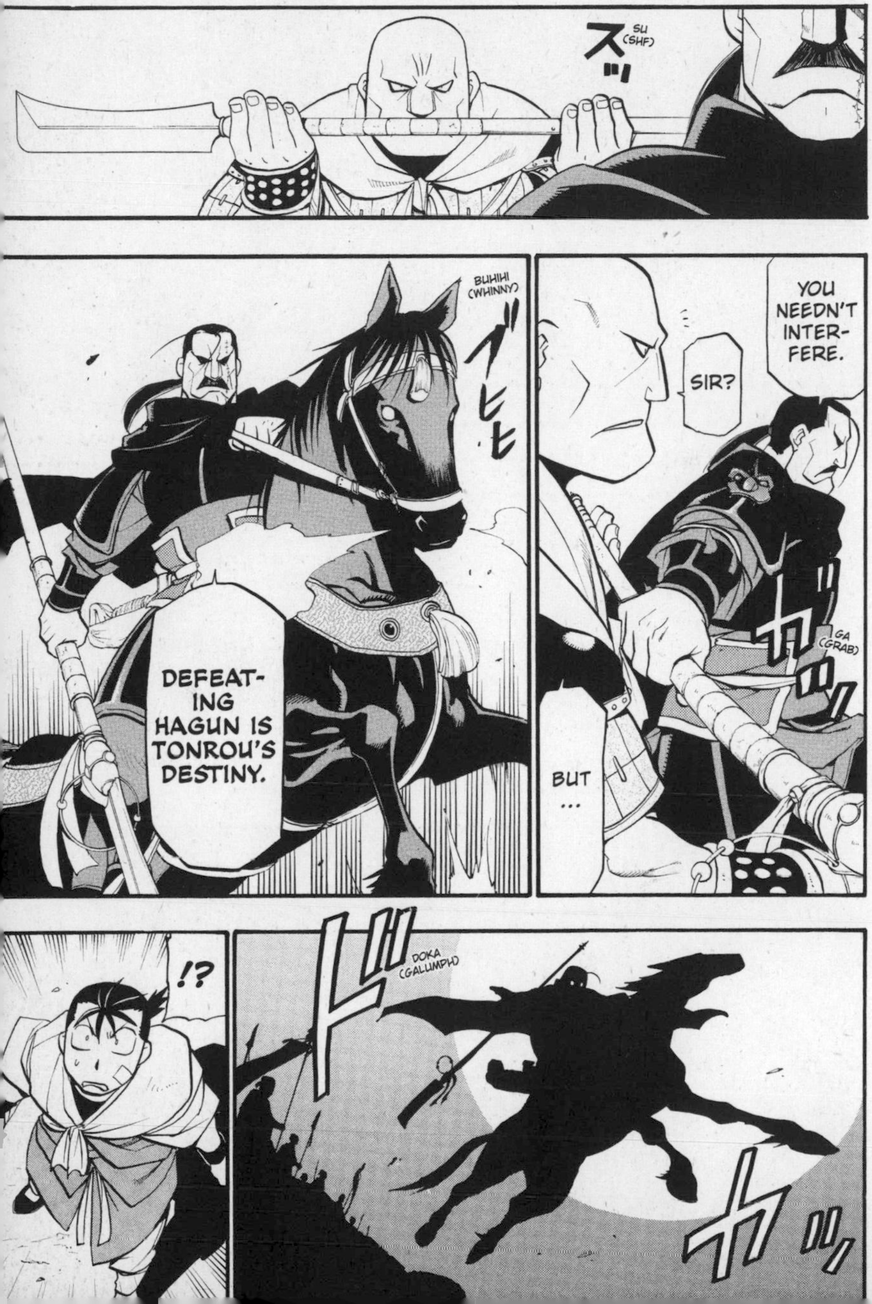
SU (SHF)
YOU NEEDN'T INTER-FERE.
SIR?
GA (GRAB)
BUT ...
BUHIHI (WHINNY)
DEFEAT-ING HAGUN IS TONROU'S DESTINY.
DOKA (GALUMPH)
!?

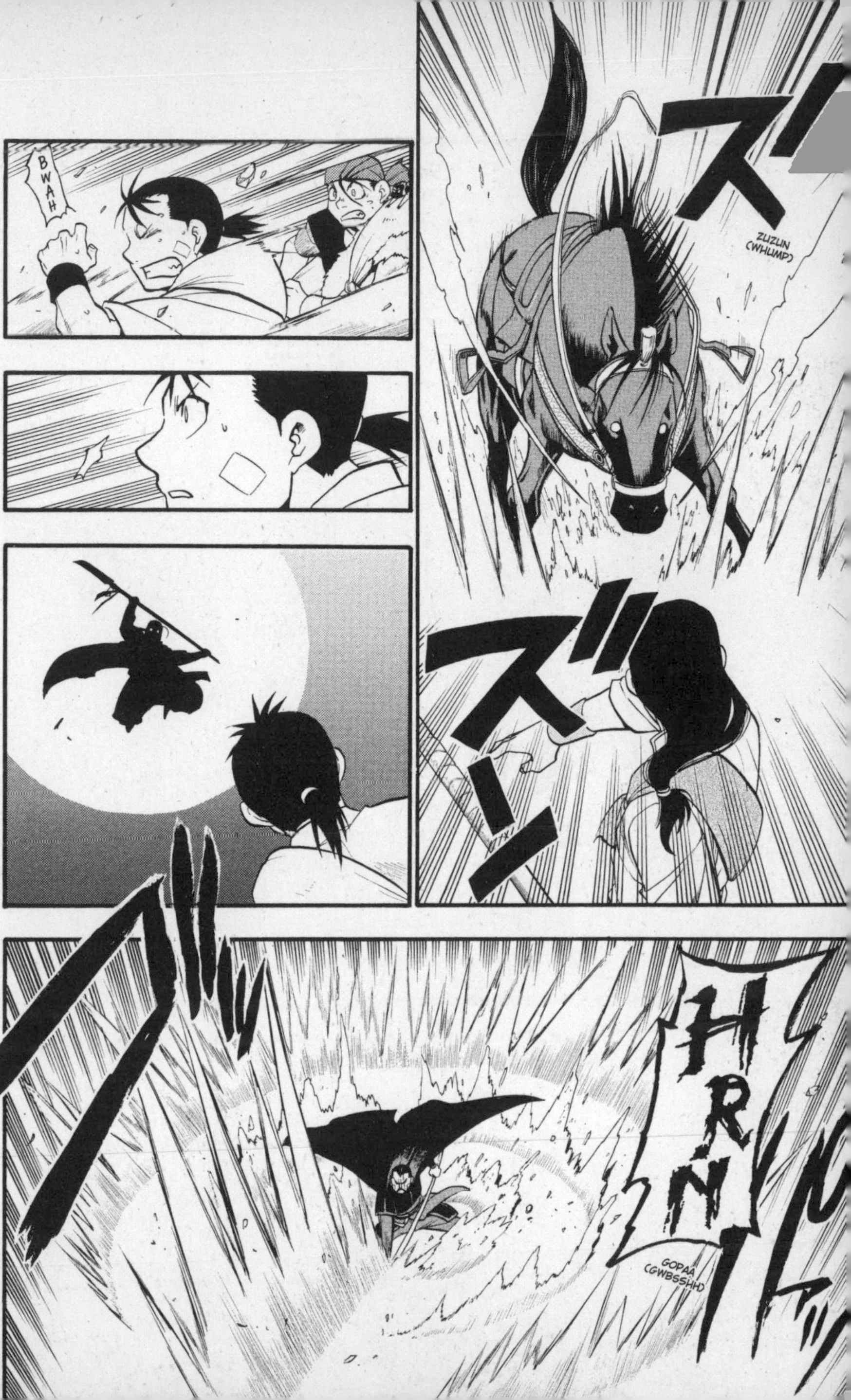
ZUZUN (WHUMP)
BWAH
HRN
GOPAA (GWBSSHH)

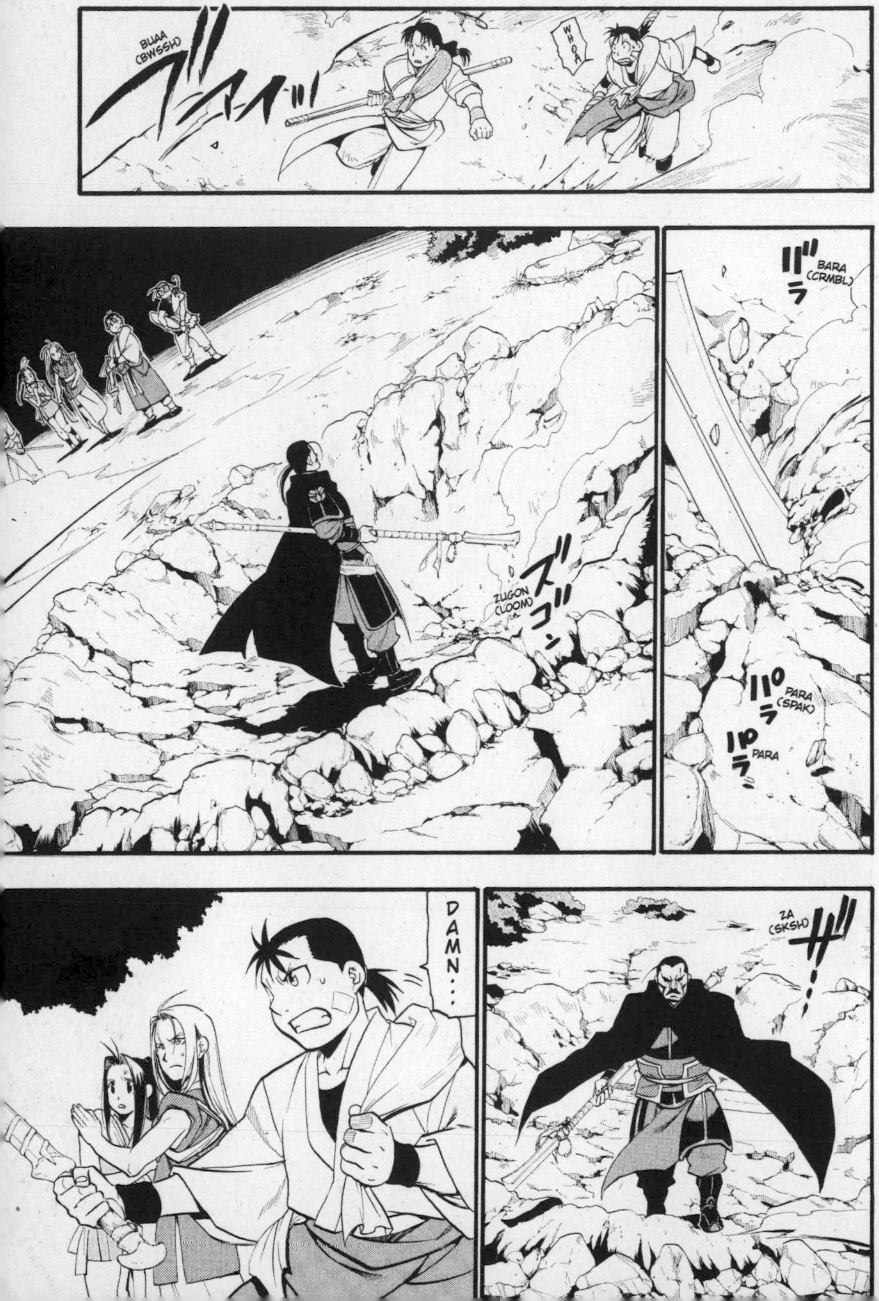
WHOA
BUAA (BWSSH)
BARA (CRMBL)
PARA (SPAK)
PARA
ZUGON (LOOM)
ZA (SKSH)
DAMN...

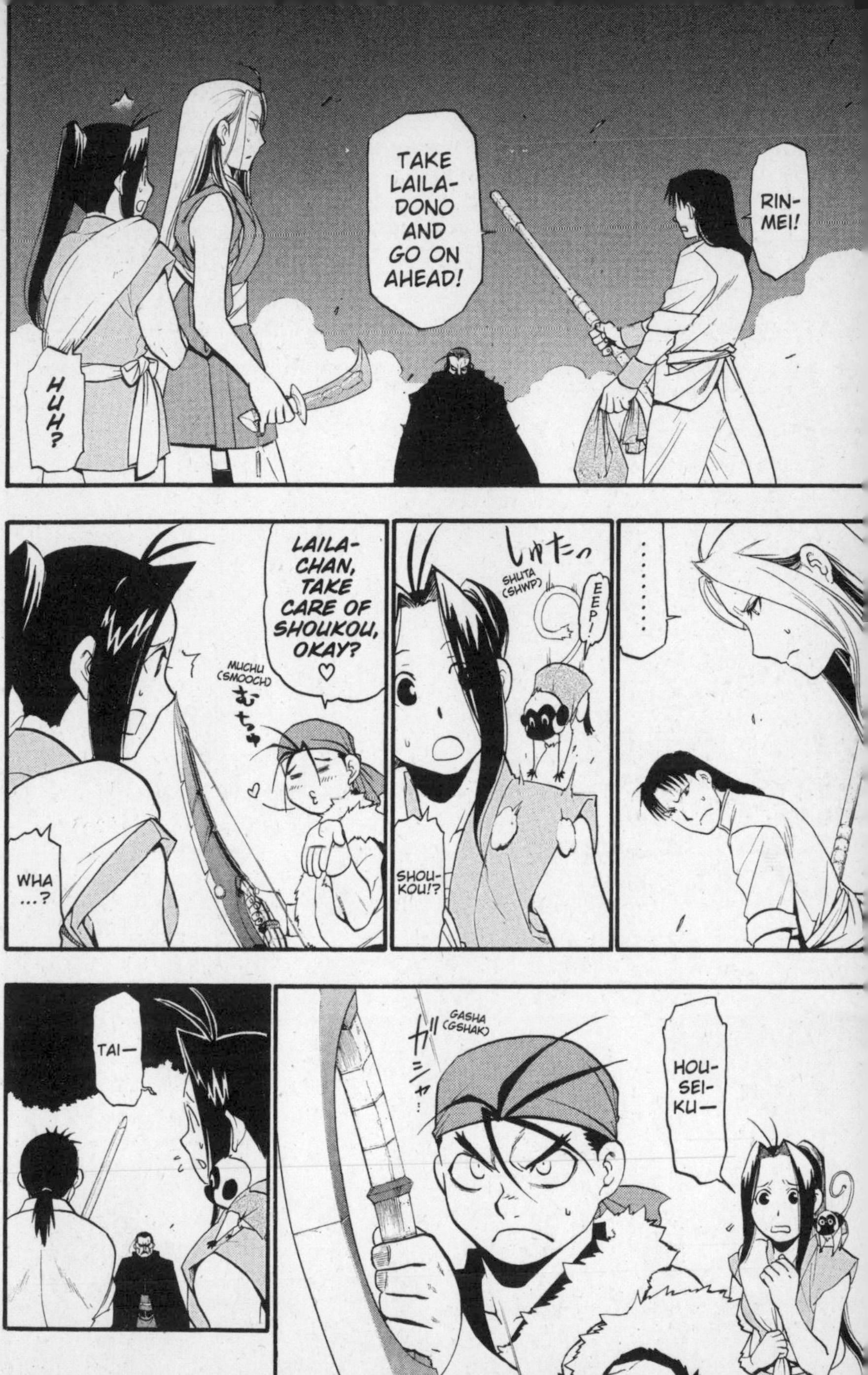
RIN-MEI!
TAKE LAILA-DONO AND GO ON AHEAD!
HUH?
......
しゅたっ
SHUTA (SHWP)
EEP!
SHOUKOU!?
LAILA-CHAN, TAKE CARE OF SHOUKOU, OKAY? ♡
MUCHU (SMOOCH)
むちゅ
WHA ...?
HOU-SEI-KU—
GASHA (GSHAK)
ガシャ
TAI—

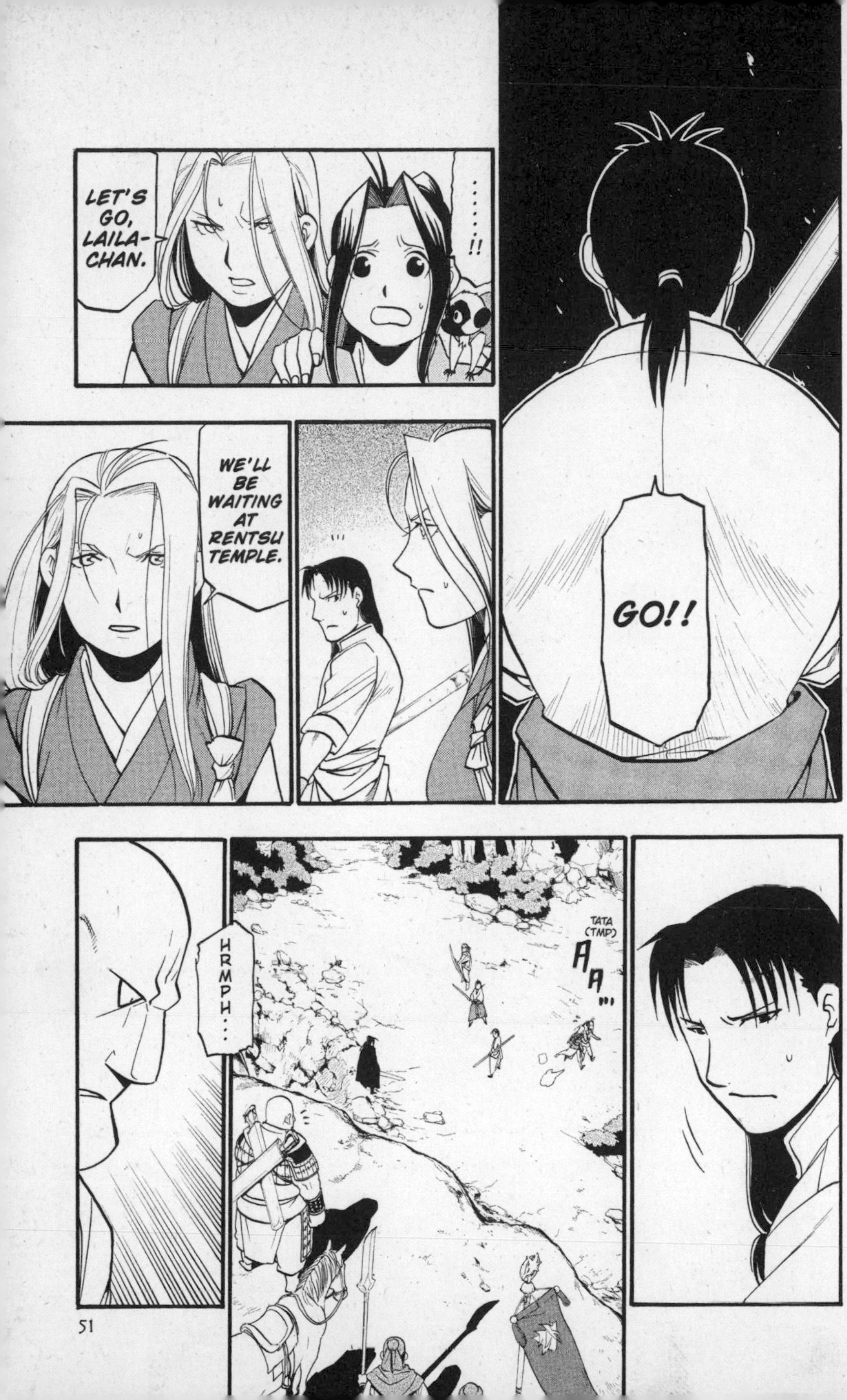
GO!!
......!!
LET'S GO, LAILA-CHAN.
WE'LL BE WAITING AT RENTSU TEMPLE.
TATA (TMP)
HRMPH...

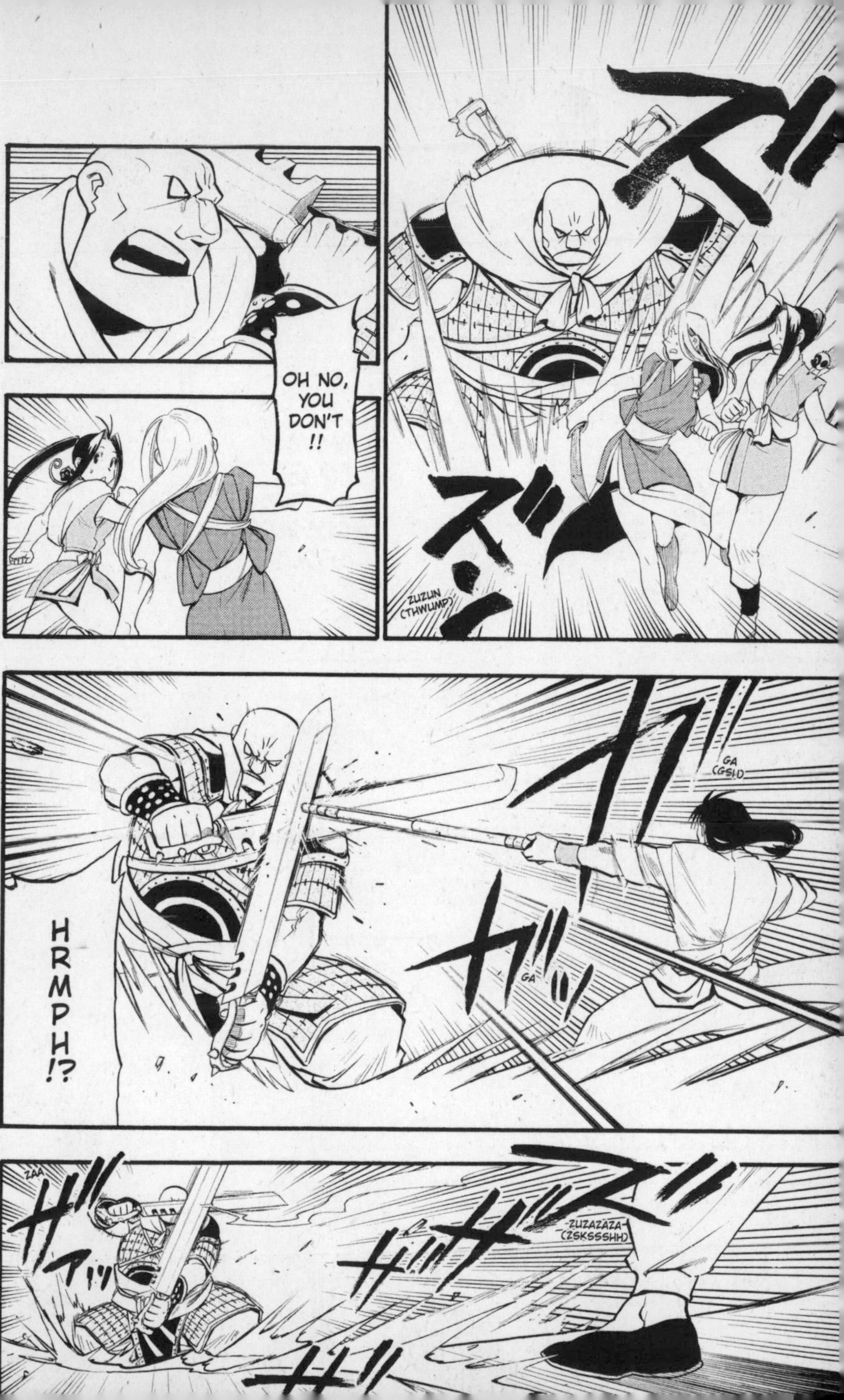
ZUZUN
(THWUMP)
OH NO, YOU DON'T !!
GA
(GSI)
GA
HRMPH!?
ZAA
ZUZAZAZA
(ZSKSSSHH)

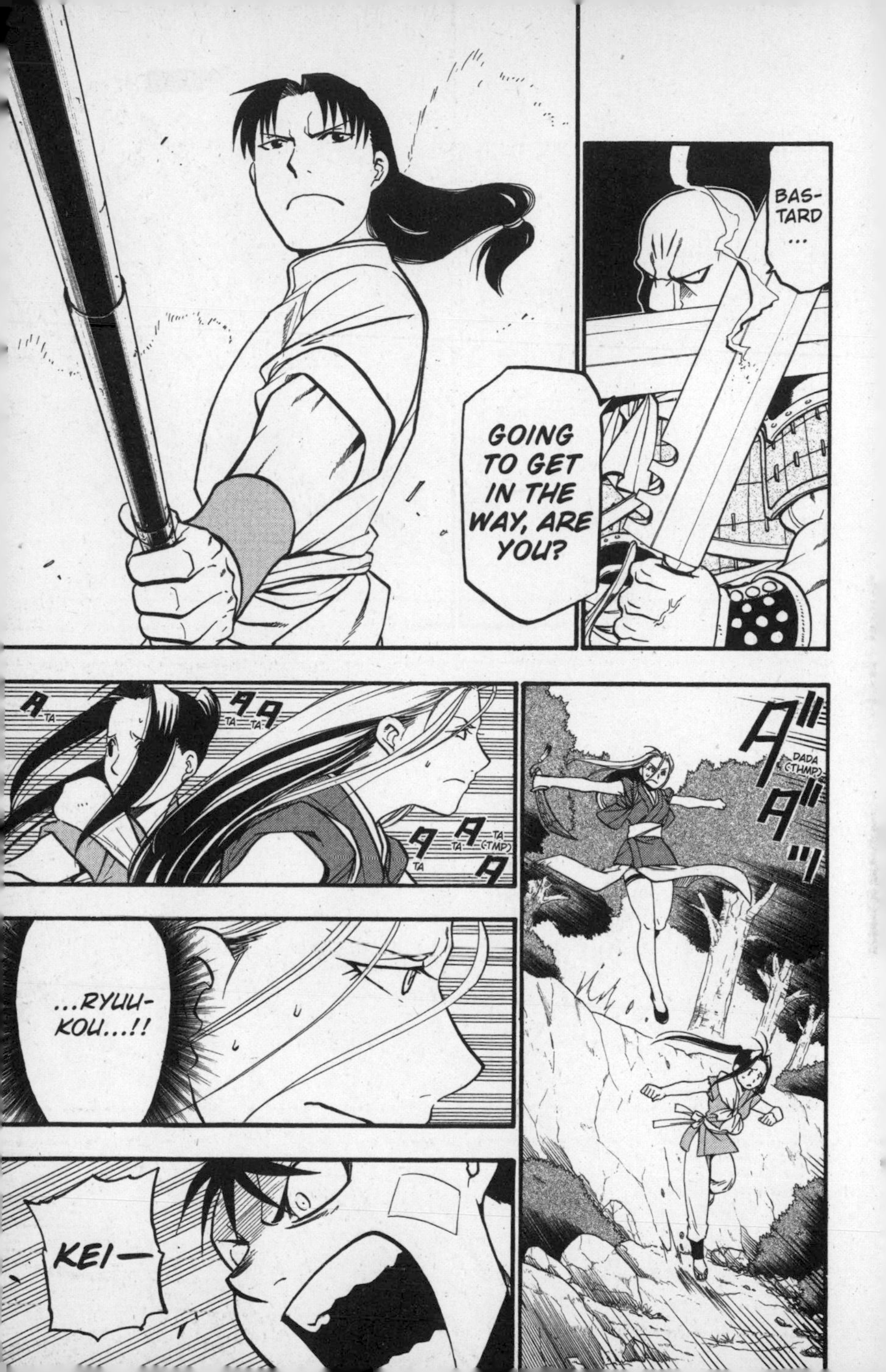
BASTARD...
GOING TO GET IN THE WAY, ARE YOU?
DADA (THMP)
TA TA TA
TA TA TA TA (TMP)
...
...RYUUKOU...!!
KEI—

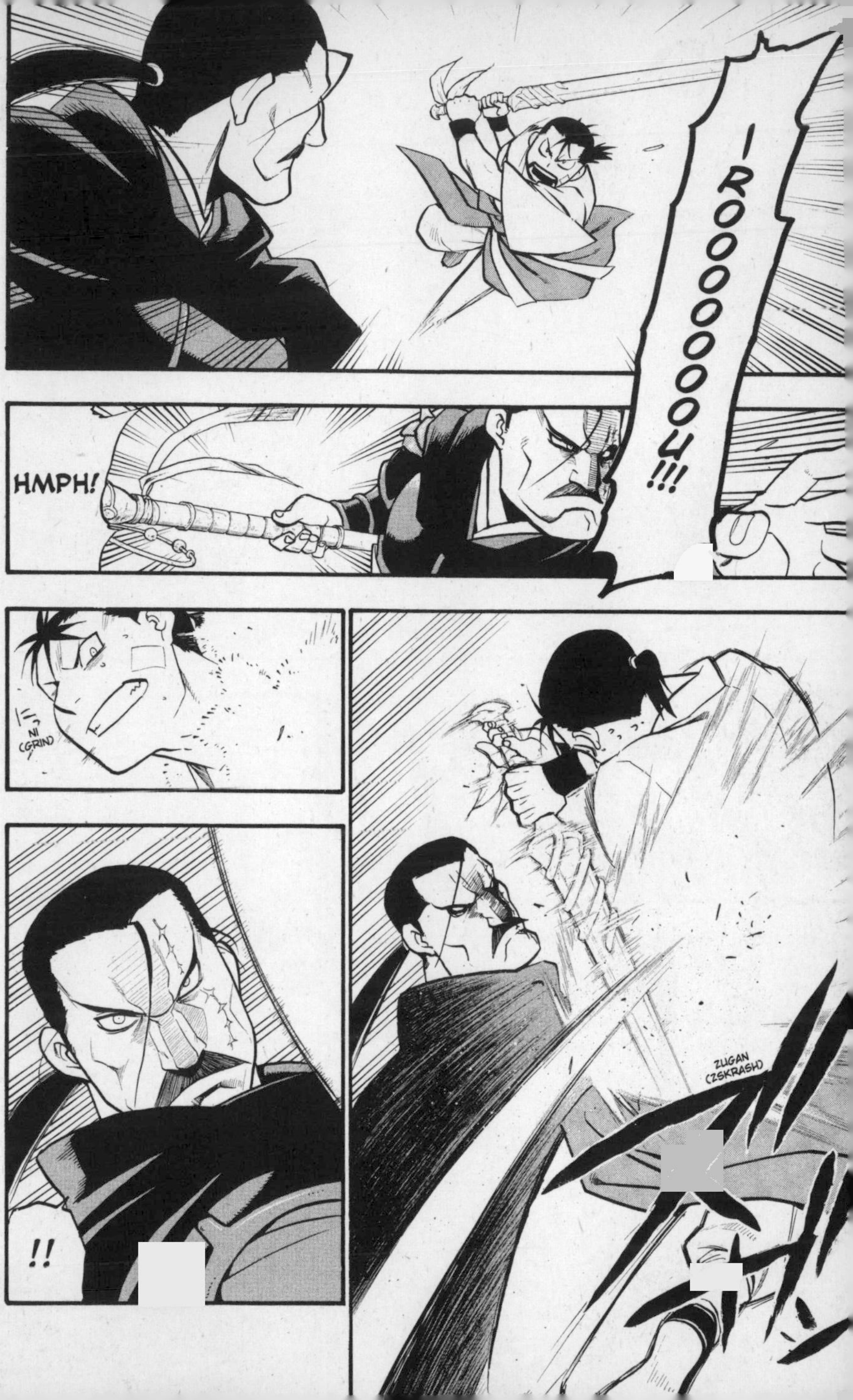
IROOOOOOOU!!!
HMPH!
ZUGAN
(ZSKRASH)
NI
(GRIN)
!!

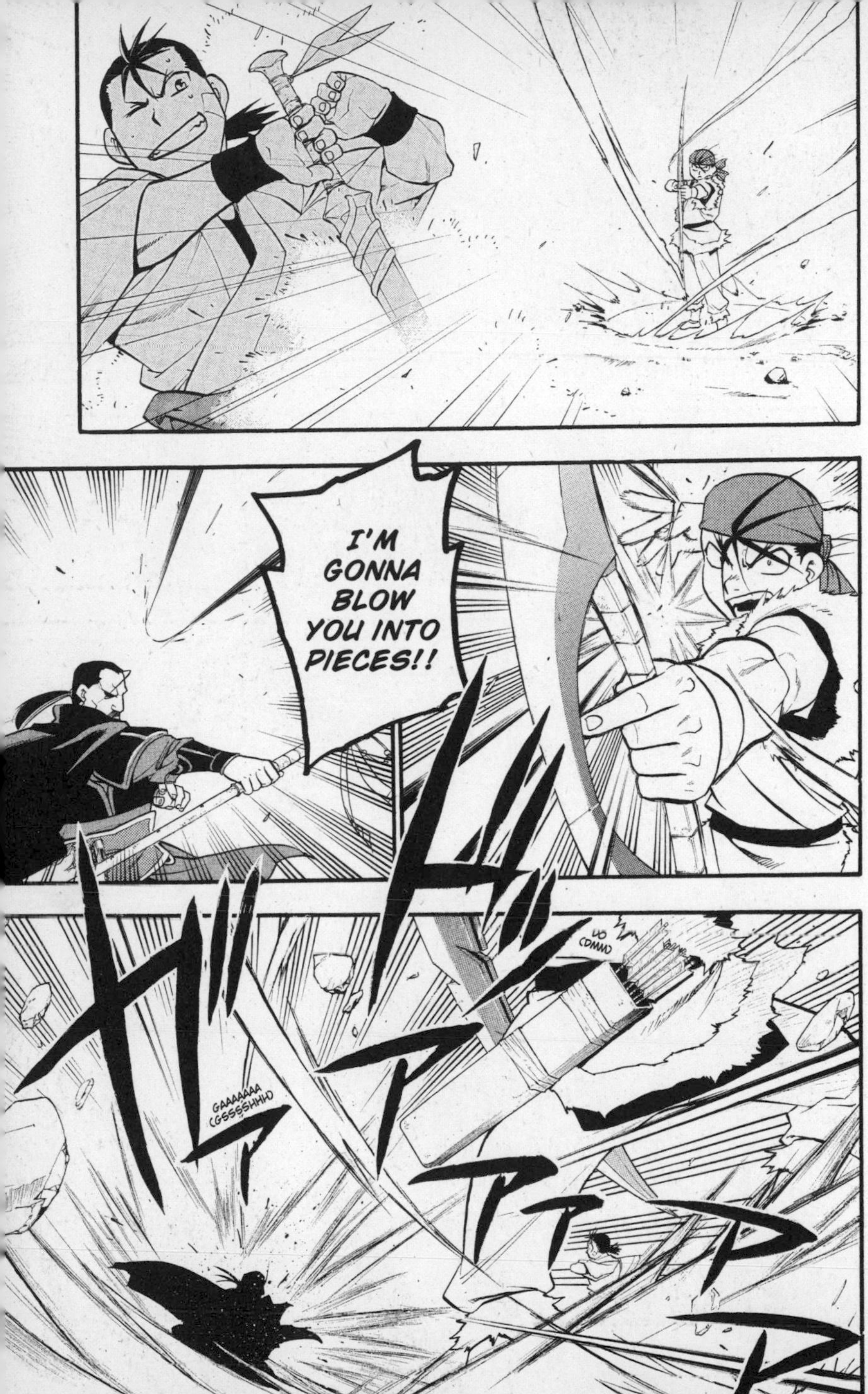
I'M GONNA BLOW YOU INTO PIECES!!
DO (DMM)
GAAAAAAA (GSSSSHHH)

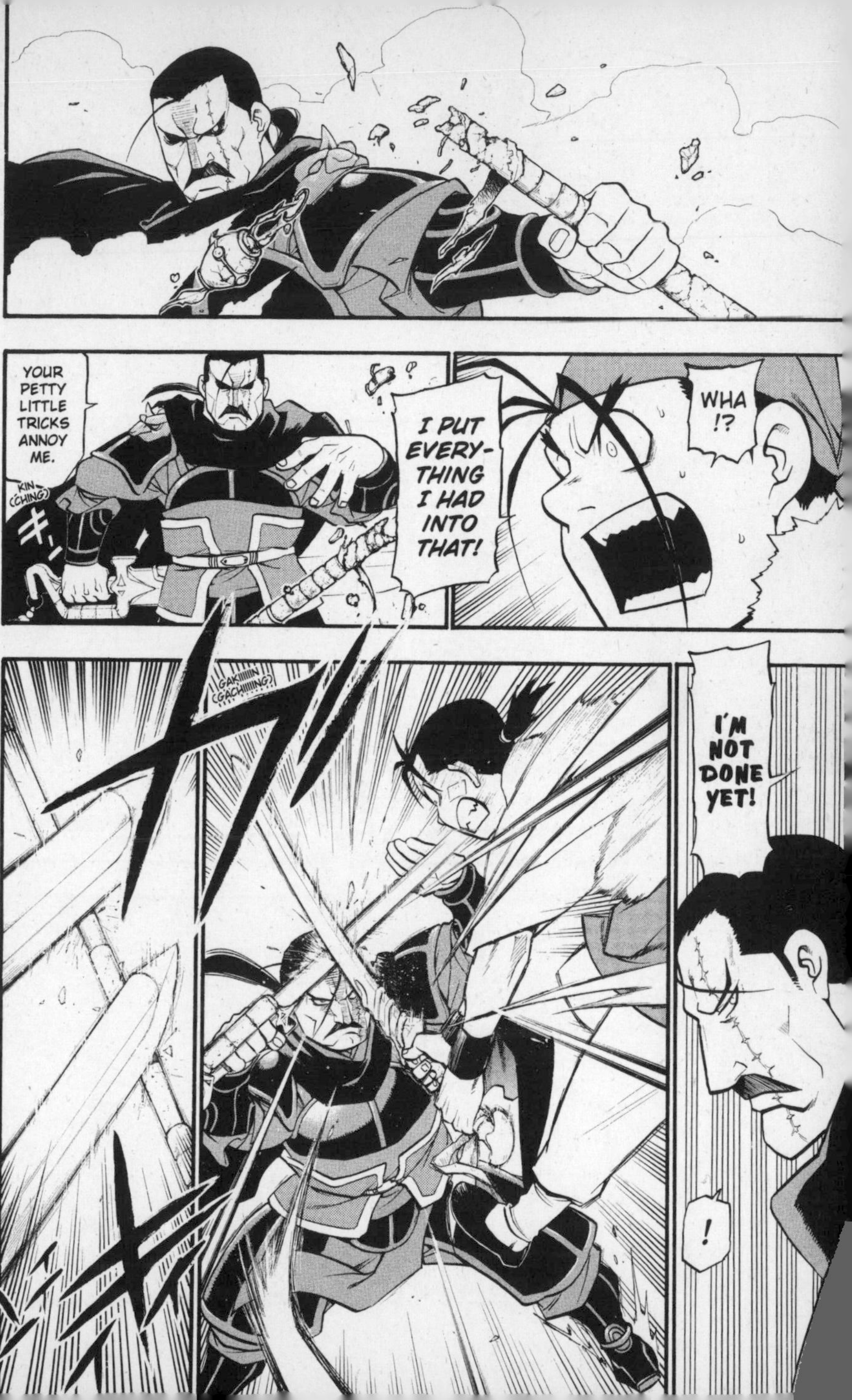
WHA !?
I PUT EVERYTHING I HAD INTO THAT!
YOUR PETTY LITTLE TRICKS ANNOY ME.
KIN (CHING)
I'M NOT DONE YET!
!
GAKIIIIIIN (GACHIIIIIING)

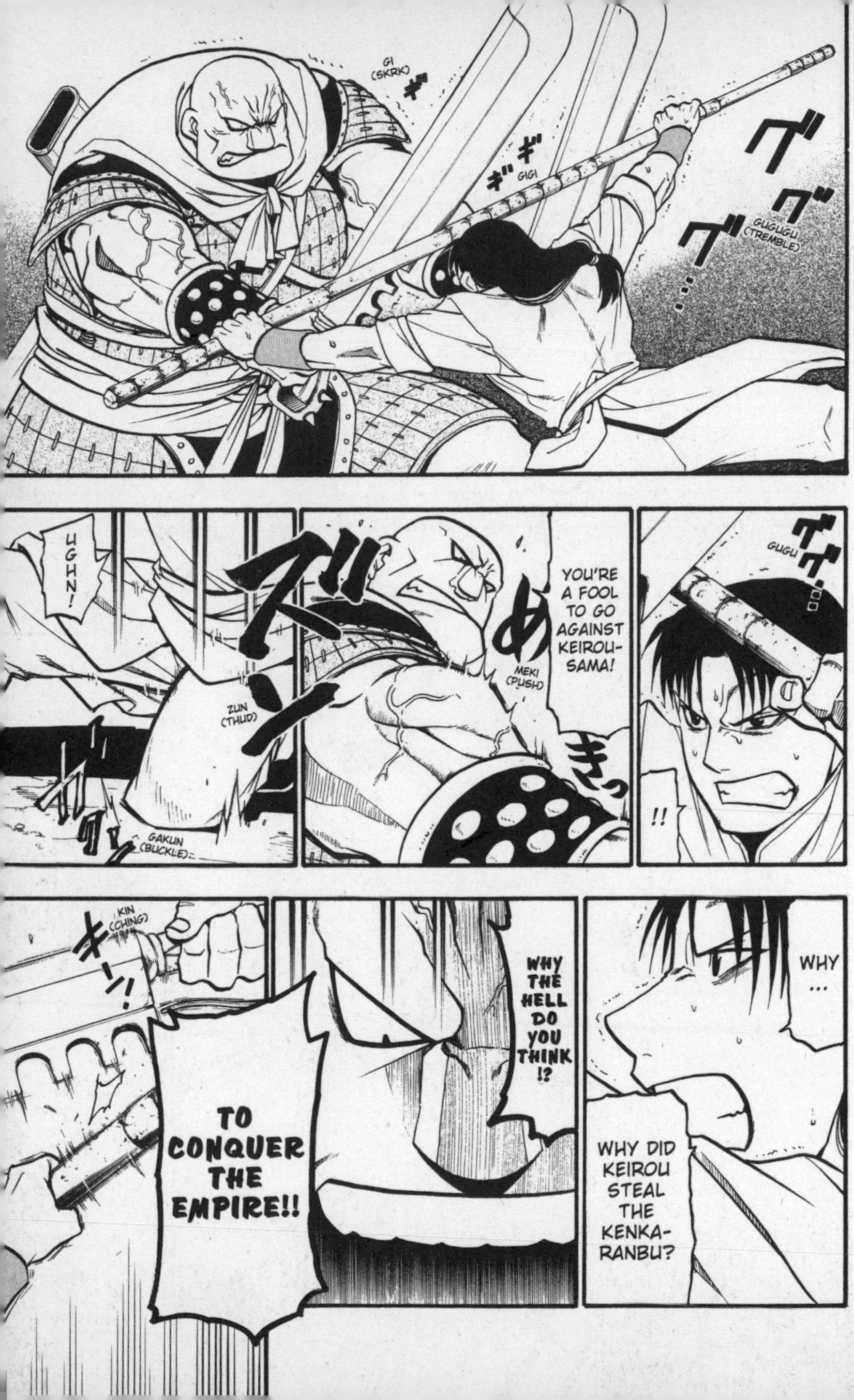
GI (SKRK)
GIGI
GUGUGU (TREMBLE)
GUGU
!!
YOU'RE A FOOL TO GO AGAINST KEIROU-SAMA!
MEKI (PUSH)
ZUN (THUD)
UGHN!
GAKUN (BUCKLE)
WHY ...
WHY DID KEIROU STEAL THE KENKA-RANBU?
WHY THE HELL DO YOU THINK!?
KIN (CHING)
TO CONQUER THE EMPIRE!!

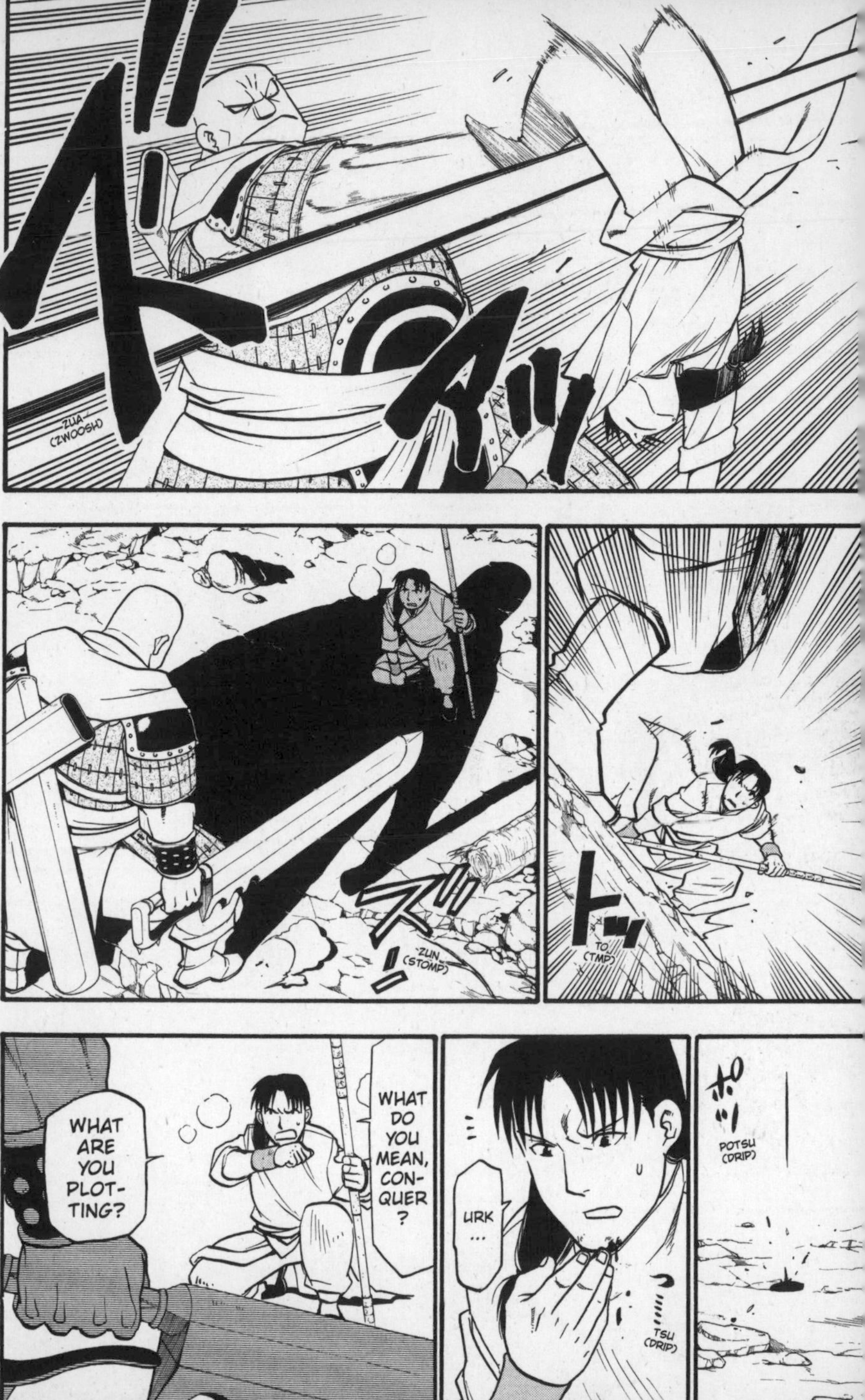
ZUA (ZWOOSH)
TO (TMP)
ZUN (STOMP)
POTSU (DRIP)
URK ...
TSU (DRIP)
WHAT DO YOU MEAN, CONQUER?
WHAT ARE YOU PLOTTING?

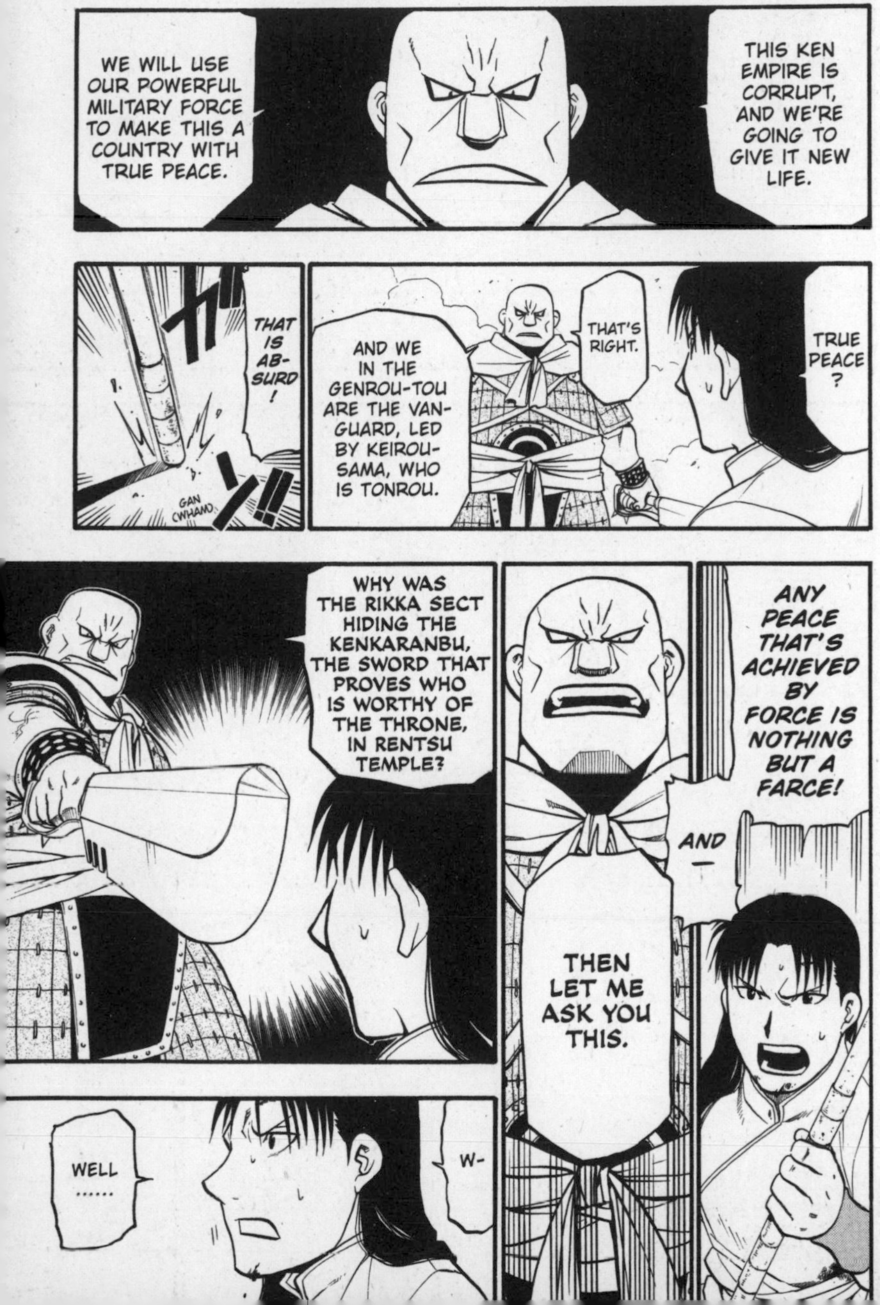
THIS KEN EMPIRE IS CORRUPT, AND WE'RE GOING TO GIVE IT NEW LIFE.
WE WILL USE OUR POWERFUL MILITARY FORCE TO MAKE THIS A COUNTRY WITH TRUE PEACE.
TRUE PEACE?
THAT'S RIGHT.
AND WE IN THE GENROU-TOU ARE THE VANGUARD, LED BY KEIROU-SAMA, WHO IS TONROU.
THAT IS ABSURD!
GAN (WHAM)
ANY PEACE THAT'S ACHIEVED BY FORCE IS NOTHING BUT A FARCE!
AND—
THEN LET ME ASK YOU THIS.
WHY WAS THE RIKKA SECT HIDING THE KENKARANBU, THE SWORD THAT PROVES WHO IS WORTHY OF THE THRONE, IN RENTSU TEMPLE?
W-
WELL ......

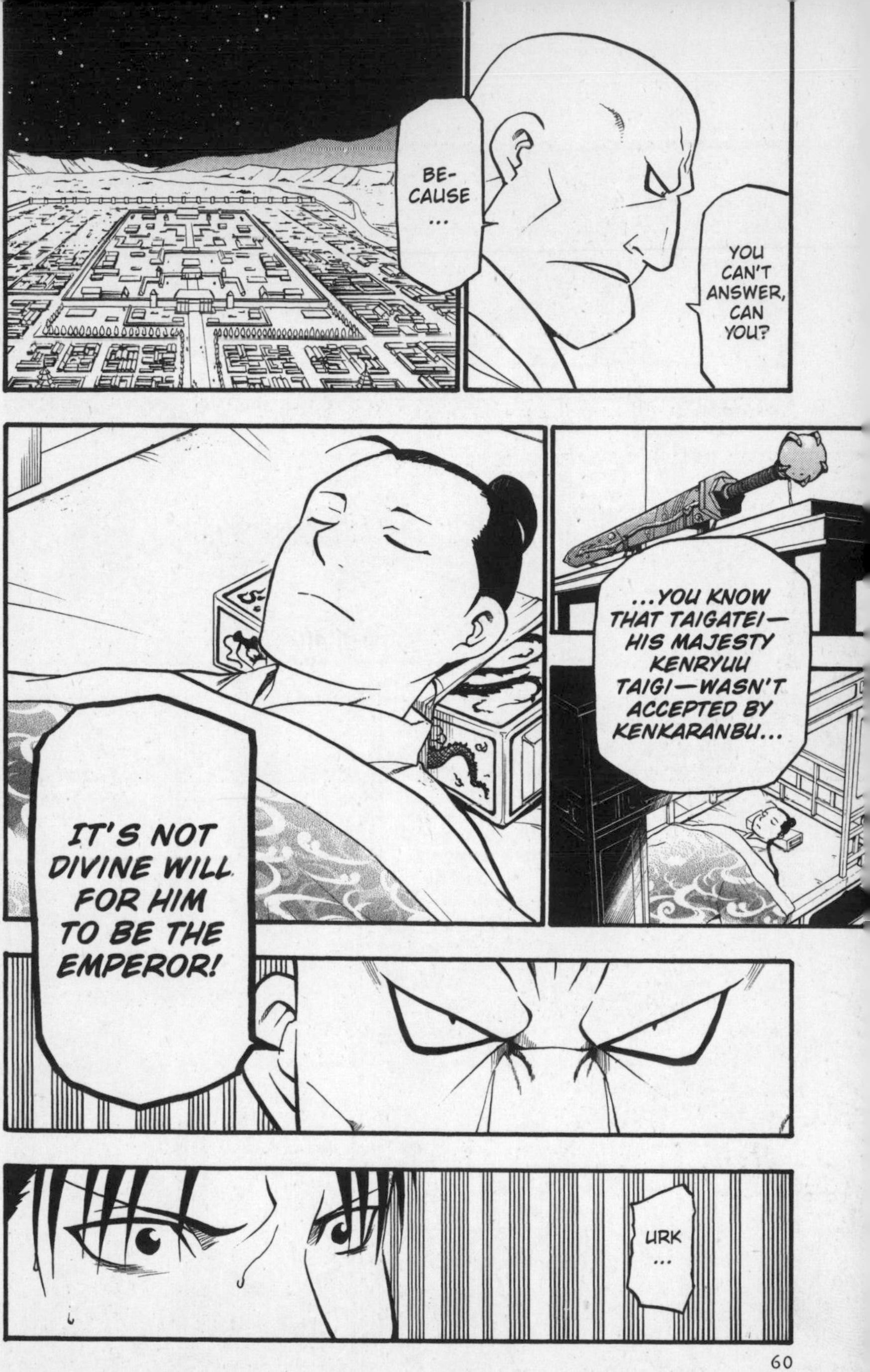
YOU CAN'T ANSWER, CAN YOU?
BE-CAUSE ...
...YOU KNOW THAT TAIGATEI—HIS MAJESTY KENRYUU TAIGI—WASN'T ACCEPTED BY KENKARANBU...
IT'S NOT DIVINE WILL FOR HIM TO BE THE EMPEROR!
URK ...

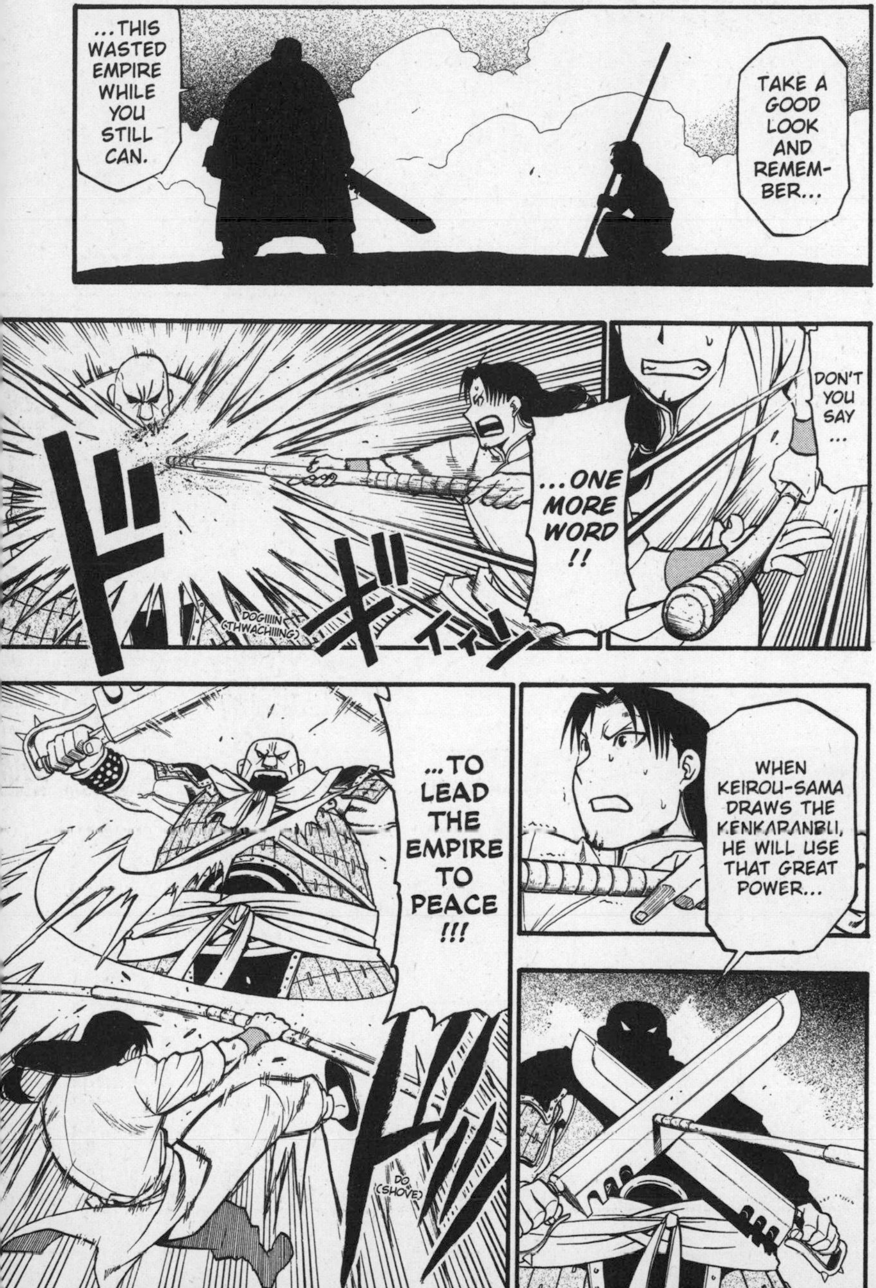
TAKE A GOOD LOOK AND REMEMBER...
...THIS WASTED EMPIRE WHILE YOU STILL CAN.
DON'T YOU SAY ...
...ONE MORE WORD !!
ドギィン
DOGIIIN (THWACHIIING)
WHEN KEIROU-SAMA DRAWS THE KENKARANBU, HE WILL USE THAT GREAT POWER...
...TO LEAD THE EMPIRE TO PEACE !!!
DO (SHOVE)

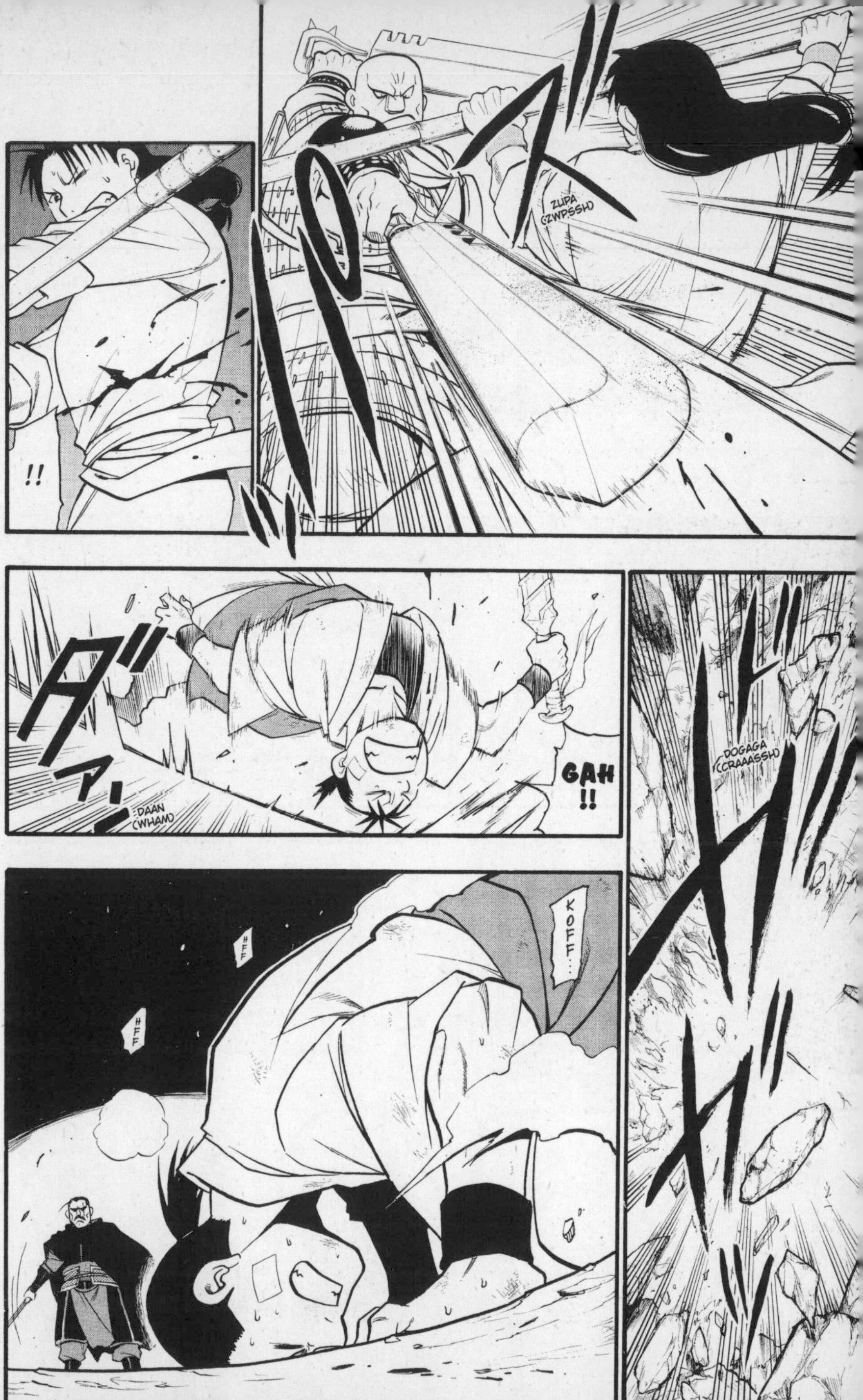
ZUPA (ZWPSSH)
!!
DOGAGA (CRAAASSH)
GAH!!
DAAN (WHAM)
KOFF...
HFF
HFF

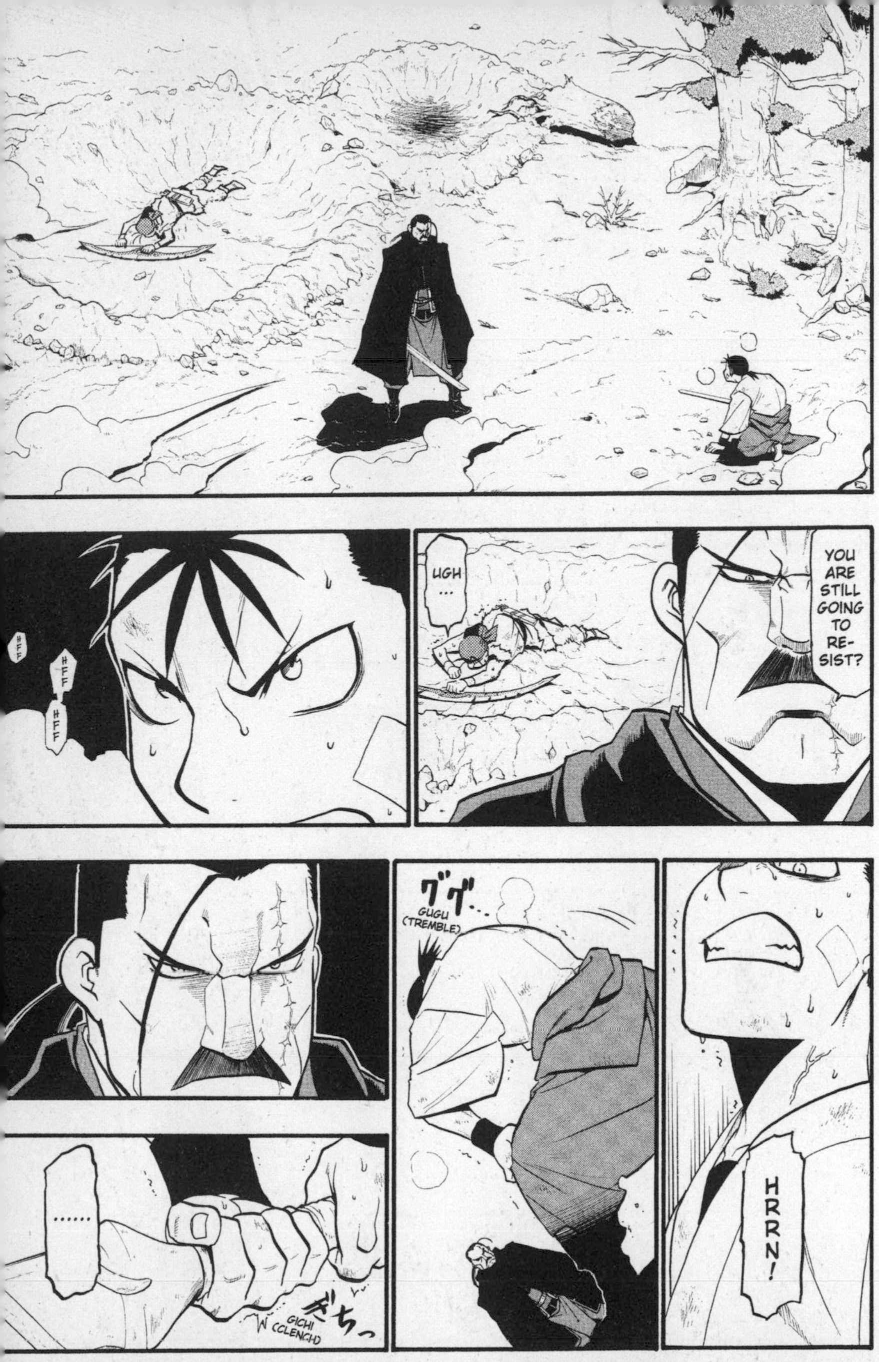
YOU ARE STILL GOING TO RE-SIST?
UGH ...
HFF
HFF
HFF
HRRN!
ググ...
GUGU (TREMBLE)
.......
ぎちっ
GICHI (CLENCH)

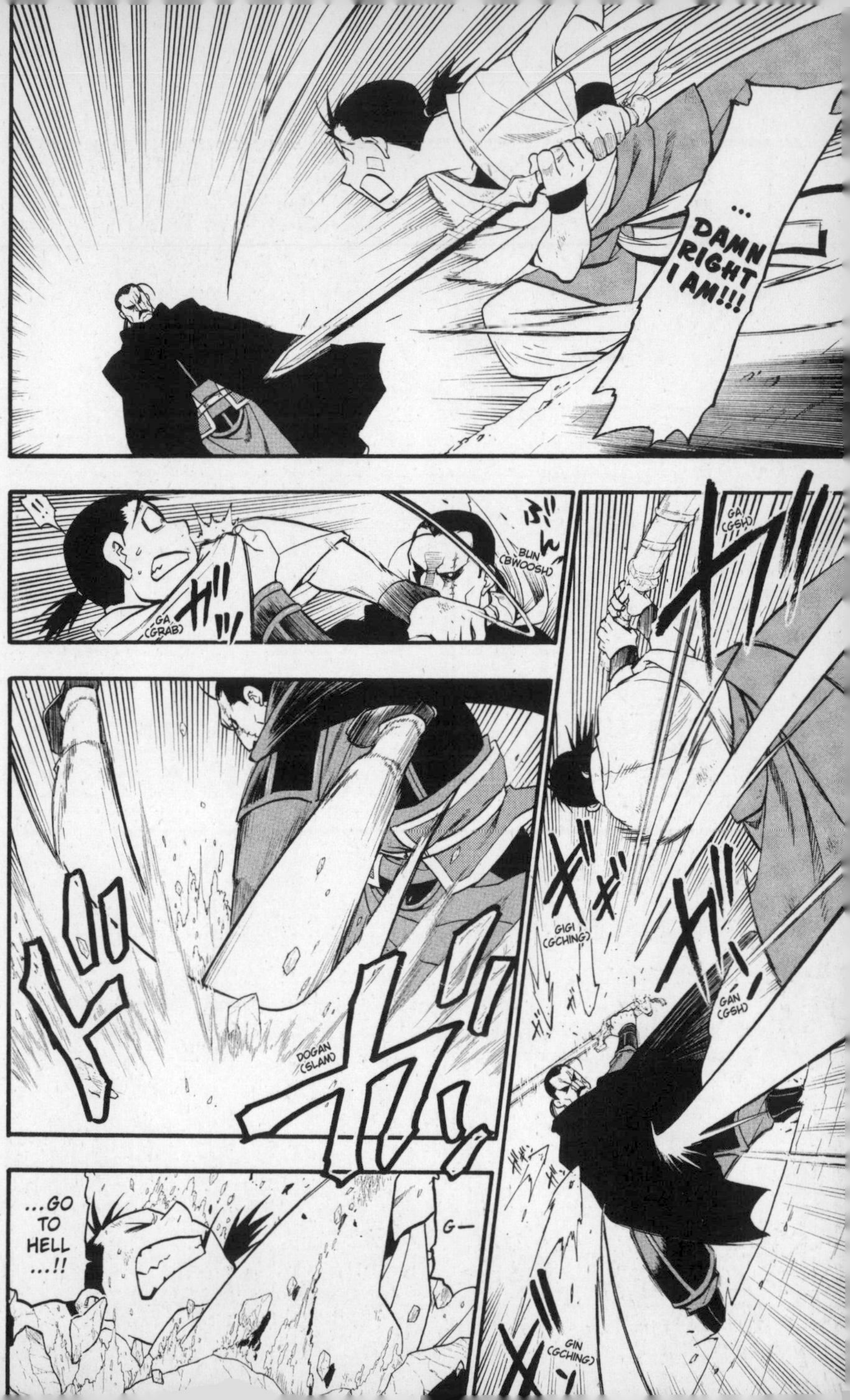

...DAMN RIGHT I AM!!!
GA (GSH)
GIGI (GCHING)
GAN (GSH)
GIN (GCHING)
!!
ぶん
BUN (BWOOSH)
GA (GRAB)
DOGAN (SLAM)
G—
...GO TO HELL ...!!

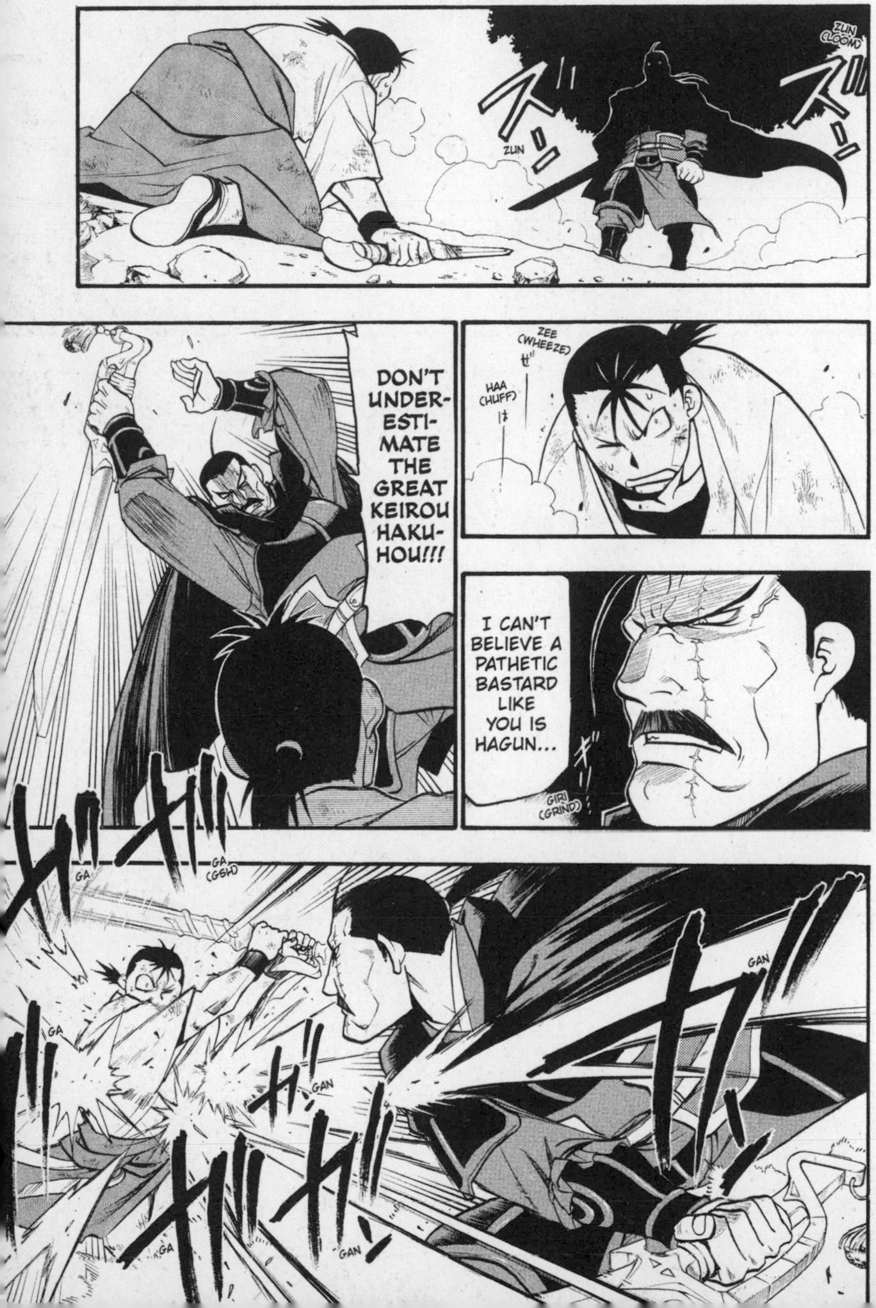
ZUN (LOOM)
ZUN
ZEE (WHEEZE)
ぜ
HAA (HUFF)
は
I CAN'T BELIEVE A PATHETIC BASTARD LIKE YOU IS HAGUN...
ギ
GIRI (GRIND)
DON'T UNDER-ESTI-MATE THE GREAT KEIROU HAKU-HOU!!!
GAN
GA (GSH)
GA
GAN
GA
GAN
GA

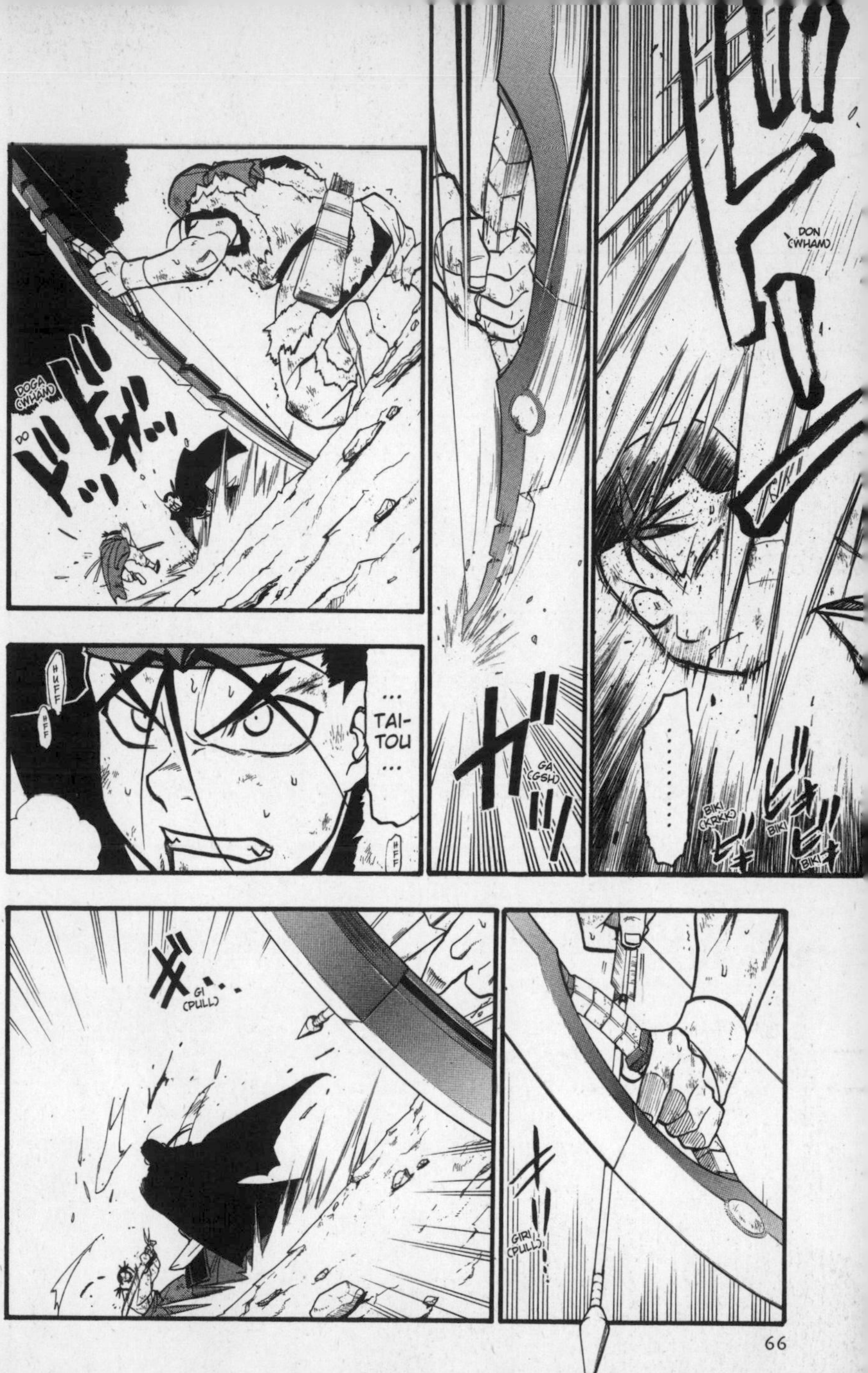
DON (WHAM)
BIKI (KRKK)
BIKI
BIKI
GA (GSH)
DOGA (WHAM)
DO
HUFF
HFF
... TAITOU ...
HFF
GIRI (PULL)
GI (PULL)

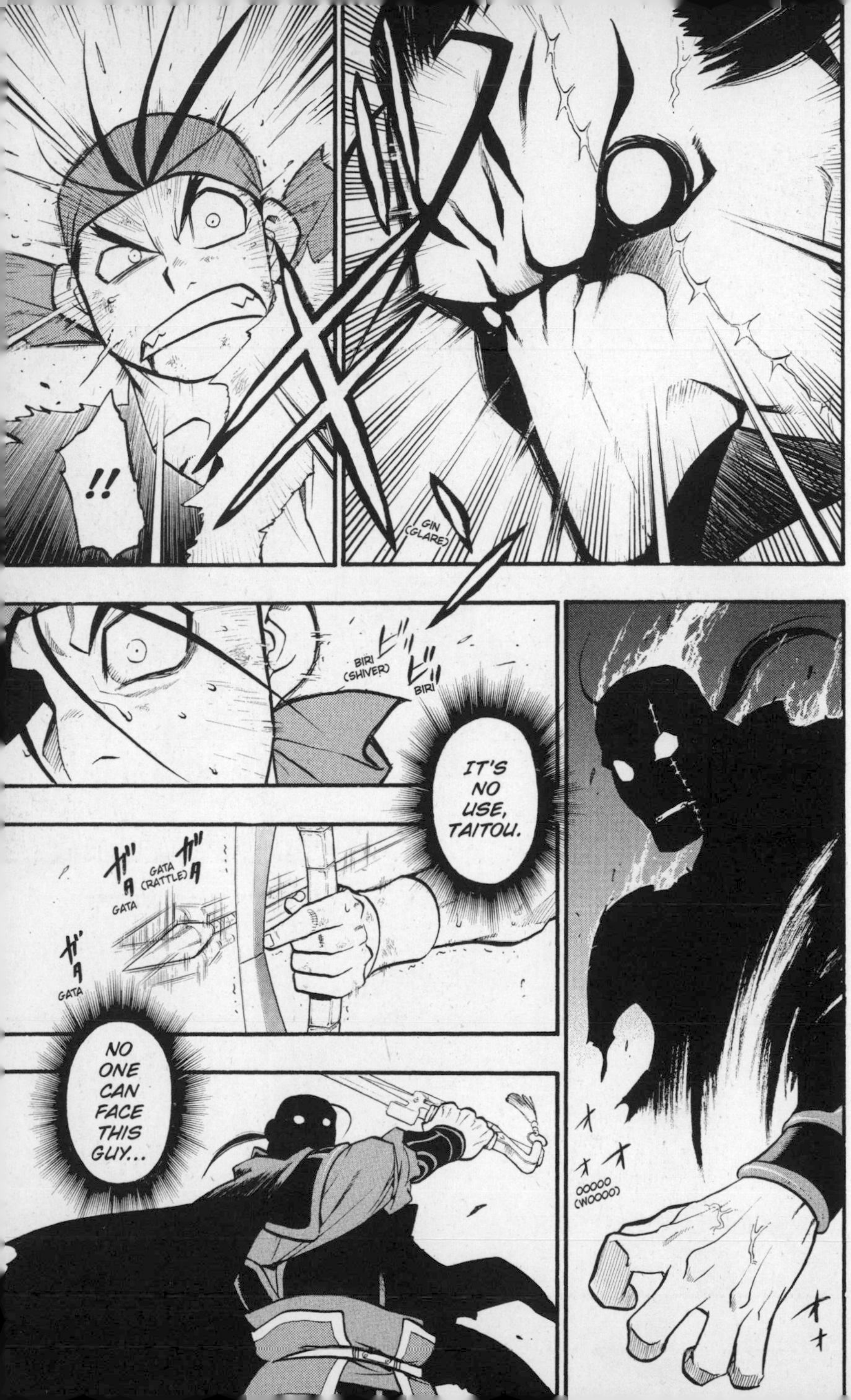
GIN (GLARE)
!!
OOOOO (WOOOO)
BIRI (SHIVER)
BIRI
IT'S NO USE, TAITOU.
GATA (RATTLE)
GATA
GATA
NO ONE CAN FACE THIS GUY...

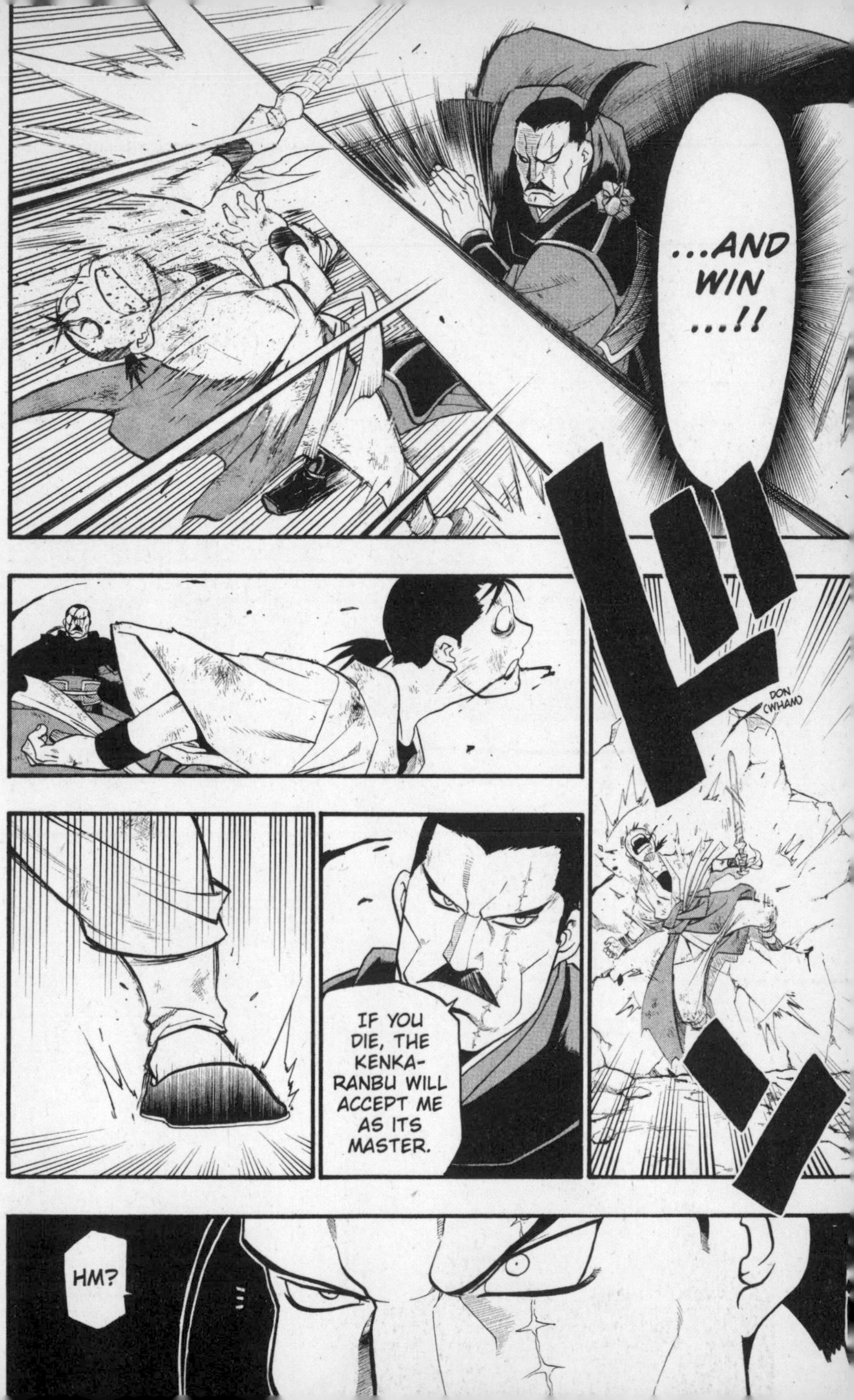
...AND WIN ...!!
DON (WHAM)
IF YOU DIE, THE KENKA-RANBU WILL ACCEPT ME AS ITS MASTER.
HM?

SSSSS

FSSSS

SSSSS

FSSSS

KOOOOOOO

FSSSH

......

GASHA
(GSHAK)

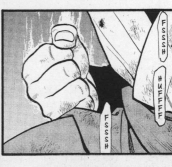

FSSSH

HUFFF

FSSSH

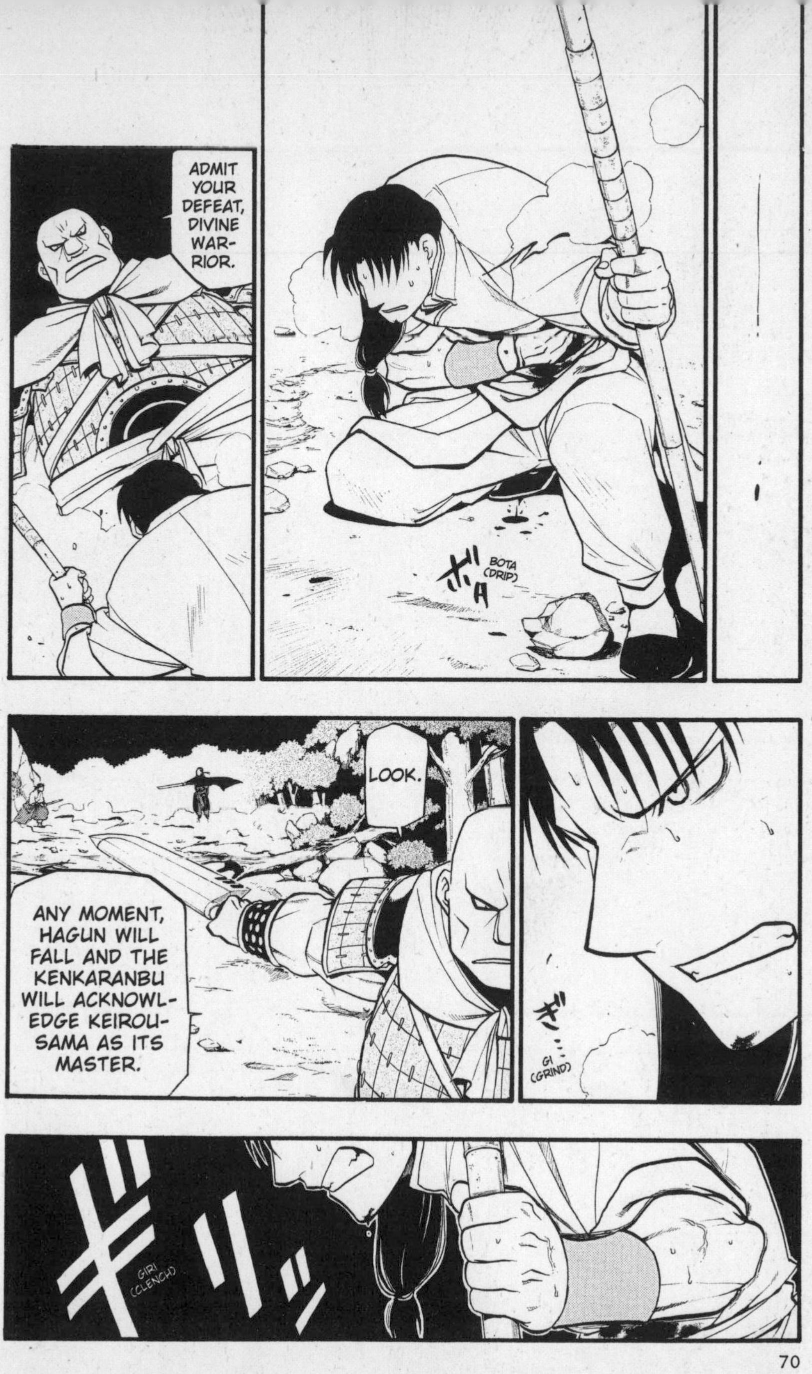
BOTA (DRIP)
ADMIT YOUR DEFEAT, DIVINE WAR-RIOR.
GI (GRIND)
LOOK.
ANY MOMENT, HAGUN WILL FALL AND THE KENKARANBU WILL ACKNOWL-EDGE KEIROU-SAMA AS ITS MASTER.
GIRI (CLENCH)

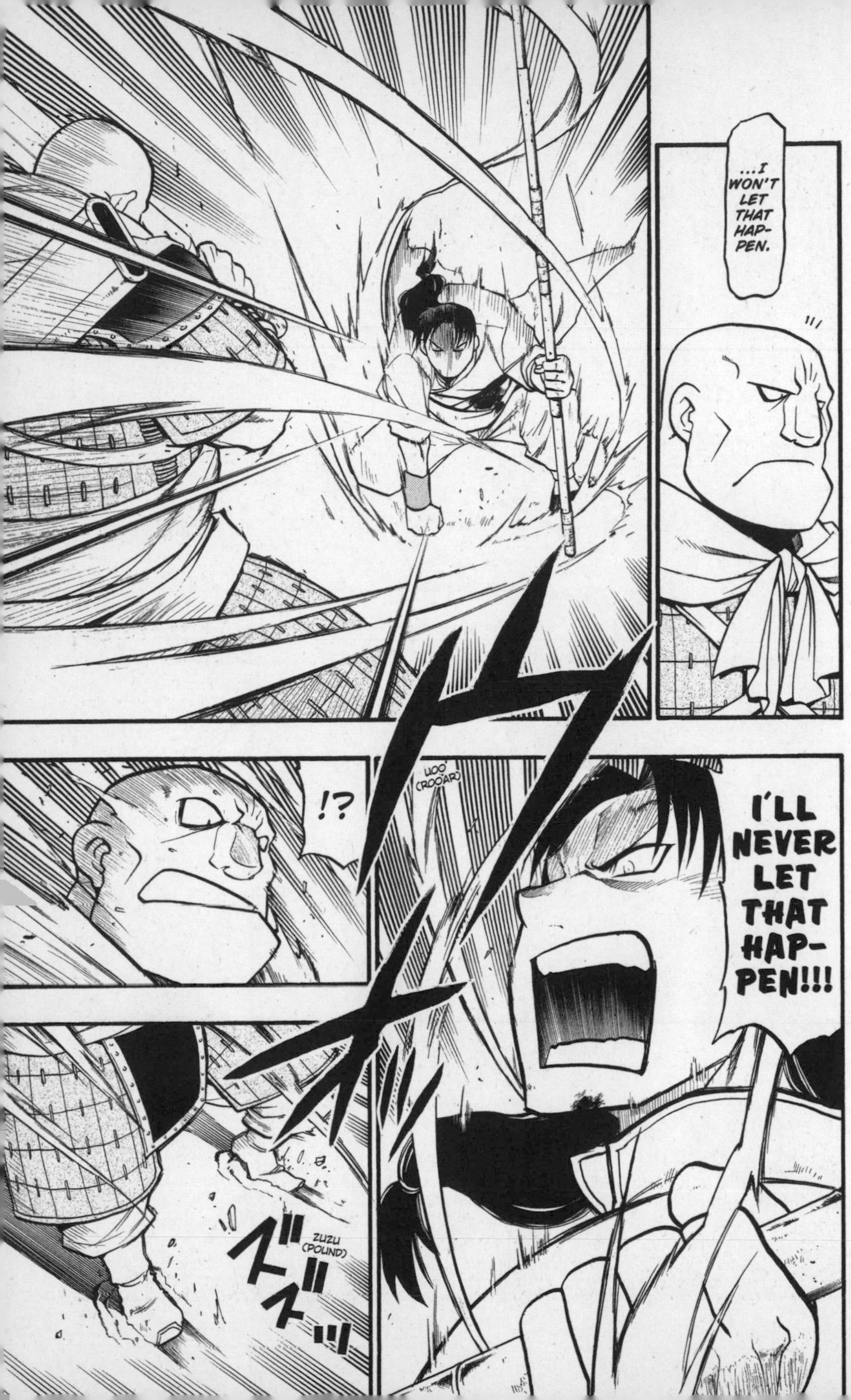

...I WON'T LET THAT HAP-PEN.
I'LL NEVER LET THAT HAP-PEN!!!
UOO (ROOAR)
!?
ZUZU (POUND)

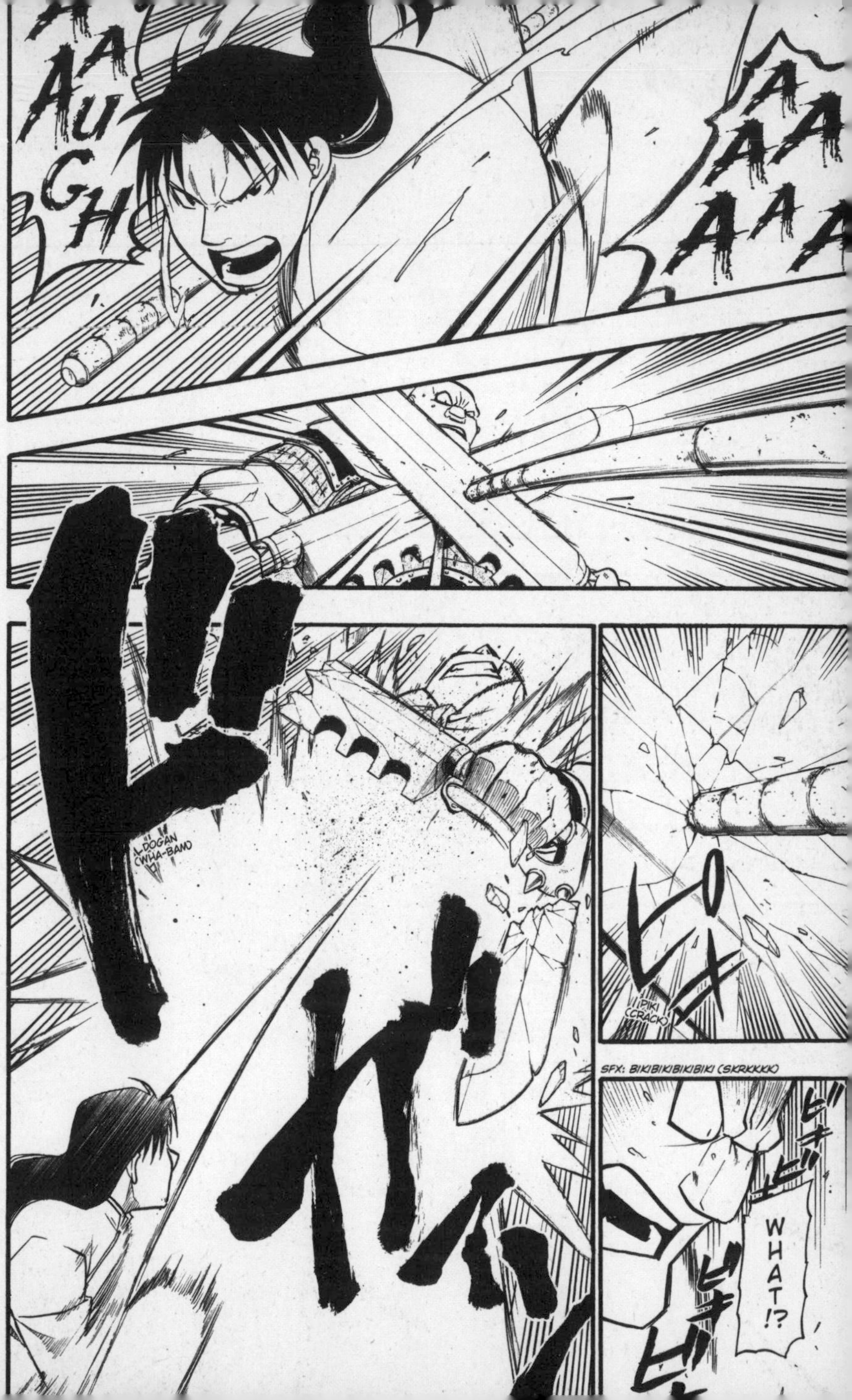

AAAAAA
AAUGH
PIKI (CRACK)
SFX: BIKIBIKIBIKIBIKI (SKRKKKK)
WHAT!?
DOGAN (WHA-BAM)

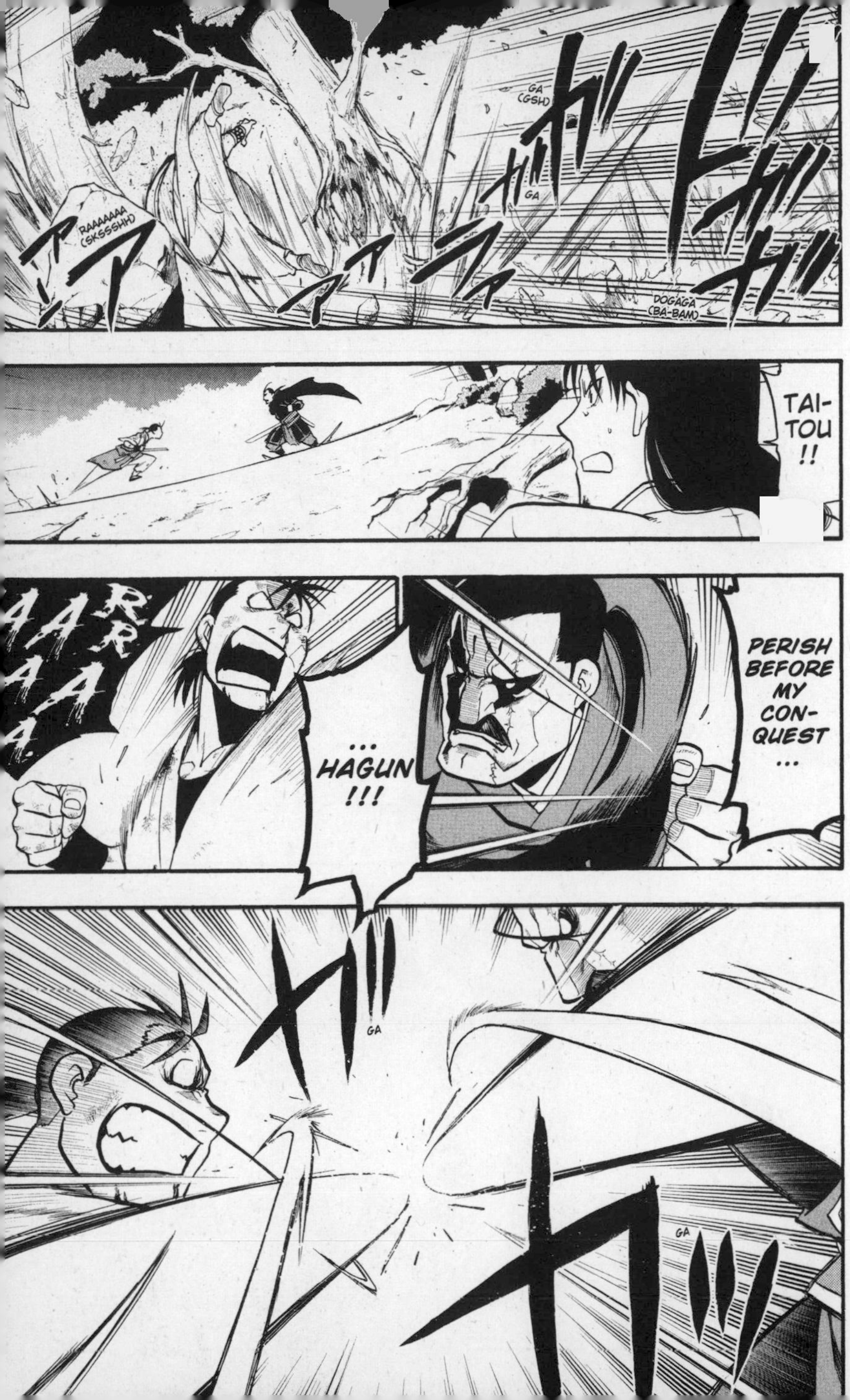
DOGAGA (BA-BAM)
GA (GSH)
GA
RAAAAAAA (SKSSSHH)
TAI-TOU !!
PERISH BEFORE MY CON-QUEST ...
... HÄGUN !!!
RRAAAAAA
GA
GA

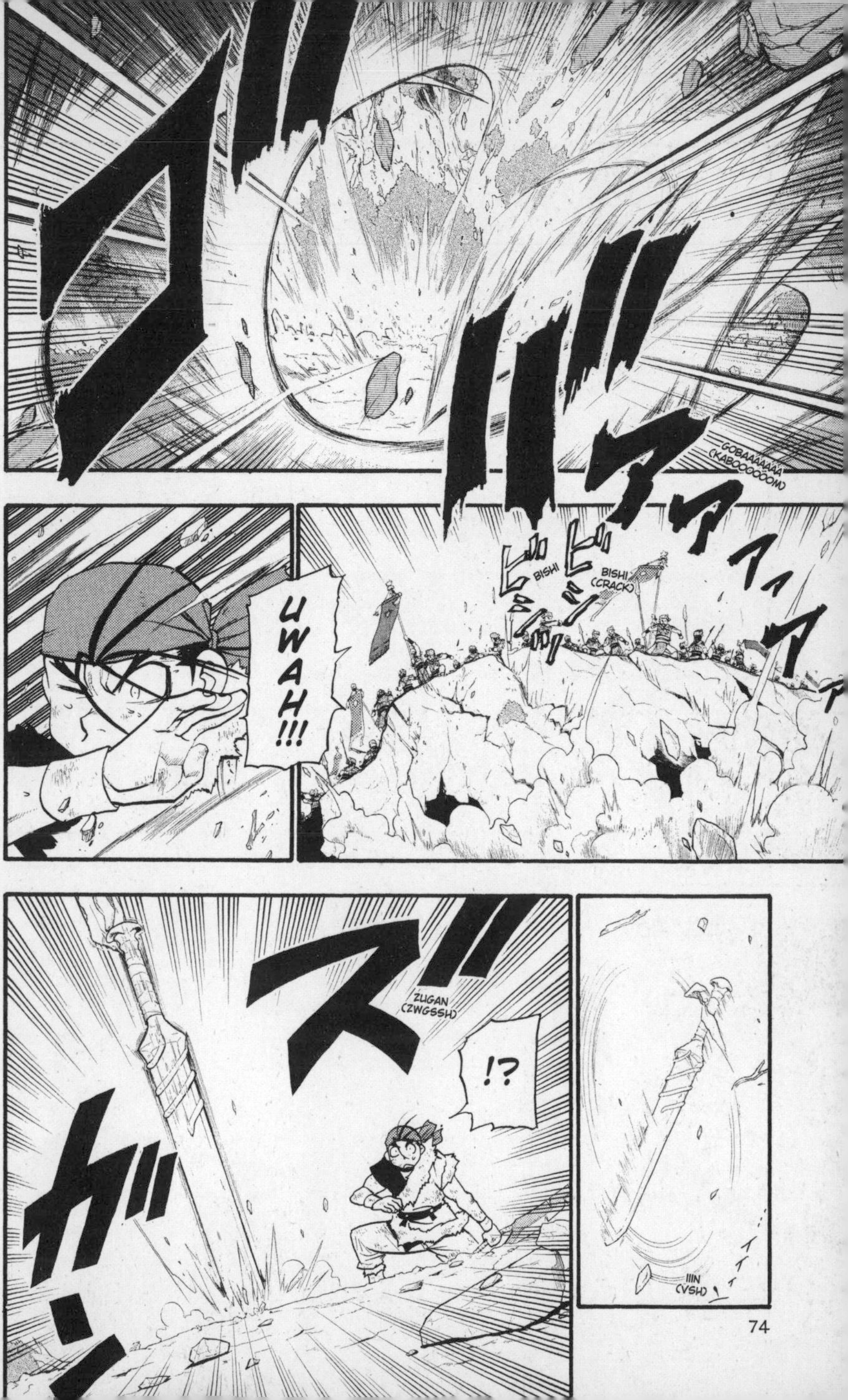
GOBAAAAAAA
(KABOOOOOOM)
BISHI
(CRACK)
BISHI
UWAH!!!
IIIN
(VSH)
ZUGAN
(ZWGSSH)
!?

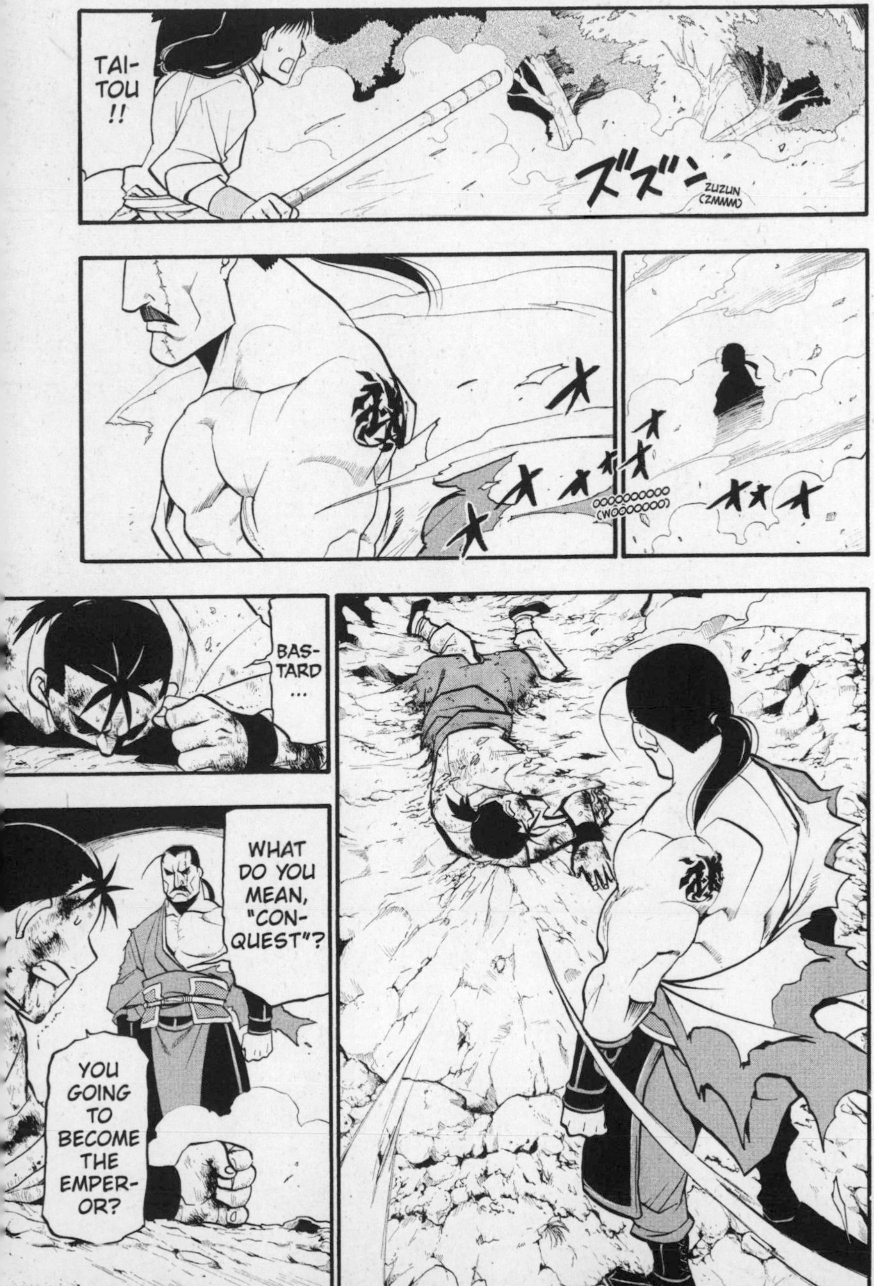
TAI-TOU!!
ズズン
ZUZUN (ZMMMM)
オオオ
OOOOOOOOOO (WOOOOOOOO)
オオオオオオオオ
BASTARD...
WHAT DO YOU MEAN, "CONQUEST"?
YOU GOING TO BECOME THE EMPEROR?

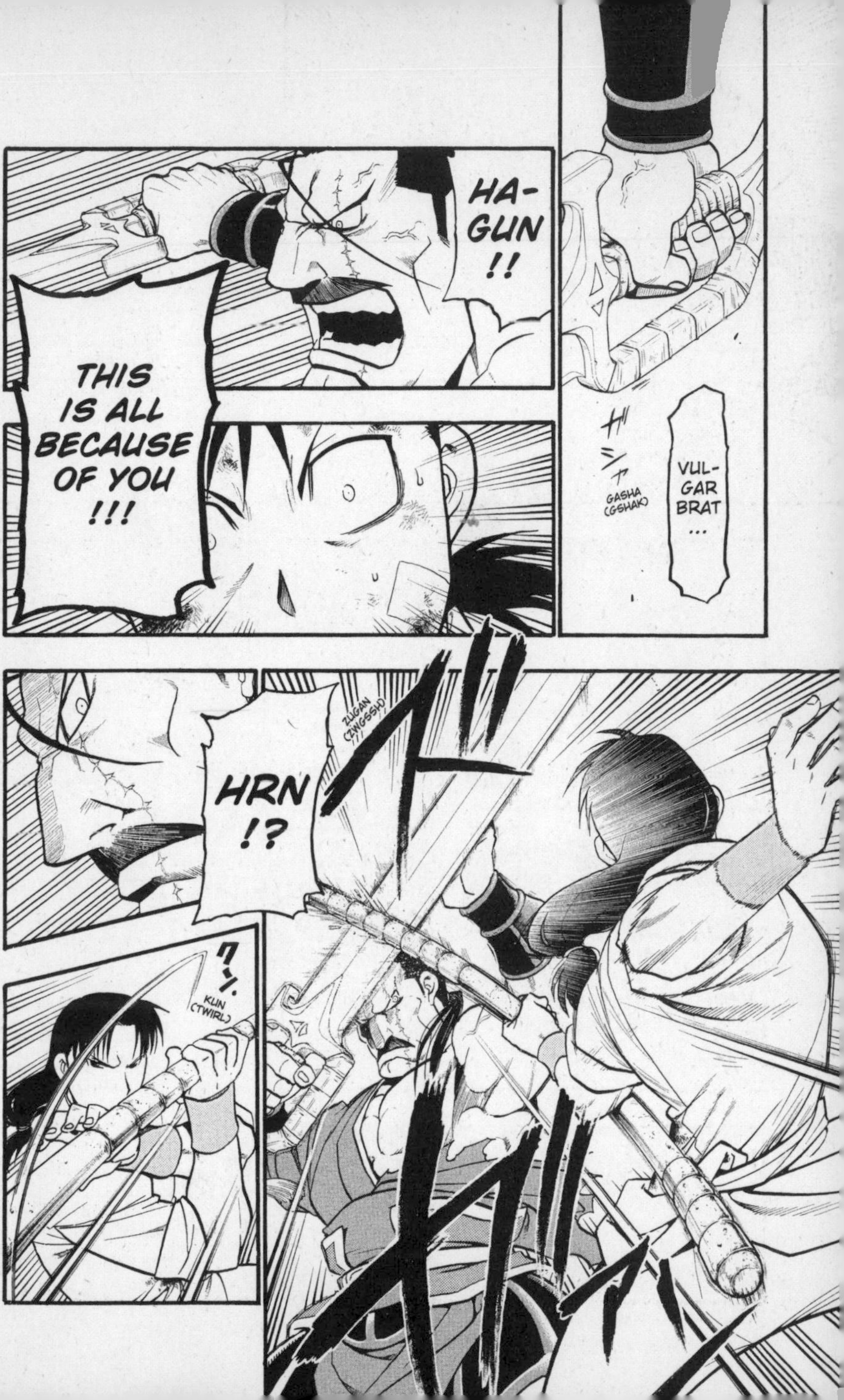
VUL-GAR BRAT...
ガシャ
GASHA (GSHAK)
HA-GUN!!
THIS IS ALL BECAUSE OF YOU!!!
ZUGAN (ZWGSSH)
HRN!?
クン
KUN (TWIRL)

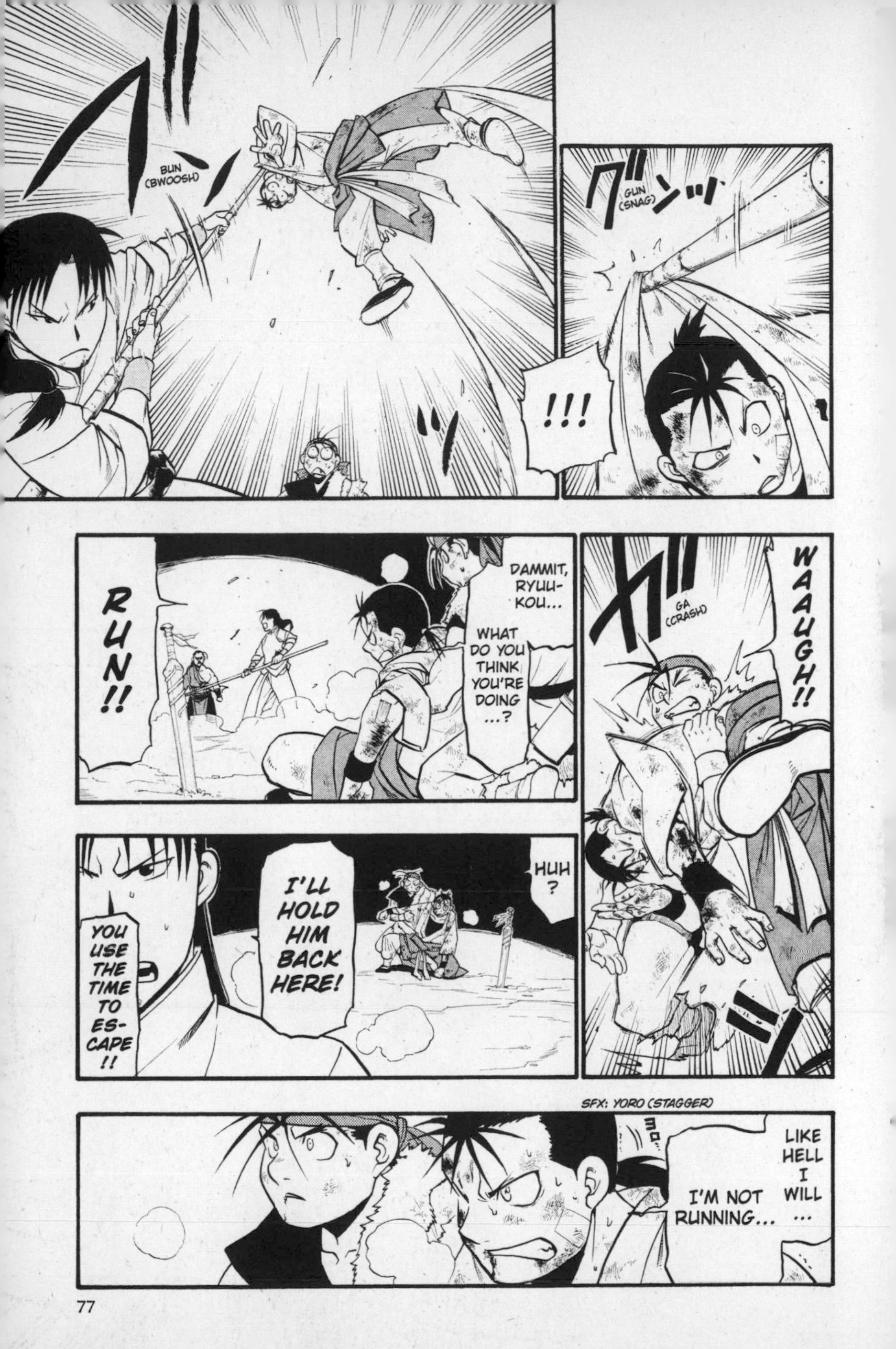
GUN (SNAG)
!!!
BUN (BWOOSH)
GA (CRASH)
WAAUGH!!
DAMMIT, RYUU-KOU...
WHAT DO YOU THINK YOU'RE DOING ...?
RUN!!
HUH ?
I'LL HOLD HIM BACK HERE!
YOU USE THE TIME TO ES-CAPE !!
SFX: YORO (STAGGER)
LIKE HELL I WILL ...
I'M NOT RUNNING...

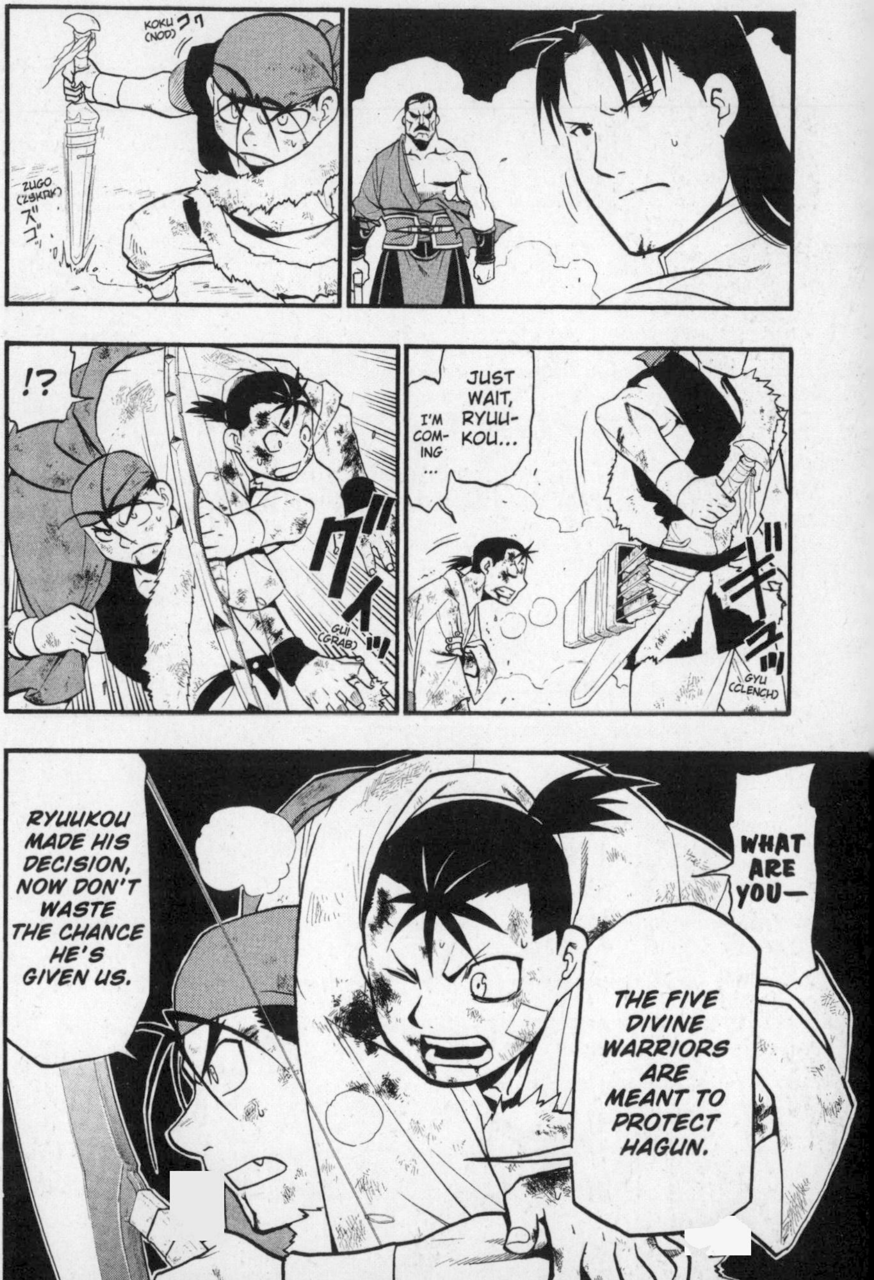
KOKU (NOD)
ZUGO (ZYKRK)
JUST WAIT, RYUUKOU...
I'M COMING...
GYU (CLENCH)
!?
GUI (GRAB)
WHAT ARE YOU—
RYUUKOU MADE HIS DECISION, NOW DON'T WASTE THE CHANCE HE'S GIVEN US.
THE FIVE DIVINE WARRIORS ARE MEANT TO PROTECT HAGUN.

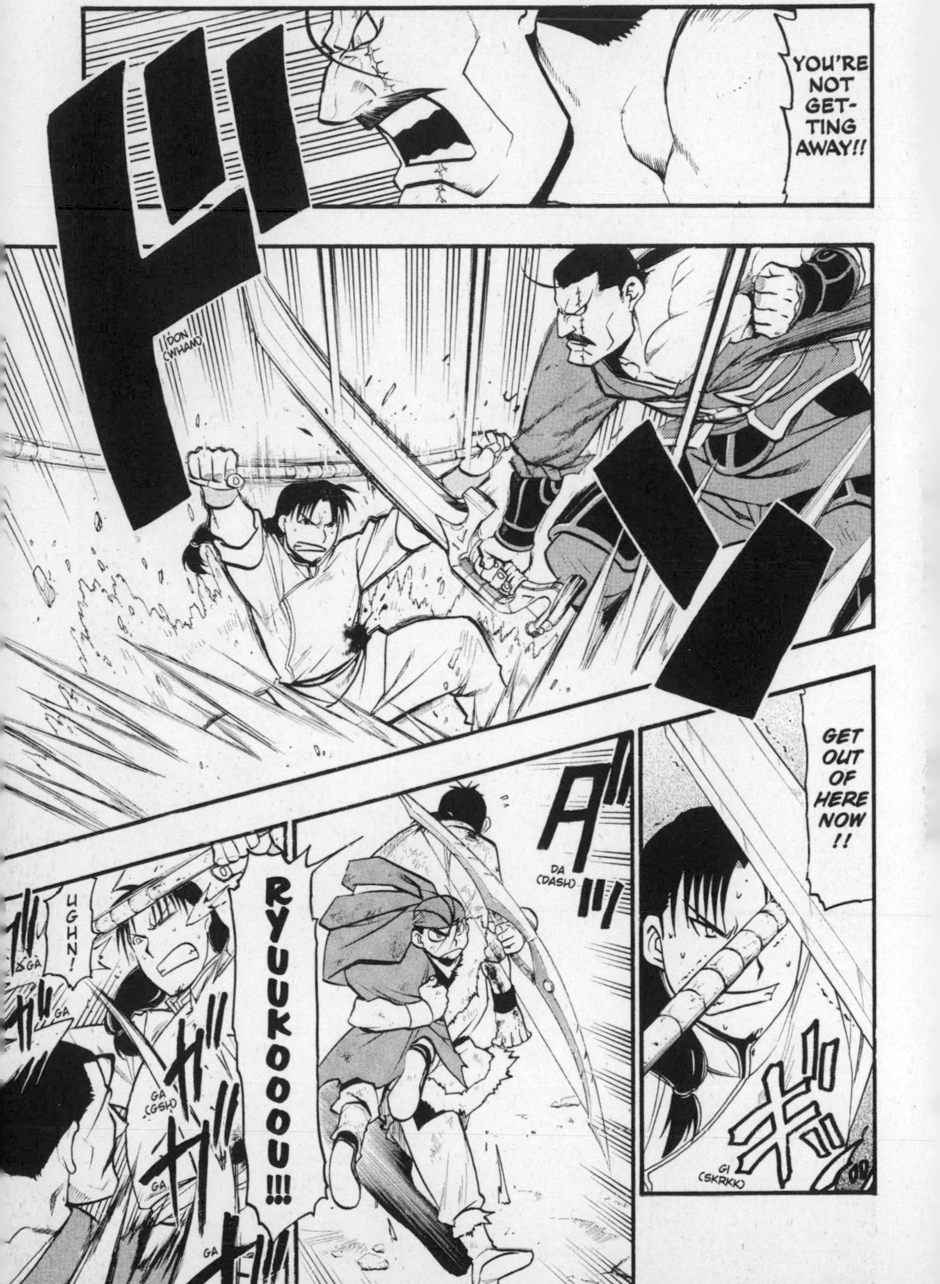
YOU'RE NOT GET-TING AWAY!!
DON (WHAM)
GET OUT OF HERE NOW!!
GI (SKRKK)
DA (DASH)
RYUUKOOOOU!!!
UGHN!
GA
GA
GA (GSH)
GA
GA

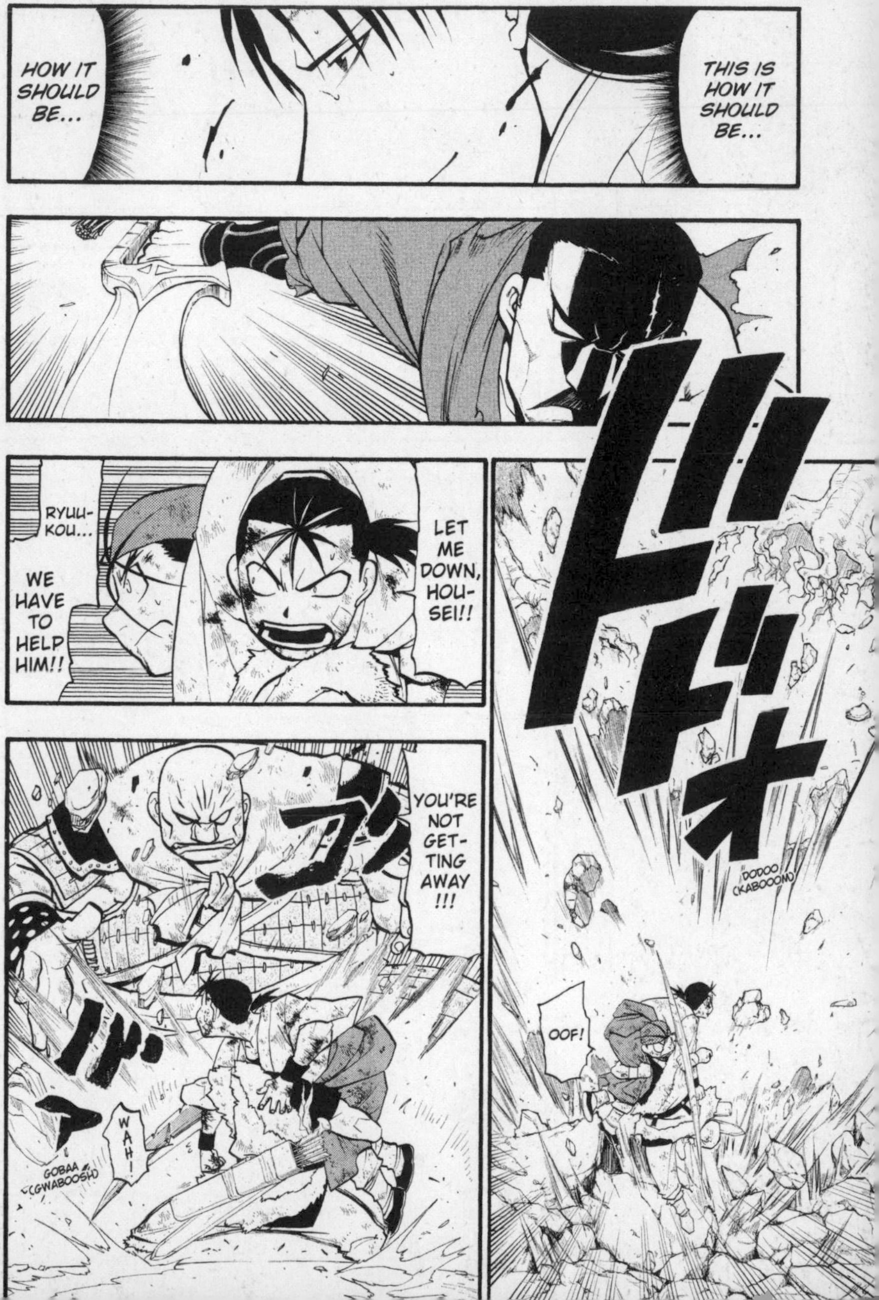
THIS IS HOW IT SHOULD BE...
HOW IT SHOULD BE...
DODOO (KABOOM)
OOF!
LET ME DOWN, HOU-SEI!!
RYUU-KOU...
WE HAVE TO HELP HIM!!
YOU'RE NOT GET-TING AWAY!!!
WAH!
GOBAA (GWABOOSH)

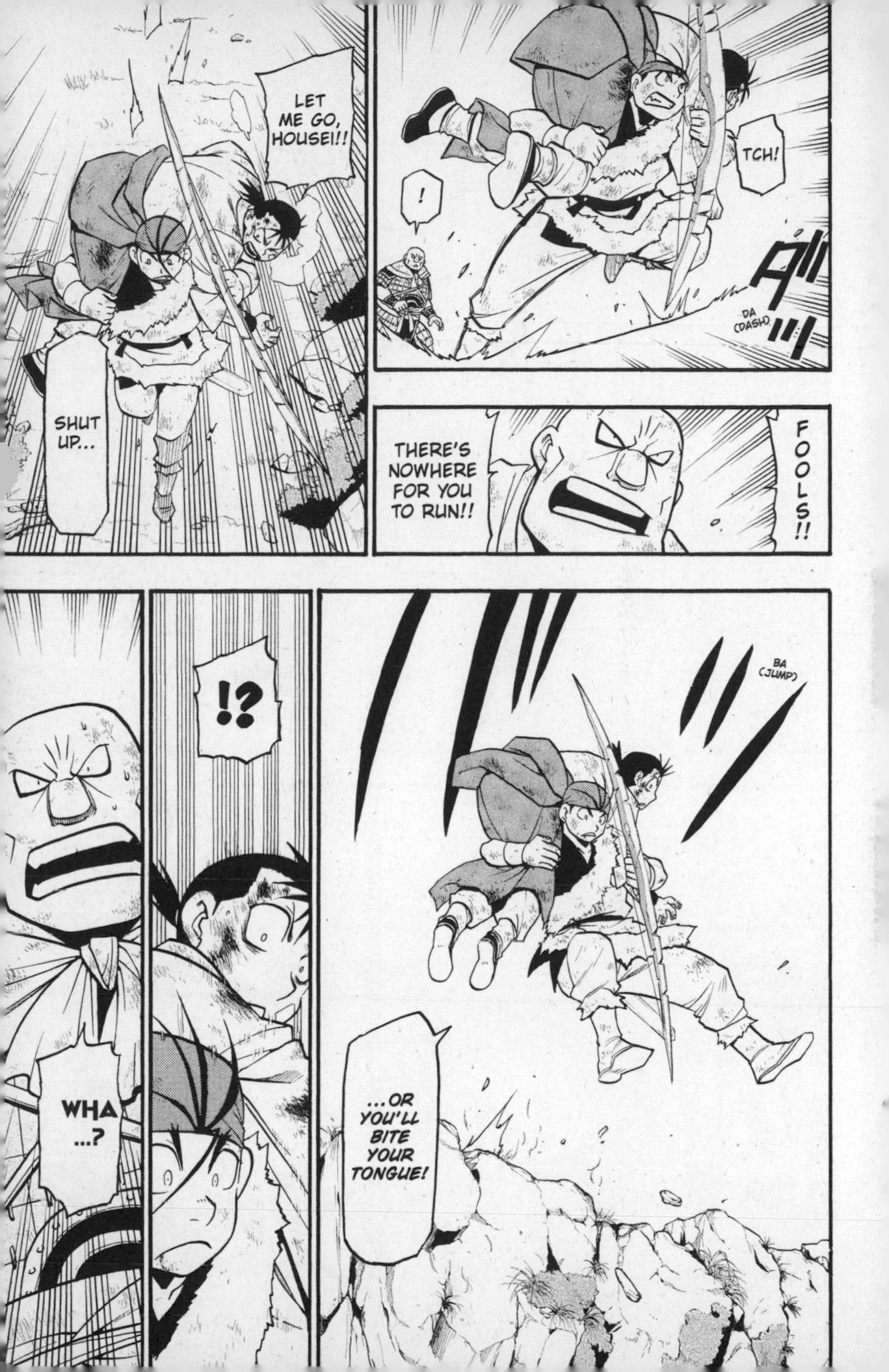
TCH!
!
DA (DASH)
FOOLS!!
THERE'S NOWHERE FOR YOU TO RUN!!
LET ME GO, HOUSEI!!
SHUT UP...
BA (JUMP)
...OR YOU'LL BITE YOUR TONGUE!
!?
WHA ...?

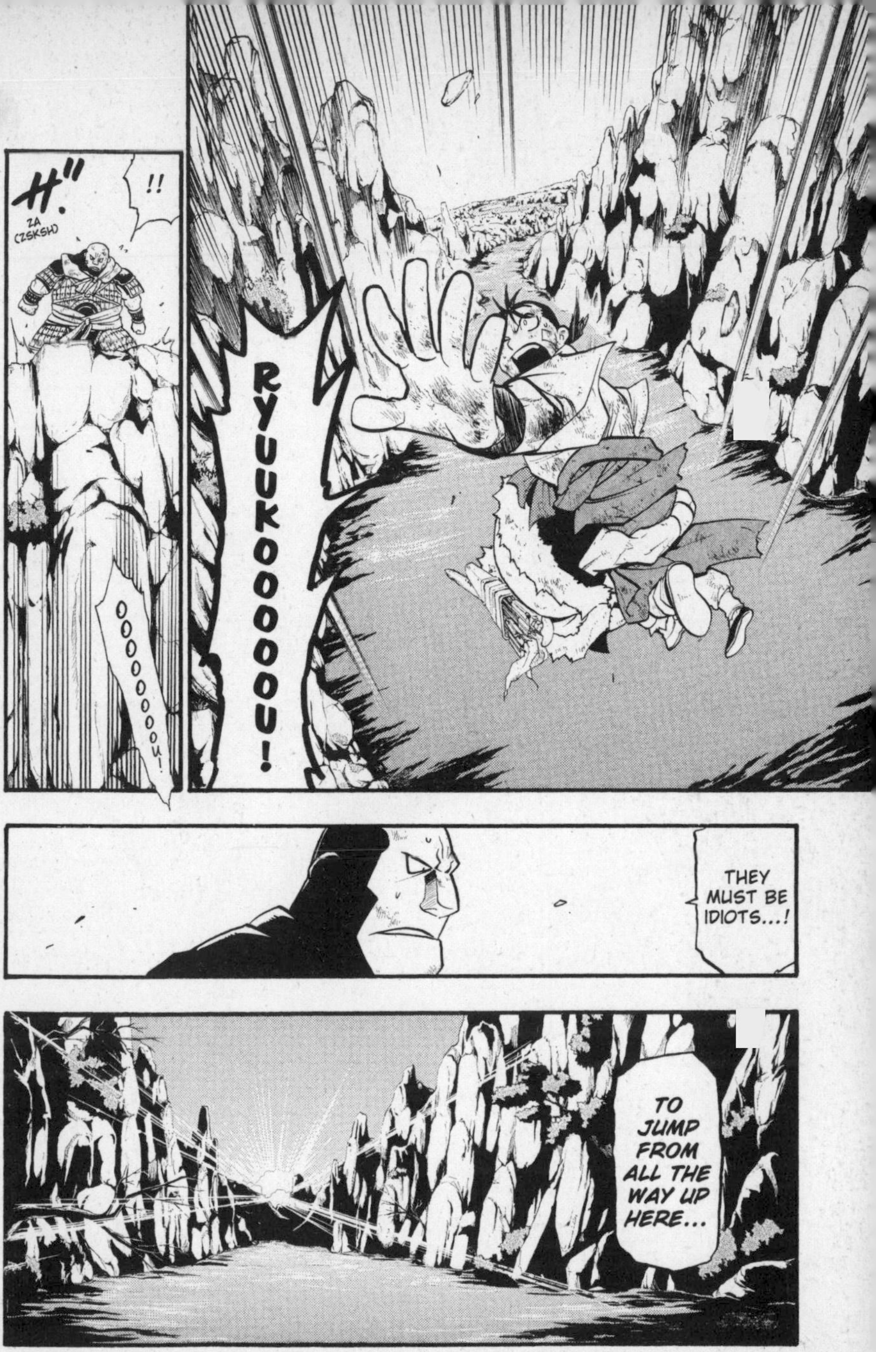
RYUUKOOOOOOOU!
!!
ZA (ZSKSH)
OOOOOOOOOU!
THEY MUST BE IDIOTS...!
TO JUMP FROM ALL THE WAY UP HERE...

# HERO TALES
獣　神　演　武

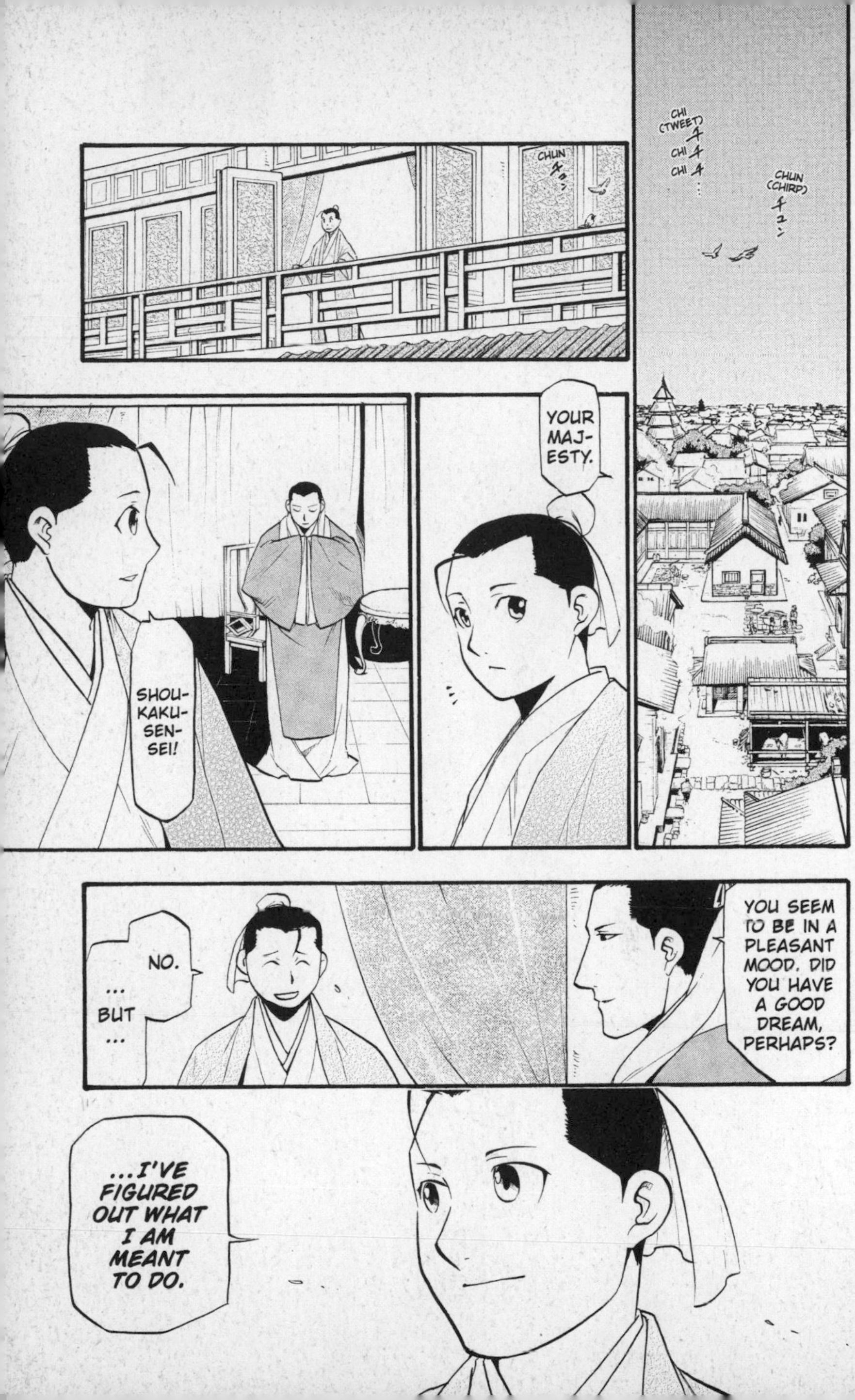
CHI (TWEET) チ
CHI チ
CHI チ …
CHUN (CHIRP) チュン
CHUN チュン
YOUR MAJ-ESTY.
SHOUKAKU-SENSEI!
YOU SEEM TO BE IN A PLEASANT MOOD. DID YOU HAVE A GOOD DREAM, PERHAPS?
NO. ... BUT ...
...I'VE FIGURED OUT WHAT I AM MEANT TO DO.

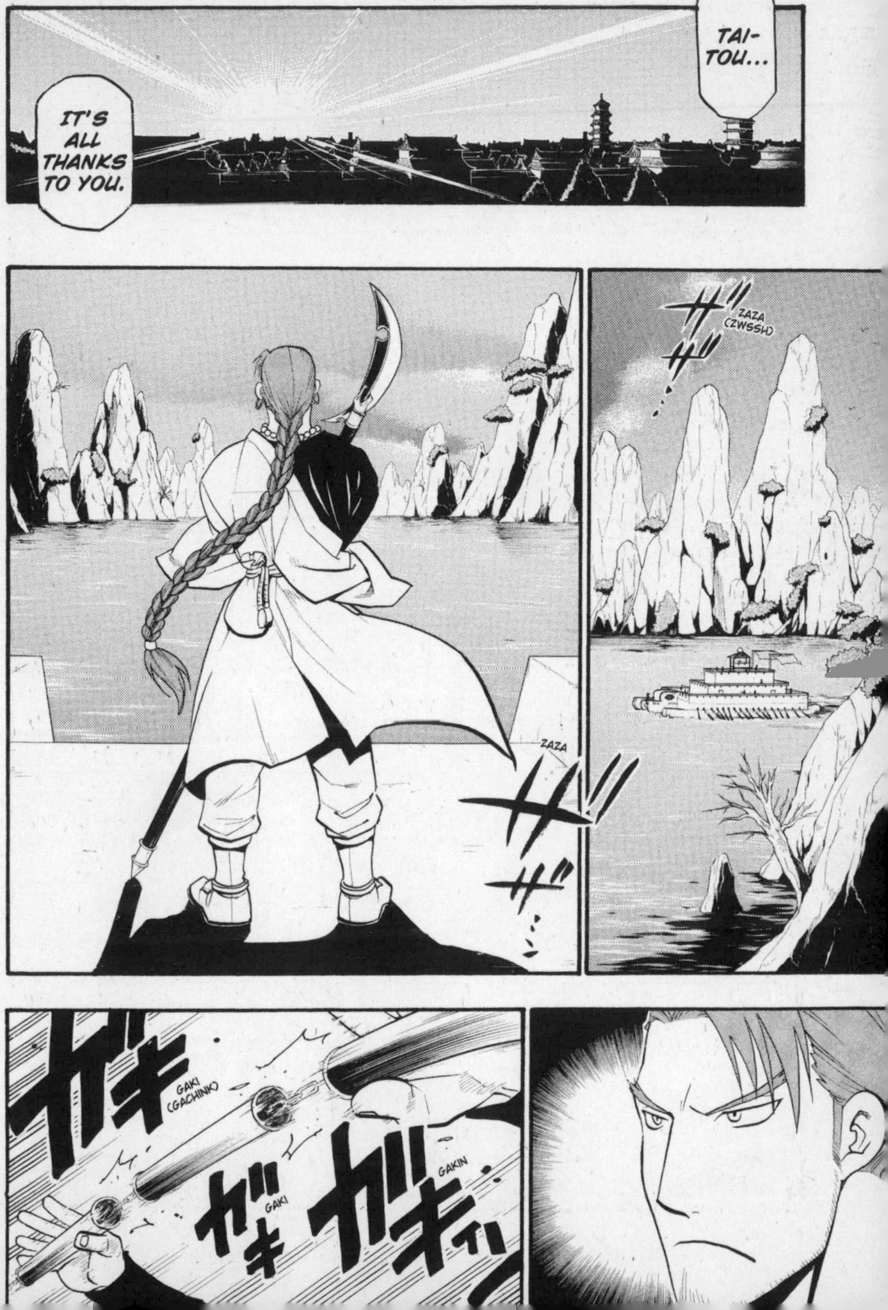
TAI-TOU...
IT'S ALL THANKS TO YOU.
ZAZA (ZWSSH)
ZAZA
GAKI (GACHINK)
GAKIN
GAKI

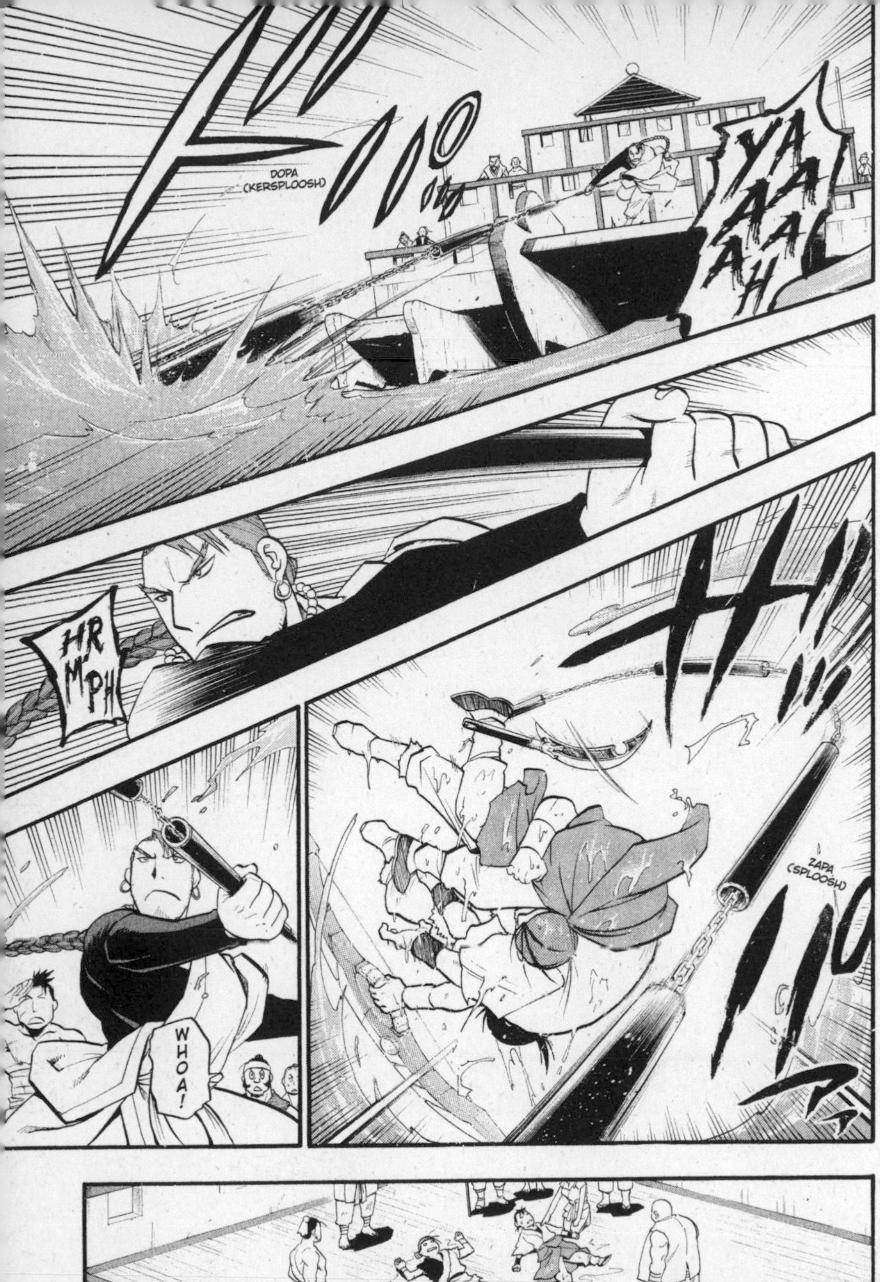
YAAAAH
DOPA (KERSPLOOSH)
HRMPH
ZAPA (SPLOOSH)
WHOA!

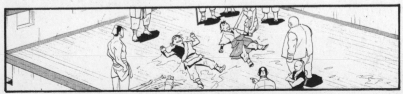

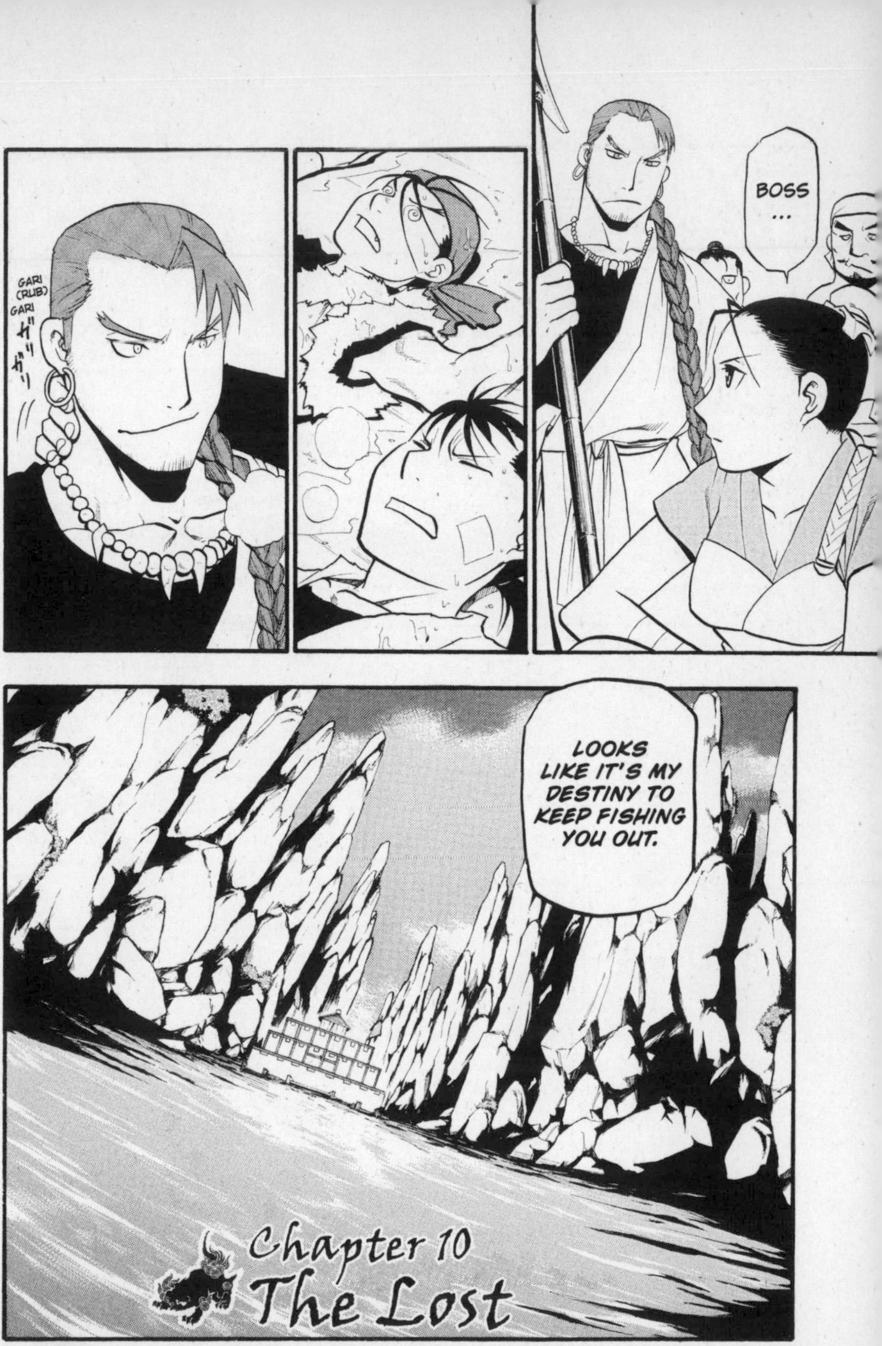
BOSS ...
GARI (RUB) GARI
ガリ ガリ
LOOKS LIKE IT'S MY DESTINY TO KEEP FISHING YOU OUT.
Chapter 10
The Lost

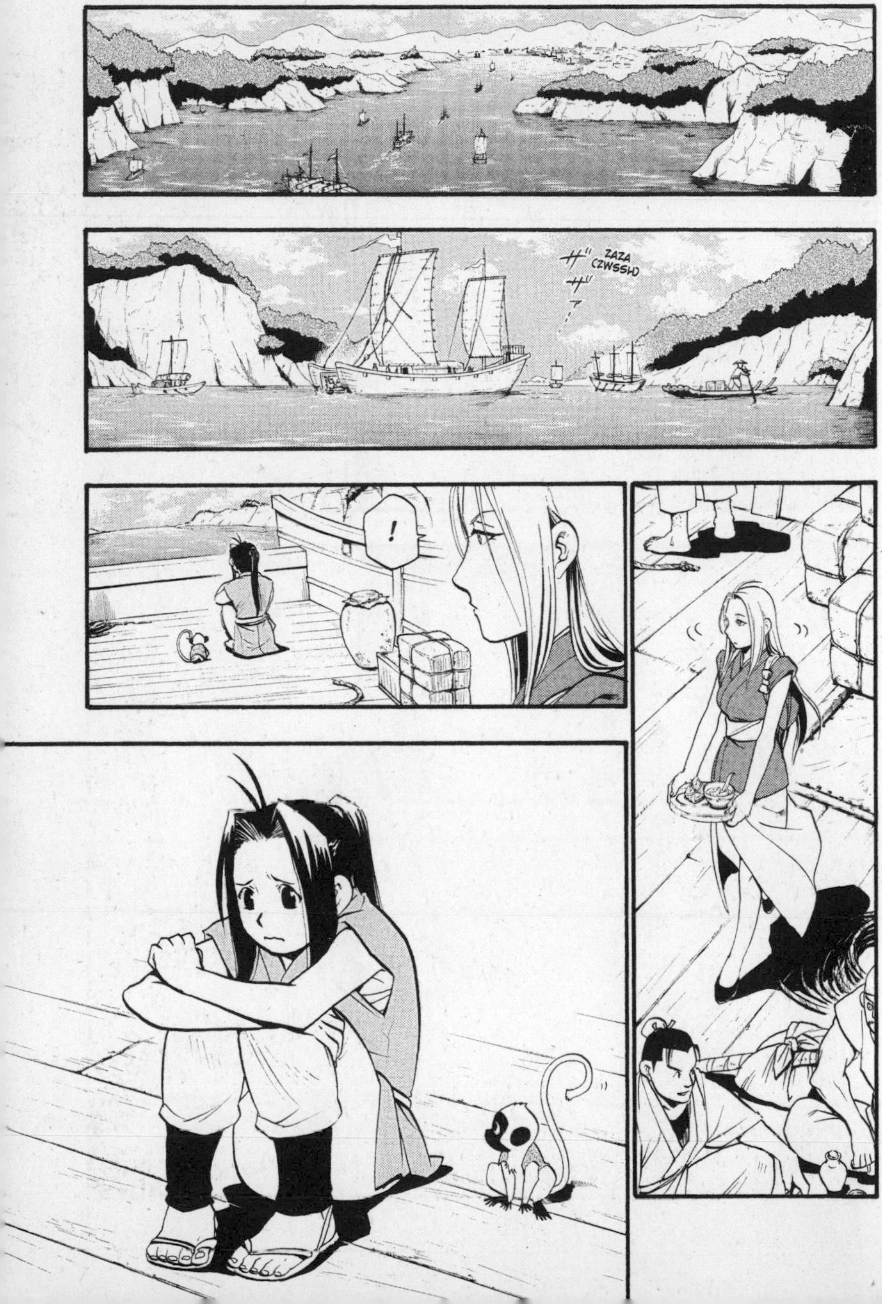
ザザァ…
ZAZA (ZWSSH)
!

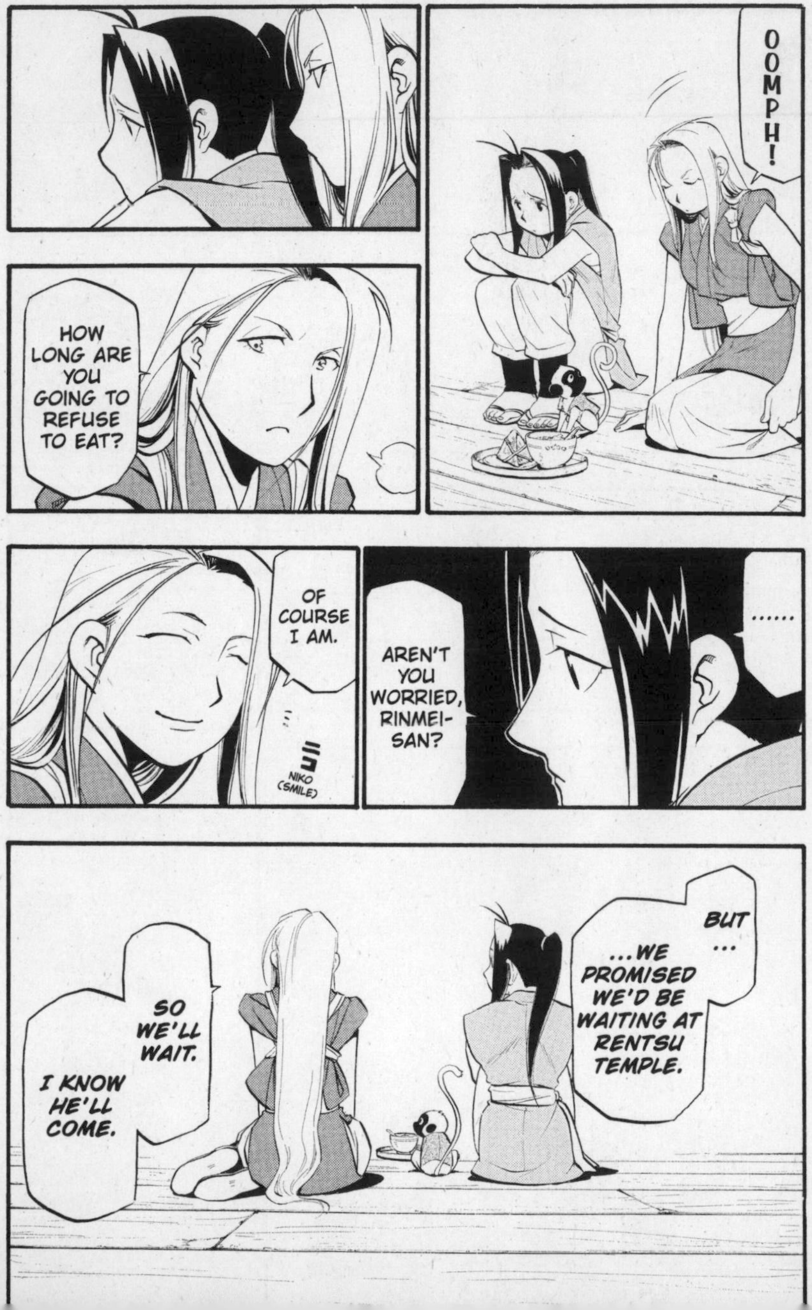
OOMPH!
HOW LONG ARE YOU GOING TO REFUSE TO EAT?
......
AREN'T YOU WORRIED, RINMEI-SAN?
OF COURSE I AM.
NIKO (SMILE)
BUT ... ...WE PROMISED WE'D BE WAITING AT RENTSU TEMPLE.
SO WE'LL WAIT.
I KNOW HE'LL COME.

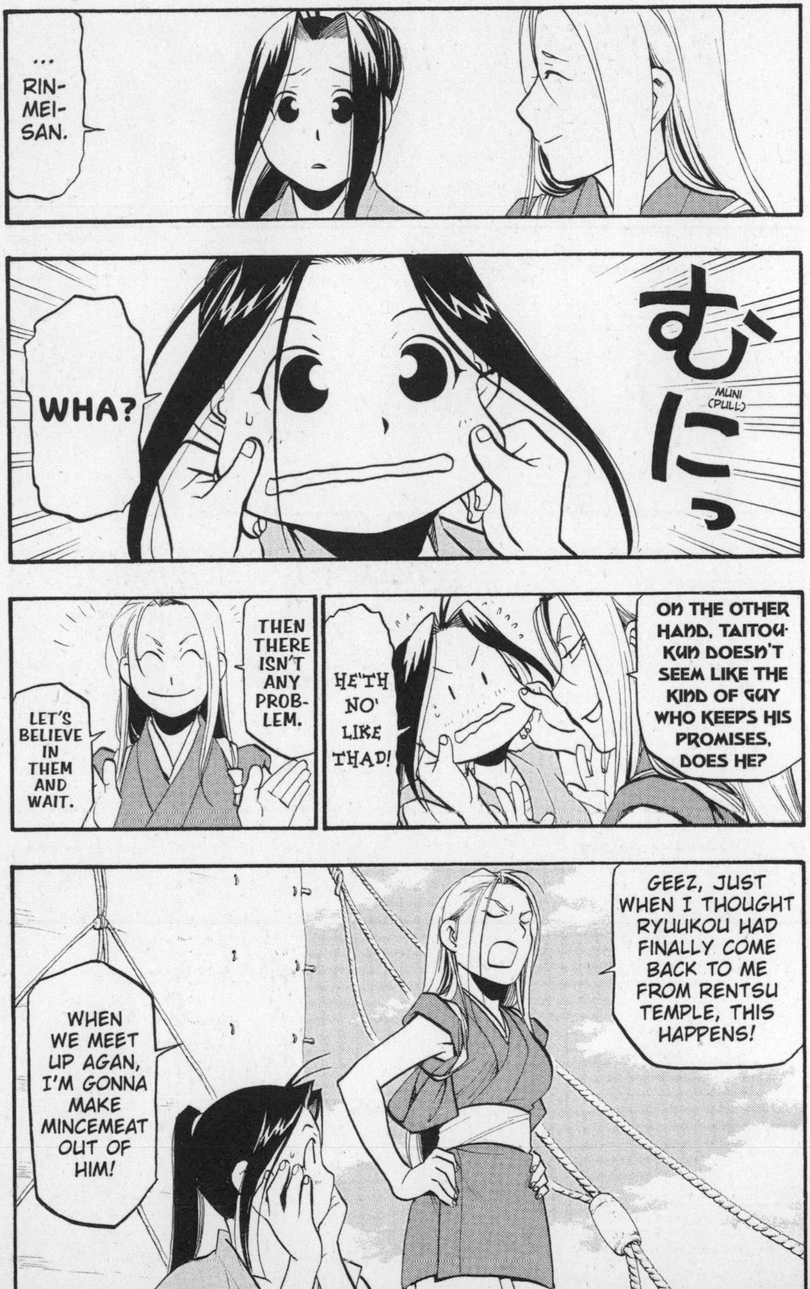

... RIN-MEI-SAN.
むにっ
MUNI (PULL)
WHA?
ON THE OTHER HAND, TAITOU-KUN DOESN'T SEEM LIKE THE KIND OF GUY WHO KEEPS HIS PROMISES, DOES HE?
HE'TH NO' LIKE THAD!
THEN THERE ISN'T ANY PROB-LEM.
LET'S BELIEVE IN THEM AND WAIT.
GEEZ, JUST WHEN I THOUGHT RYUUKOU HAD FINALLY COME BACK TO ME FROM RENTSU TEMPLE, THIS HAPPENS!
WHEN WE MEET UP AGAN, I'M GONNA MAKE MINCEMEAT OUT OF HIM!

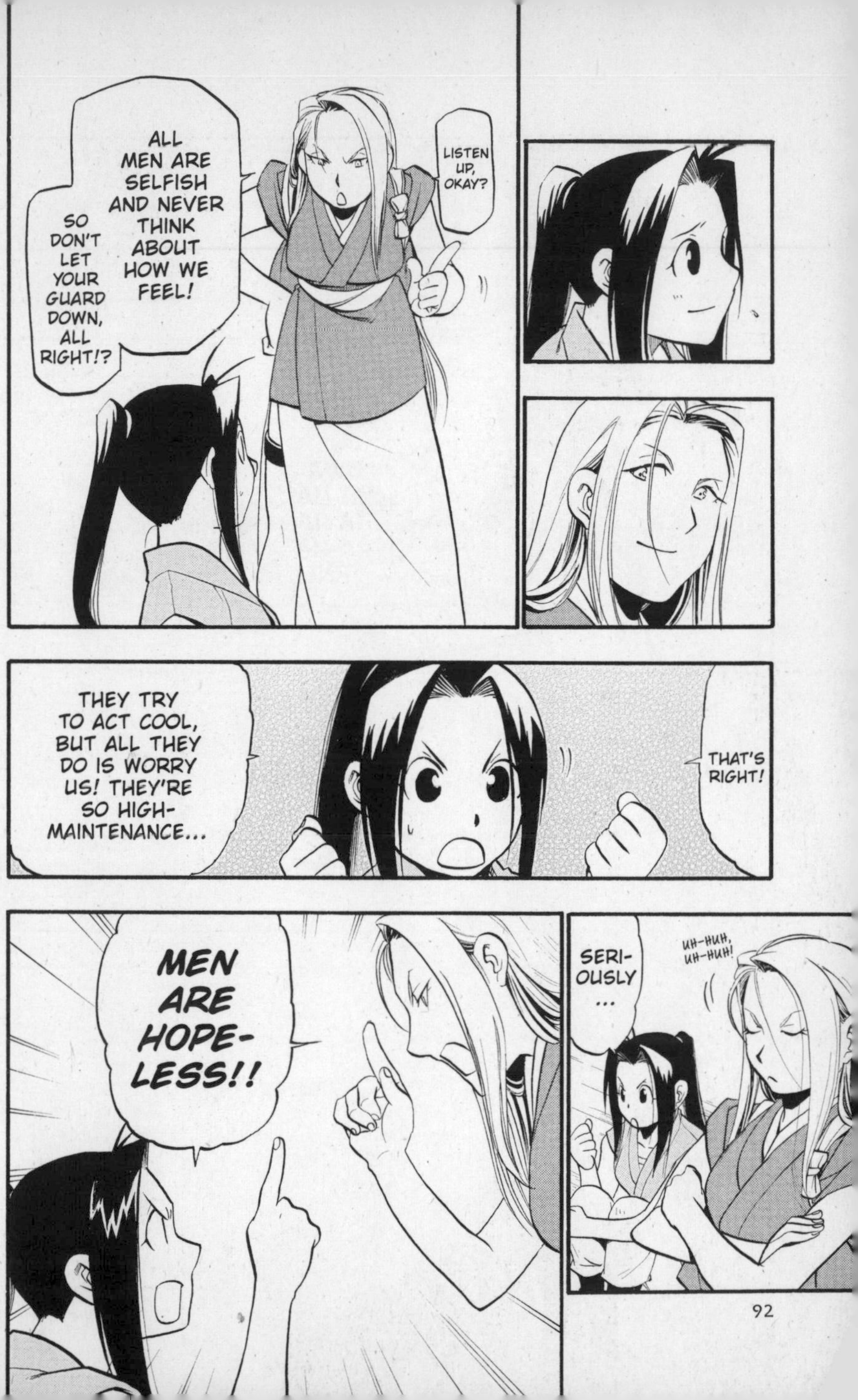
LISTEN UP, OKAY?
ALL MEN ARE SELFISH AND NEVER THINK ABOUT HOW WE FEEL!
SO DON'T LET YOUR GUARD DOWN, ALL RIGHT!?
THAT'S RIGHT!
THEY TRY TO ACT COOL, BUT ALL THEY DO IS WORRY US! THEY'RE SO HIGH-MAINTENANCE...
UH-HUH, UH-HUH!
SERI-OUSLY ...
MEN ARE HOPE-LESS!!

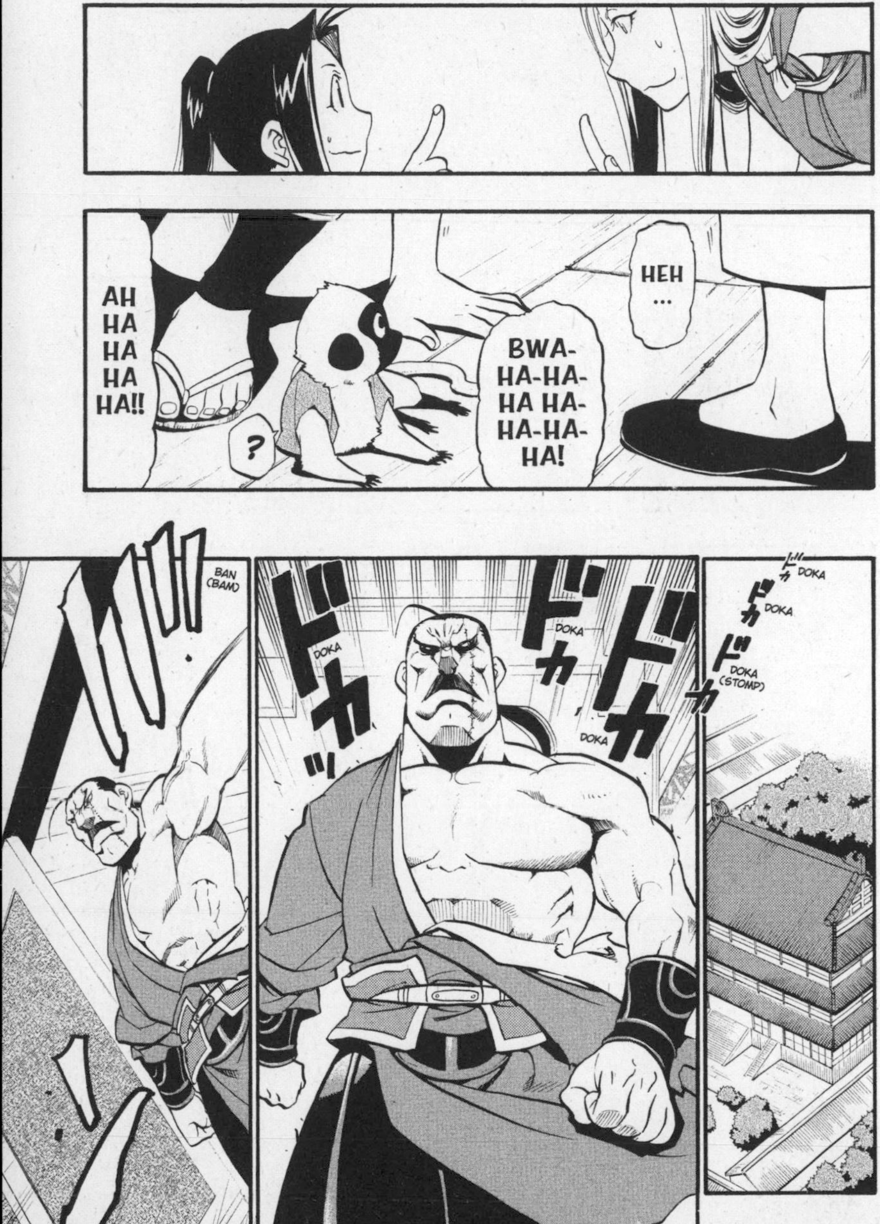
HEH...
BWA-HA-HA-HA HA-HA-HA-HA-HA!
?
AH HA HA HA HA!!
DOKA
DOKA
DOKA (STOMP)
DOKA
DOKA
DOKA
BAN (BAM)

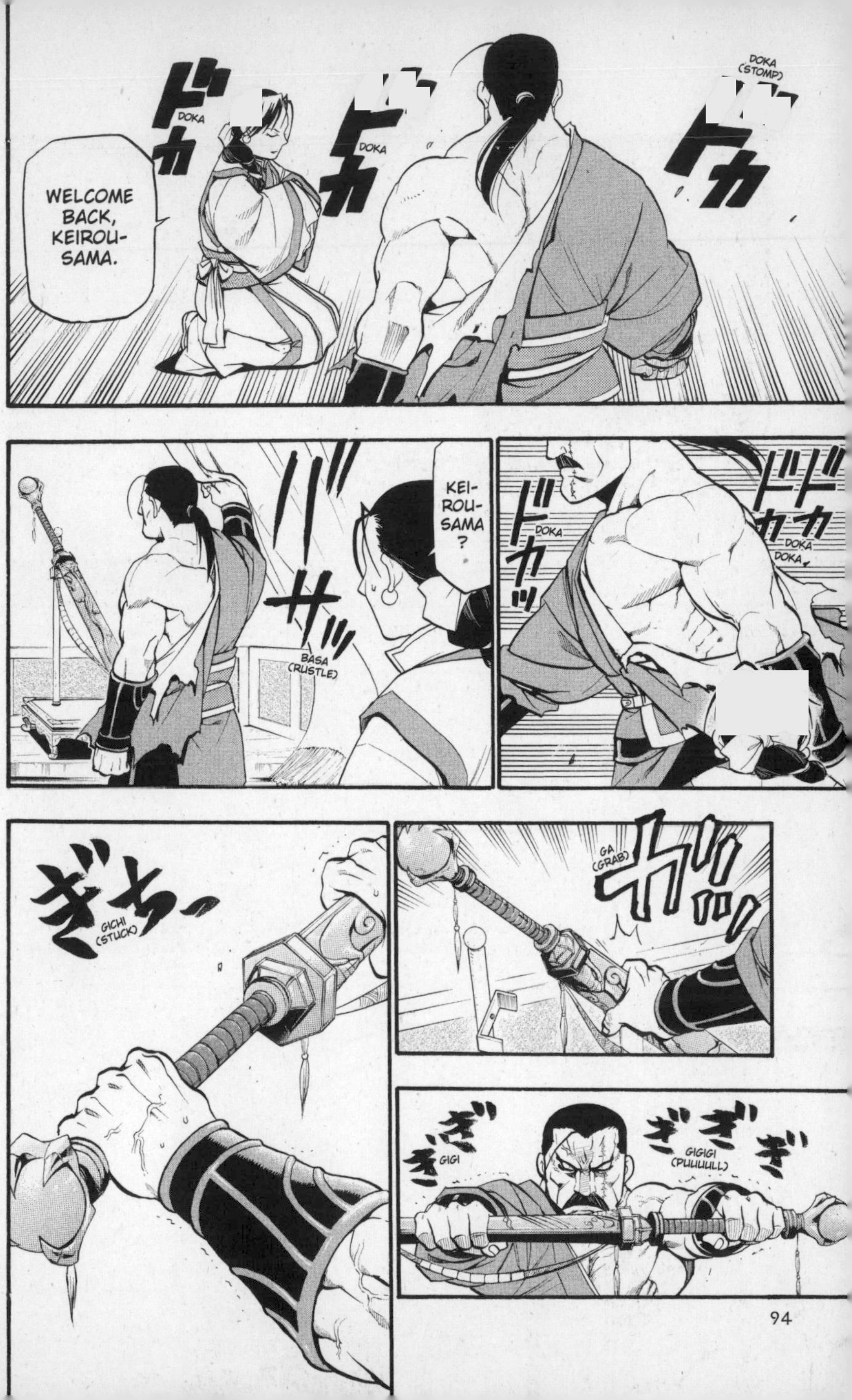
DOKA (STOMP)
DOKA
DOKA
WELCOME BACK, KEIROU-SAMA.
DOKA DOKA
DOKA
KEI-ROU-SAMA?
BASA (RUSTLE)
GA (GRAB)
GIGIGI (PUUUULL)
GIGI
GICHI (STUCK)

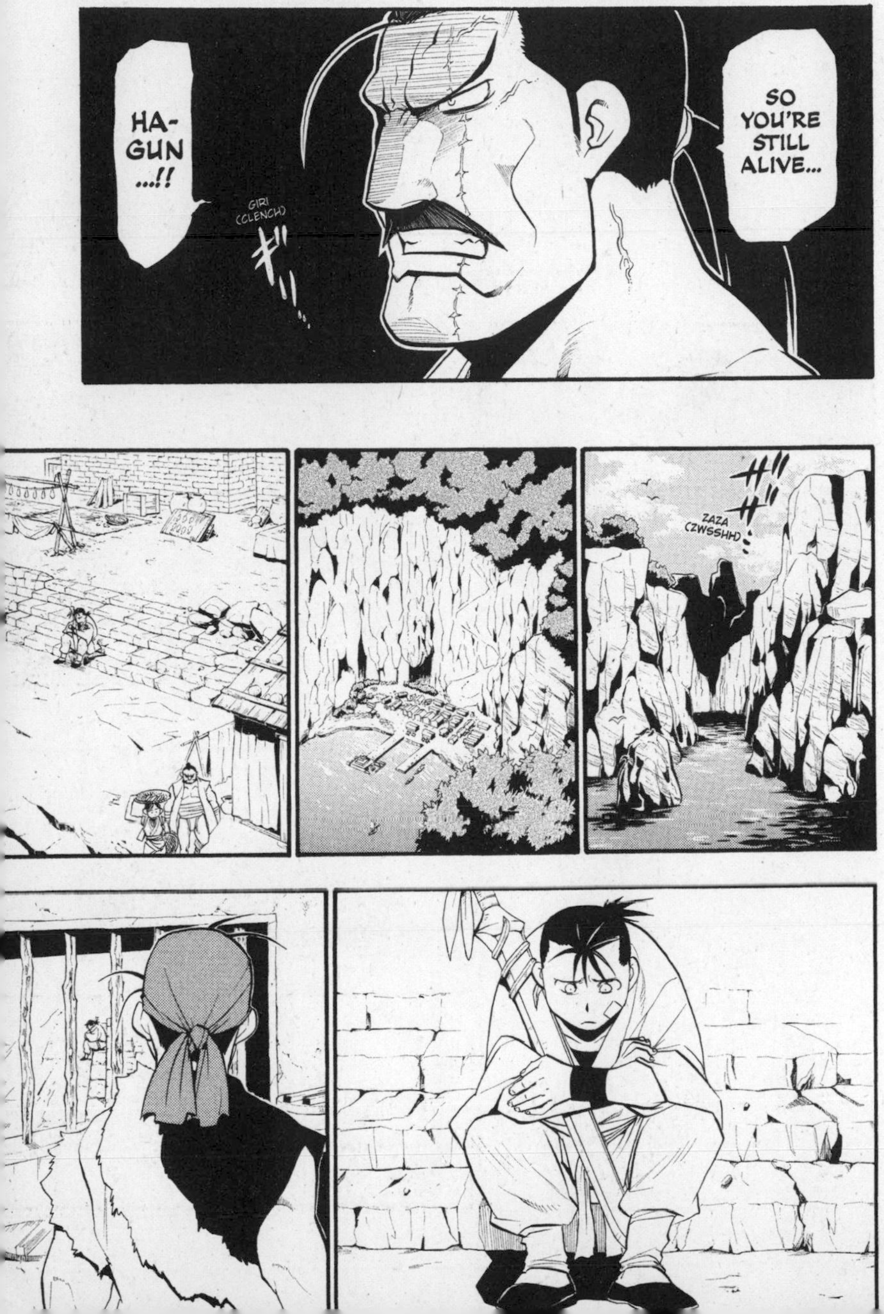
SO YOU'RE STILL ALIVE...
GIRI (CLENCH)
HA-GUN ...!!
ZAZA (ZWSSHH)

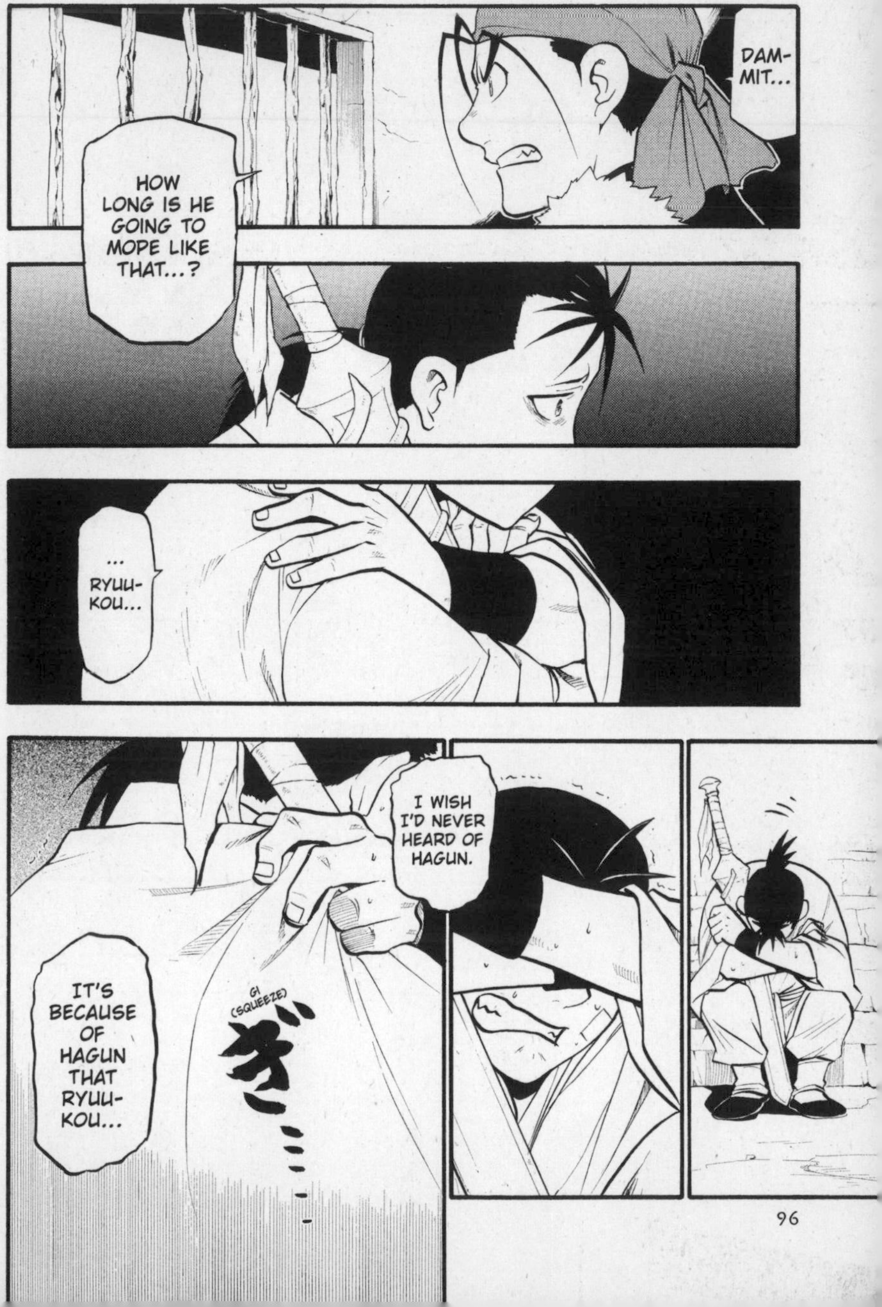
DAM-
MIT...
HOW LONG IS HE GOING TO MOPE LIKE THAT...?
... RYUU-KOU...
I WISH I'D NEVER HEARD OF HAGUN.
IT'S BECAUSE OF HAGUN THAT RYUU-KOU...
GI (SQUEEZE)

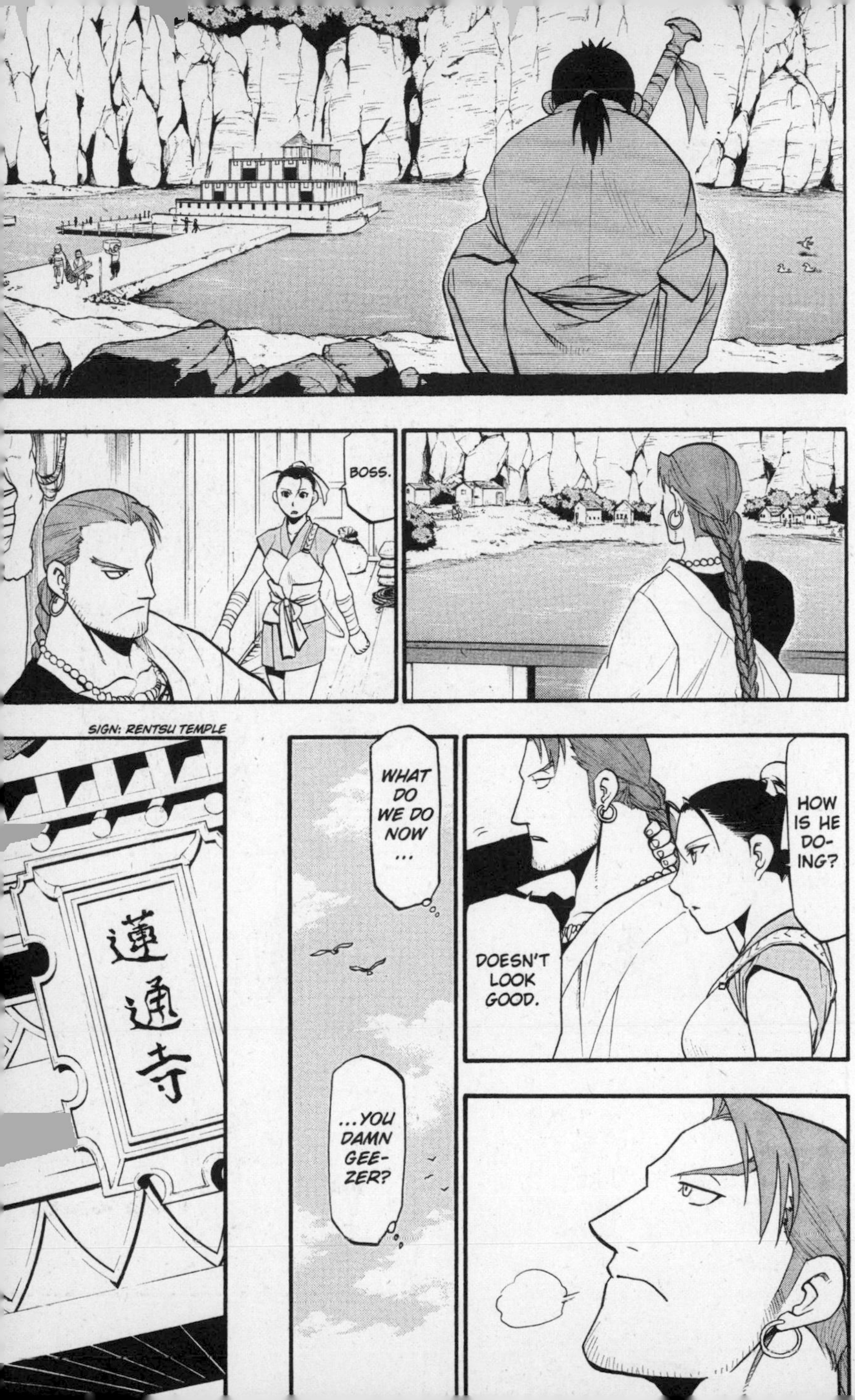
BOSS.
HOW IS HE DOING?
DOESN'T LOOK GOOD.
WHAT DO WE DO NOW...
...YOU DAMN GEEZER?
SIGN: RENTSU TEMPLE
蓮通寺

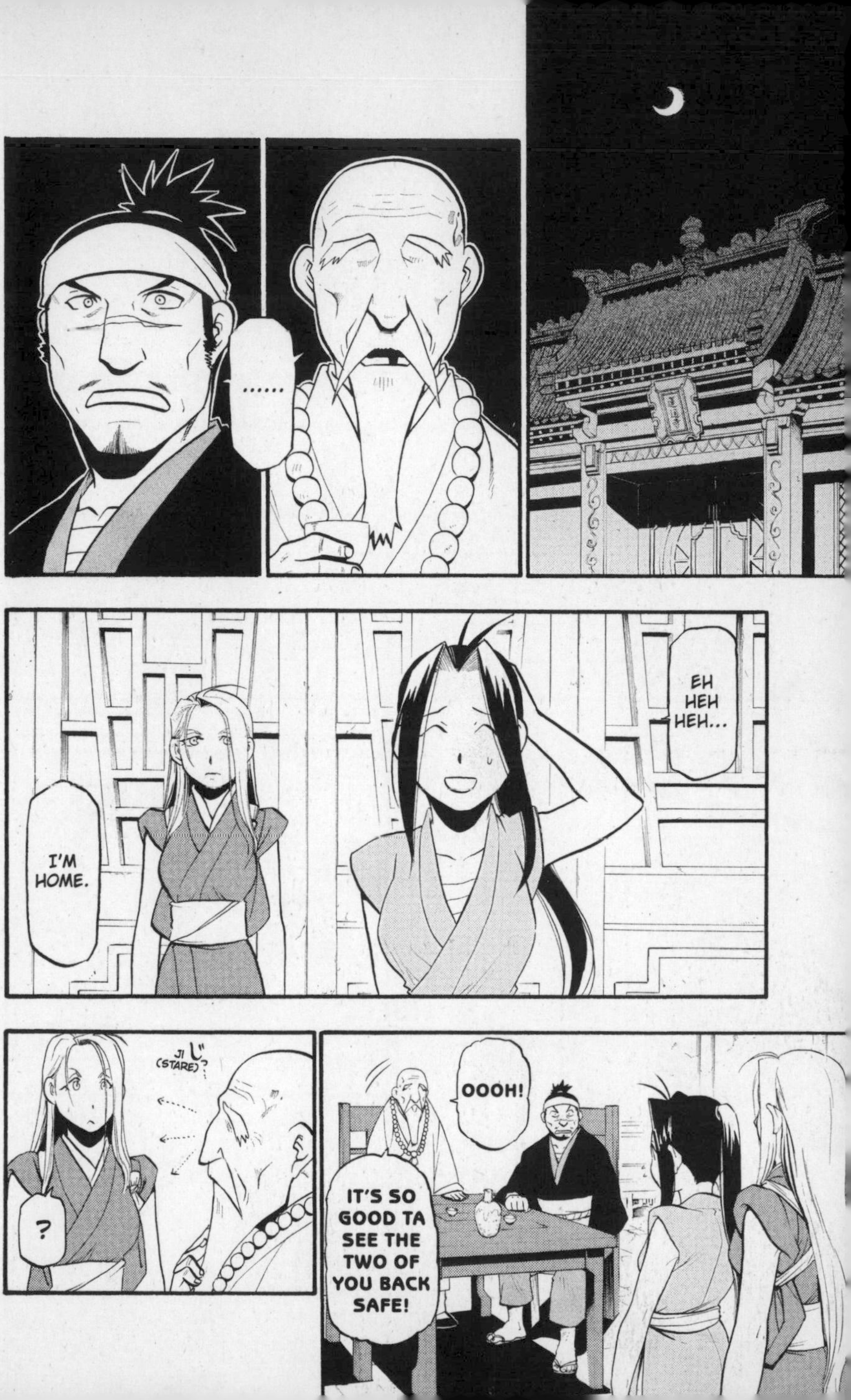
......
EH HEH HEH...
I'M HOME.
OOOH!
IT'S SO GOOD TA SEE THE TWO OF YOU BACK SAFE!
JI じ (STARE)
?

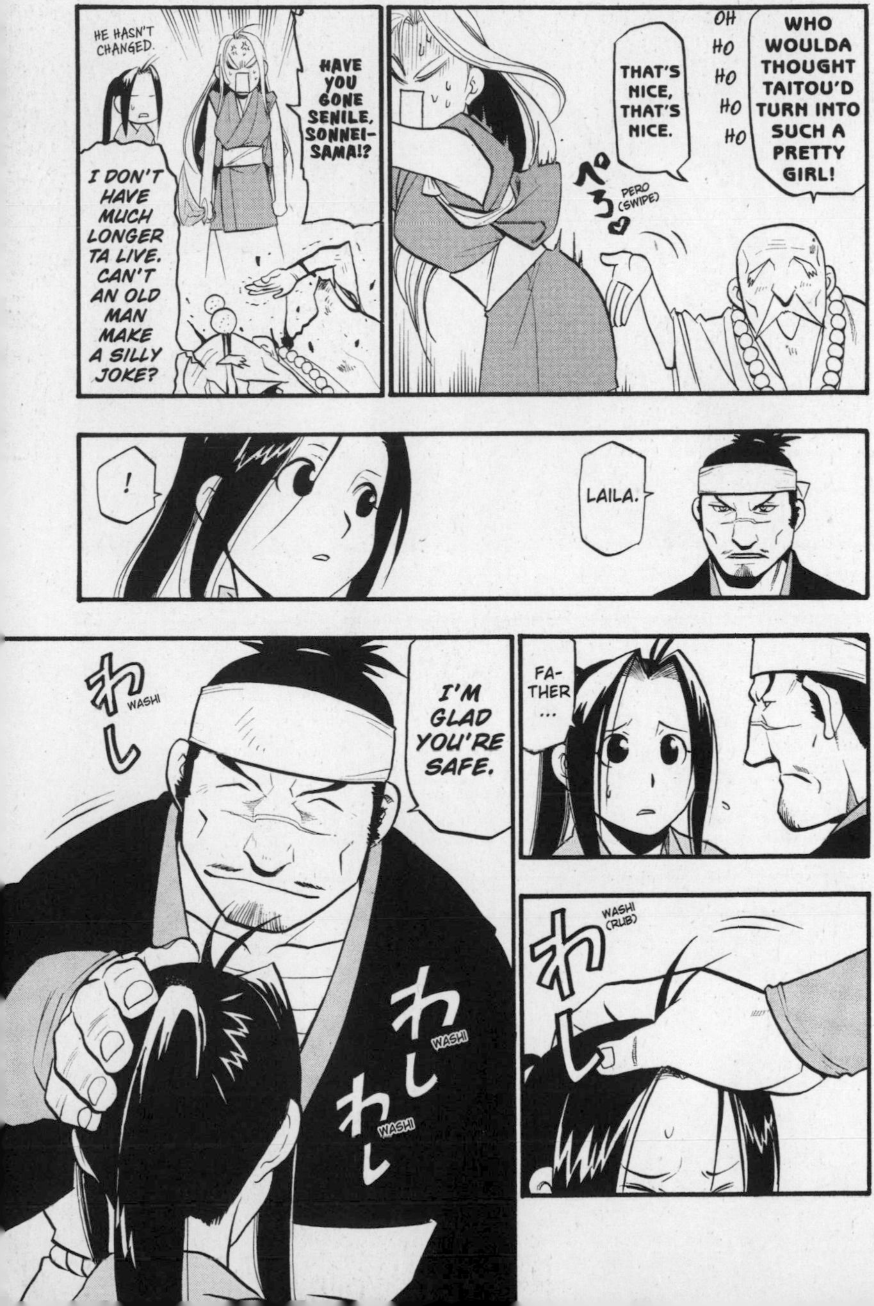
WHO WOULDA THOUGHT TAITOU'D TURN INTO SUCH A PRETTY GIRL!
OH HO HO HO HO
THAT'S NICE, THAT'S NICE.
ぺろ
PERO (SWIPE)
HAVE YOU GONE SENILE, SONNEI-SAMA!?
HE HASN'T CHANGED.
I DON'T HAVE MUCH LONGER TA LIVE. CAN'T AN OLD MAN MAKE A SILLY JOKE?
LAILA.
!
FA-THER...
わし
WASHI (RUB)
I'M GLAD YOU'RE SAFE.
わし
WASHI
わし
WASHI
わし
WASHI

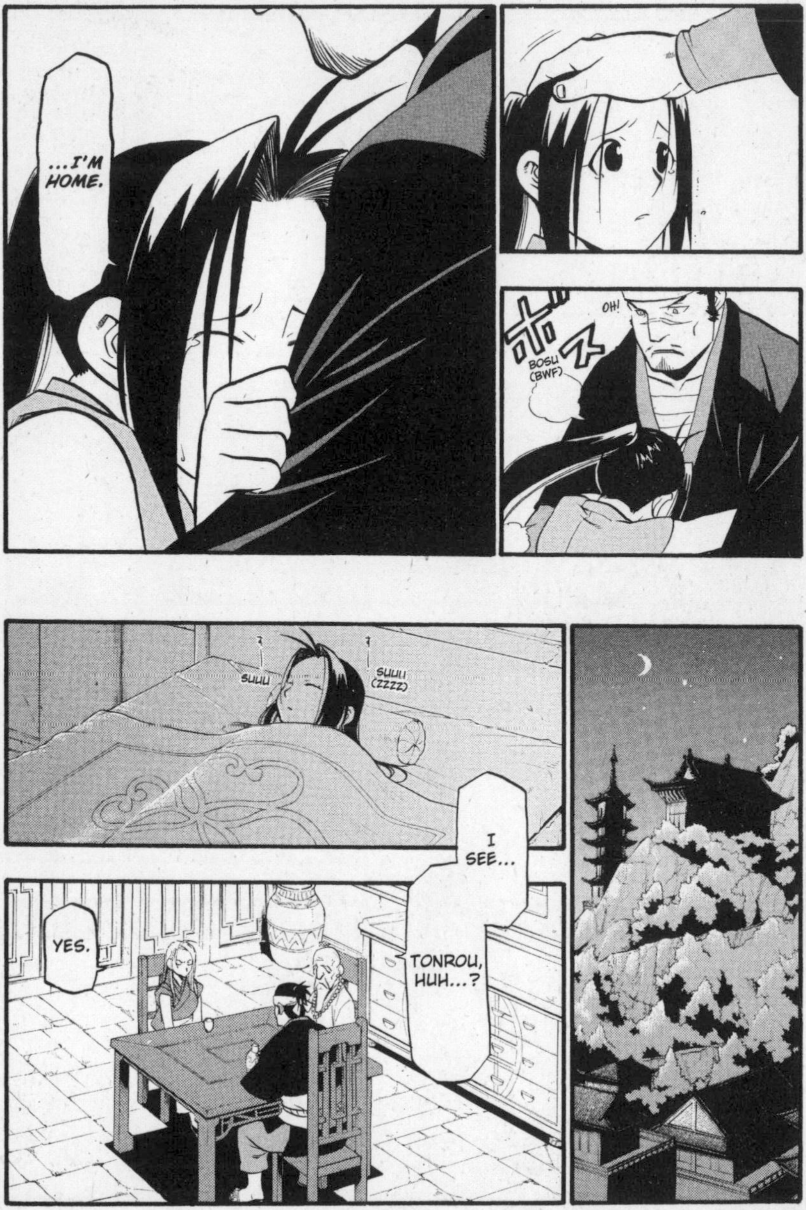
OH!
BOSU
(BWF)
...I'M HOME.
SUUU
SUUU
(ZZZZ)
I SEE...
TONROU, HUH...?
YES.

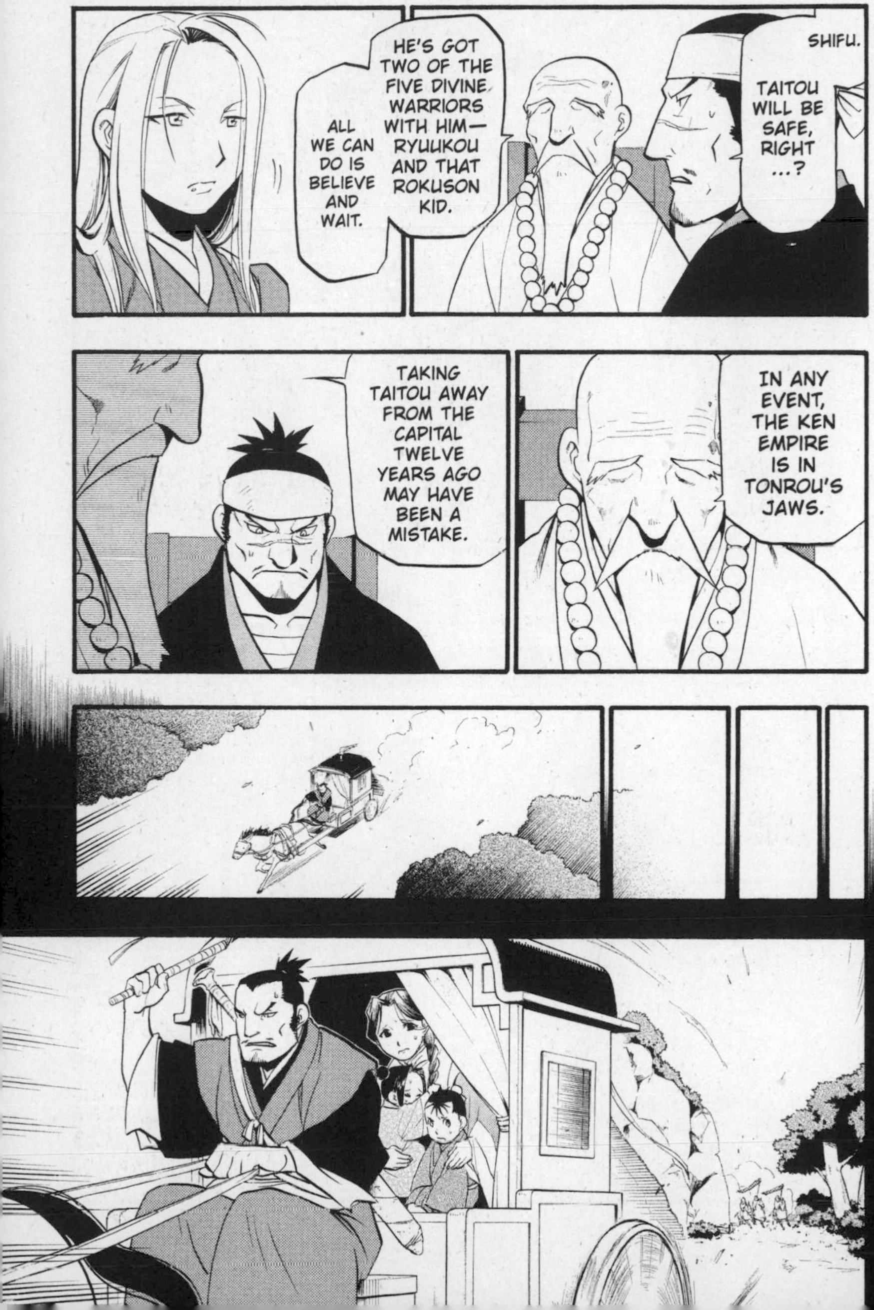
SHIFU.
TAITOU WILL BE SAFE, RIGHT ...?
HE'S GOT TWO OF THE FIVE DIVINE WARRIORS WITH HIM—RYUUKOU AND THAT ROKUSON KID.
ALL WE CAN DO IS BELIEVE AND WAIT.
IN ANY EVENT, THE KEN EMPIRE IS IN TONROU'S JAWS.
TAKING TAITOU AWAY FROM THE CAPITAL TWELVE YEARS AGO MAY HAVE BEEN A MISTAKE.

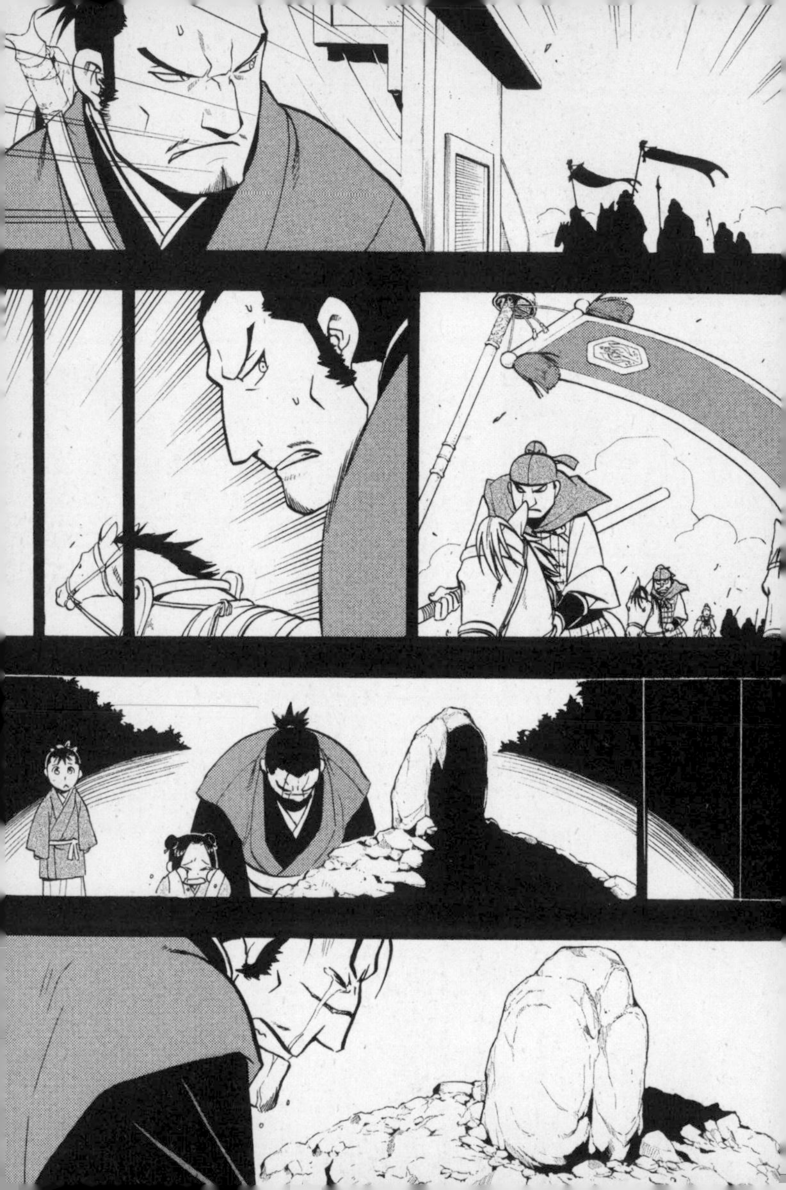

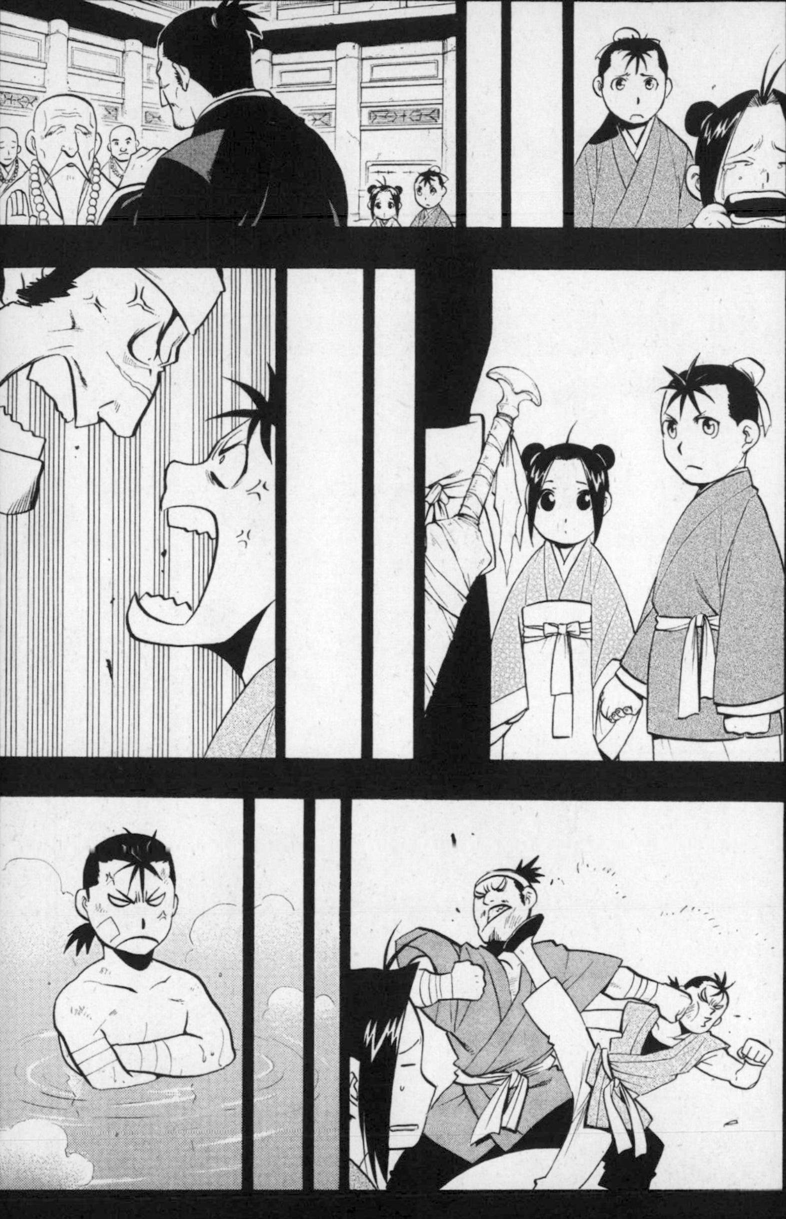

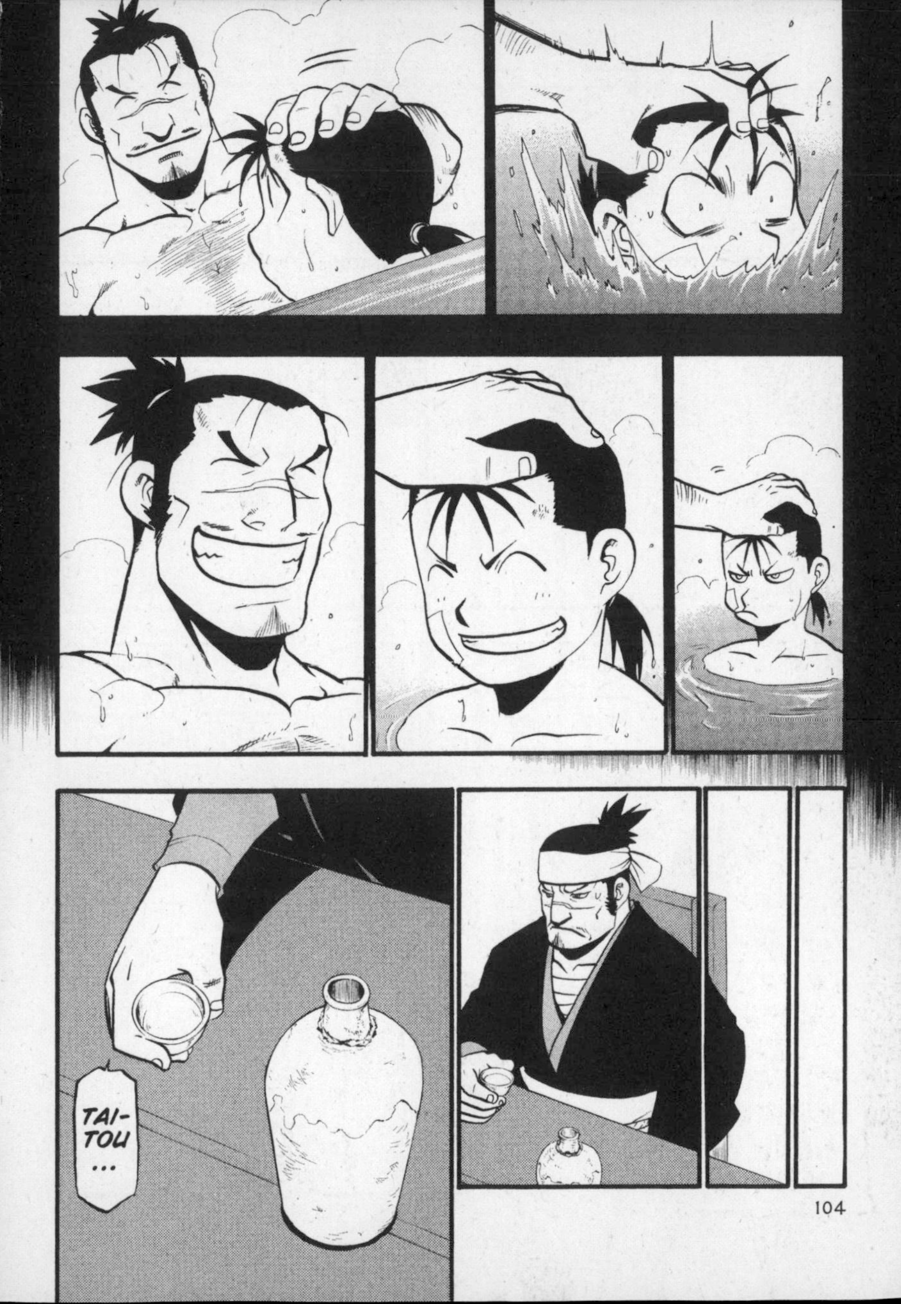
TAI-TOU ...

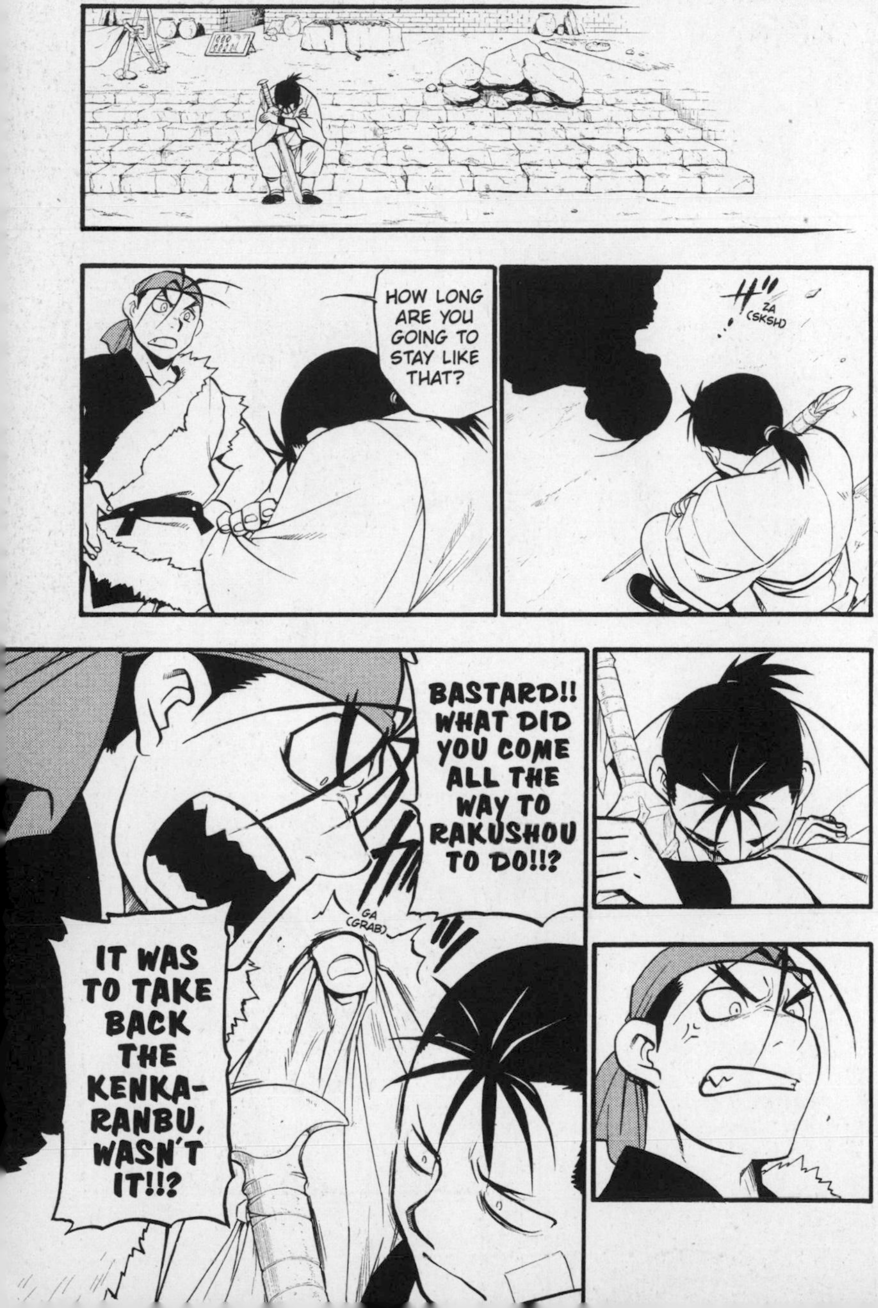
ZA (SKSH)
HOW LONG ARE YOU GOING TO STAY LIKE THAT?
BASTARD!! WHAT DID YOU COME ALL THE WAY TO RAKUSHOU TO DO!!?
GA (GRAB)
IT WAS TO TAKE BACK THE KENKA-RANBU, WASN'T IT!!?

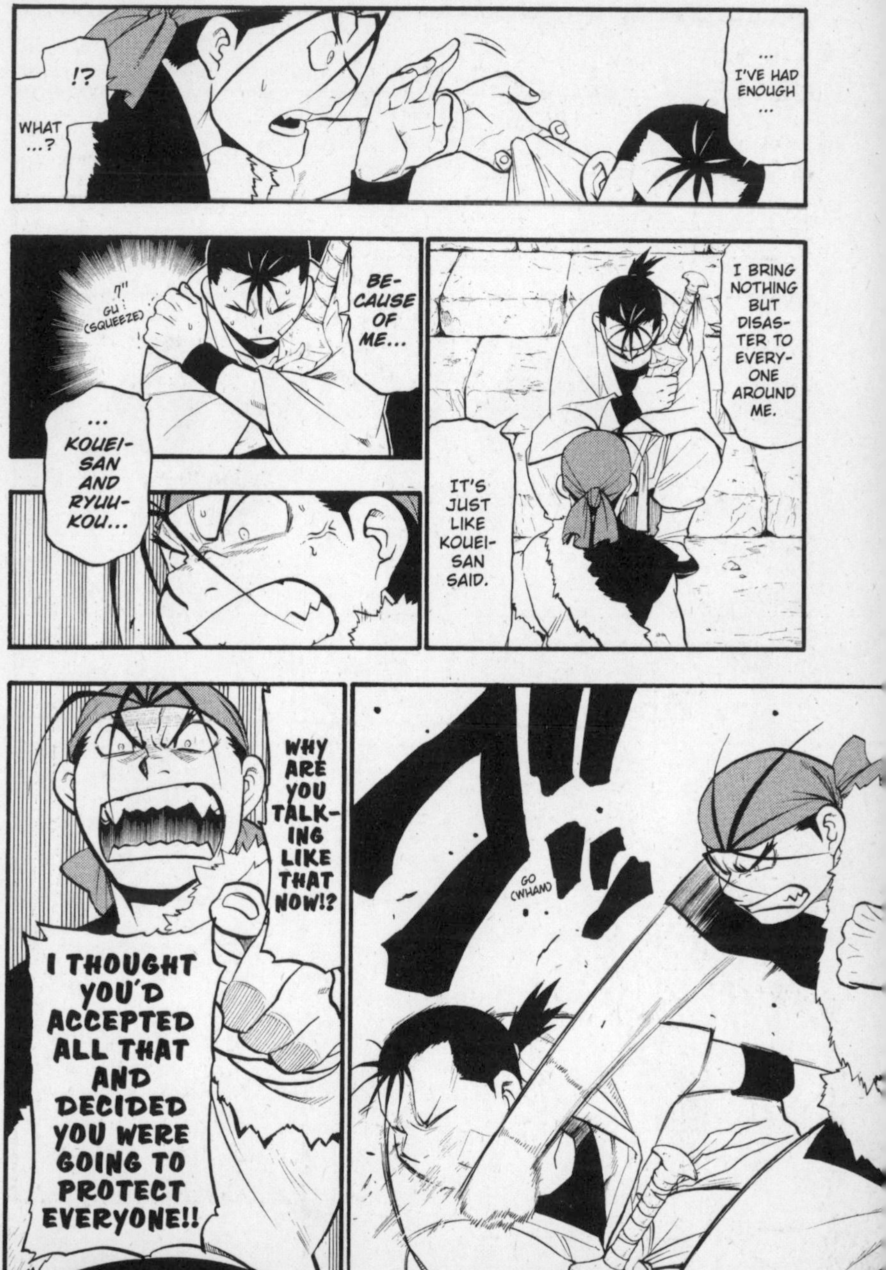

... I'VE HAD ENOUGH ...
!?
WHAT ...?
I BRING NOTHING BUT DISASTER TO EVERYONE AROUND ME.
IT'S JUST LIKE KOUEI-SAN SAID.
BECAUSE OF ME...
GU (SQUEEZE)
... KOUEI-SAN AND RYUUKOU...
GO (WHAM)
WHY ARE YOU TALKING LIKE THAT NOW!?
I THOUGHT YOU'D ACCEPTED ALL THAT AND DECIDED YOU WERE GOING TO PROTECT EVERYONE!!

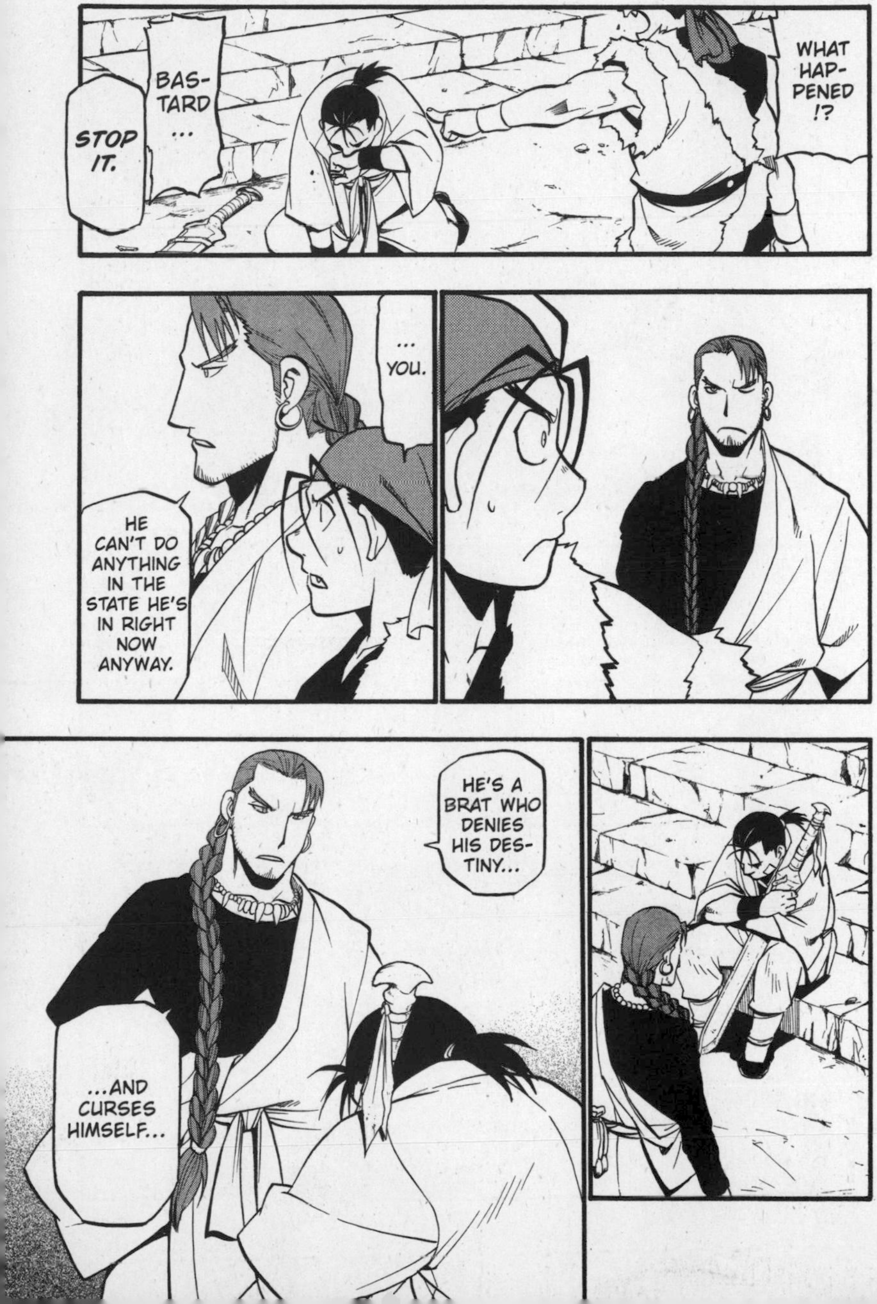
WHAT HAP-PENED !?
BAS-TARD ...
STOP IT.
... YOU.
HE CAN'T DO ANYTHING IN THE STATE HE'S IN RIGHT NOW ANYWAY.
HE'S A BRAT WHO DENIES HIS DES-TINY...
...AND CURSES HIMSELF...

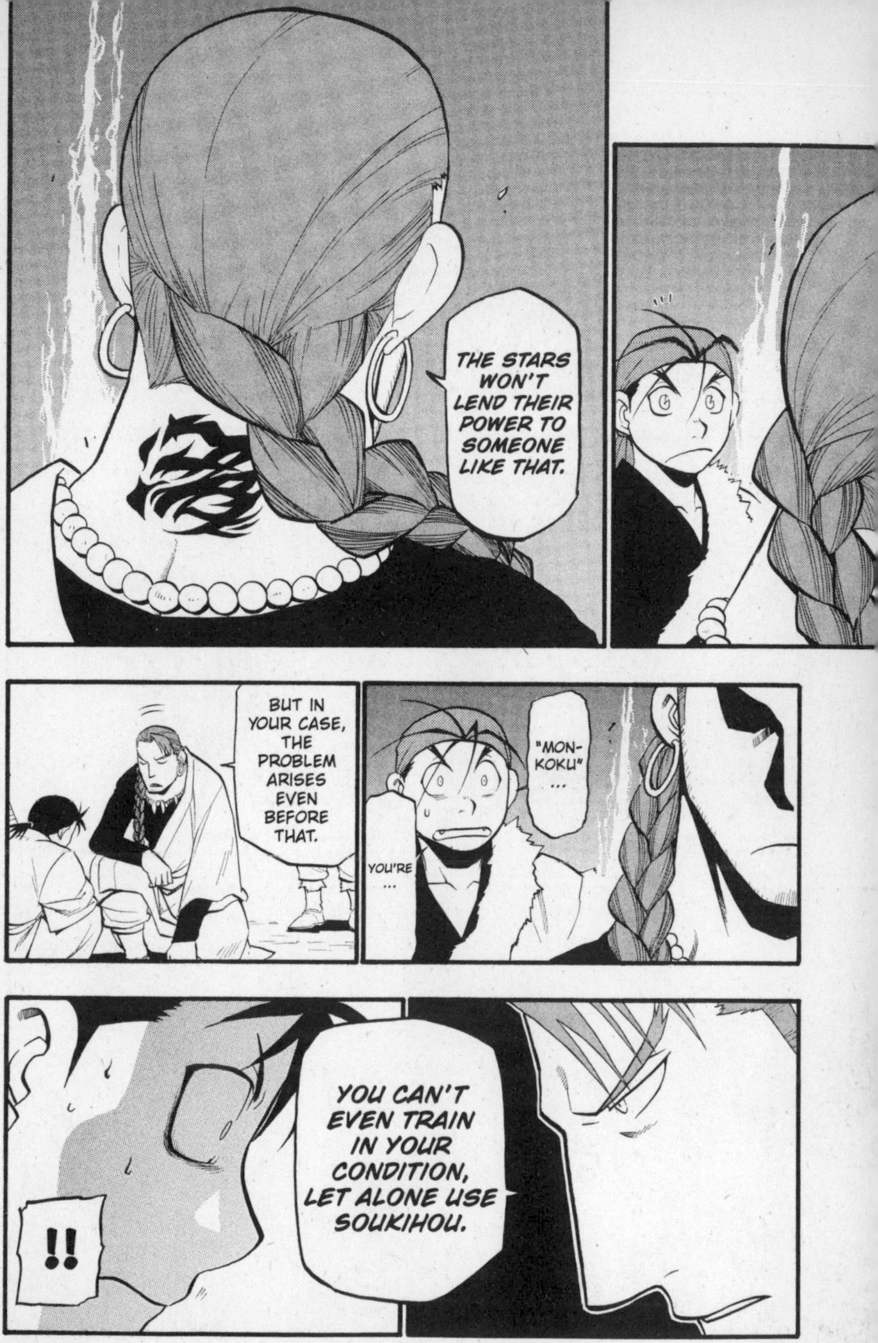
THE STARS WON'T LEND THEIR POWER TO SOMEONE LIKE THAT.
"MON-KOKU" ...
YOU'RE ...
BUT IN YOUR CASE, THE PROBLEM ARISES EVEN BEFORE THAT.
YOU CAN'T EVEN TRAIN IN YOUR CONDITION, LET ALONE USE SOUKIHOU.
!!

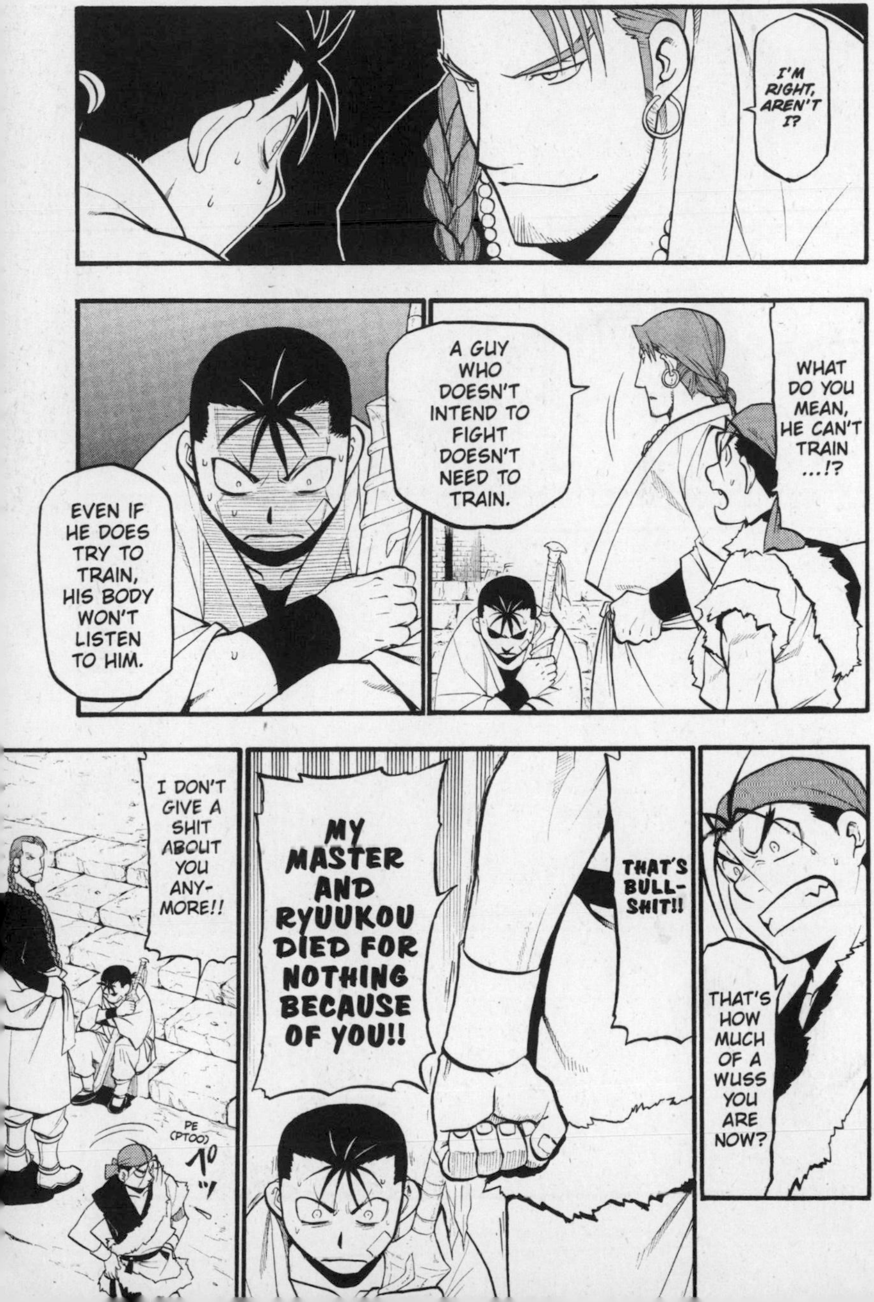
I'M RIGHT, AREN'T I?
WHAT DO YOU MEAN, HE CAN'T TRAIN ...!?
A GUY WHO DOESN'T INTEND TO FIGHT DOESN'T NEED TO TRAIN.
EVEN IF HE DOES TRY TO TRAIN, HIS BODY WON'T LISTEN TO HIM.
THAT'S HOW MUCH OF A WUSS YOU ARE NOW?
THAT'S BULLSHIT!!
MY MASTER AND RYUUKOU DIED FOR NOTHING BECAUSE OF YOU!!
I DON'T GIVE A SHIT ABOUT YOU ANYMORE!!
PE (PTOO)

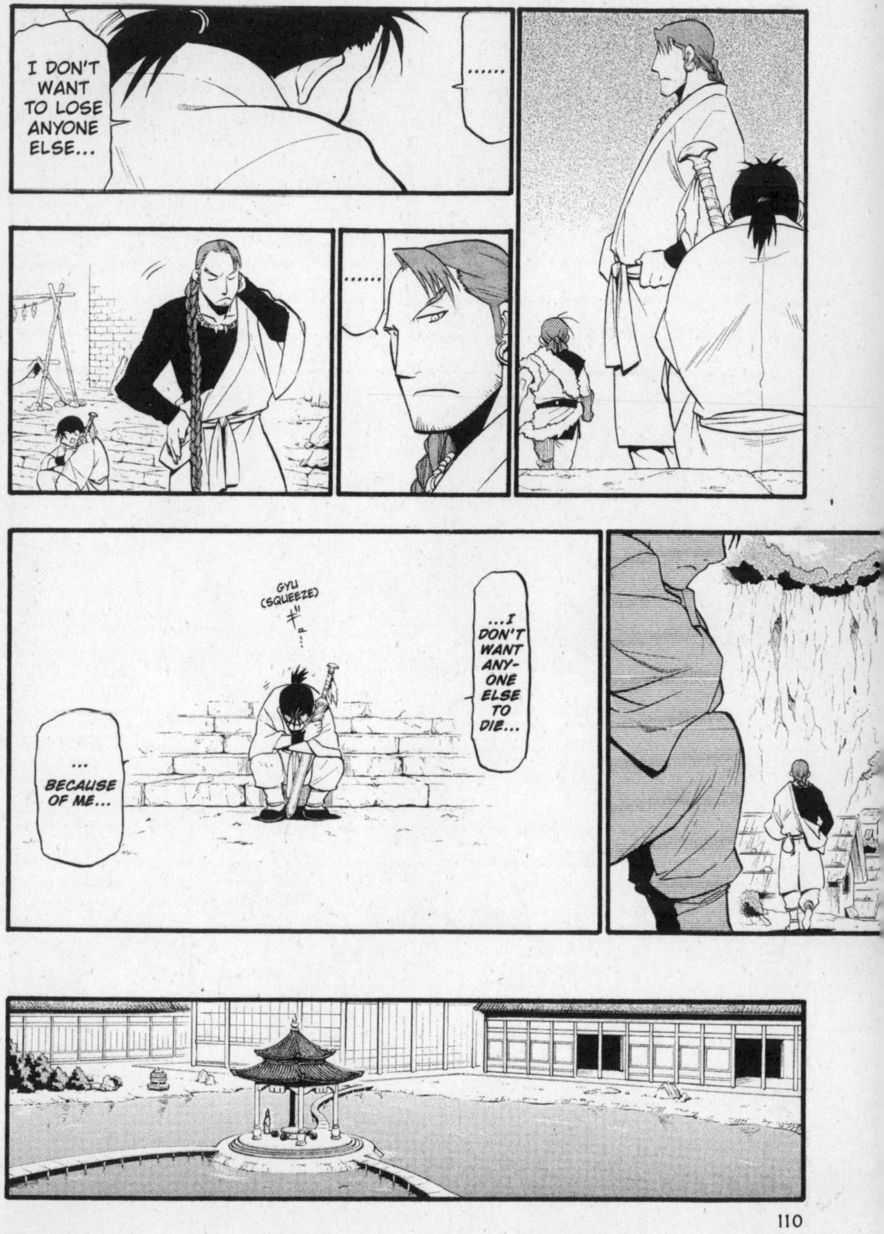
I DON'T WANT TO LOSE ANYONE ELSE...
......
......
...I DON'T WANT ANY-ONE ELSE TO DIE...
GYU (SQUEEZE)
... BECAUSE OF ME...

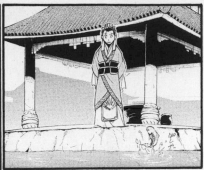

YOU CALLED, YOUR MAJESTY?
YES, I'VE BEEN WAITING FOR YOU, TAKI.
TAKI, DO YOU RE-MEMBER TAITOU?
... YES.
HE WAS A WILD AND FREE MAN.
I WISH THAT I COULD LIVE LIKE THAT TOO.
HA HA HA!
... YOUR MAJ-ESTY.

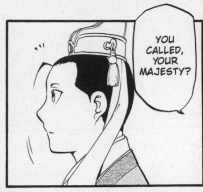

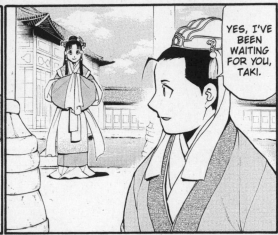

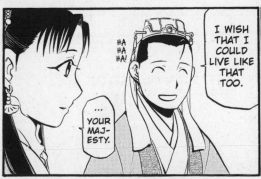

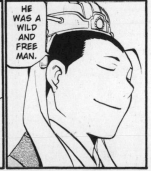

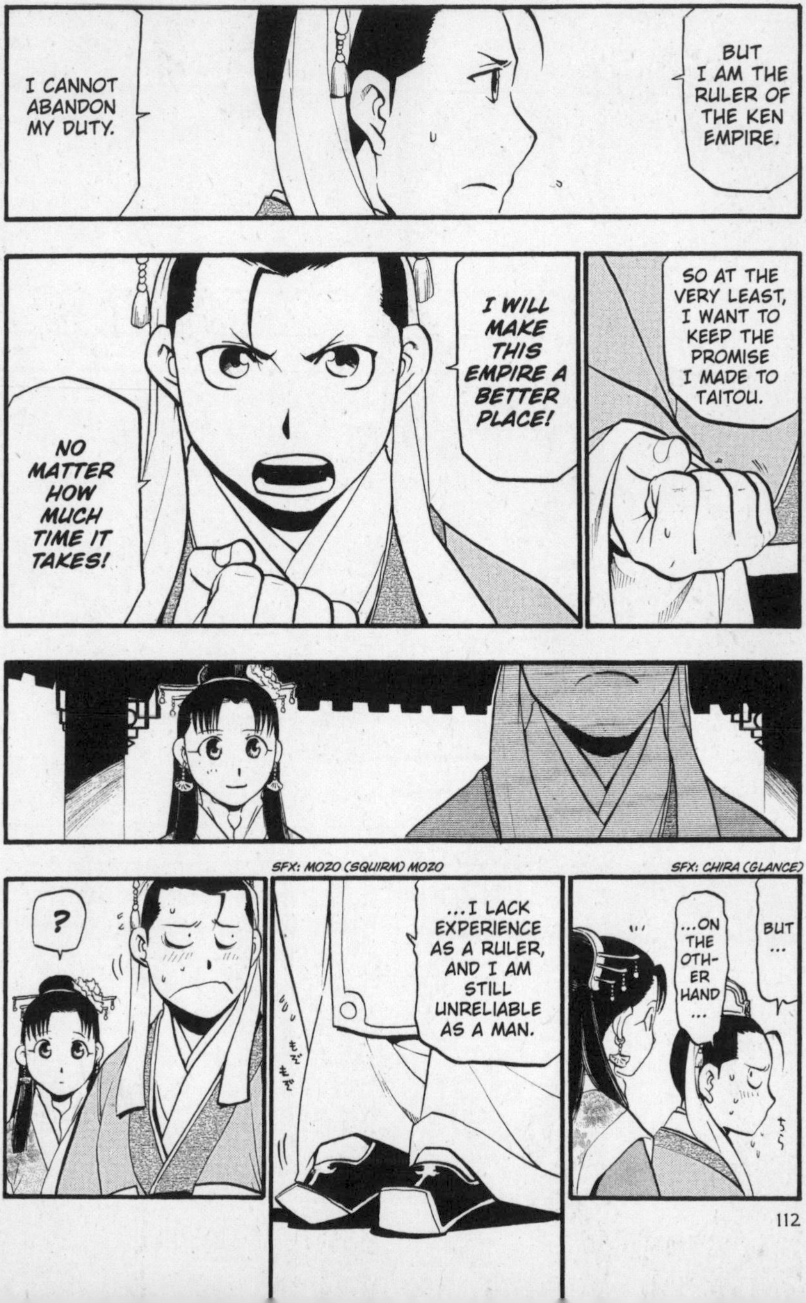
BUT I AM THE RULER OF THE KEN EMPIRE.
I CANNOT ABANDON MY DUTY.
SO AT THE VERY LEAST, I WANT TO KEEP THE PROMISE I MADE TO TAITOU.
I WILL MAKE THIS EMPIRE A BETTER PLACE!
NO MATTER HOW MUCH TIME IT TAKES!
SFX: CHIRA (GLANCE)
BUT ...
...ON THE OTH-ER HAND ...
SFX: MOZO (SQUIRM) MOZO
...I LACK EXPERIENCE AS A RULER, AND I AM STILL UNRELIABLE AS A MAN.
?

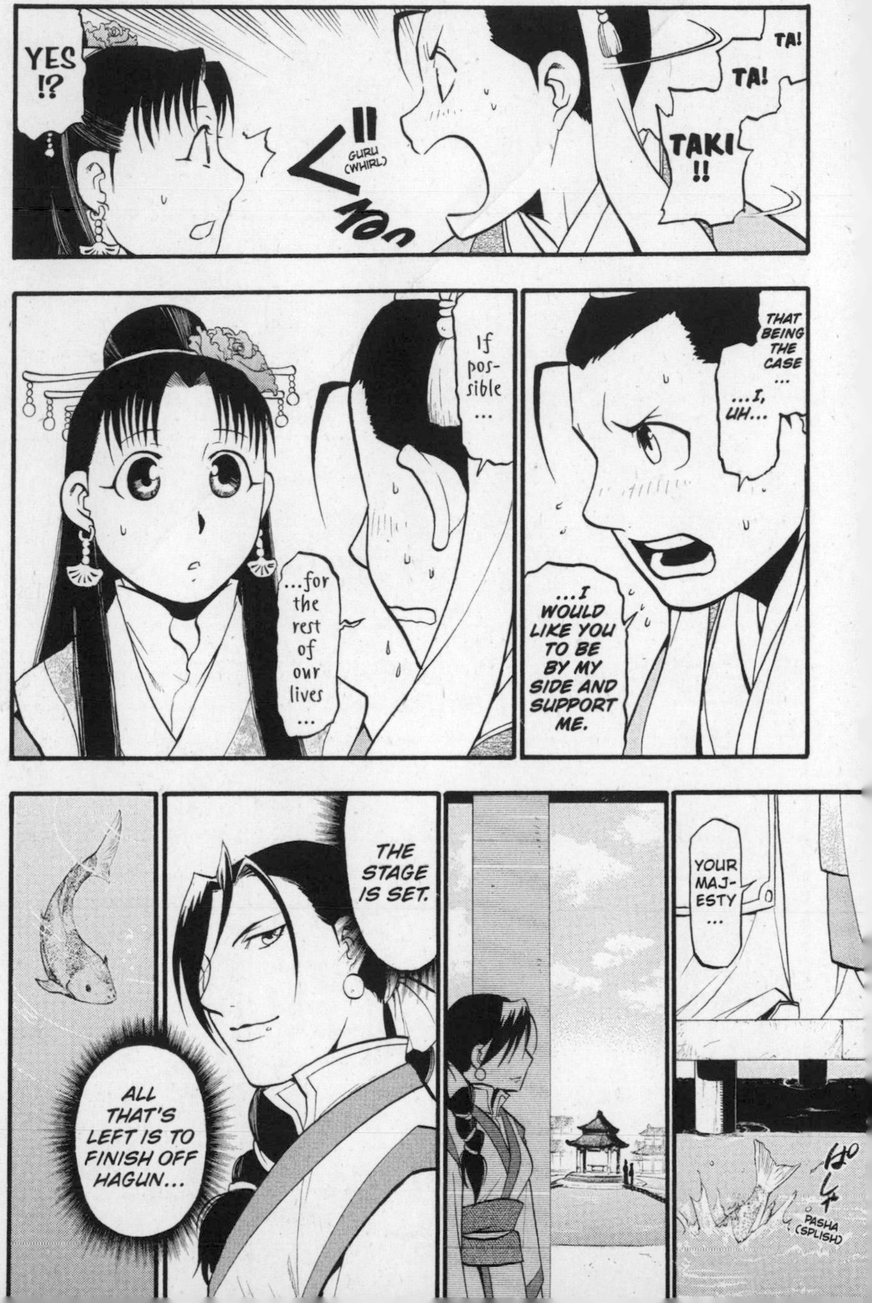
TA!
TA!
TAKI!!
GURU (WHIRL)
YES!?
THAT BEING THE CASE...
...I, UH...
...I WOULD LIKE YOU TO BE BY MY SIDE AND SUPPORT ME.
If possible...
...for the rest of our lives...
YOUR MAJESTY...
PASHA (SPLISH)
THE STAGE IS SET.
ALL THAT'S LEFT IS TO FINISH OFF HAGUN...

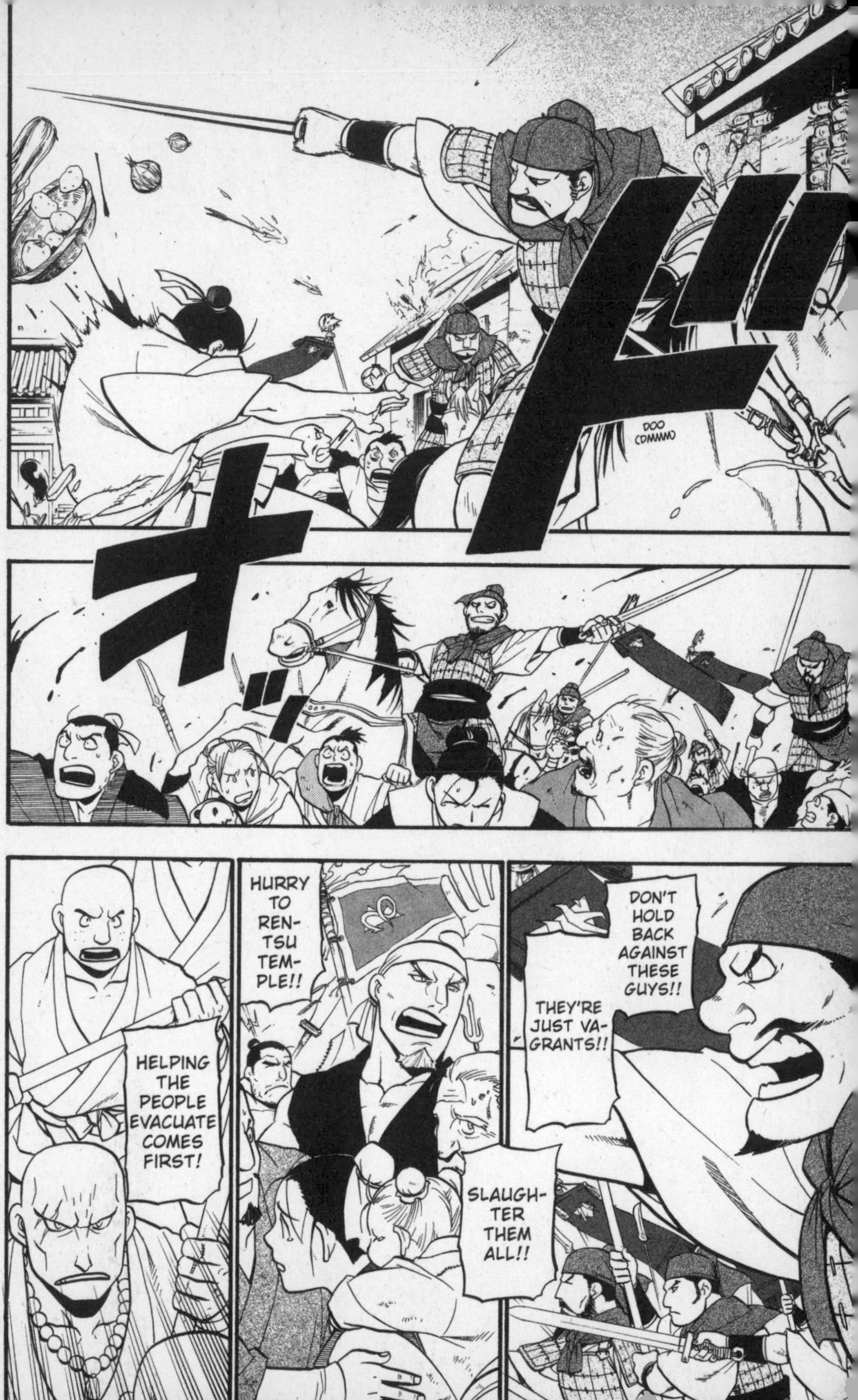
DOO (DMMMM)
DON'T HOLD BACK AGAINST THESE GUYS!!
THEY'RE JUST VAGRANTS!!
SLAUGHTER THEM ALL!!
HURRY TO RENTSU TEMPLE!!
HELPING THE PEOPLE EVACUATE COMES FIRST!

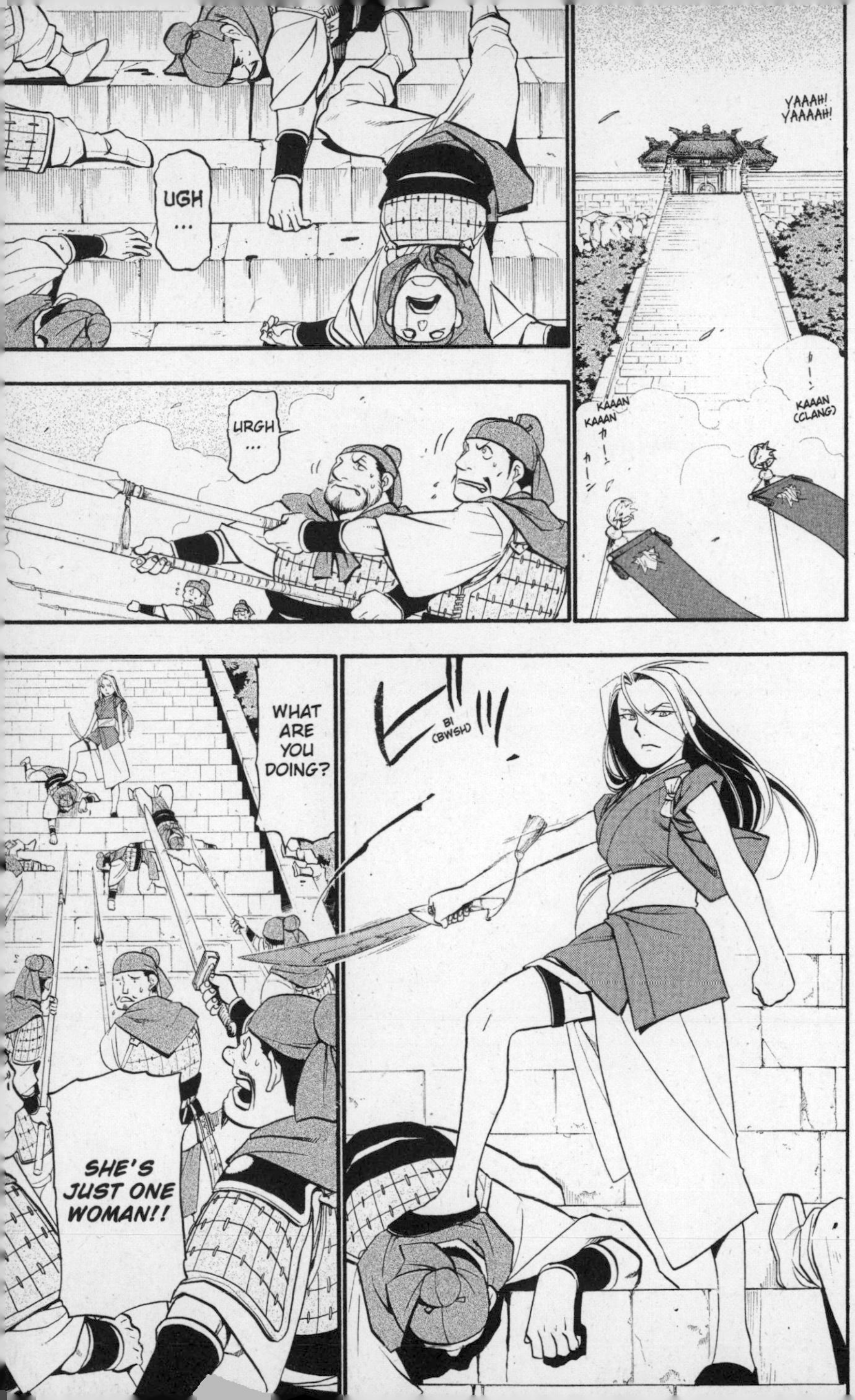

YAAAH! YAAAAH!
KAAAN (CLANG)
KAAAN KAAAN
UGH ...
URGH ...
BI (BWSH)
WHAT ARE YOU DOING?
SHE'S JUST ONE WOMAN!!

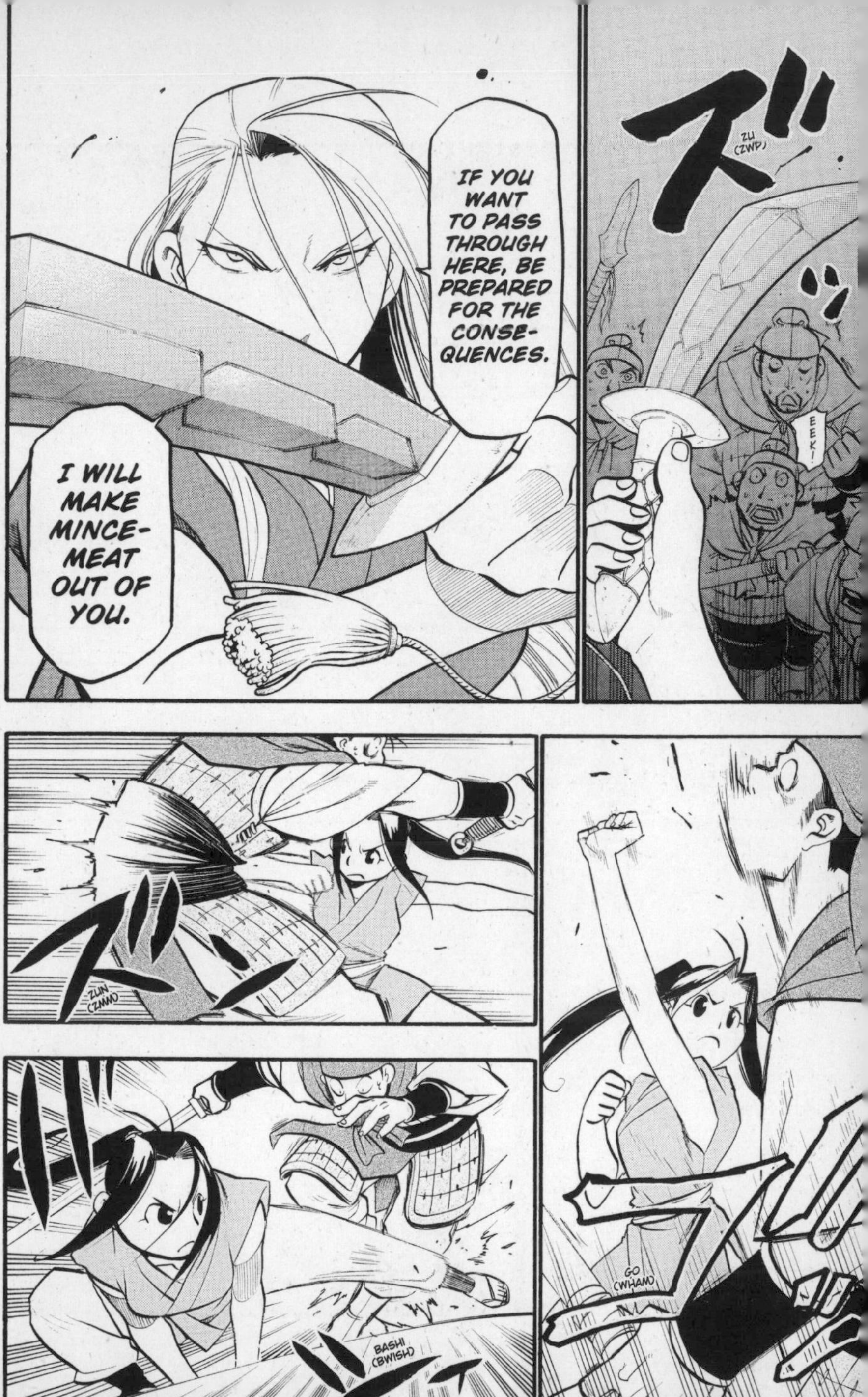
ZU (ZWP)
EEK!
IF YOU WANT TO PASS THROUGH HERE, BE PREPARED FOR THE CONSE-QUENCES.
I WILL MAKE MINCE-MEAT OUT OF YOU.
GO (WHAM)
ZUN (ZMM)
BASHI (BWISH)

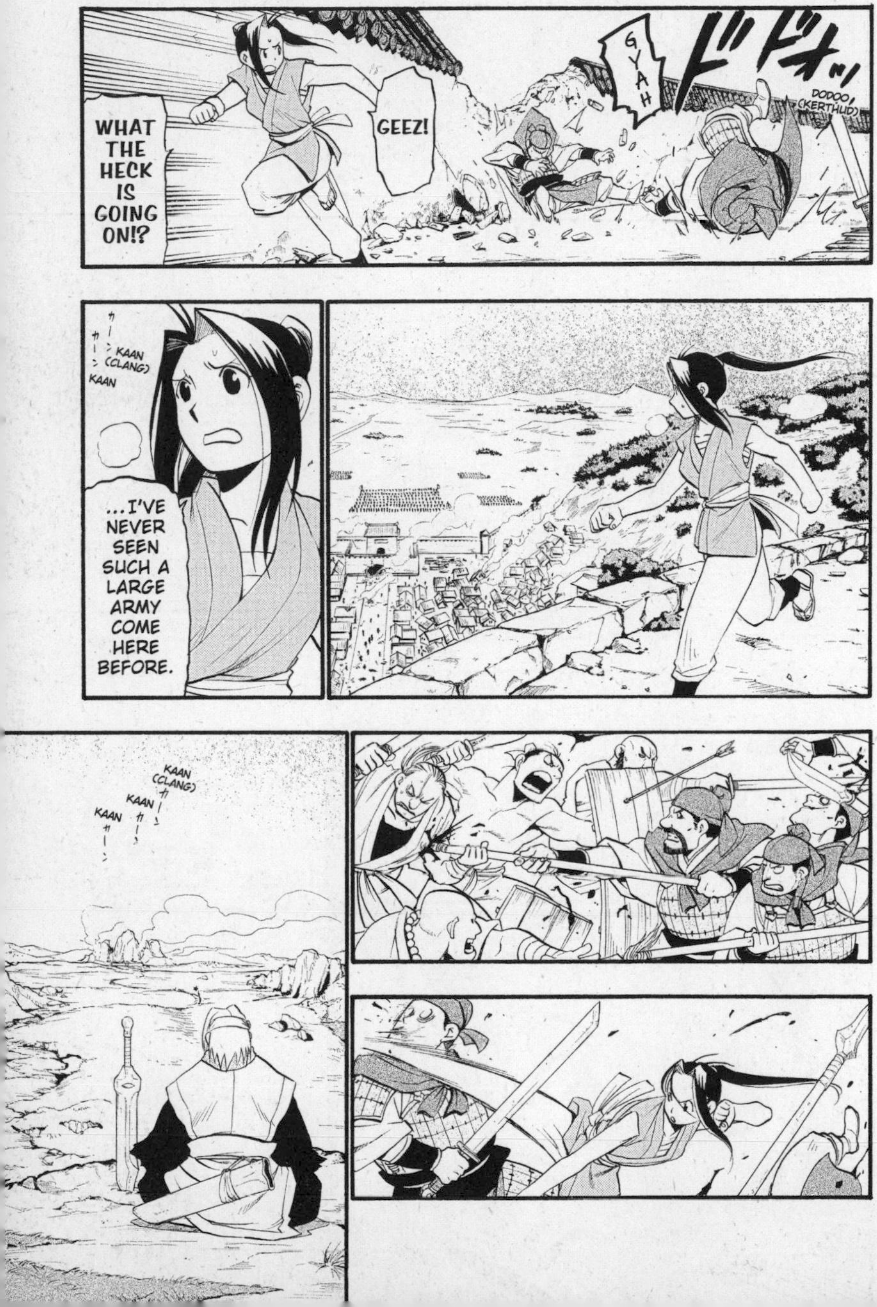
ドドオッ
DODOO (KERTHUD)
GYAH
GEEZ!
WHAT THE HECK IS GOING ON!?
カーン
カーン
KAAN (CLANG)
KAAN
...I'VE NEVER SEEN SUCH A LARGE ARMY COME HERE BEFORE.
KAAN (CLANG)
KAAN
KAAN
カーン
カーン
カーン

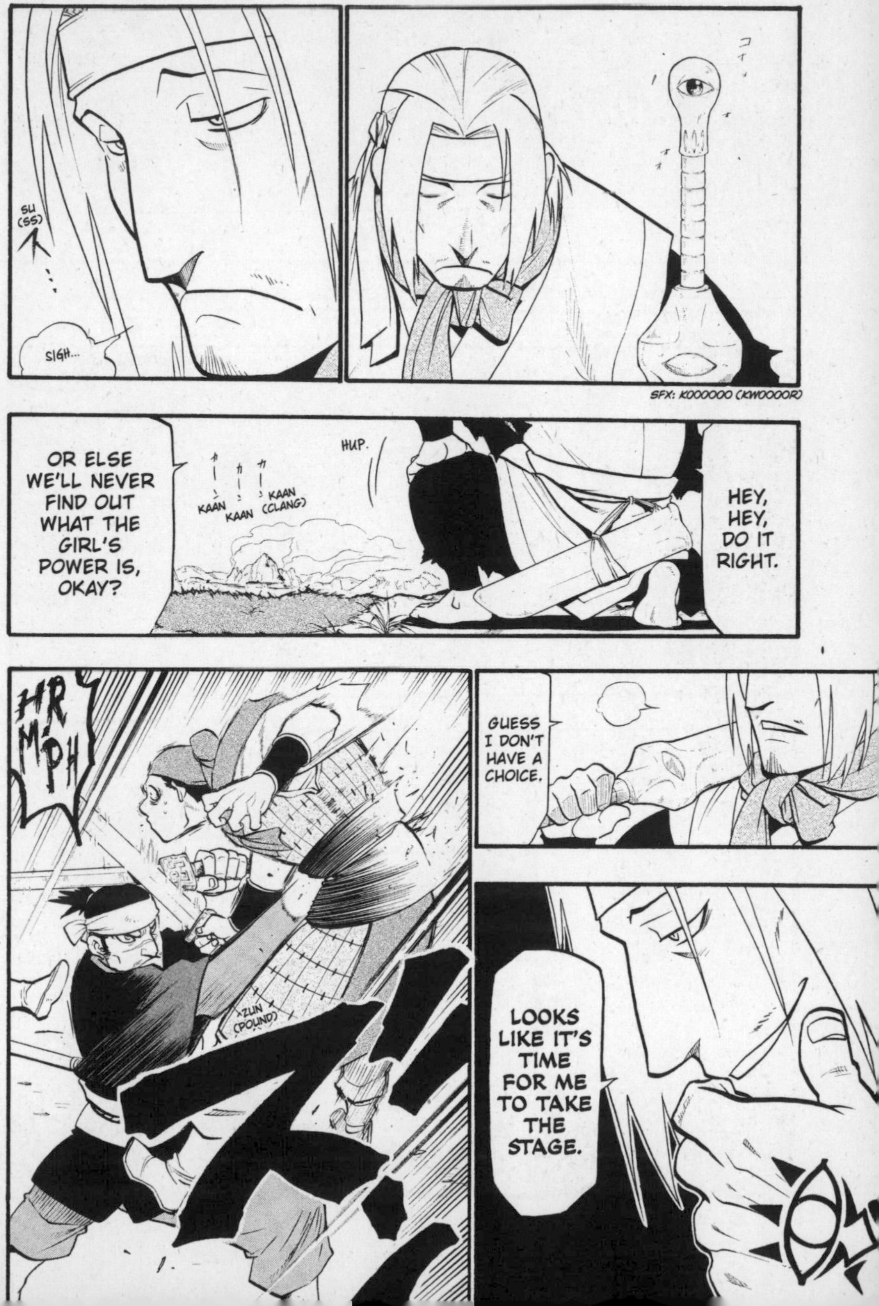
SFX: KOOOOO (KWOOOOR)
SU (SS)
SIGH...
HEY, HEY, DO IT RIGHT.
HUP.
KAAN KAAN KAAN (CLANG)
OR ELSE WE'LL NEVER FIND OUT WHAT THE GIRL'S POWER IS, OKAY?
GUESS I DON'T HAVE A CHOICE.
LOOKS LIKE IT'S TIME FOR ME TO TAKE THE STAGE.
HRMPH
ZUN (POUND)

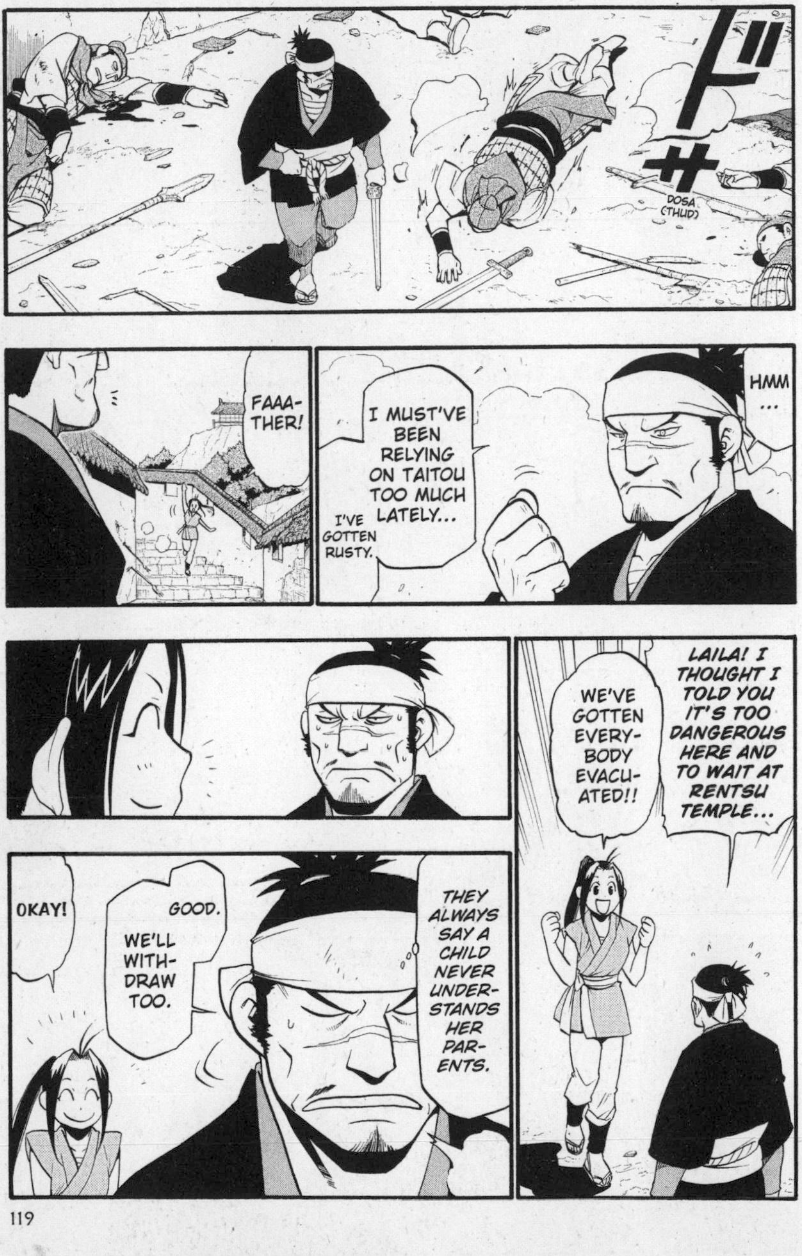
DOSA (THUD)
HMM...
I MUST'VE BEEN RELYING ON TAITOU TOO MUCH LATELY...
I'VE GOTTEN RUSTY.
FAAA-THER!
LAILA! I THOUGHT I TOLD YOU IT'S TOO DANGEROUS HERE AND TO WAIT AT RENTSU TEMPLE...
WE'VE GOTTEN EVERY-BODY EVACU-ATED!!
THEY ALWAYS SAY A CHILD NEVER UNDER-STANDS HER PAR-ENTS.
GOOD.
WE'LL WITH-DRAW TOO.
OKAY!

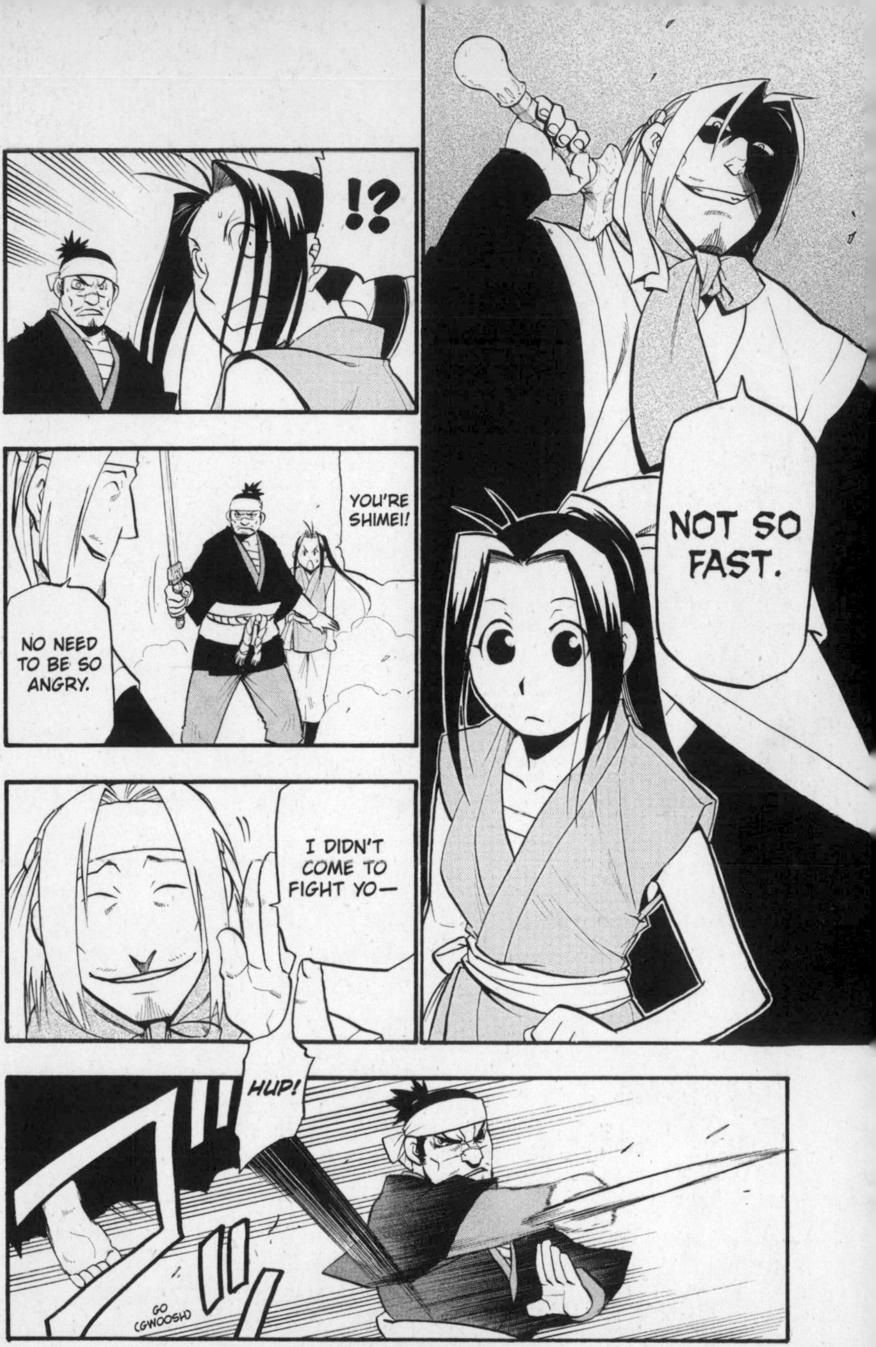
NOT SO FAST.
!?
YOU'RE SHIMEI!
NO NEED TO BE SO ANGRY.
I DIDN'T COME TO FIGHT YO—
HUP!
GO
(GWOOSH)

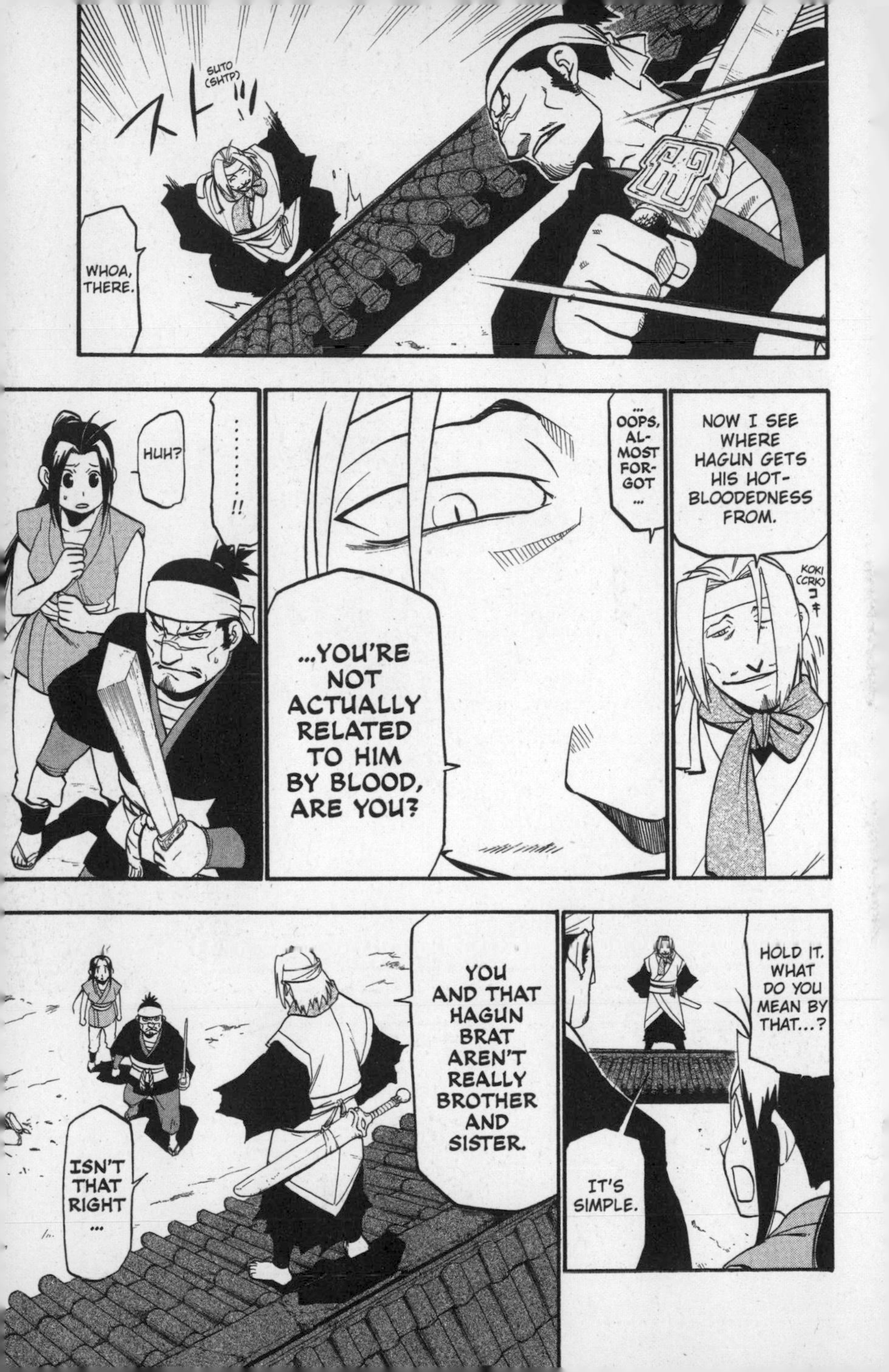
SUTO (SHTP)
ストッ
WHOA, THERE.
NOW I SEE WHERE HAGUN GETS HIS HOT-BLOODEDNESS FROM.
KOKI (CRK)
コキ
...OOPS, AL-MOST FOR-GOT...
...YOU'RE NOT ACTUALLY RELATED TO HIM BY BLOOD, ARE YOU?
......!!
HUH?
HOLD IT. WHAT DO YOU MEAN BY THAT...?
IT'S SIMPLE.
YOU AND THAT HAGUN BRAT AREN'T REALLY BROTHER AND SISTER.
ISN'T THAT RIGHT...

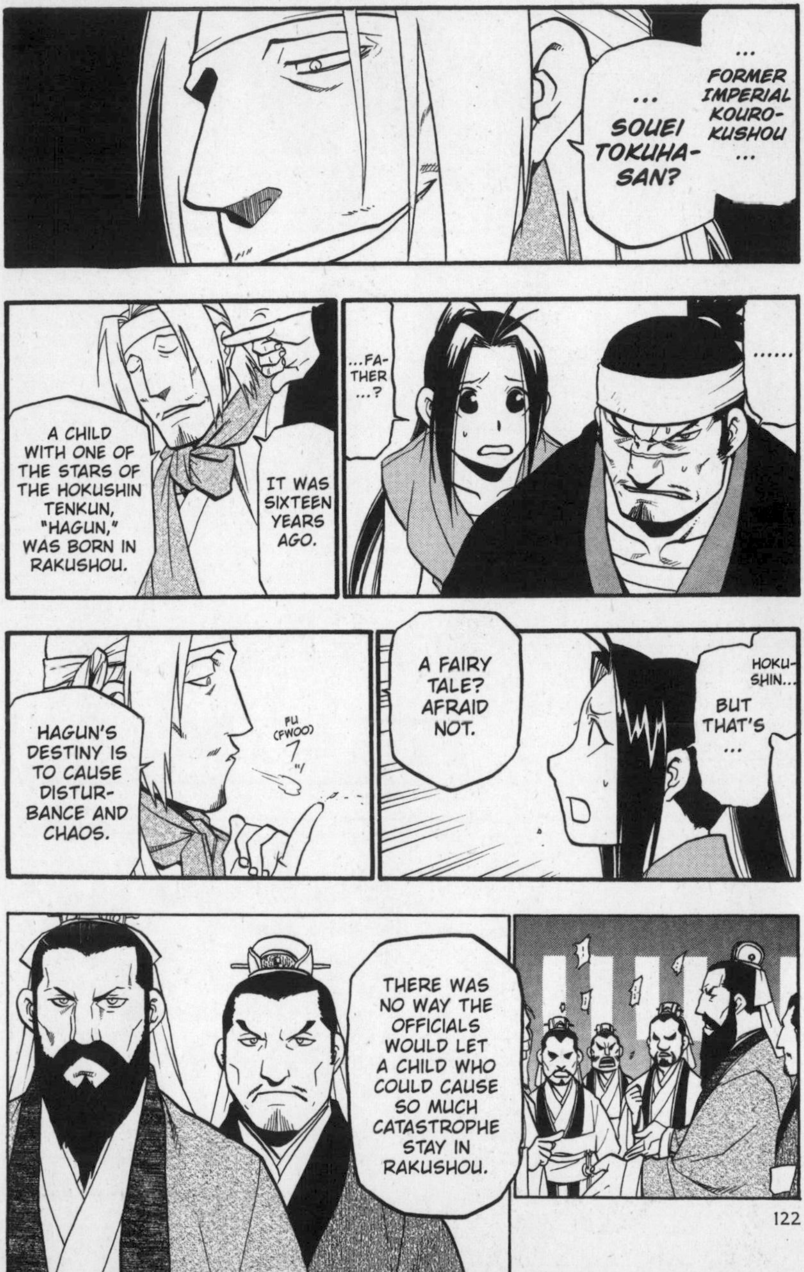
... FORMER IMPERIAL KOURO-KUSHOU ...
... SOUEI TOKUHA-SAN?
......
...FA-THER ...?
IT WAS SIXTEEN YEARS AGO.
A CHILD WITH ONE OF THE STARS OF THE HOKUSHIN TENKUN, "HAGUN," WAS BORN IN RAKUSHOU.
HOKU-SHIN... BUT THAT'S ...
A FAIRY TALE? AFRAID NOT.
FU (FWOO)
HAGUN'S DESTINY IS TO CAUSE DISTUR-BANCE AND CHAOS.
THERE WAS NO WAY THE OFFICIALS WOULD LET A CHILD WHO COULD CAUSE SO MUCH CATASTROPHE STAY IN RAKUSHOU.

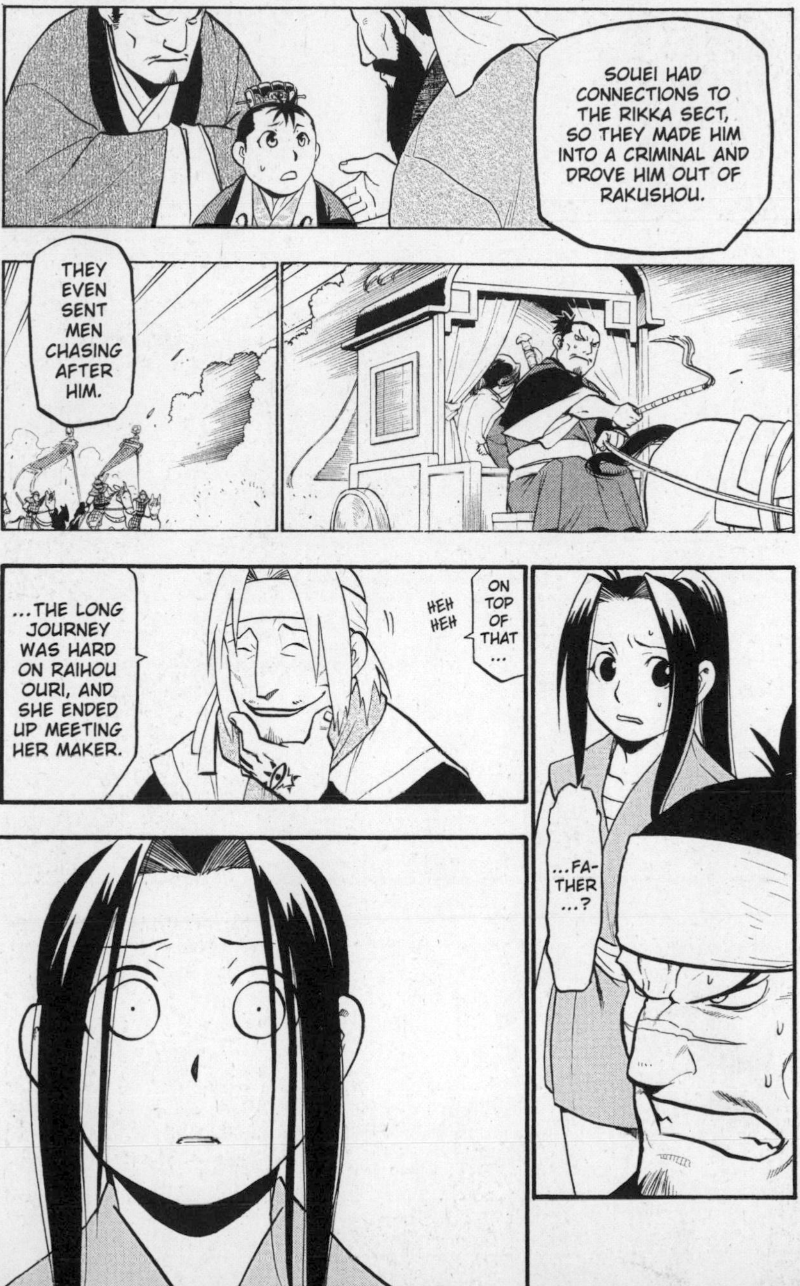
SOUEI HAD CONNECTIONS TO THE RIKKA SECT, SO THEY MADE HIM INTO A CRIMINAL AND DROVE HIM OUT OF RAKUSHOU.
THEY EVEN SENT MEN CHASING AFTER HIM.
...FA-THER ...?
ON TOP OF THAT ...
HEH HEH
...THE LONG JOURNEY WAS HARD ON RAIHOU OURI, AND SHE ENDED UP MEETING HER MAKER.

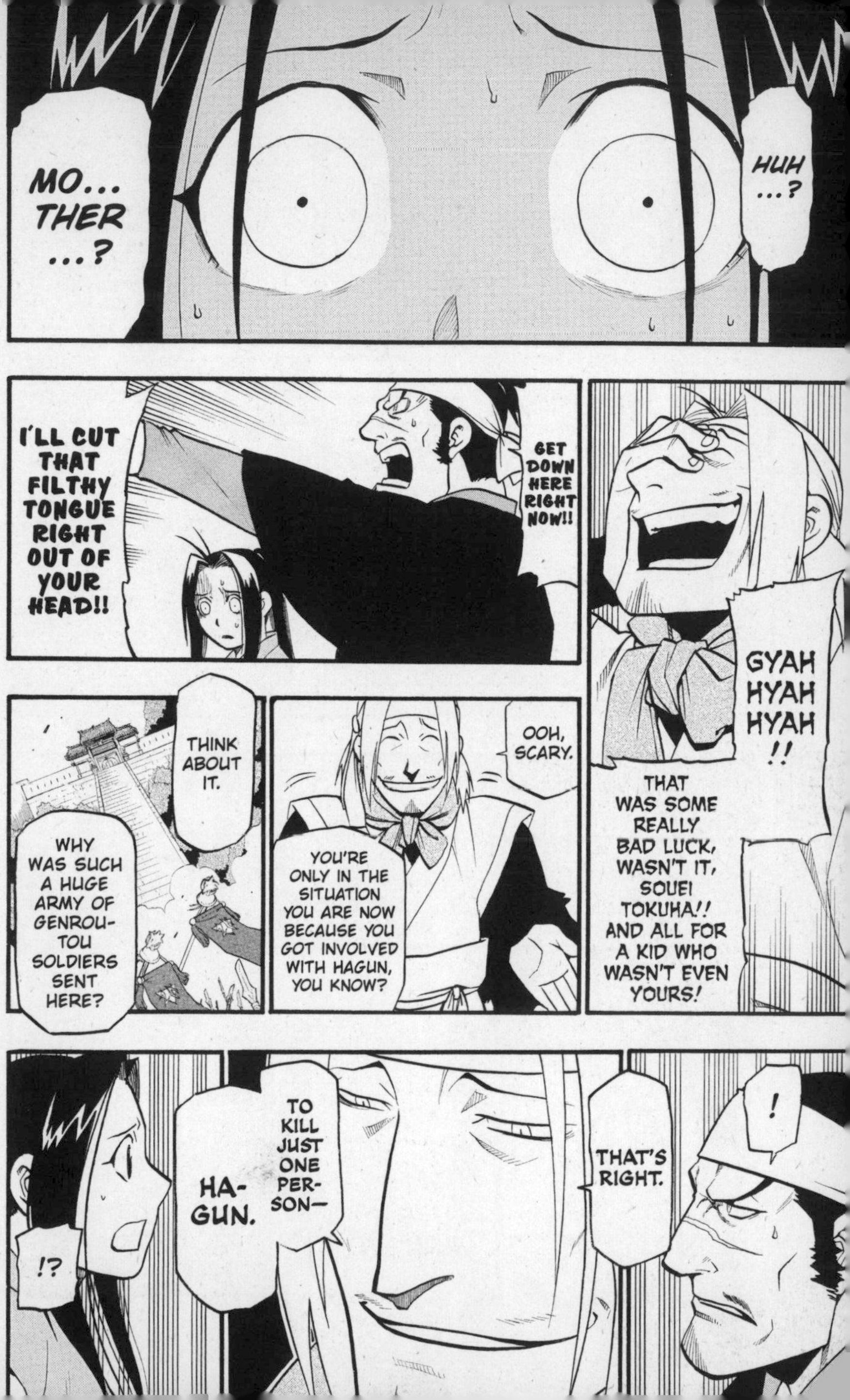

HUH ...?
MO... THER ...?
GYAH HYAH HYAH !!
THAT WAS SOME REALLY BAD LUCK, WASN'T IT, SOUEI TOKUHA!! AND ALL FOR A KID WHO WASN'T EVEN YOURS!
GET DOWN HERE RIGHT NOW!!
I'LL CUT THAT FILTHY TONGUE RIGHT OUT OF YOUR HEAD!!
OOH, SCARY.
YOU'RE ONLY IN THE SITUATION YOU ARE NOW BECAUSE YOU GOT INVOLVED WITH HAGUN, YOU KNOW?
THINK ABOUT IT.
WHY WAS SUCH A HUGE ARMY OF GENROU-TOU SOLDIERS SENT HERE?
!
THAT'S RIGHT.
TO KILL JUST ONE PER-SON—
HA-GUN.
!?

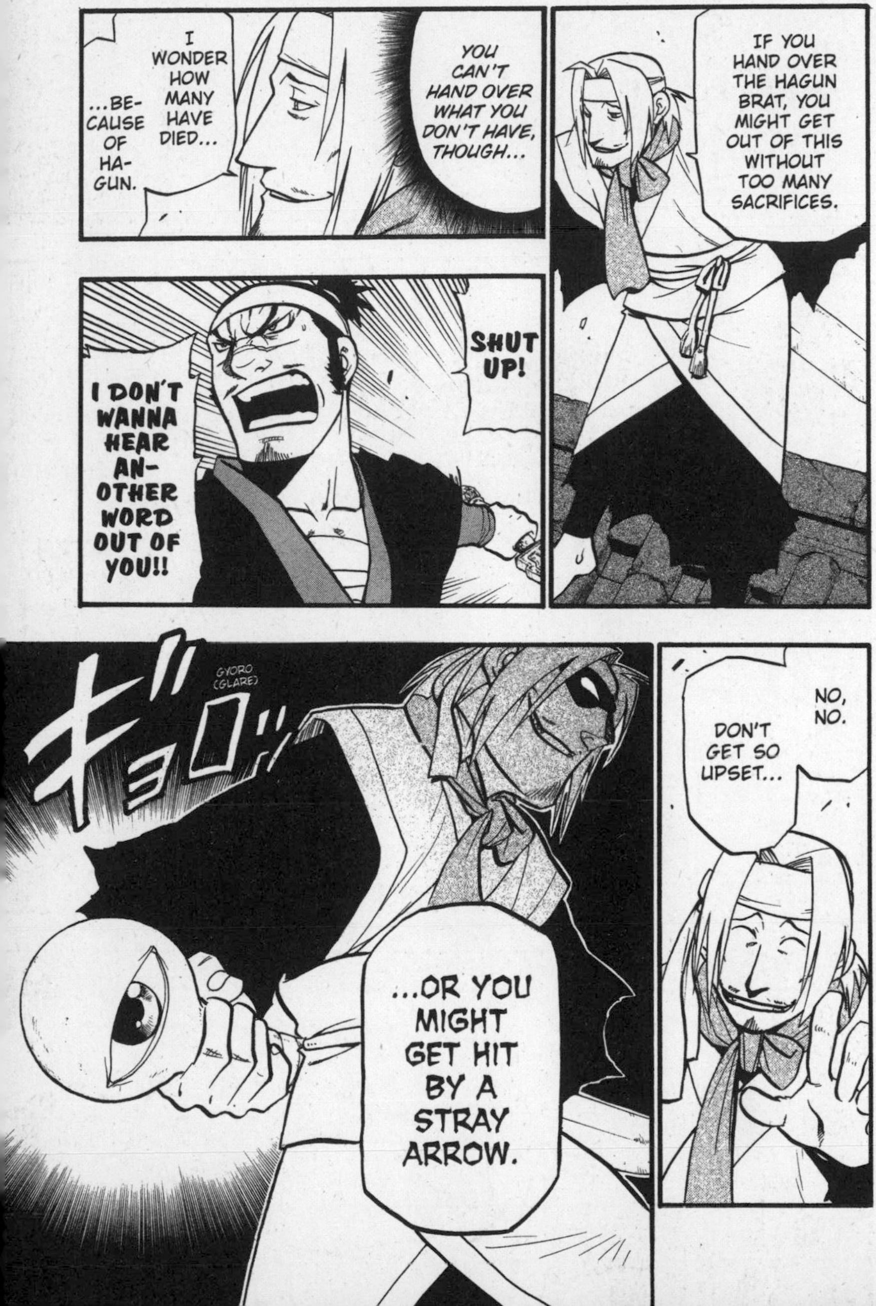
IF YOU HAND OVER THE HAGUN BRAT, YOU MIGHT GET OUT OF THIS WITHOUT TOO MANY SACRIFICES.
YOU CAN'T HAND OVER WHAT YOU DON'T HAVE, THOUGH...
I WONDER HOW MANY HAVE DIED...
...BE-CAUSE OF HA-GUN.
SHUT UP!
I DON'T WANNA HEAR AN-OTHER WORD OUT OF YOU!!
NO, NO.
DON'T GET SO UPSET...
GYORO (GLARE)
...OR YOU MIGHT GET HIT BY A STRAY ARROW.

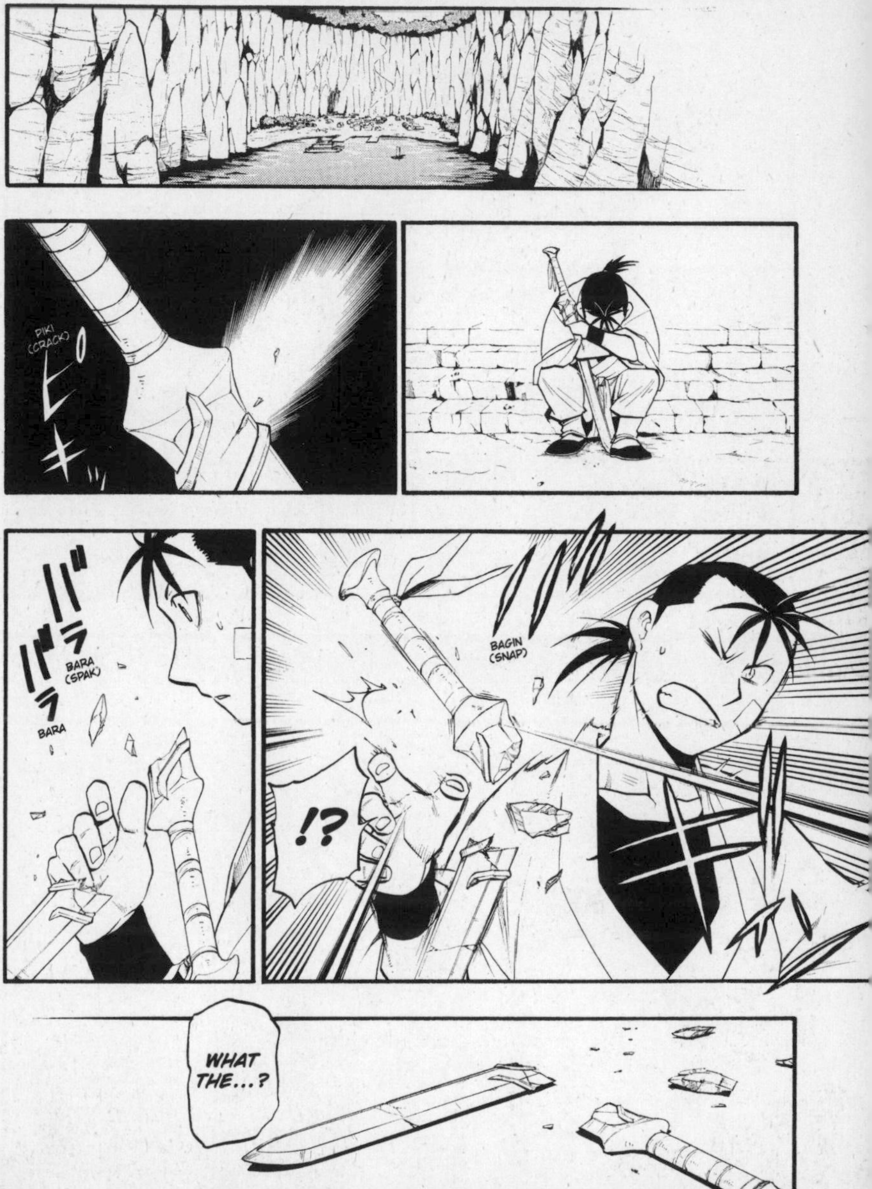
PIKI
(CRACK)
BAGIN
(SNAP)
!?
BARA
(SPAK)
BARA
WHAT THE...?

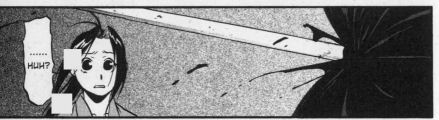

...... HUH?

FATHERRRR!!!

DOO (THUD)

OH.

SO IT WASN'T AN ARROW, IT WAS A SPEAR, HUH?

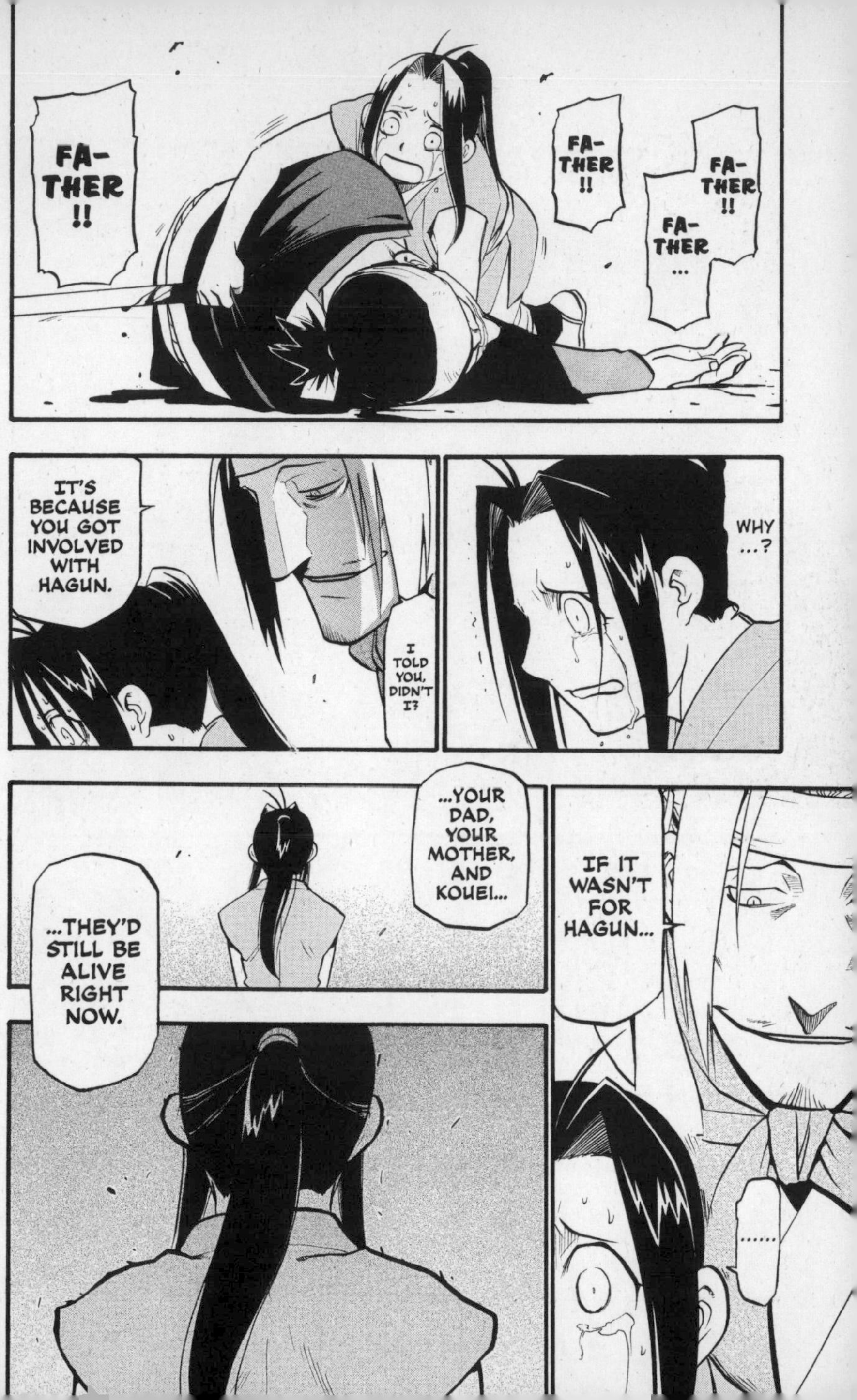
FA-THER!!
FA-THER...
FA-THER!!
FA-THER!!
WHY...?
IT'S BECAUSE YOU GOT INVOLVED WITH HAGUN.
I TOLD YOU, DIDN'T I?
IF IT WASN'T FOR HAGUN...
...YOUR DAD, YOUR MOTHER, AND KOUEI...
...THEY'D STILL BE ALIVE RIGHT NOW.
......

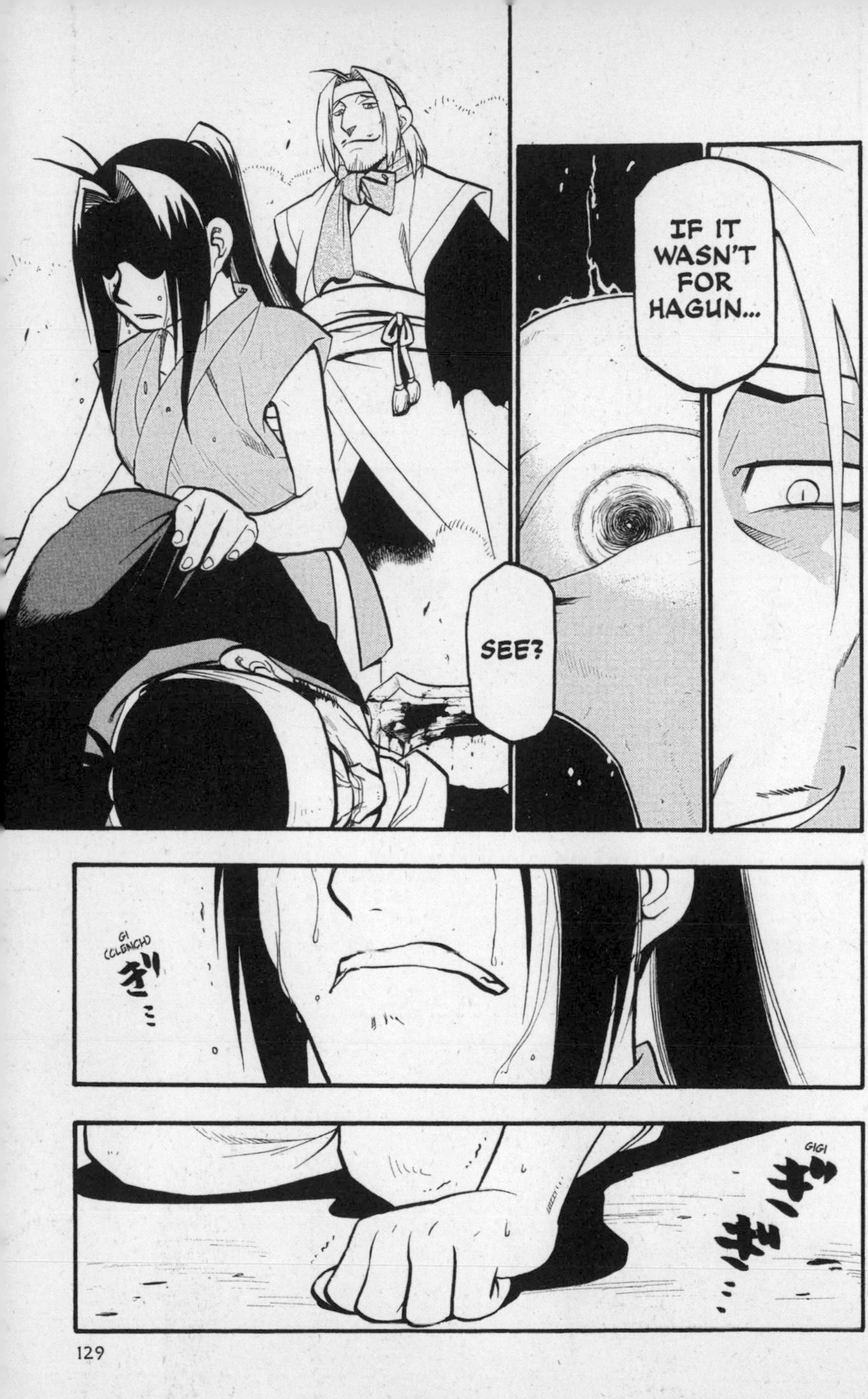
IF IT WASN'T FOR HAGUN...
SEE?
GI (CLENCH)
GIGI

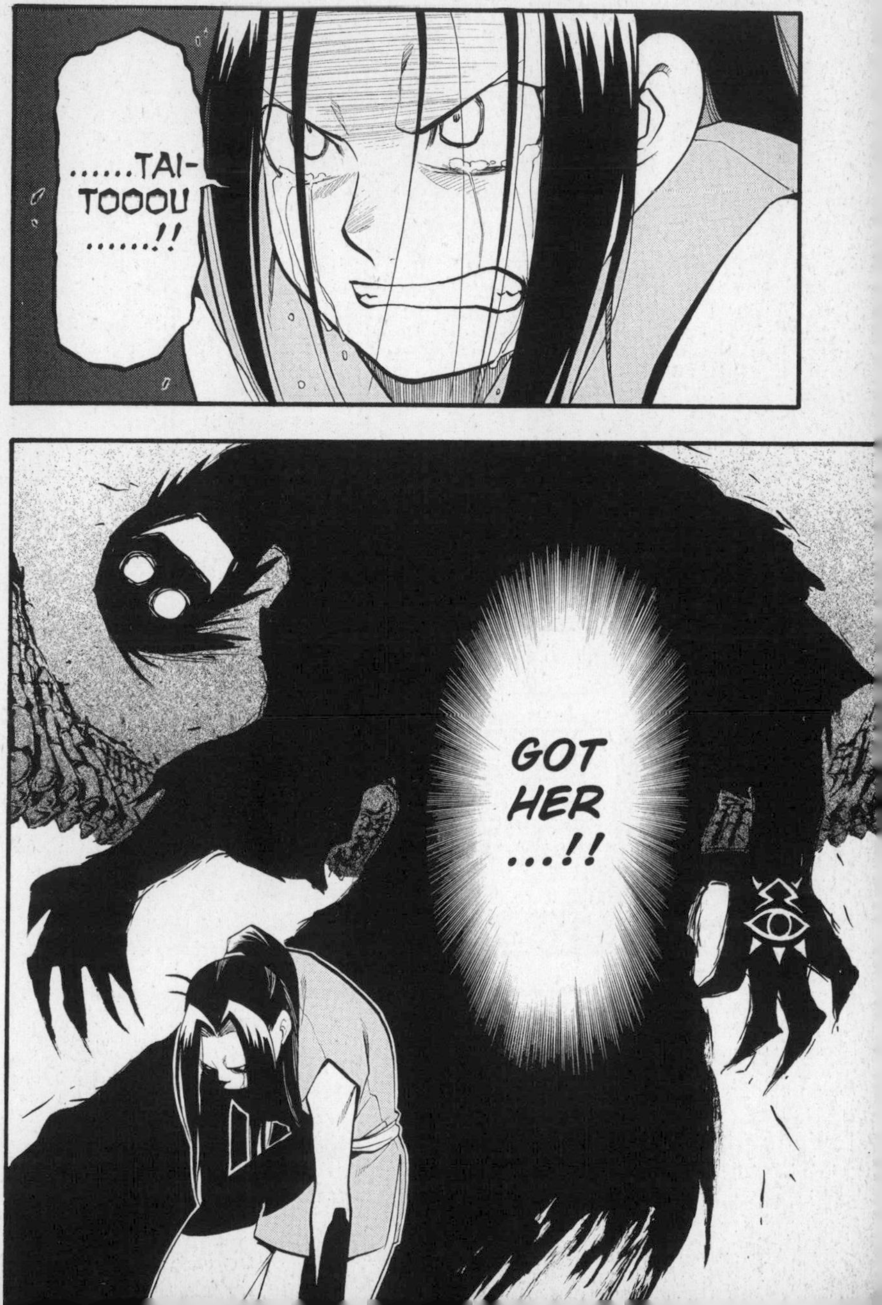
......TAI-
TOOOU
......!!
GOT
HER
...!!

HERO TALES
獣　神　演　武

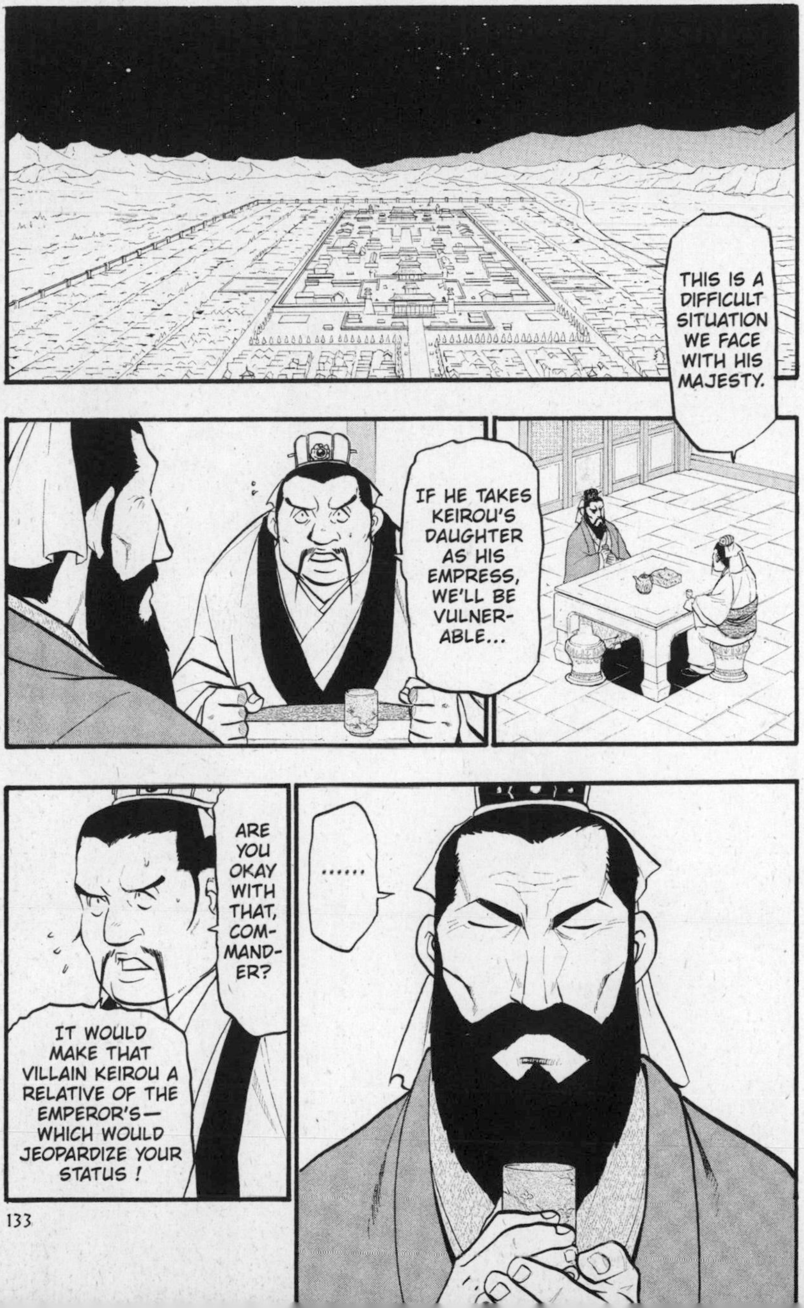
THIS IS A DIFFICULT SITUATION WE FACE WITH HIS MAJESTY.
IF HE TAKES KEIROU'S DAUGHTER AS HIS EMPRESS, WE'LL BE VULNER-ABLE...
......
ARE YOU OKAY WITH THAT, COM-MAND-ER?
IT WOULD MAKE THAT VILLAIN KEIROU A RELATIVE OF THE EMPEROR'S— WHICH WOULD JEOPARDIZE YOUR STATUS !

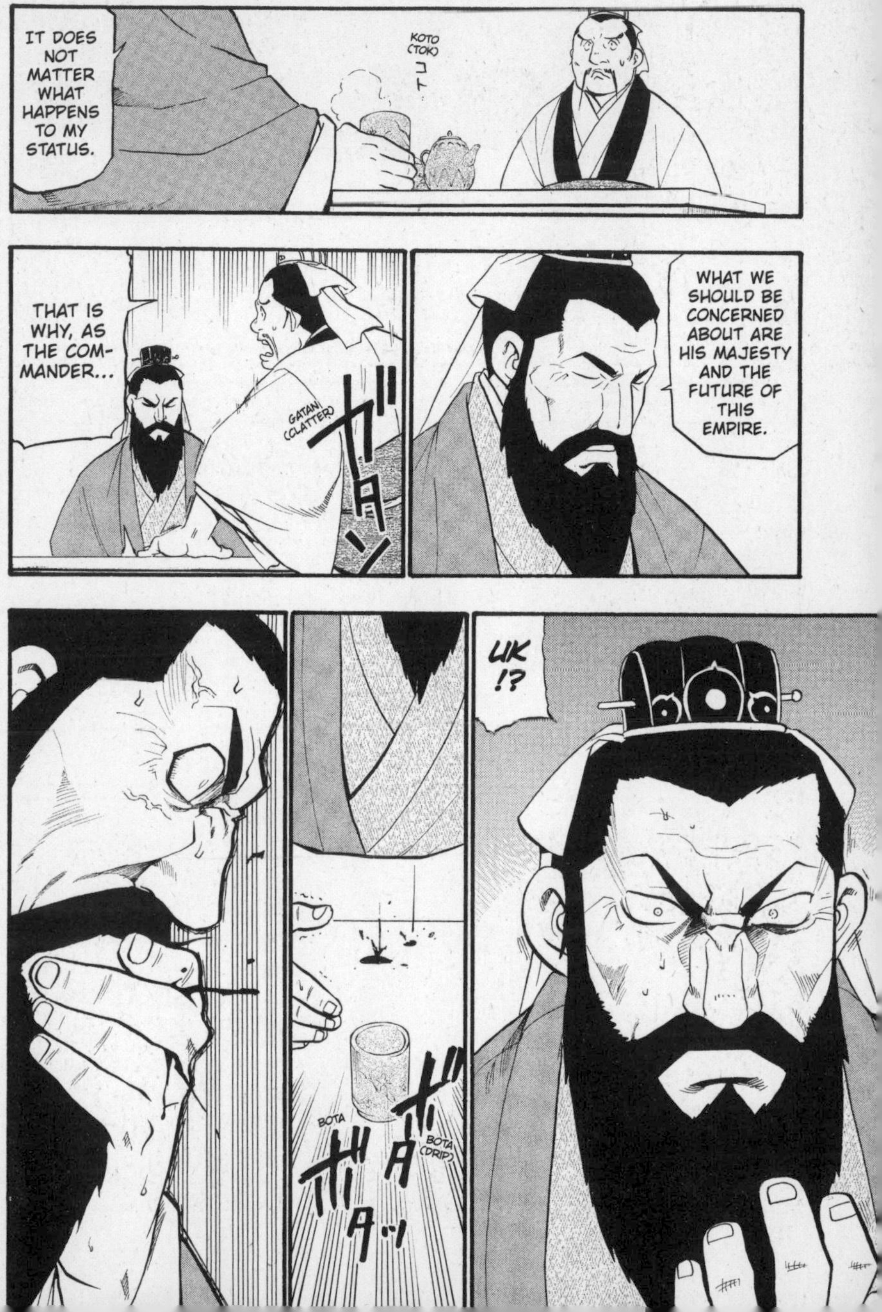
KOTO (TOK)
IT DOES NOT MATTER WHAT HAPPENS TO MY STATUS.
WHAT WE SHOULD BE CONCERNED ABOUT ARE HIS MAJESTY AND THE FUTURE OF THIS EMPIRE.
THAT IS WHY, AS THE COM-MANDER...
GATAN (CLATTER)
UK!?
BOTA
BOTA (DRIP)

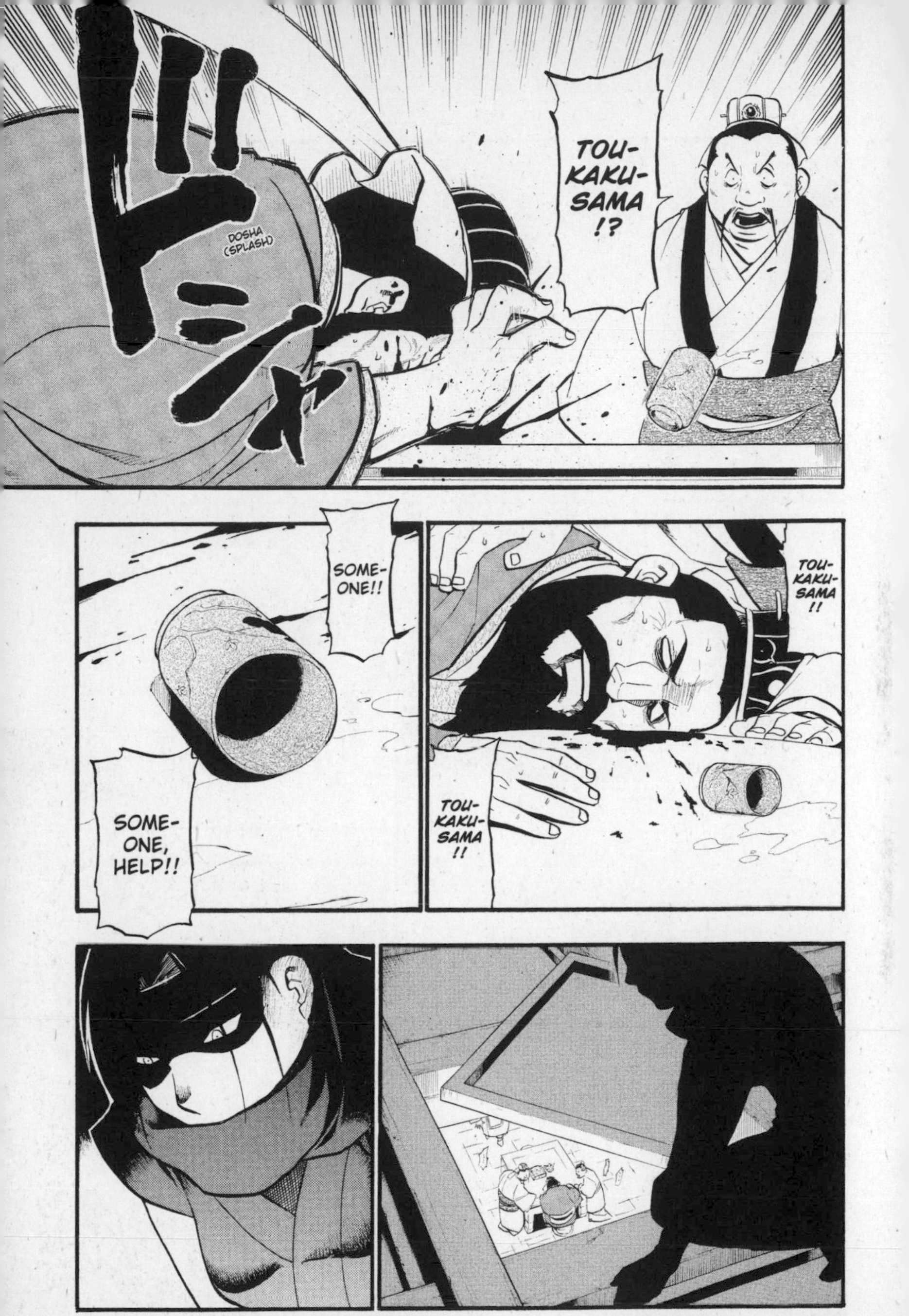
TOU-KAKU-SAMA!?
DOSHA (SPLASH)
TOU-KAKU-SAMA!!
TOU-KAKU-SAMA!!
SOME-ONE!!
SOME-ONE, HELP!!

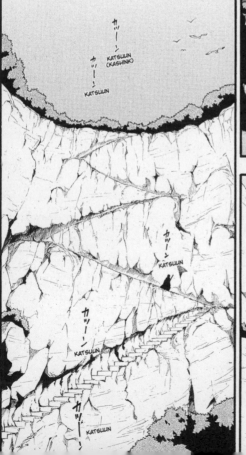

カツ──ン！
KATSULIN
(KASHINK)

カツ──ン！
KATSULIN

カツ──ン！
KATSULIN

カツ──ン！
KATSULIN

カツ──ン！
KATSULIN

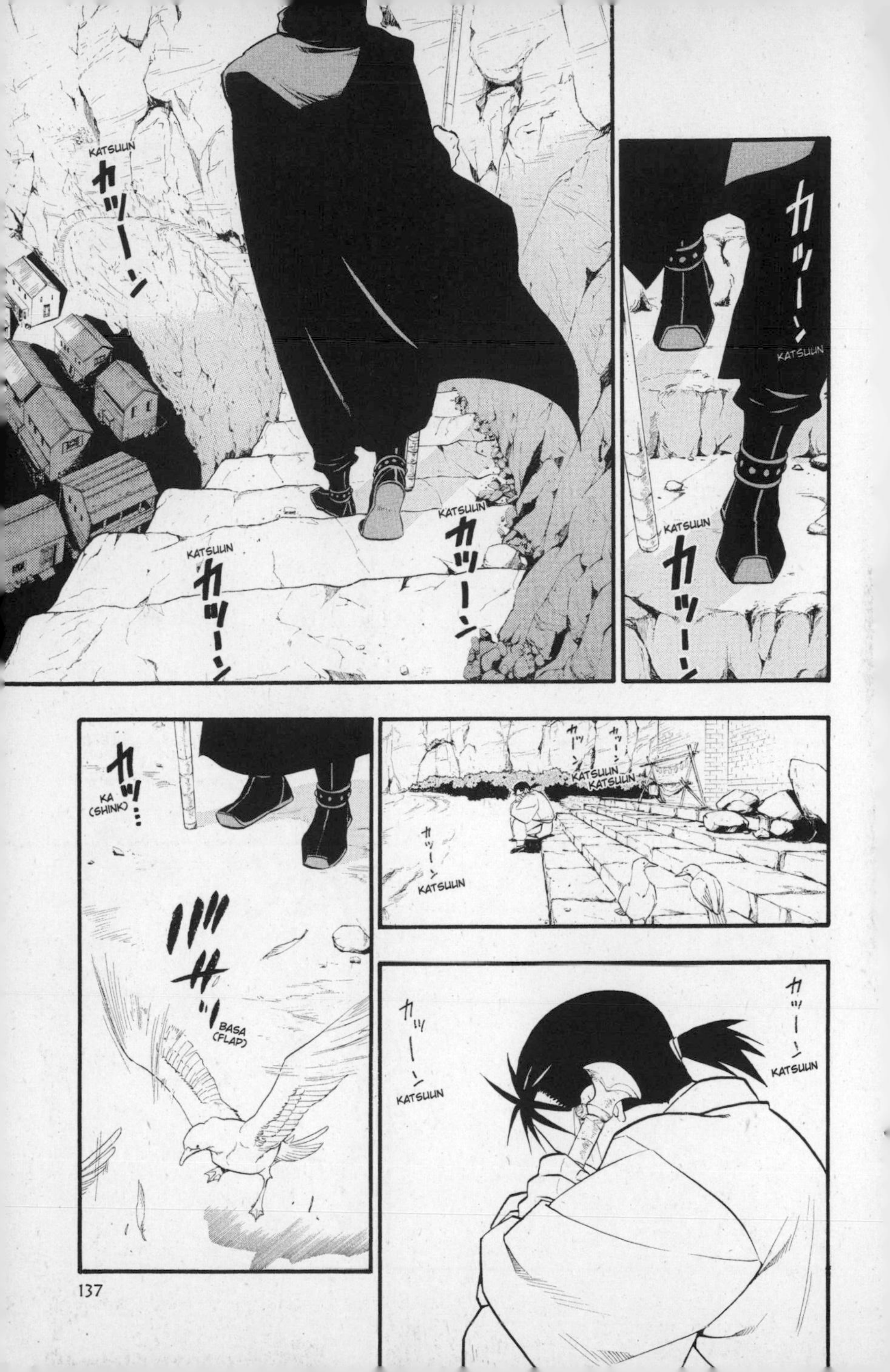
カツーン
KATSUUN
カツーン
KATSUUN
KATSUUN
カツーン
KATSUUN
カツーン
KATSUUN
カツーン
カツーン
カツーン
KATSUUN
KATSUUN
カツーン
KATSUUN
カツーン
KATSUUN
カツーン
KATSUUN
カッ!…
KA (SHINK)
バサッ
BASA (FLAP)

IT'S BEEN A WHILE, TAITOU.

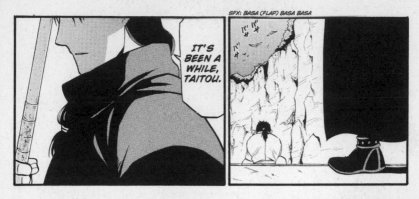

AH...

AHH...

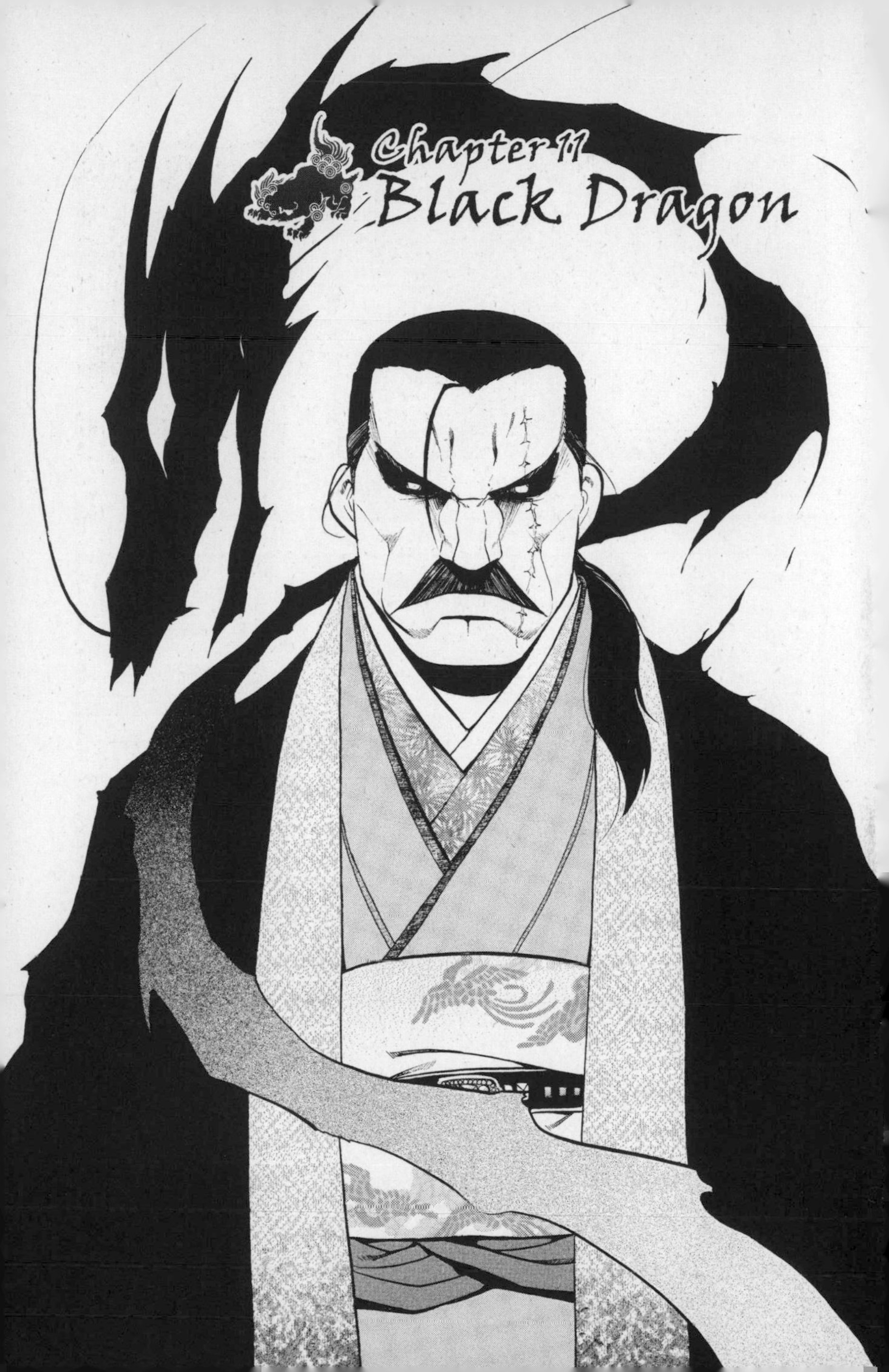
Chapter 11
Black Dragon

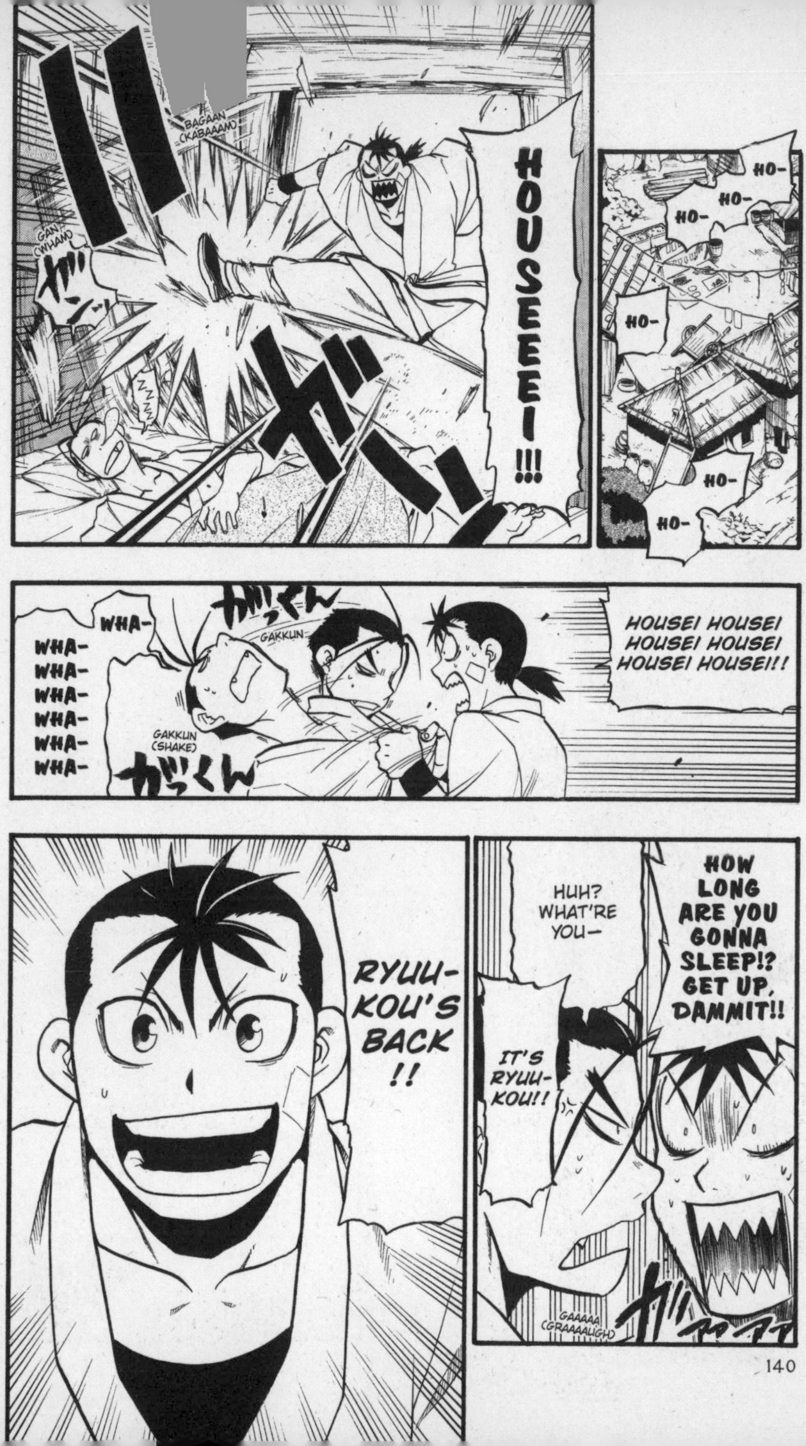
HO-
HO-
HO-
HO-
HO-
HO-
BAGAAN (KABAAAM)
HOUSEEEI!!!
GAN (WHAM)
HOUSEI HOUSEI HOUSEI HOUSEI HOUSEI HOUSEI!!
GAKKUN
WHA-
WHA- WHA- WHA- WHA- WHA- WHA-
GAKKUN (SHAKE)
HOW LONG ARE YOU GONNA SLEEP!? GET UP, DAMMIT!!
HUH? WHAT'RE YOU—
IT'S RYUU-KOU!!
GAAAAA (GRAAAAUGH)
RYUU-KOU'S BACK!!

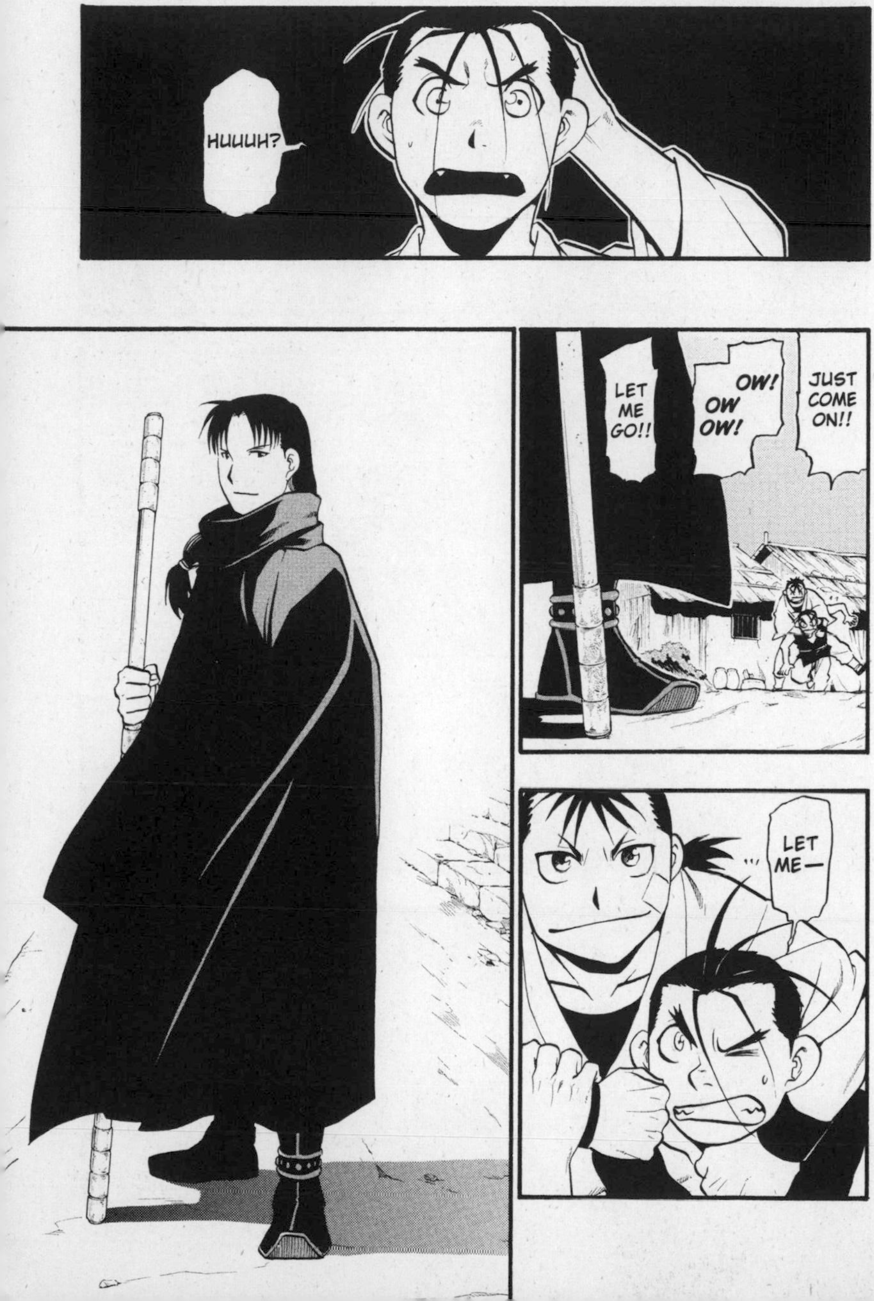
HUUUH?
JUST COME ON!!
OW! OW OW!
LET ME GO!!
... LET ME—

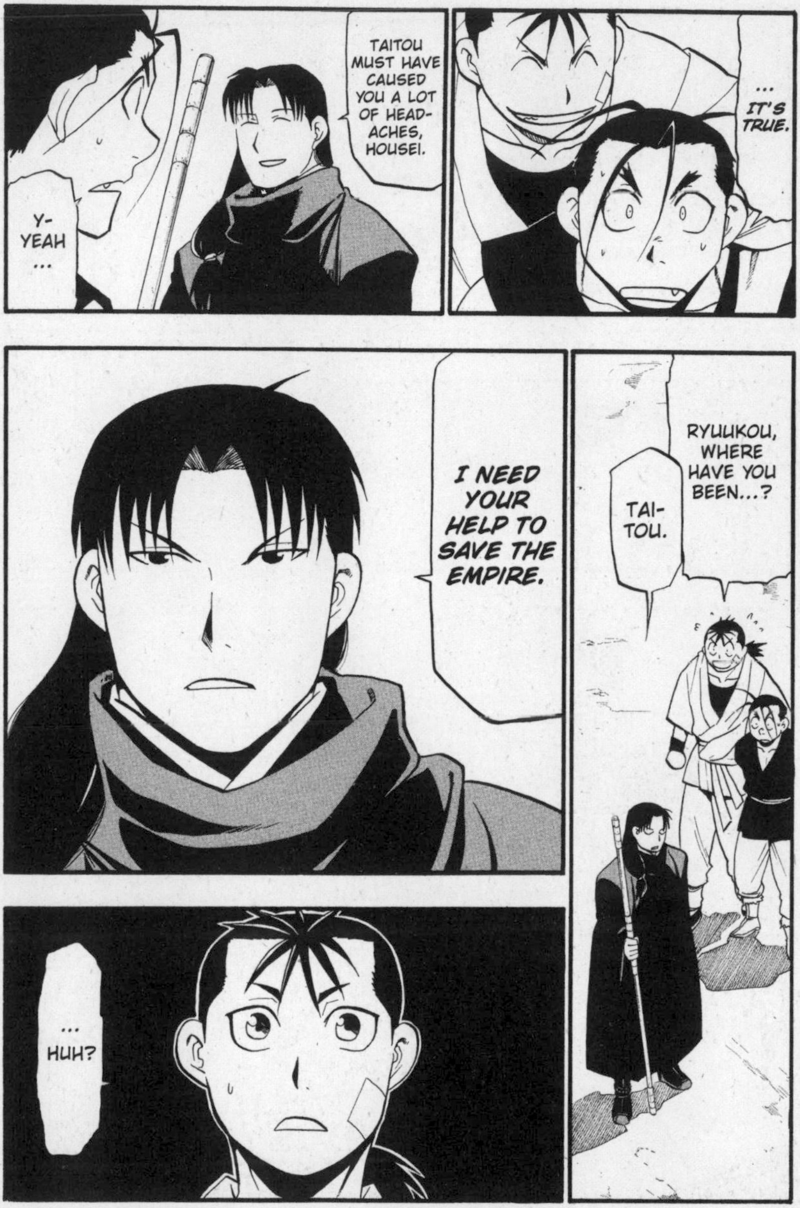
... IT'S TRUE.
TAITOU MUST HAVE CAUSED YOU A LOT OF HEAD-ACHES, HOUSEI.
Y-YEAH ...
RYUUKOU, WHERE HAVE YOU BEEN...?
TAI-TOU.
I NEED YOUR HELP TO SAVE THE EMPIRE.
... HUH?

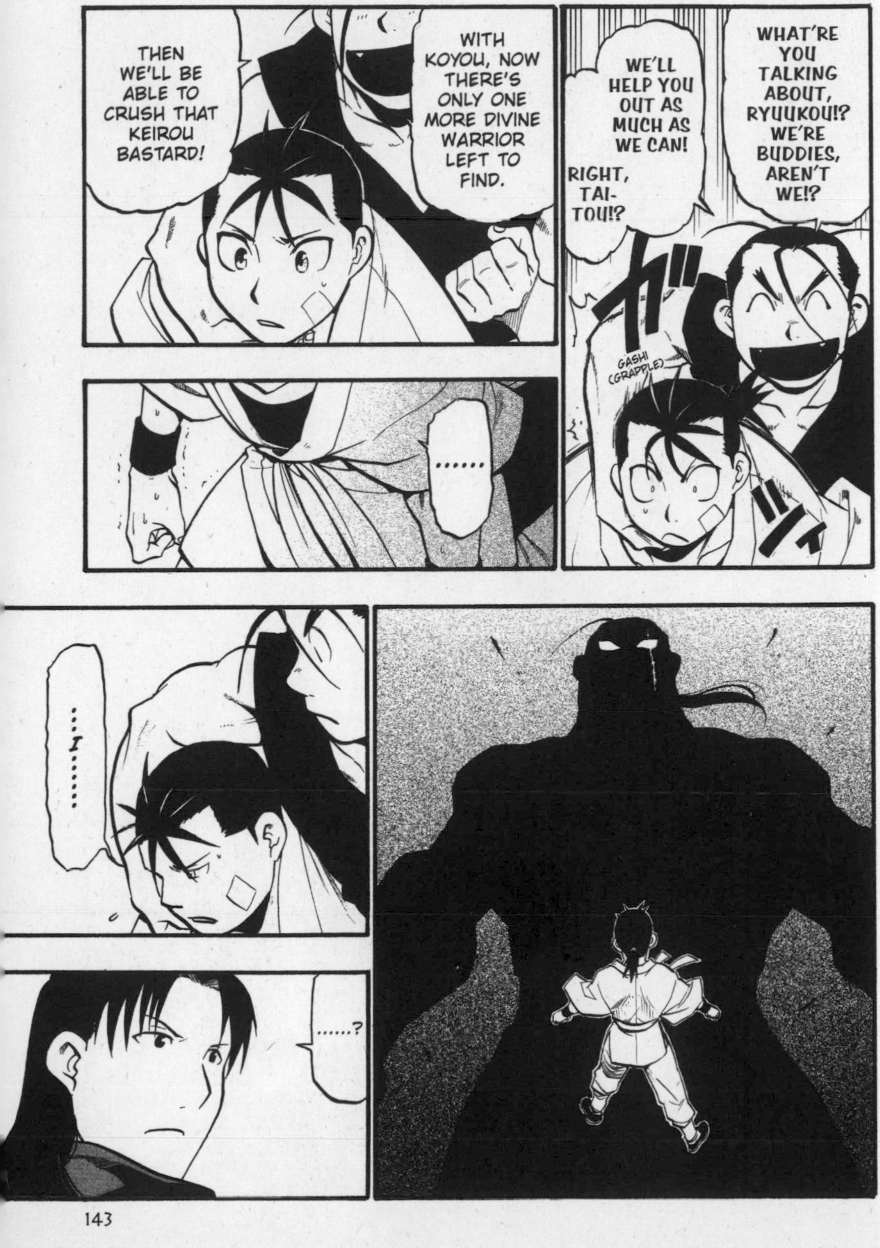
WHAT'RE YOU TALKING ABOUT, RYUUKOU!? WE'RE BUDDIES, AREN'T WE!?
WE'LL HELP YOU OUT AS MUCH AS WE CAN!
RIGHT, TAI-TOU!?
GASHI (GRAPPLE)
WITH KOYOU, NOW THERE'S ONLY ONE MORE DIVINE WARRIOR LEFT TO FIND.
THEN WE'LL BE ABLE TO CRUSH THAT KEIROU BASTARD!
......
...I......
......?

DON'T MEAN TO INTERRUPT, BUT...

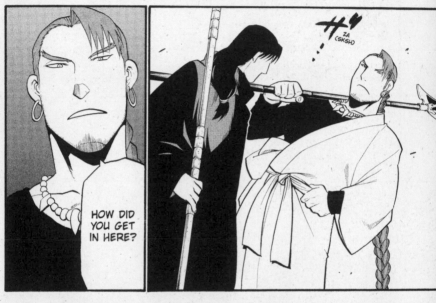

HOW DID YOU GET IN HERE?

ZA (CKSH)

I HAVE SUBOR-DINATES WATCHING THE PERIMETER OF OUR BASE.

KASHA (CKSHAK)

?

SLIPPING PAST THEM IS SOMETHING A THIEF WOULD DO.

I SERIOUSLY DOUBT...

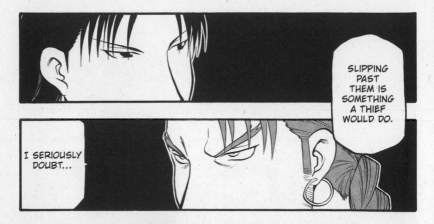

...IT'S SOME-THING YOU COULD PULL OFF!

KO-YOU!?

HEY!!

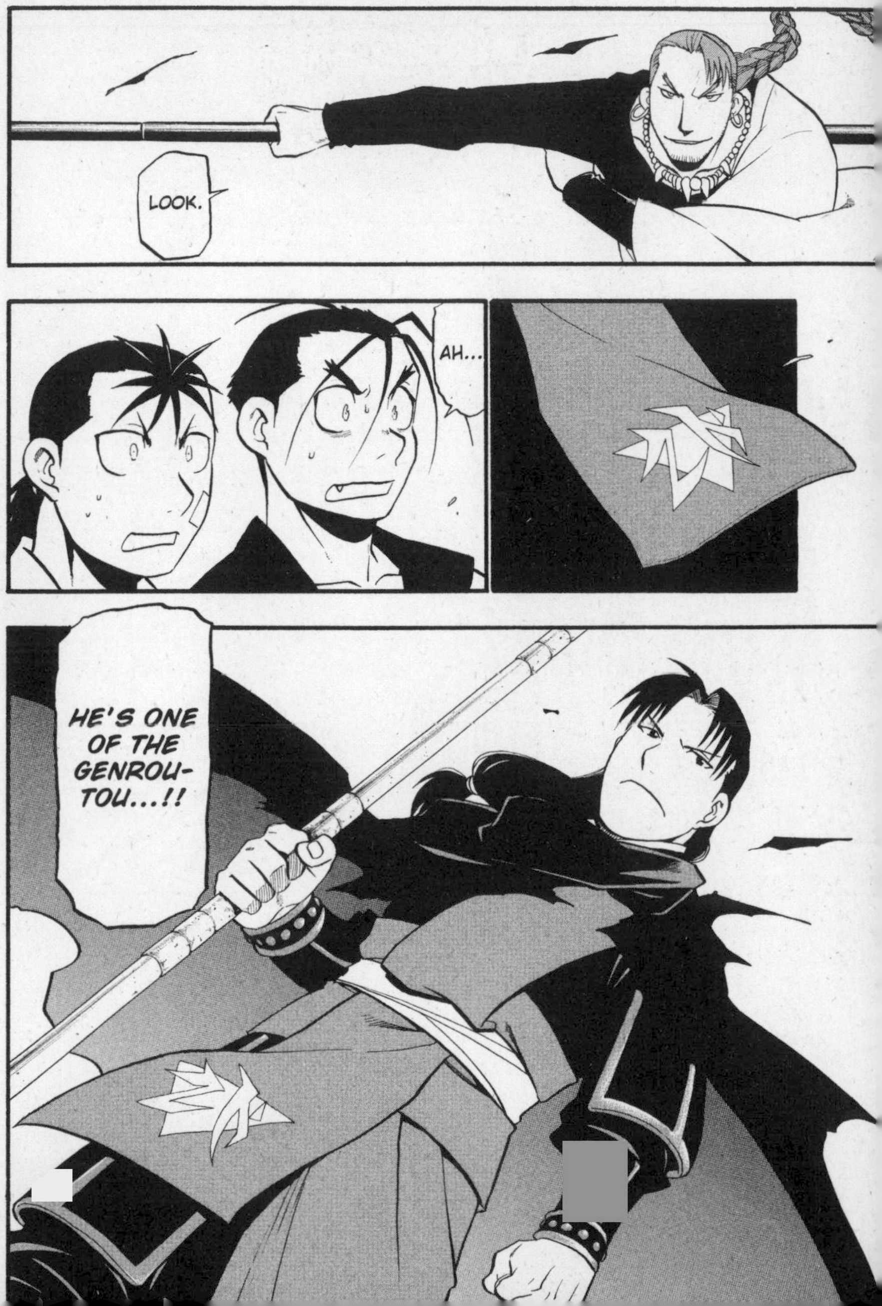
LOOK.
AH...
HE'S ONE OF THE GENROU-TOU...!!

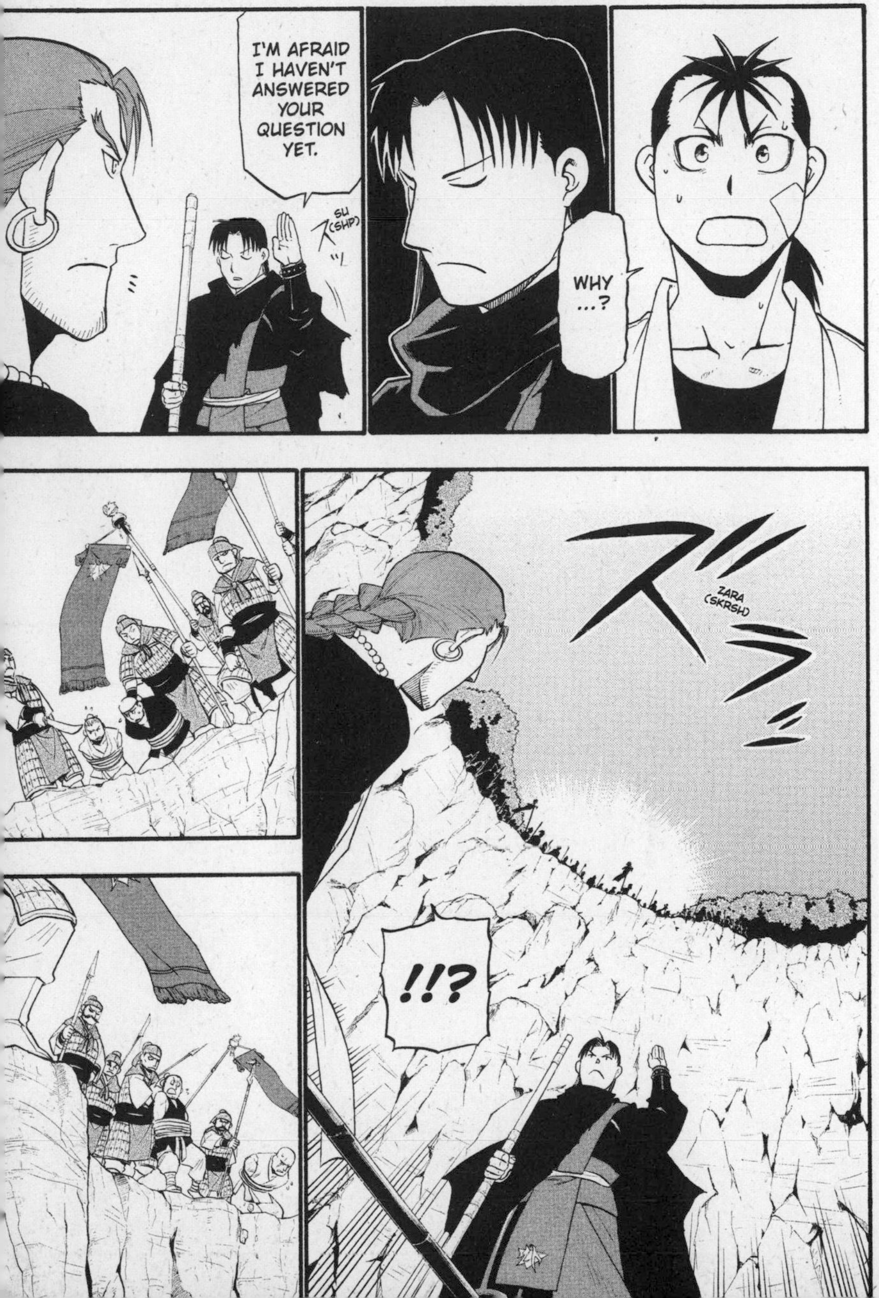
WHY ...?
I'M AFRAID I HAVEN'T ANSWERED YOUR QUESTION YET.
SU (SHP)
ZARA (SKRSH)
!!?

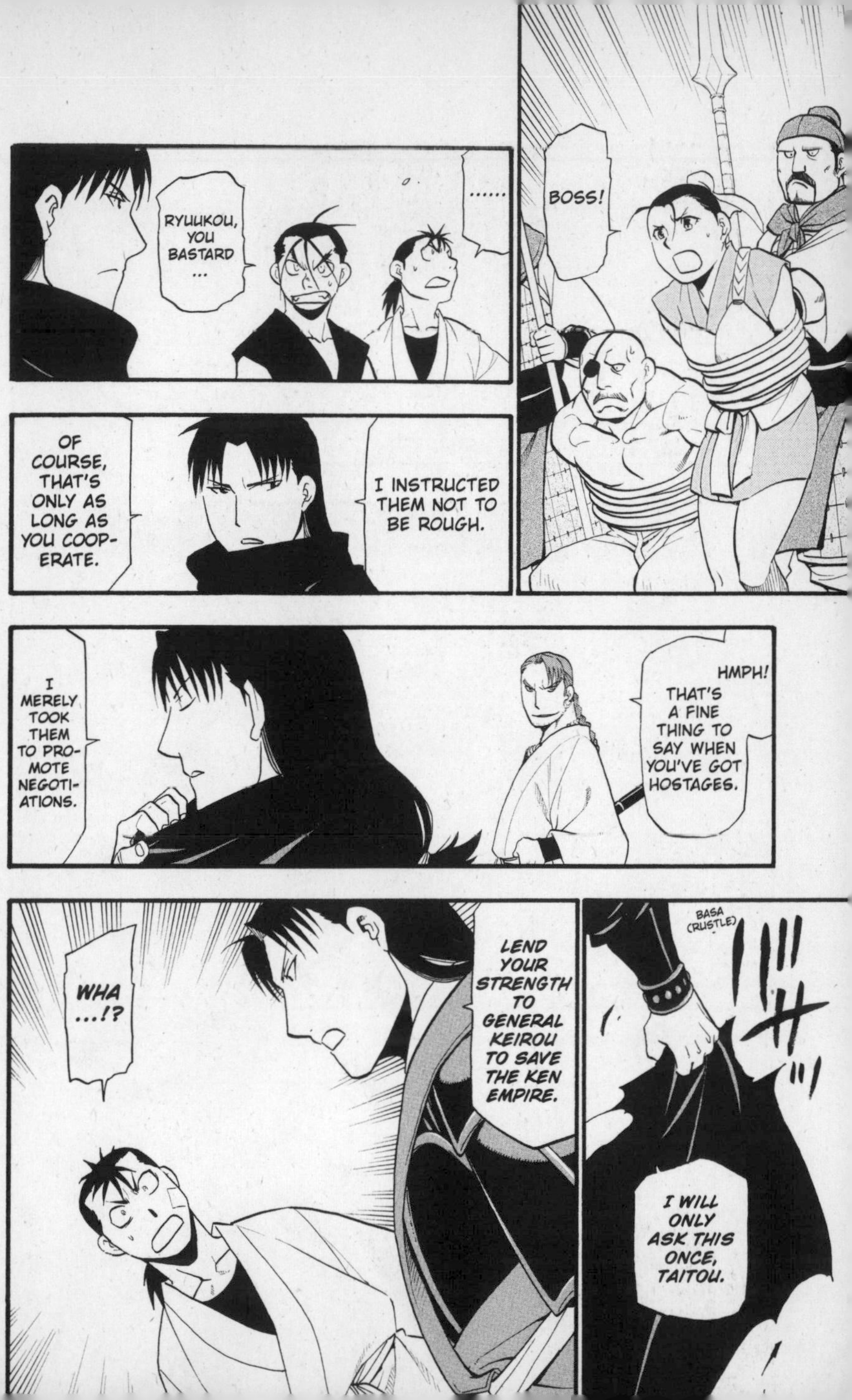
BOSS!
......
RYUUKOU, YOU BASTARD ...
I INSTRUCTED THEM NOT TO BE ROUGH.
OF COURSE, THAT'S ONLY AS LONG AS YOU COOPERATE.
HMPH! THAT'S A FINE THING TO SAY WHEN YOU'VE GOT HOSTAGES.
I MERELY TOOK THEM TO PROMOTE NEGOTIATIONS.
BASA (RUSTLE)
I WILL ONLY ASK THIS ONCE, TAITOU.
LEND YOUR STRENGTH TO GENERAL KEIROU TO SAVE THE KEN EMPIRE.
WHA ...!?

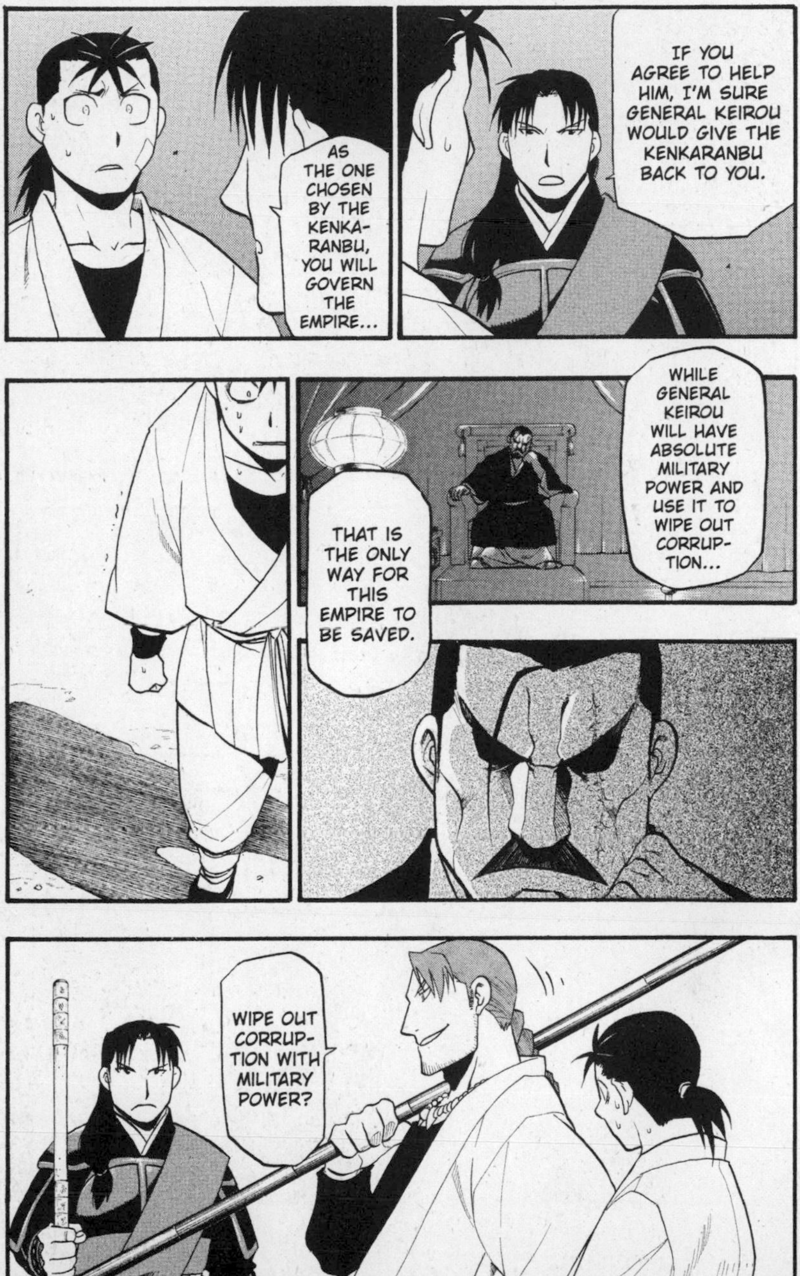
IF YOU AGREE TO HELP HIM, I'M SURE GENERAL KEIROU WOULD GIVE THE KENKARANBU BACK TO YOU.
AS THE ONE CHOSEN BY THE KENKA-RANBU, YOU WILL GOVERN THE EMPIRE...
WHILE GENERAL KEIROU WILL HAVE ABSOLUTE MILITARY POWER AND USE IT TO WIPE OUT CORRUP-TION...
THAT IS THE ONLY WAY FOR THIS EMPIRE TO BE SAVED.
WIPE OUT CORRUP-TION WITH MILITARY POWER?

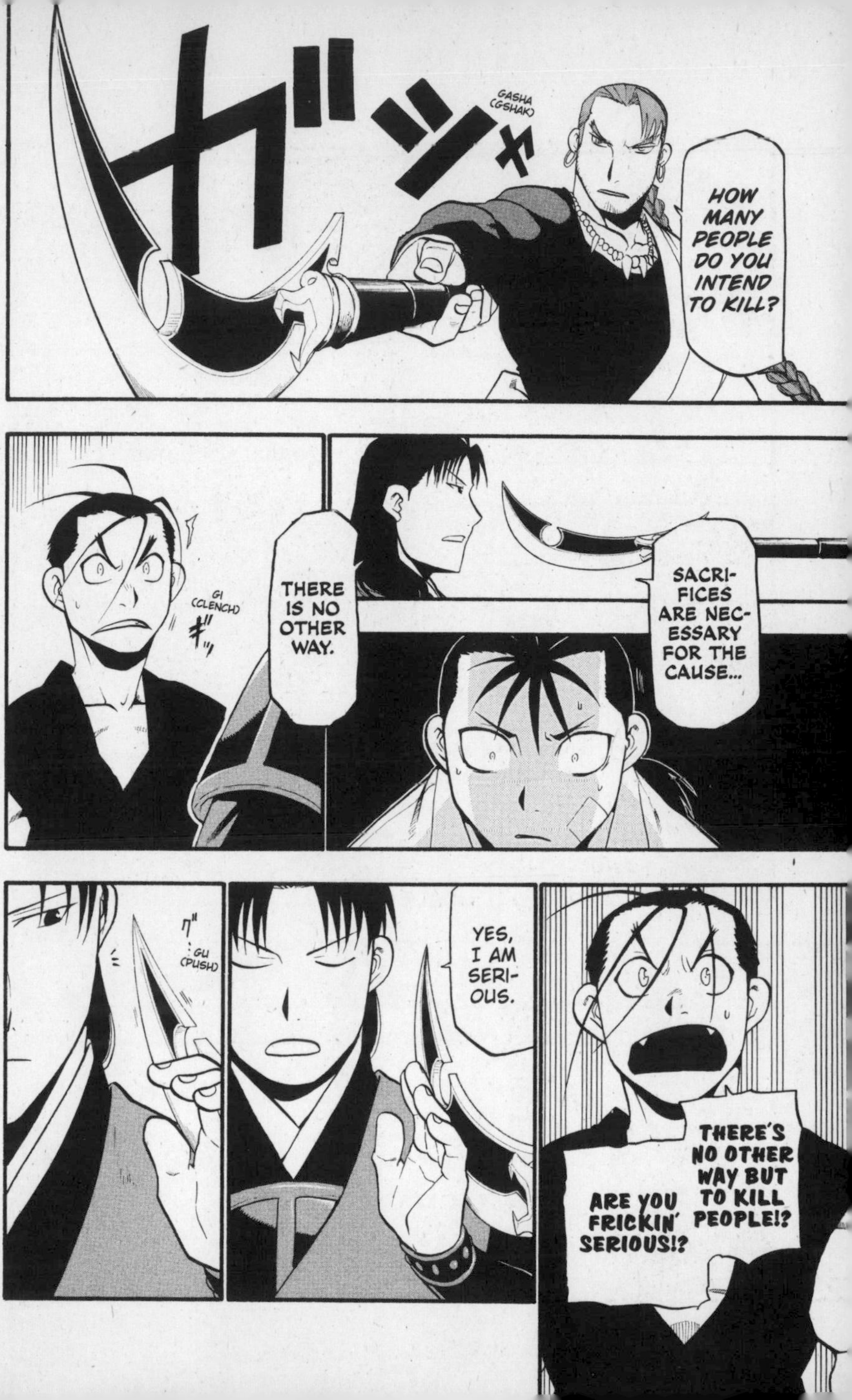
GASHA (GSHAK)
HOW MANY PEOPLE DO YOU INTEND TO KILL?
SACRI-FICES ARE NEC-ESSARY FOR THE CAUSE...
THERE IS NO OTHER WAY.
GI (CLENCH)
THERE'S NO OTHER WAY BUT TO KILL PEOPLE!?
ARE YOU FRICKIN' SERIOUS!?
YES, I AM SERI-OUS.
GU (PUSH)

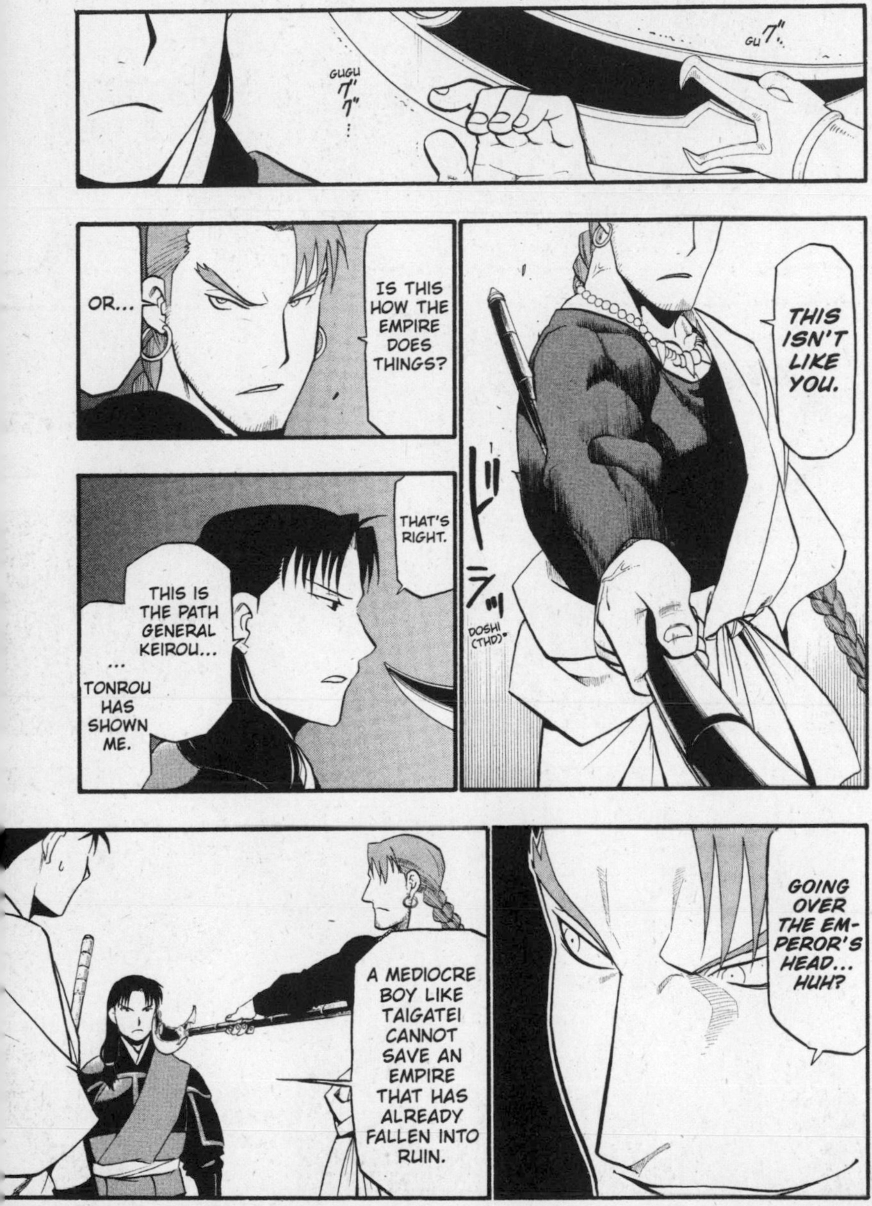
GU
GUGU
THIS ISN'T LIKE YOU.
DOSHI (THD)
IS THIS HOW THE EMPIRE DOES THINGS?
OR...
THAT'S RIGHT.
THIS IS THE PATH GENERAL KEIROU...
... TONROU HAS SHOWN ME.
GOING OVER THE EMPEROR'S HEAD... HUH?
A MEDIOCRE BOY LIKE TAIGATEI CANNOT SAVE AN EMPIRE THAT HAS ALREADY FALLEN INTO RUIN.

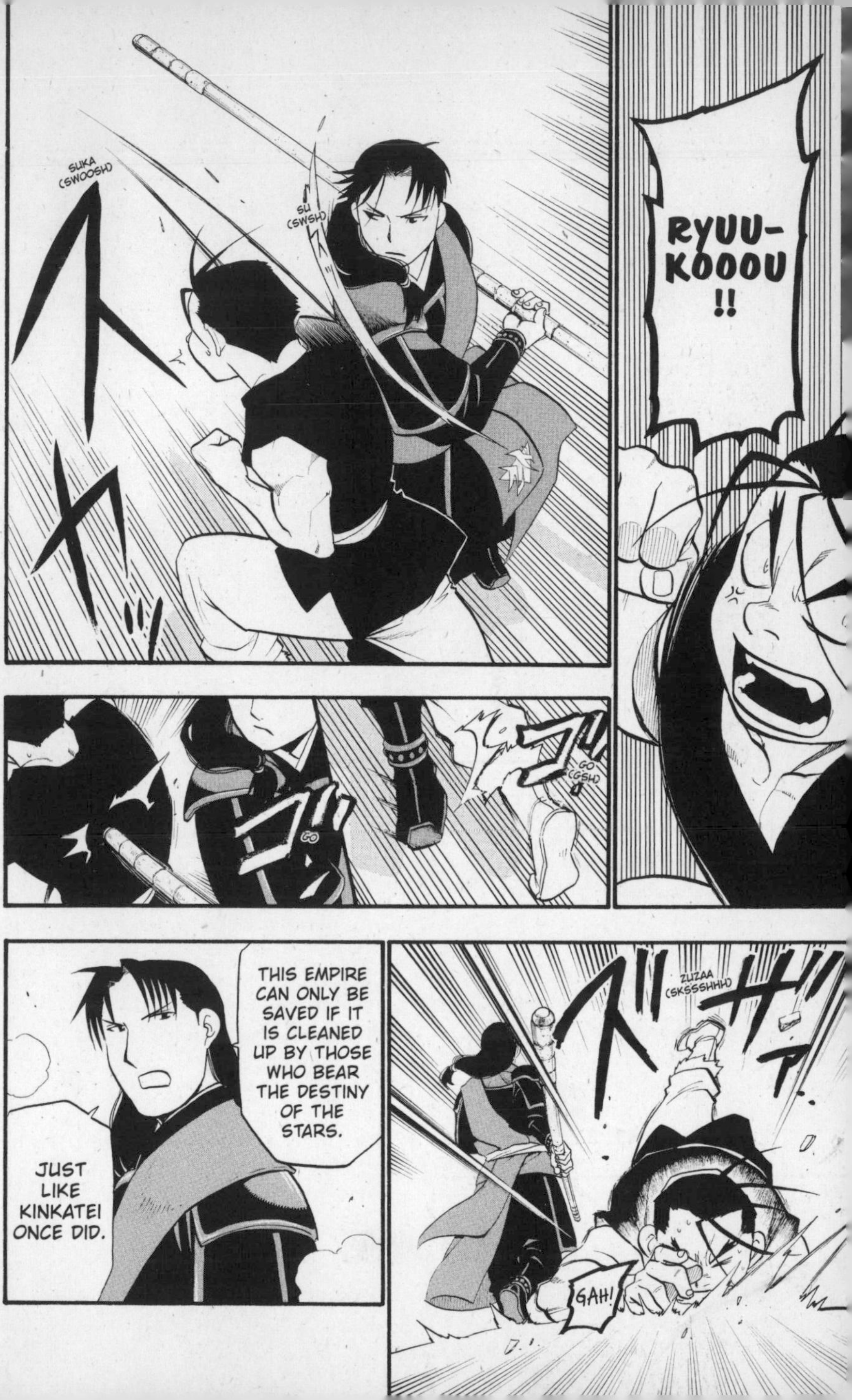
RYUU-KOOOU!!
SU (SWSH)
SUKA (SWOOSH)
GO (GSH)
GO
ZUZAA (SKSSSHHH)
GAH!
THIS EMPIRE CAN ONLY BE SAVED IF IT IS CLEANED UP BY THOSE WHO BEAR THE DESTINY OF THE STARS.
JUST LIKE KINKATEI ONCE DID.

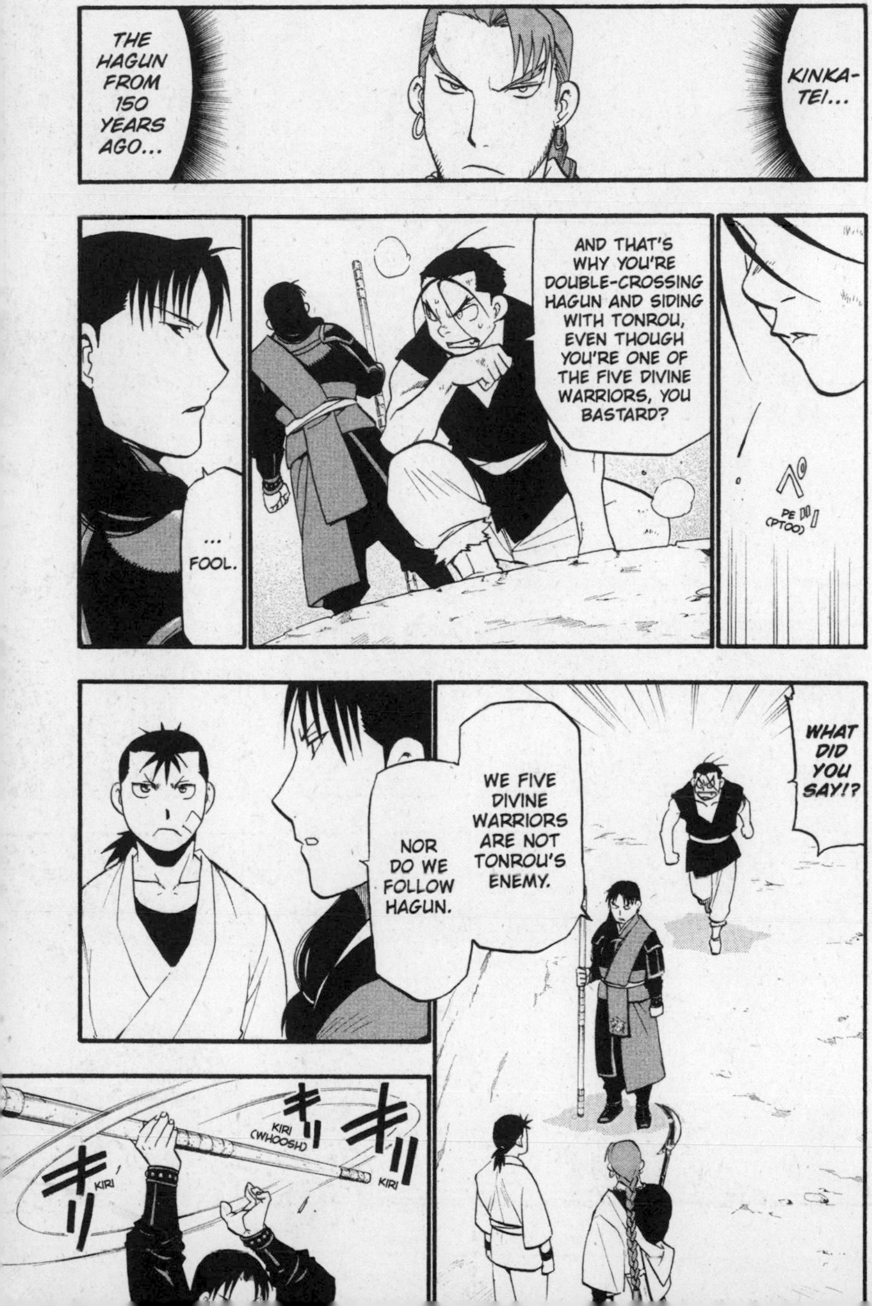
KINKA-TEI...
THE HAGUN FROM 150 YEARS AGO...
PE (PTOO)
AND THAT'S WHY YOU'RE DOUBLE-CROSSING HAGUN AND SIDING WITH TONROU, EVEN THOUGH YOU'RE ONE OF THE FIVE DIVINE WARRIORS, YOU BASTARD?
... FOOL.
WHAT DID YOU SAY!?
WE FIVE DIVINE WARRIORS ARE NOT TONROU'S ENEMY.
NOR DO WE FOLLOW HAGUN.
KIRI (WHOOSH)
KIRI
KIRI

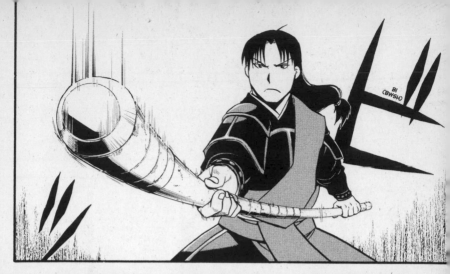

BI (BWSH)
THE FIVE DIVINE WARRIORS ARE CALLED TO PROTECT THE EARTH FROM THE FIERCE STARS THAT THROW THIS WORLD INTO STRIFE.
I WILL DO WHATEVER I MUST TO ACCOMPLISH THAT...
ARE YOU SERIOUS?
I CANNOT ALLOW MY PERSONAL FEELINGS TO INTERFERE WITH...

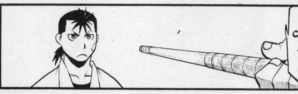

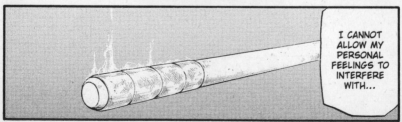

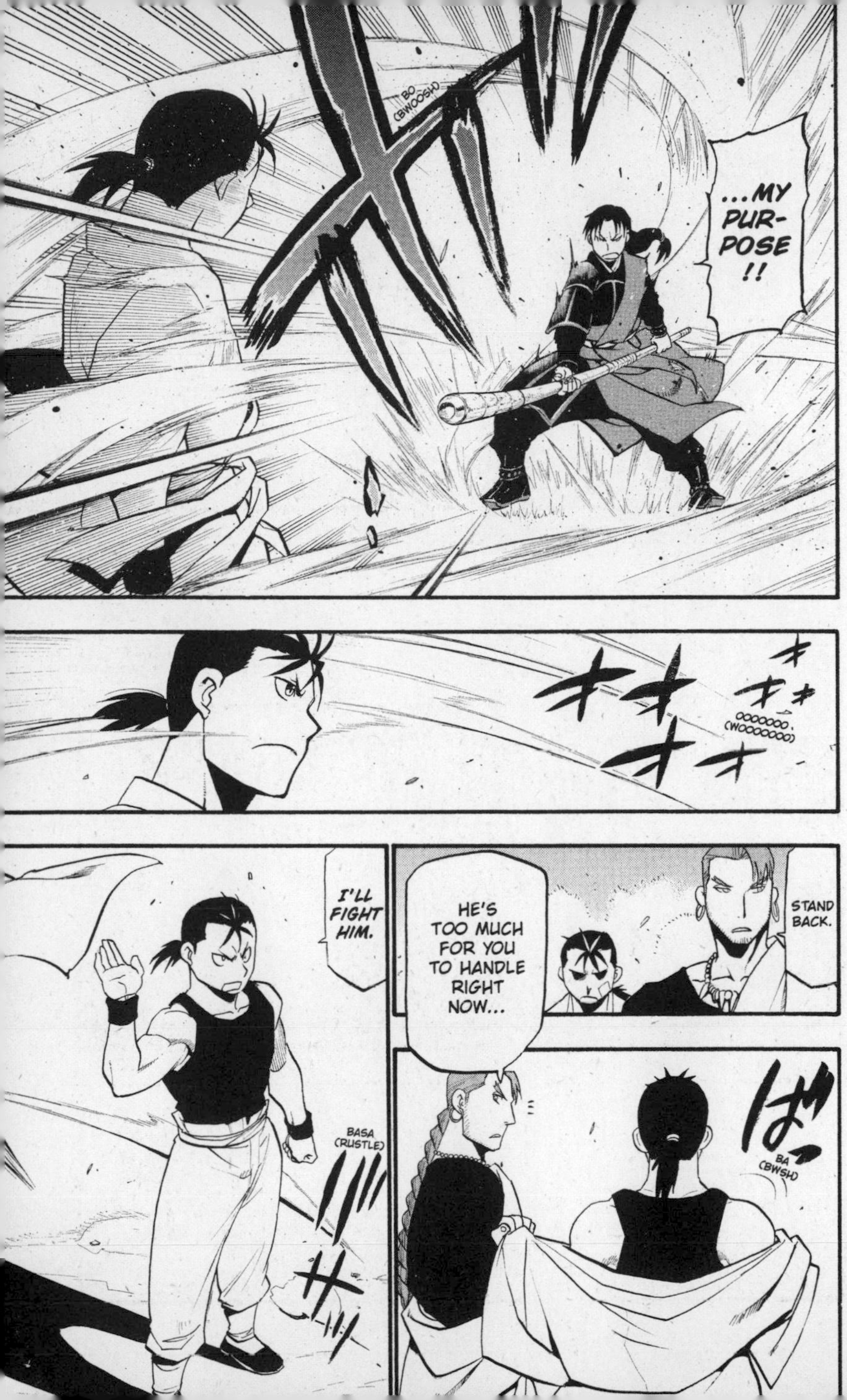
...MY PURPOSE!!
BO (BWOOSH)
OOOOOOO. (WOOOOOOO)
STAND BACK.
HE'S TOO MUCH FOR YOU TO HANDLE RIGHT NOW...
BA (BWSH)
I'LL FIGHT HIM.
BASA (RUSTLE)

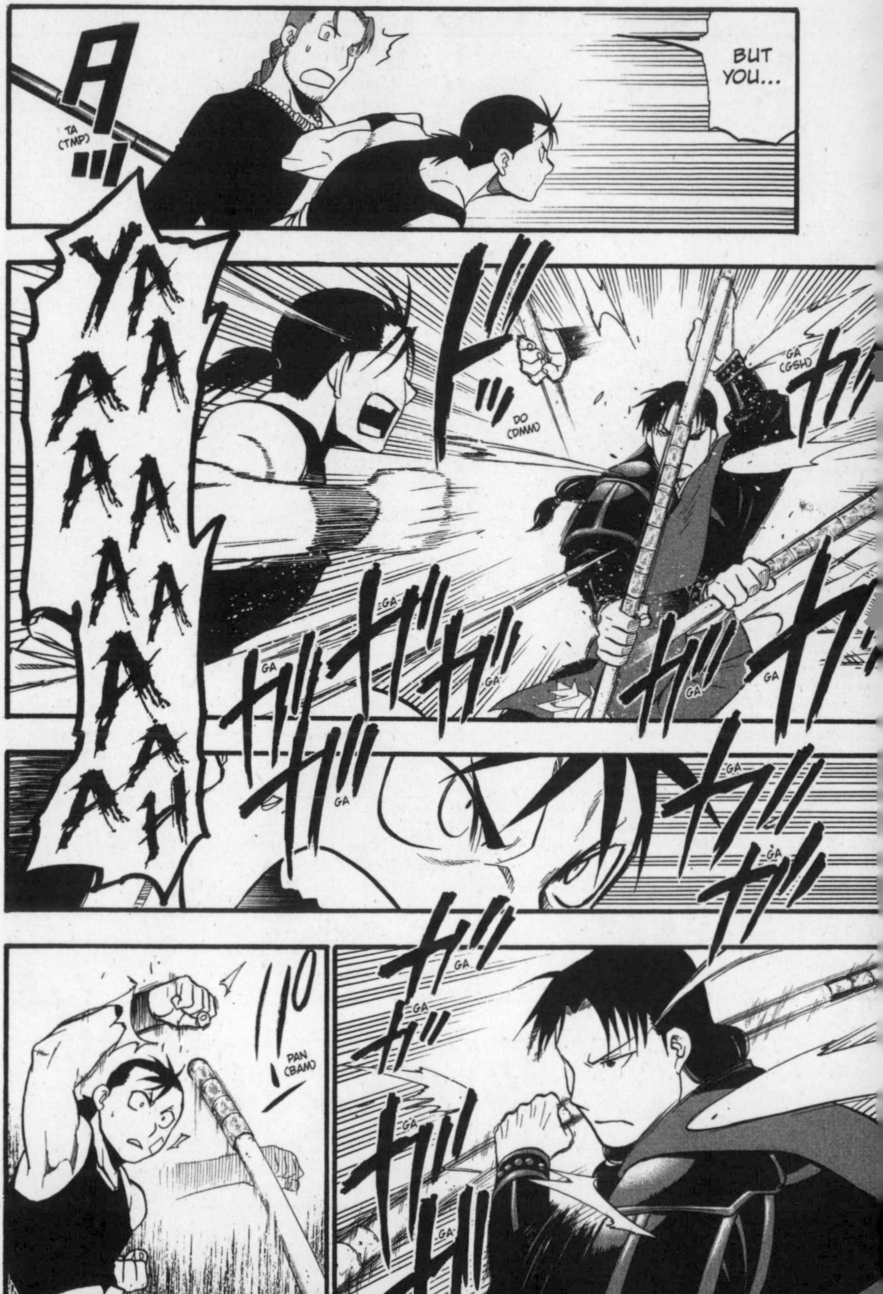

BUT YOU...
TA (TMP)
YAAAAAAAAAAAH
GA (GSH)
DO (DOMM)
GA
GA
GA
GA
GA
GA
GA
GA
GA
GA
GA
PAN (BAM)

DON
COMMO

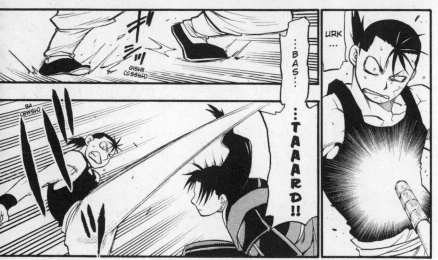

GISH!!!
(GSSSH)

BA
(BWSH)

...BAS...

...TAAARD!!

URK
...

DOGAGA
(BWGSSH)

GA
GA GA
GA
GA GA

157

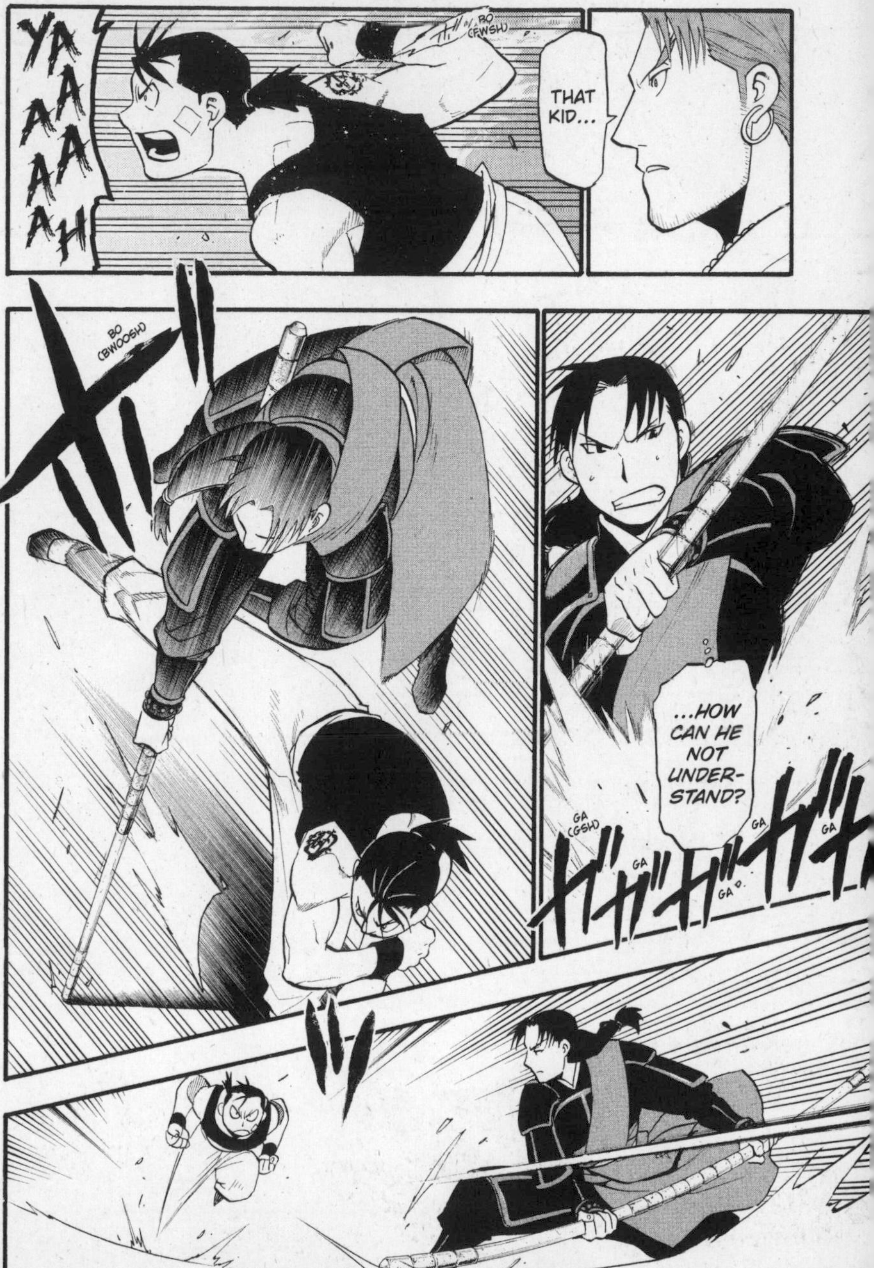
THAT KID...
BO (FWSH)
YAAAAAAH
...HOW CAN HE NOT UNDERSTAND?
GA (GSH)
GA
GA
GA
GA
BO (BWOOSH)

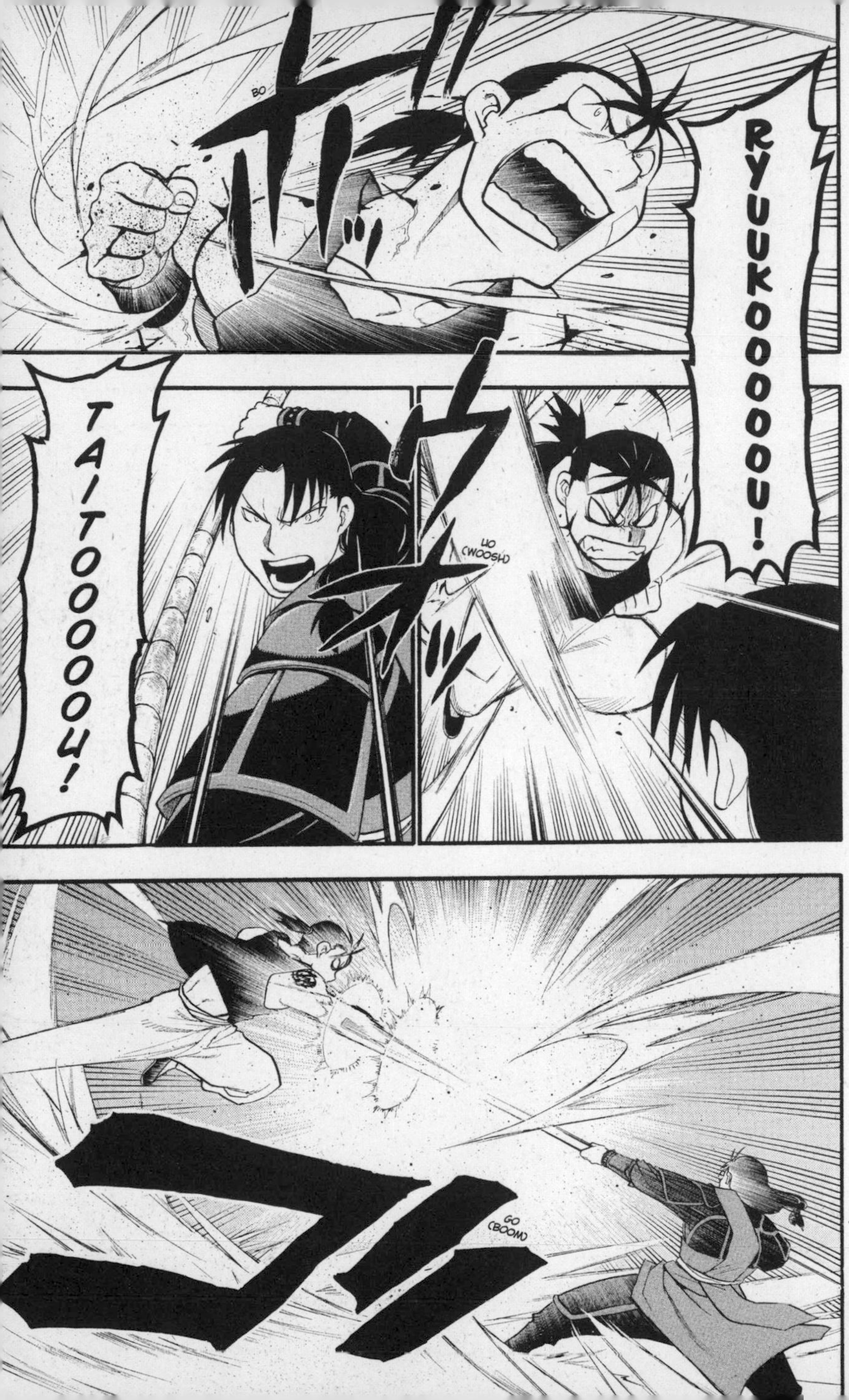
RYUUKOOOOOU!
BO
HO (WOOSH)
TAITOOOOOU!
GO (BOOM)

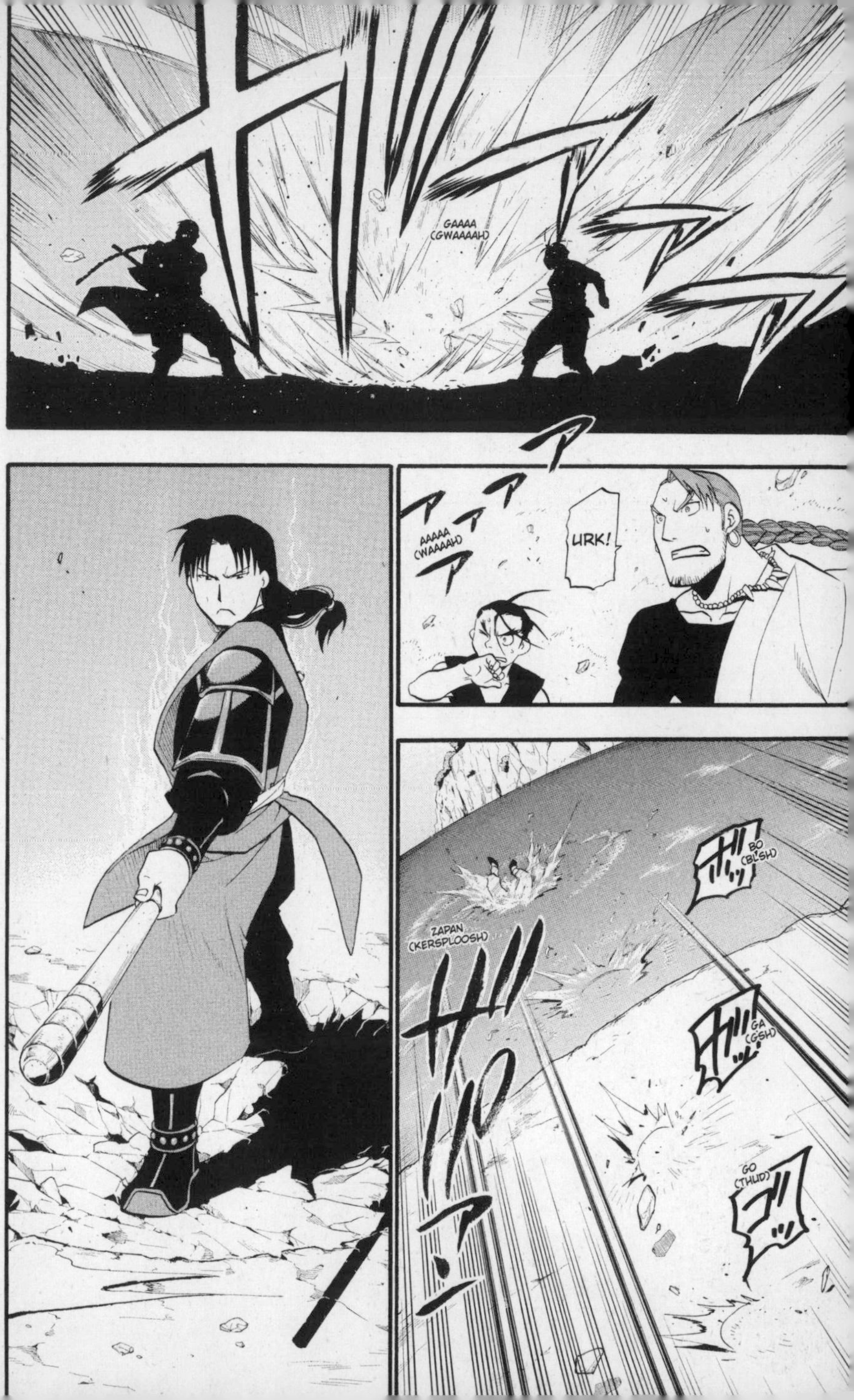
GAAAA (GWAAAAH)
URK!
AAAAA (WAAAAH)
BO (BL'SH)
ZAPAN (KERSPLOOSH)
GA (G'SH)
GO (THUD)

BWAH

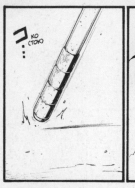

KO
(TOK)

...!?

GARAN

GARA
(CLATTER)

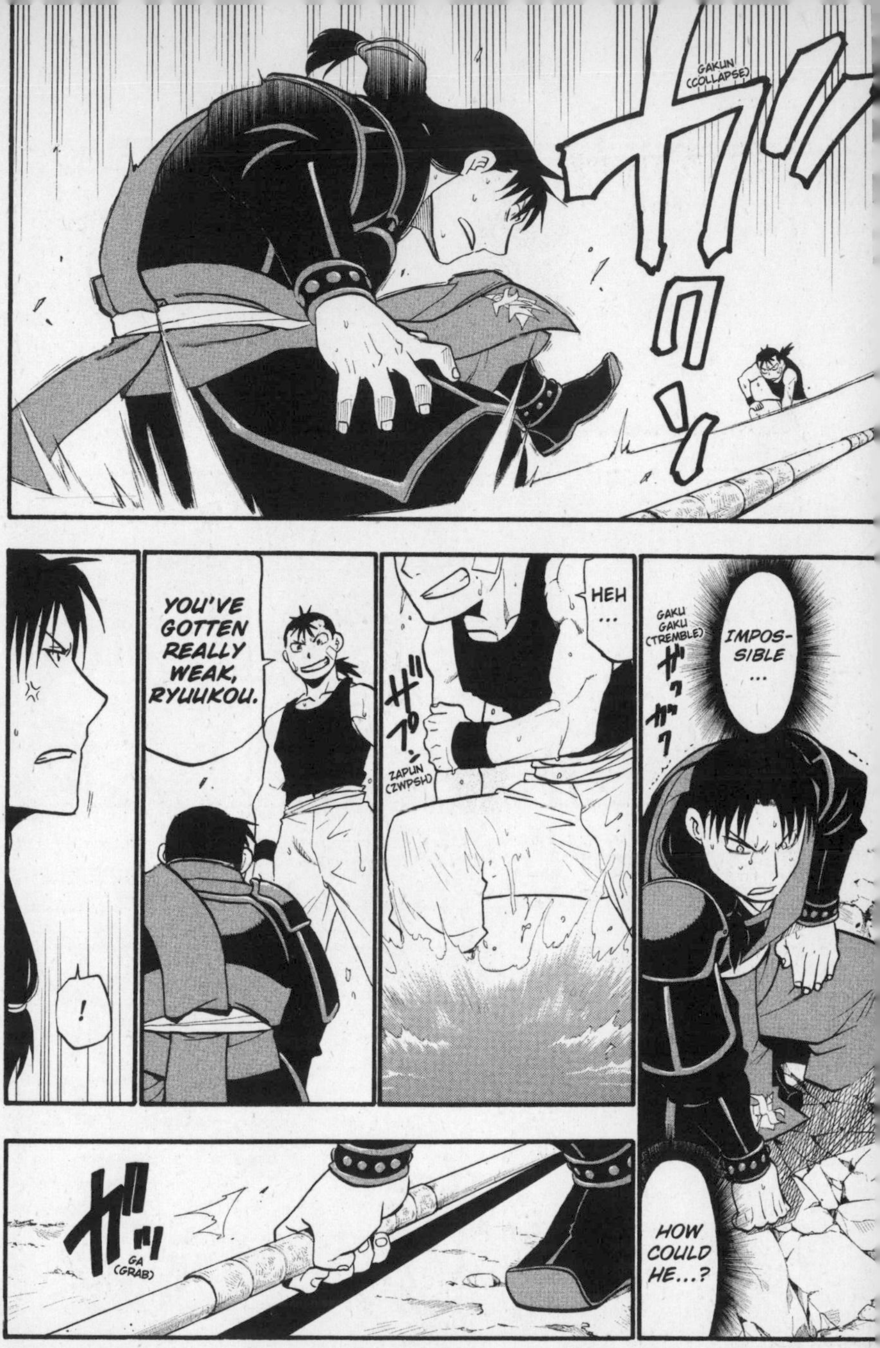
GAKUN (COLLAPSE)
IMPOS-SIBLE...
GAKU GAKU (TREMBLE)
HOW COULD HE...?
HEH...
ZAPUN (ZWPSH)
YOU'VE GOTTEN REALLY WEAK, RYUUKOU.
!
GA (GRAB)

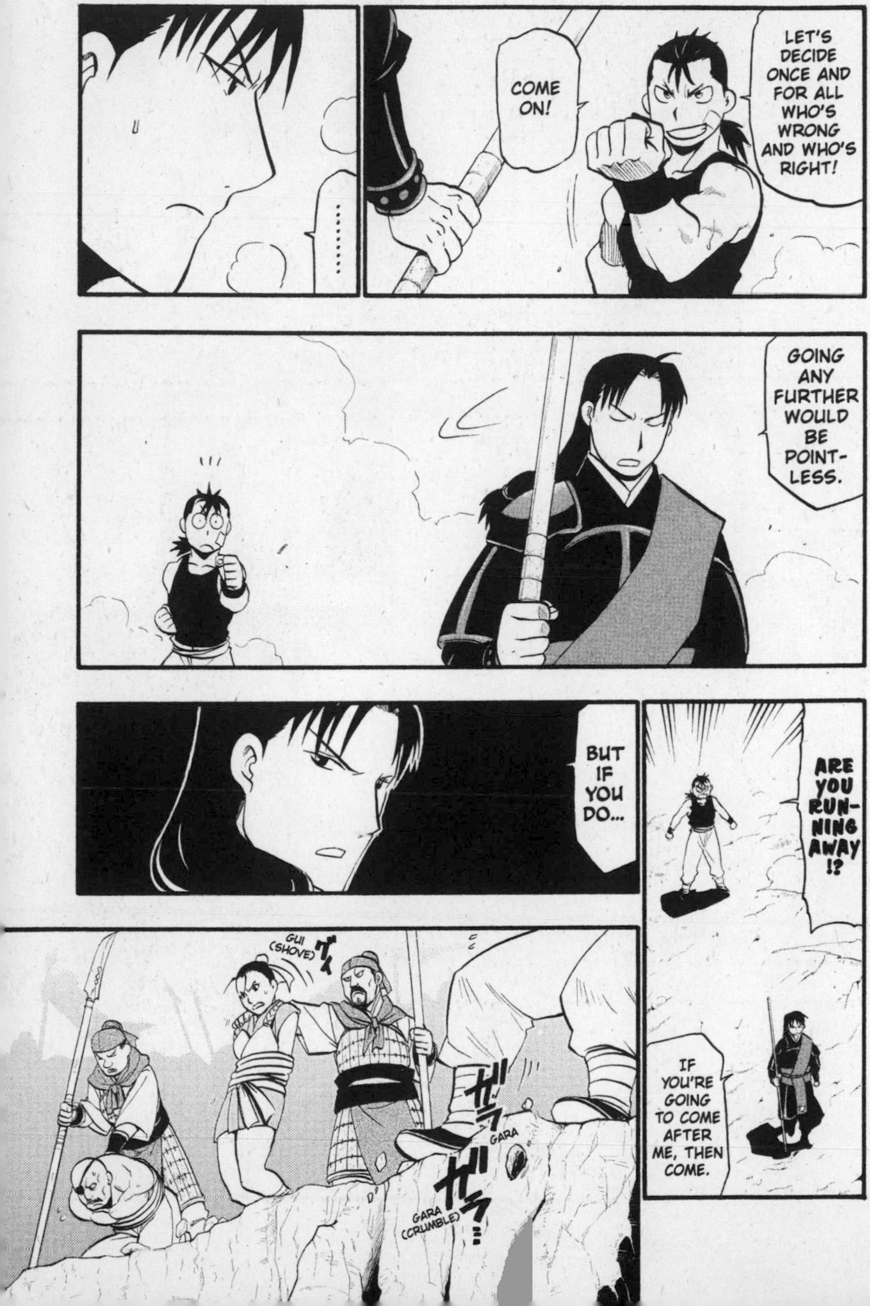
LET'S DECIDE ONCE AND FOR ALL WHO'S WRONG AND WHO'S RIGHT!
COME ON!
......
GOING ANY FURTHER WOULD BE POINTLESS.
ARE YOU RUN-NING AWAY!?
IF YOU'RE GOING TO COME AFTER ME, THEN COME.
BUT IF YOU DO...
GUI (SHOVE)
GARA
GARA (CRUMBLE)

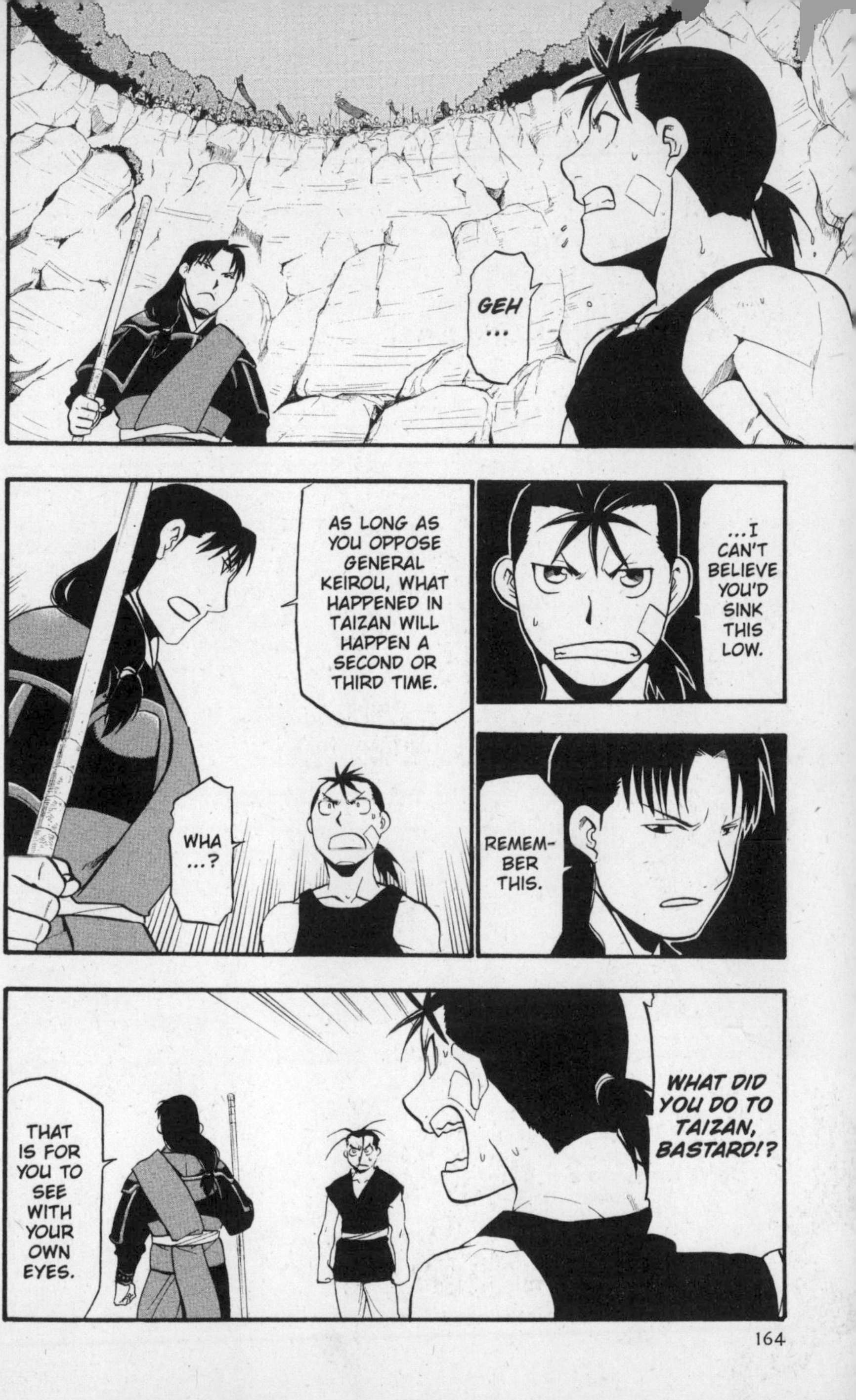
GEH ...
...I CAN'T BELIEVE YOU'D SINK THIS LOW.
REMEMBER THIS.
AS LONG AS YOU OPPOSE GENERAL KEIROU, WHAT HAPPENED IN TAIZAN WILL HAPPEN A SECOND OR THIRD TIME.
WHA ...?
WHAT DID YOU DO TO TAIZAN, BASTARD!?
THAT IS FOR YOU TO SEE WITH YOUR OWN EYES.

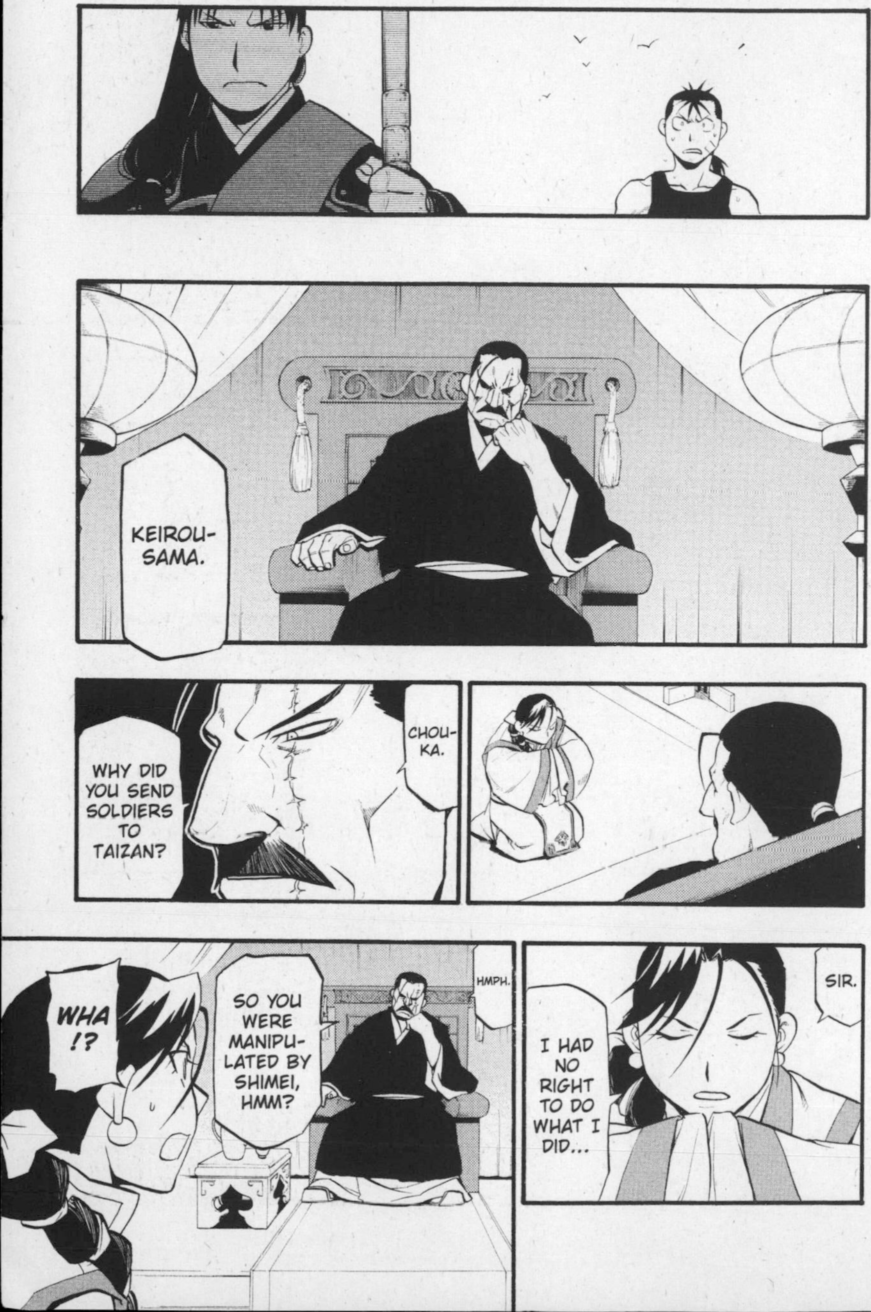
KEIROU-SAMA.
CHOU-KA.
WHY DID YOU SEND SOLDIERS TO TAIZAN?
SIR.
I HAD NO RIGHT TO DO WHAT I DID...
HMPH.
SO YOU WERE MANIPULATED BY SHIMEI, HMM?
WHA!?

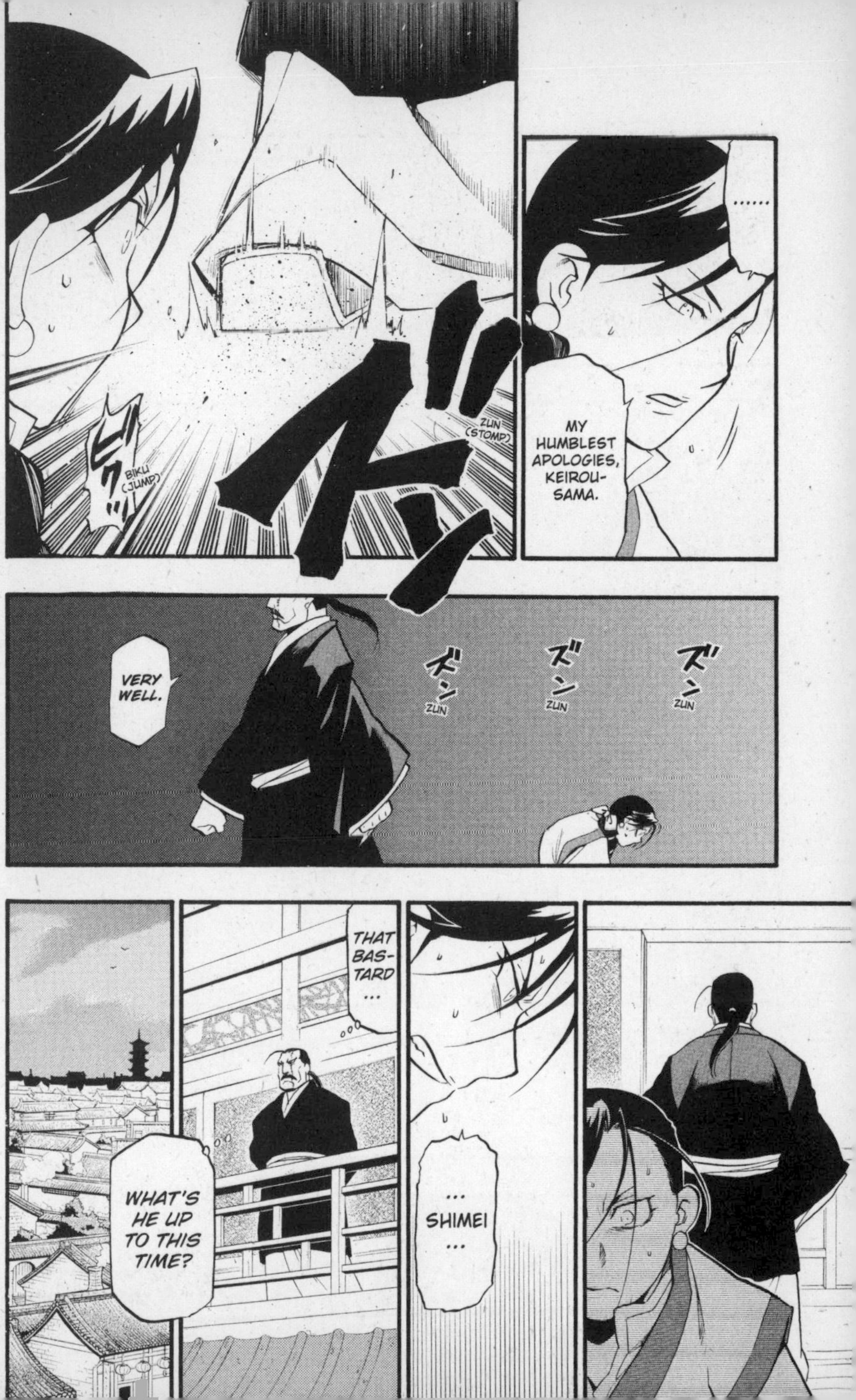
......
MY HUMBLEST APOLOGIES, KEIROU-SAMA.
ZUN (STOMP)
BIKU (JUMP)
ZUN
ZUN
ZUN
VERY WELL.
... SHIMEI ...
THAT BASTARD ...
WHAT'S HE UP TO THIS TIME?

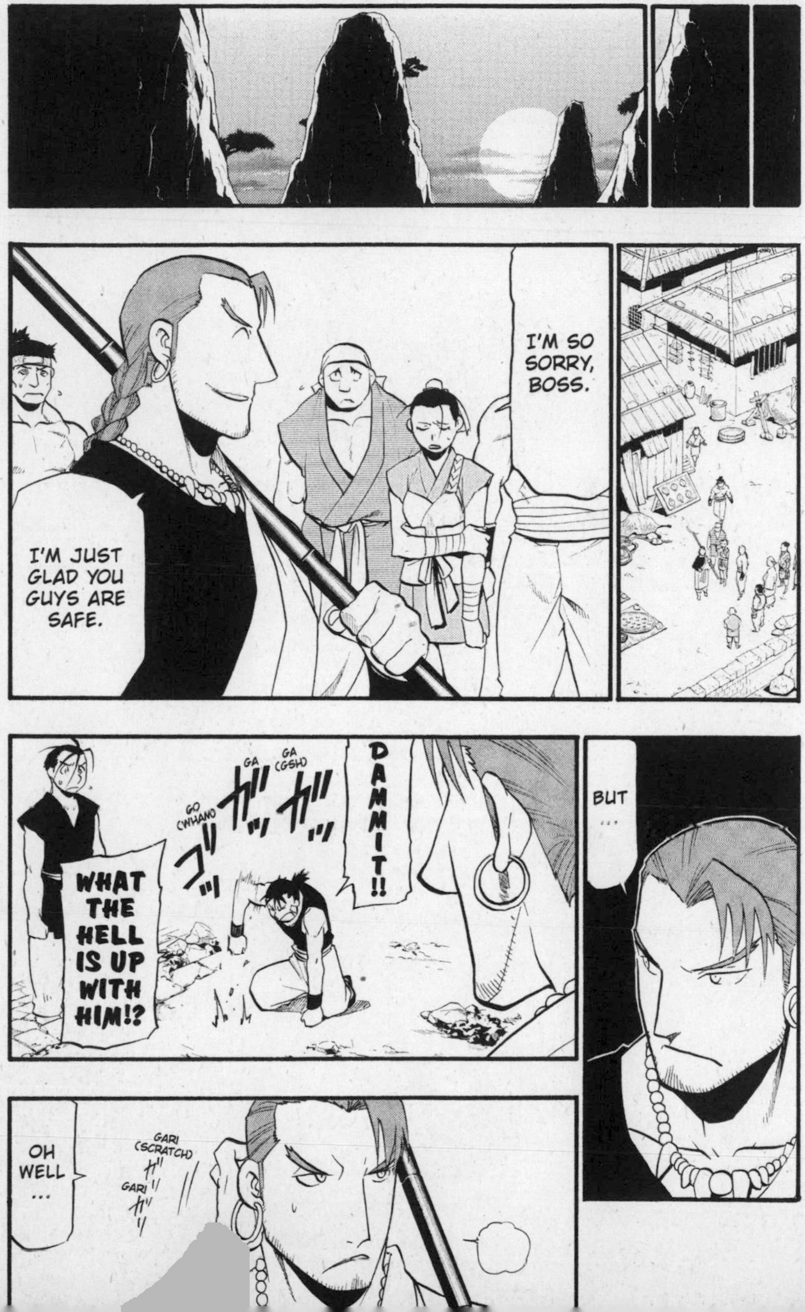
I'M SO SORRY, BOSS.
I'M JUST GLAD YOU GUYS ARE SAFE.
BUT ...
DAMMIT!!
GA (GSH)
GA
GO (WHAM)
WHAT THE HELL IS UP WITH HIM!?
GARI (SCRATCH)
GARI
OH WELL ...

...TO TAI-ZAN.

LET'S GO...

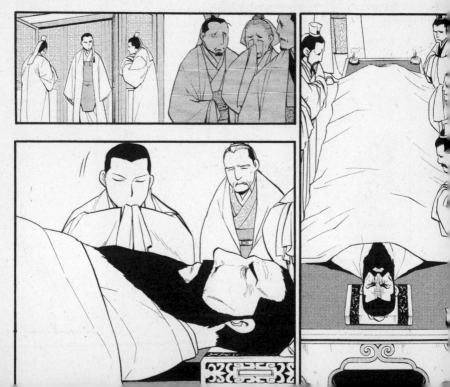

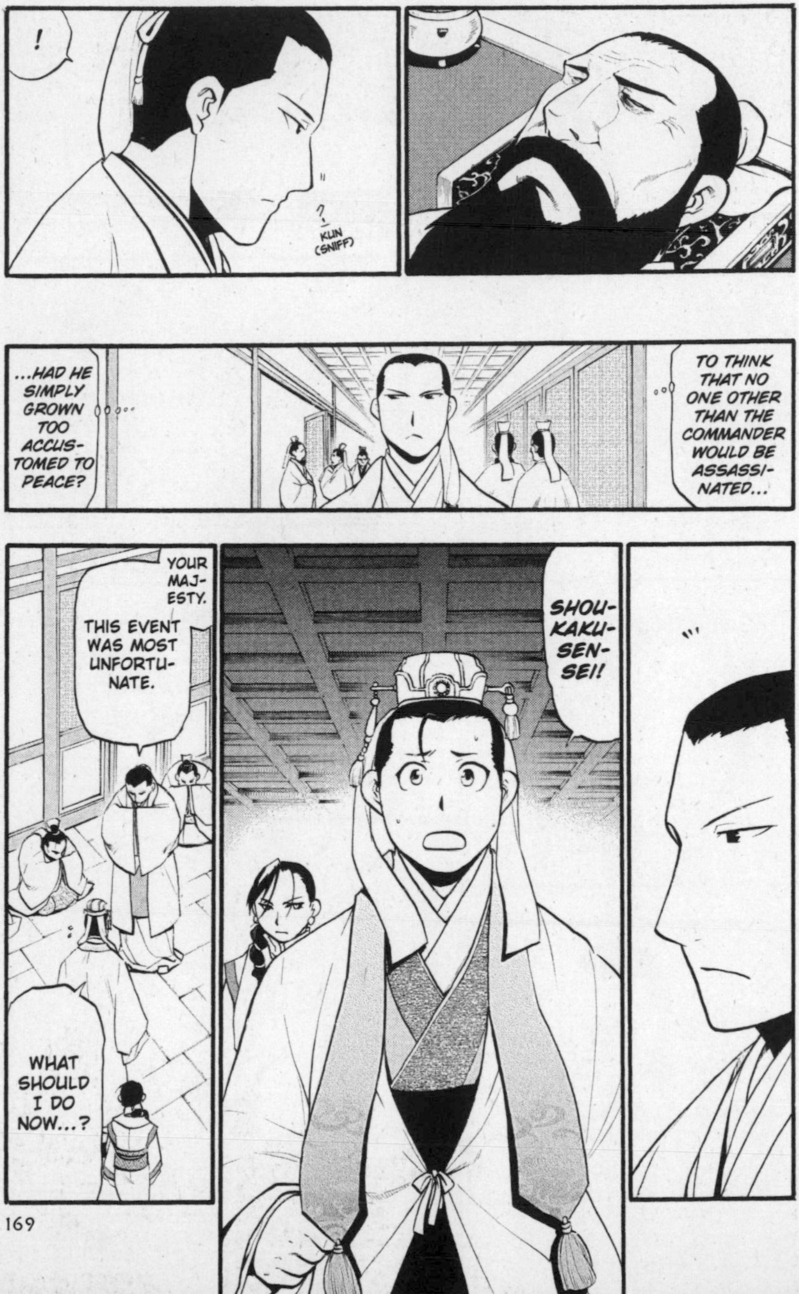
!
?
KUN (SNIFF)
TO THINK THAT NO ONE OTHER THAN THE COMMANDER WOULD BE ASSASSINATED...
...HAD HE SIMPLY GROWN TOO ACCUSTOMED TO PEACE?
SHOU-KAKU-SEN-SEI!
YOUR MAJ-ESTY.
THIS EVENT WAS MOST UNFORTU-NATE.
WHAT SHOULD I DO NOW...?

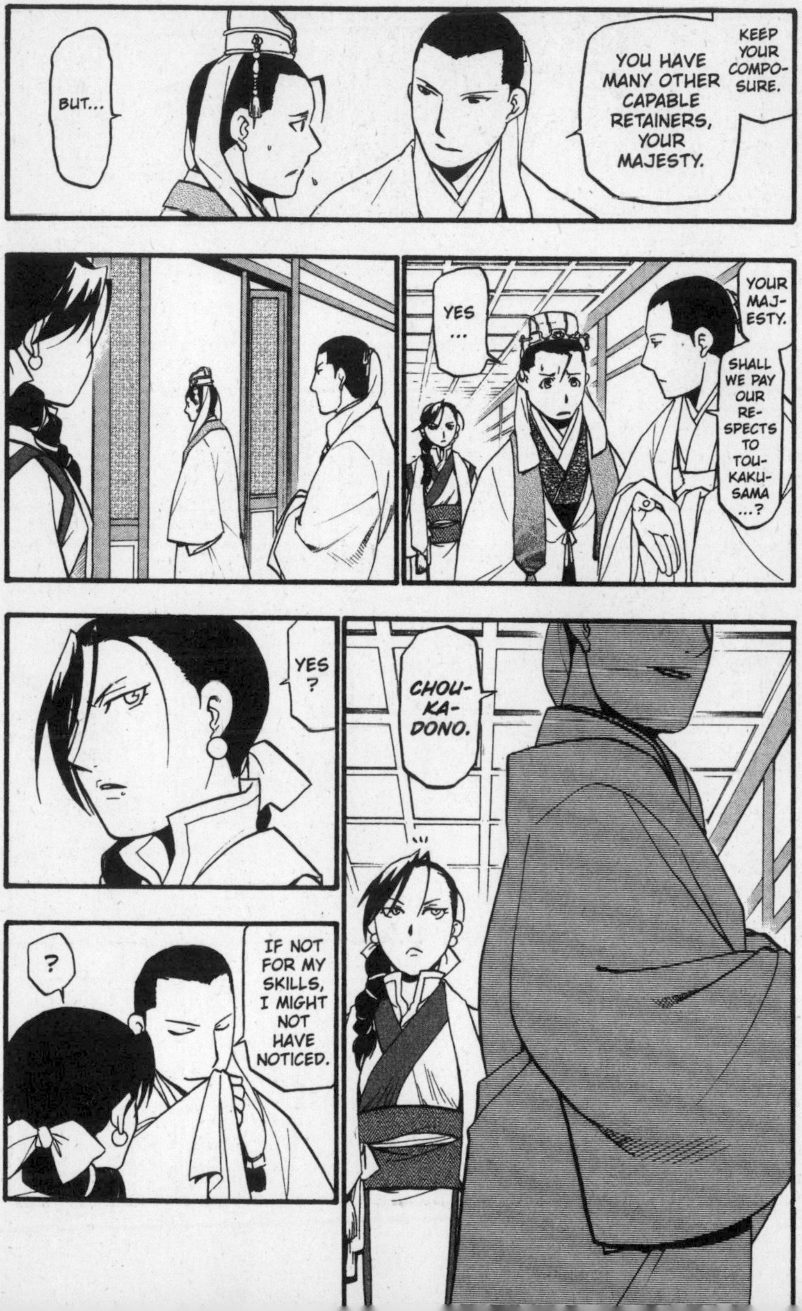
KEEP YOUR COMPOSURE.
YOU HAVE MANY OTHER CAPABLE RETAINERS, YOUR MAJESTY.
BUT...
YOUR MAJESTY.
SHALL WE PAY OUR RESPECTS TO TOUKAKU-SAMA...?
YES...
CHOUKA-DONO.
YES?
IF NOT FOR MY SKILLS, I MIGHT NOT HAVE NOTICED.
?

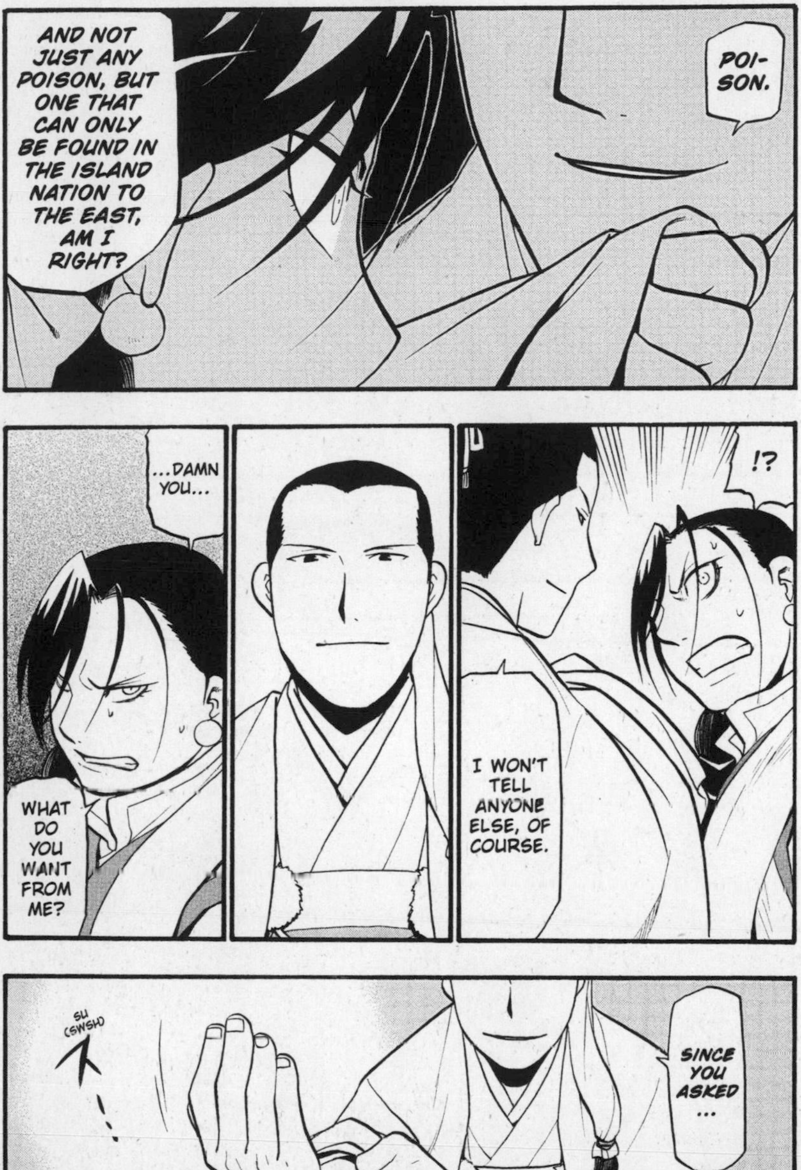
POI-SON.
AND NOT JUST ANY POISON, BUT ONE THAT CAN ONLY BE FOUND IN THE ISLAND NATION TO THE EAST, AM I RIGHT?
!?
I WON'T TELL ANYONE ELSE, OF COURSE.
...DAMN YOU...
WHAT DO YOU WANT FROM ME?
SINCE YOU ASKED ...
SU (SWSH)

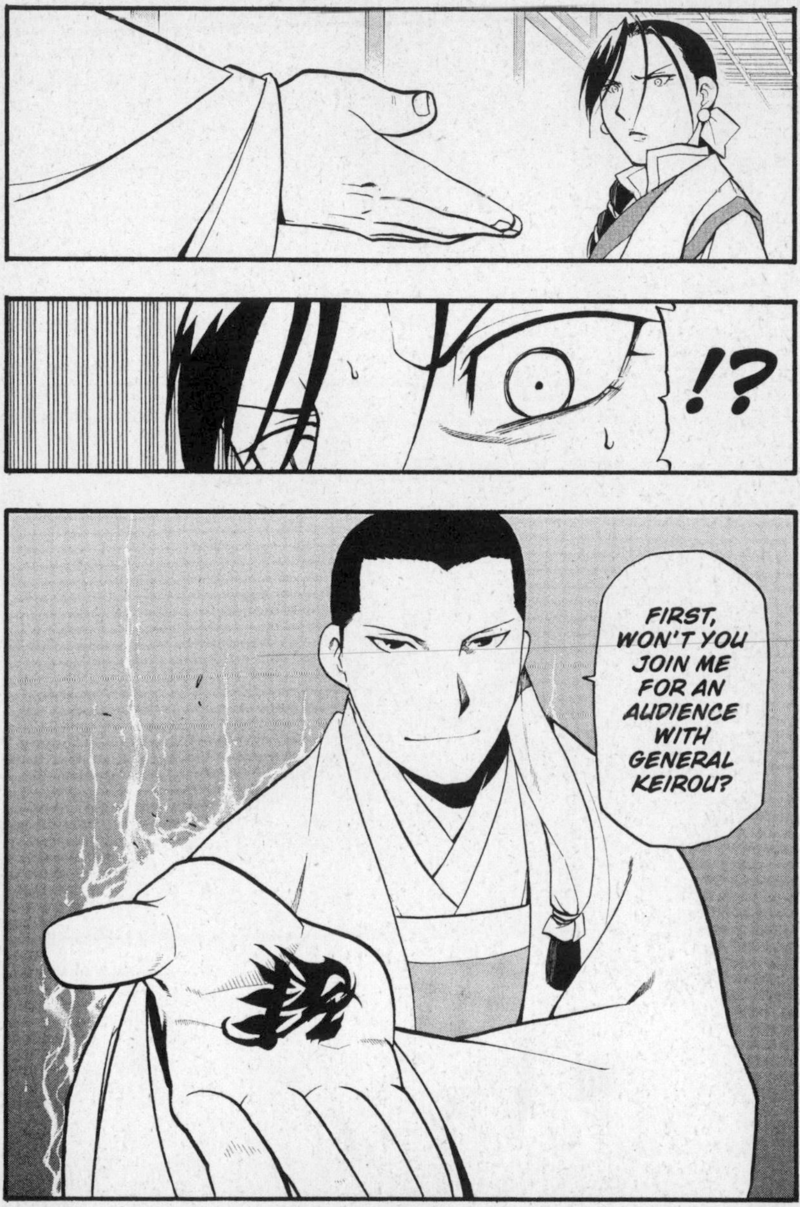
!?
FIRST, WON'T YOU JOIN ME FOR AN AUDIENCE WITH GENERAL KEIROU?

Hero Tales 3
The End

HERO TALES
獣　神　演　武

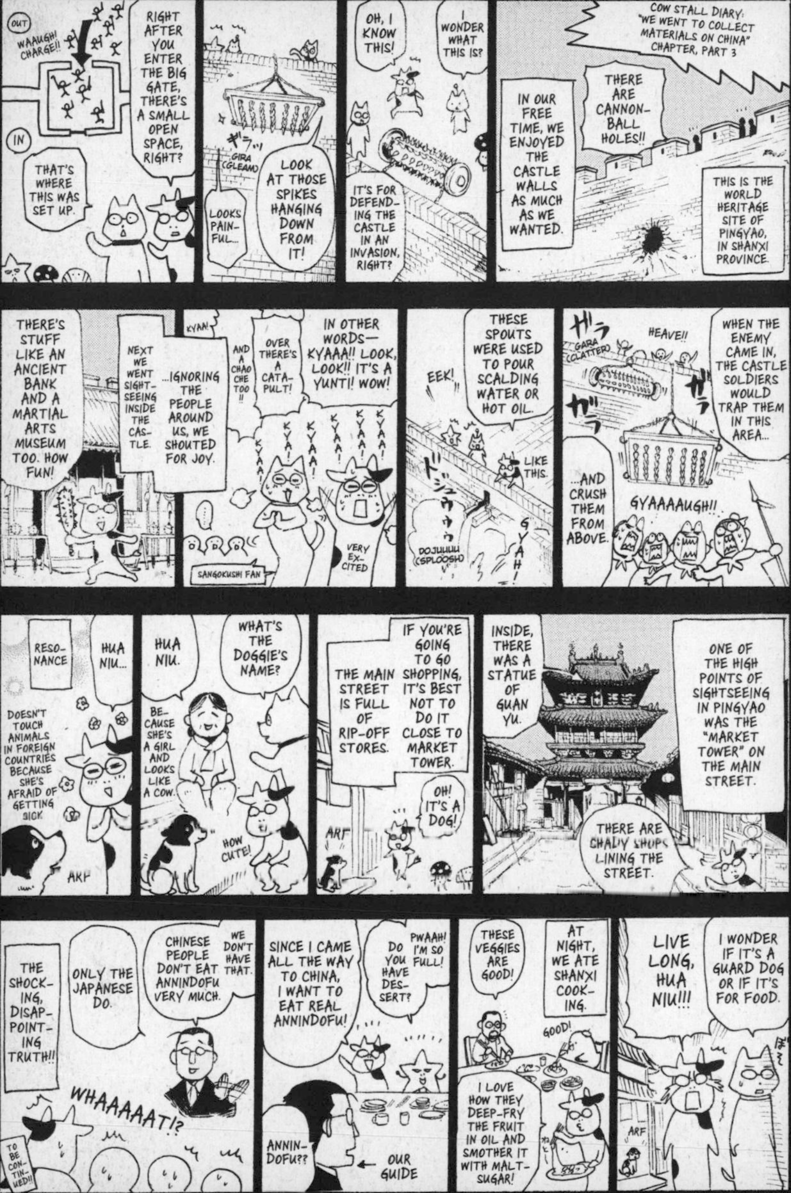
COW STALL DIARY: "WE WENT TO COLLECT MATERIALS ON CHINA" CHAPTER, PART 3
THIS IS THE WORLD HERITAGE SITE OF PINGYAO, IN SHANXI PROVINCE.
THERE ARE CANNON-BALL HOLES!!
IN OUR FREE TIME, WE ENJOYED THE CASTLE WALLS AS MUCH AS WE WANTED.
I WONDER WHAT THIS IS?
OH, I KNOW THIS!
IT'S FOR DEFENDING THE CASTLE IN AN INVASION, RIGHT?
GIRA (GLEAM)
LOOK AT THOSE SPIKES HANGING DOWN FROM IT!
LOOKS PAINFUL...
RIGHT AFTER YOU ENTER THE BIG GATE, THERE'S A SMALL OPEN SPACE, RIGHT?
OUT
WAAUGH! CHARGE!!
IN
THAT'S WHERE THIS WAS SET UP.
WHEN THE ENEMY CAME IN, THE CASTLE SOLDIERS WOULD TRAP THEM IN THIS AREA...
HEAVE!!
GARA (CLATTER)
...AND CRUSH THEM FROM ABOVE.
GYAAAAAUGH!!
THESE SPOUTS WERE USED TO POUR SCALDING WATER OR HOT OIL.
EEK!
LIKE THIS.
DOJUUUU (SPLOOSH)
GYAH!
IN OTHER WORDS— KYAAA!! LOOK, LOOK!! IT'S A YUNTI! WOW!
OVER THERE'S A CATAPULT!
AND A CHAO CHE TOO!!
KYAN!
...IGNORING THE PEOPLE AROUND US, WE SHOUTED FOR JOY.
NEXT WE WENT SIGHT-SEEING INSIDE THE CASTLE.
KYAA! KYAA! KYAA! KYAA! KYAA!
VERY EXCITED
SANGOKUSHI FAN
THERE'S STUFF LIKE AN ANCIENT BANK AND A MARTIAL ARTS MUSEUM TOO. HOW FUN!
ONE OF THE HIGH POINTS OF SIGHTSEEING IN PINGYAO WAS THE "MARKET TOWER" ON THE MAIN STREET.
INSIDE, THERE WAS A STATUE OF GUAN YU.
THERE ARE SHADY SHOPS LINING THE STREET.
IF YOU'RE GOING TO GO SHOPPING, IT'S BEST NOT TO DO IT CLOSE TO MARKET TOWER.
THE MAIN STREET IS FULL OF RIP-OFF STORES.
OH! IT'S A DOG!
ARF
WHAT'S THE DOGGIE'S NAME?
HUA NIU.
BECAUSE SHE'S A GIRL AND LOOKS LIKE A COW.
HOW CUTE!
HUA NIU...
RESONANCE
DOESN'T TOUCH ANIMALS IN FOREIGN COUNTRIES BECAUSE SHE'S AFRAID OF GETTING SICK
ARF
I WONDER IF IT'S A GUARD DOG OR IF IT'S FOR FOOD.
LIVE LONG, HUA NIU!!!
ARF
AT NIGHT, WE ATE SHANXI COOKING.
THESE VEGGIES ARE GOOD!
GOOD!
I LOVE HOW THEY DEEP-FRY THE FRUIT IN OIL AND SMOTHER IT WITH MALT-SUGAR!
PWAAH! I'M SO FULL!
DO YOU HAVE DESSERT?
SINCE I CAME ALL THE WAY TO CHINA, I WANT TO EAT REAL ANNINDOFU!
ANNINDOFU??
OUR GUIDE
WE DON'T HAVE THAT.
CHINESE PEOPLE DON'T EAT ANNINDOFU VERY MUCH.
ONLY THE JAPANESE DO.
THE SHOCKING, DISAPPOINTING TRUTH!!
WHAAAAAAT!?
TO BE CONTINUED!!

SFX: BOSO (MUTTER)

SFX: NETO (GOOEY)

Common Honorifics:

**No honorific:** Indicates familiarity or closeness; if used without permission or reason, addressing someone in this manner would constitute an insult.

**-san:** The Japanese equivalent of Mr./Mrs./Miss. If a situation calls for politeness, this is the fail-safe honorific.

**-sama:** Conveys great respect; may also indicate that the social status of the speaker is lower than that of the addressee.

**-dono:** A polite, formal honorific suffix.

**-kun:** Used most often when referring to boys, this indicates affection or familiarity. Occasionally used by older men among their peers, but it may also be used by anyone referring to a person of lower standing.

**-chan:** An affectionate honorific indicating familiarity used mostly in reference to girls; also used in reference to cute persons or animals of either gender.

**-sensei:** A respectful term for teachers, artists, or high-level professionals.

### Pg. 29
**Rasenkon**
"*Rasen*" means "spiral," although in this case, the second character, which normally means "line," is replaced with a character that is pronounced the same but means "to drill or pierce." "*Kon*" means "staff." So this weapon's name could be translated as "Spiral Staff."

**Rinsenka**
"*Rinsen*," when written with different characters, means "to prepare for battle." "*Ka*," in this case, is written with a character for "flower".

### Pg. 122
**Kourokushou**
"*Kourokushou*" was an official government position/title. The Kourokushou was one of the nine officials of the ancient Chinese government.

### Pg. 175
**Pingyao**
Pingyao is a city in the province of Shanxi, China, known for its ancient city walls. It was designated a UNESCO World Heritage Site in 1997.

**Yunti**
A *yunti*, or "cloud ladder," is a ladder used in ancient China to scale the walls of fortified cities.

**Chao Che**
A *chao che*, or "nest cart" was a mobile observation cart used to peer into a city during an invasion.

**Sangokushi**
*The Romance of the Three Kingdoms* (*Sangokushi* in Japanese) is a classic Chinese historical novel written by Luo Guanzhong in the 1300s. The story takes place from the final years of the Han Dynasty through the Three Kingdoms period, from the late 160s to 280. The novel weaves together a rich collection of characters and stories based on actual events during this tumultuous period. Arguably the most well-known of these figures is Guan Yu, a warrior whose honor and bravery in battle, though largely fictionalized with the passage of time and the publication of works such as *The Romance of the Three Kingdoms*, has lead many people to see him as something of a deity, and he is still worshipped in many parts of China today.

**Ancient bank**
Pingyao was once the financial capital of China. It is home to the first bank in China.

**Hua Niu**
The dog's name is written with the characters for "flower" and "cow."

**Annindofu**
*Annindofu*, or *douhua* in Chinese, is a dessert dish. In Japan, it is made of agar-agar, water, apricot kernel or almond powder, sugar, and milk. In China, it is typically made with an extra-soft form of tofu.

# HERO TALES③

**HUANG JIN-ZHOU**
**HIROMU ARAKAWA**

**Translation: Amy Forsyth**

**Lettering: Abigail Blackman**

HERO TALES: JUUSHIN ENBU Vol. 3 © HUANG JIN-ZHOU • GENCO •
FLAG ©2007 HERO TALES PRODUCTION PARTNERS © 2008 Hiromu
Arakawa / SQUARE ENIX. All rights reserved. First published Japan in
2008 by SQUARE ENIX CO. LTD. English translation rights arranged with
SQUARE ENIX CO. LTD. and Hachette Book Group through Tuttle-Mori
Agency, Inc. Translation © 2010 by SQUARE ENIX CO., LTD.

Yen Press
Hachette Book Group
237 Park Avenue, New York, NY 10017

Visit our Web sites at www.HachetteBookGroup.com and
www.YenPress.com

Yen Press is an imprint of Hachette Book Group, Inc. The Yen Press name
and logo are trademarks of Hachette Book Group, Inc.

First Yen Press Edition: June 2010

ISBN: 978-0-316-08501-4

10  9  8  7  6  5  4  3  2  1

BVG

Printed in the United States of America